JIMMY SNIFFLES
Double Trouble

Librarian Reviewer
Katharine Kan
Graphic novel reviewer and Library Consultant, Panama City, FL
MLS in Library and Information Studies, University of Hawaii at
Manoa, HI

Reading Consultant
Elizabeth Stedem
Educator/Consultant, Colorado Springs, CO
MA in Elementary Education, University of Denver, CO

STONE ARCH BOOKS
MINNEAPOLIS   SAN DIEGO

Graphic Sparks are published by Stone Arch Books,
151 Good Counsel Drive, P.O. Box 669,
Mankato, Minnesota 56002.
www.stonearchbooks.com

Library of Congress Cataloging-in-Publication Data
Nickel, Scott.
    Double Trouble / by Scott Nickel; illustrated by Steve Harpster.
    p. cm. — (Graphic Sparks. Jimmy Sniffles)
    ISBN-13: 978-1-59889-314-4 (library binding)
    ISBN-10: 1-59889-314-9 (library binding)
    ISBN-13: 978-1-59889-409-7 (paperback)
    ISBN-10: 1-59889-409-9 (paperback)
    1. Graphic novels. I. Harpster, Steve. II. Title.
PN6727.N544D68 2007
741.5'973—dc22   2006028025

Summary: Jimmy Sniffles' archenemy, the creepy Dr. Von Snotenstein, devises a truly
stinky plan. He creates an evil twin from a single hair of Jimmy's nose. Then he gives the
new Jimmy Two more powers than our favorite Super Sneezer. Good versus evil in a literal
nose-to-nose battle!

Art Director: Heather Kindseth
Graphic Designer: Brann Garvey

1 2 3 4 5 6 11 10 09 08 07 06

Printed in the United States of America

JIMMY SNIFFLES
Double Trouble

by Scott Nickel
illustrated by Steve Harpster

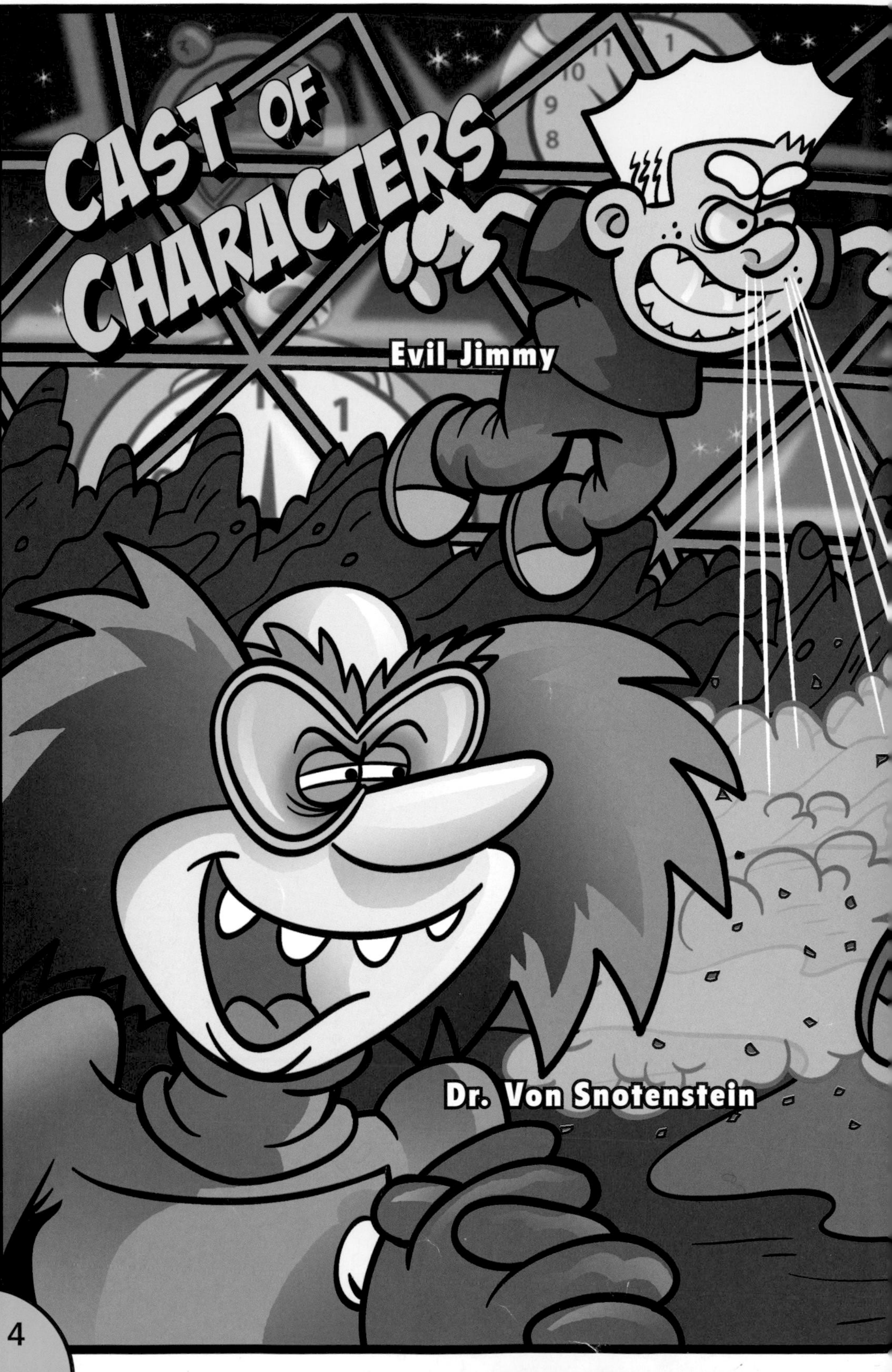
CAST OF CHARACTERS
Evil Jimmy
Dr. Von Snotenstein

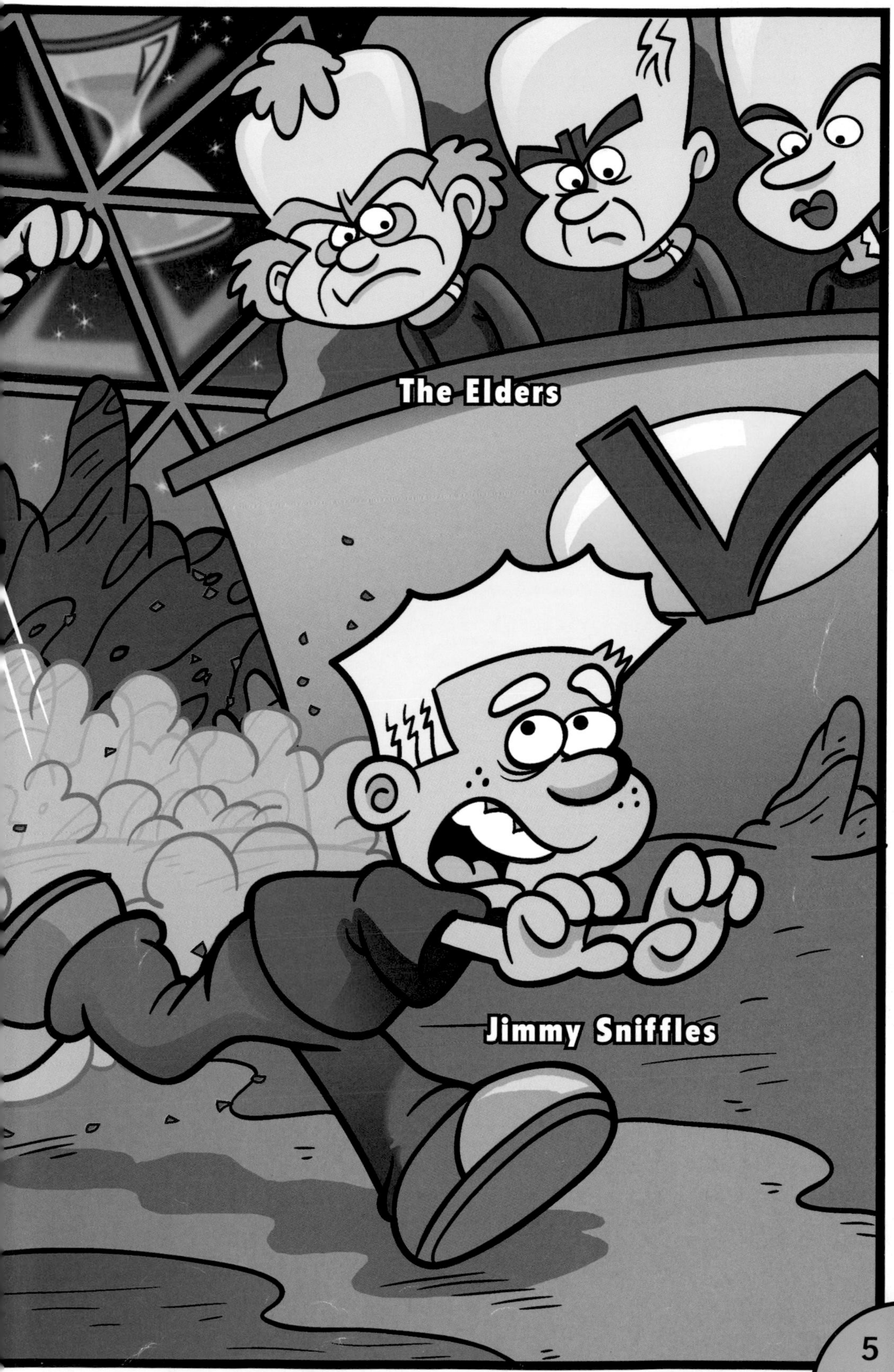
The Elders
Jimmy Sniffles

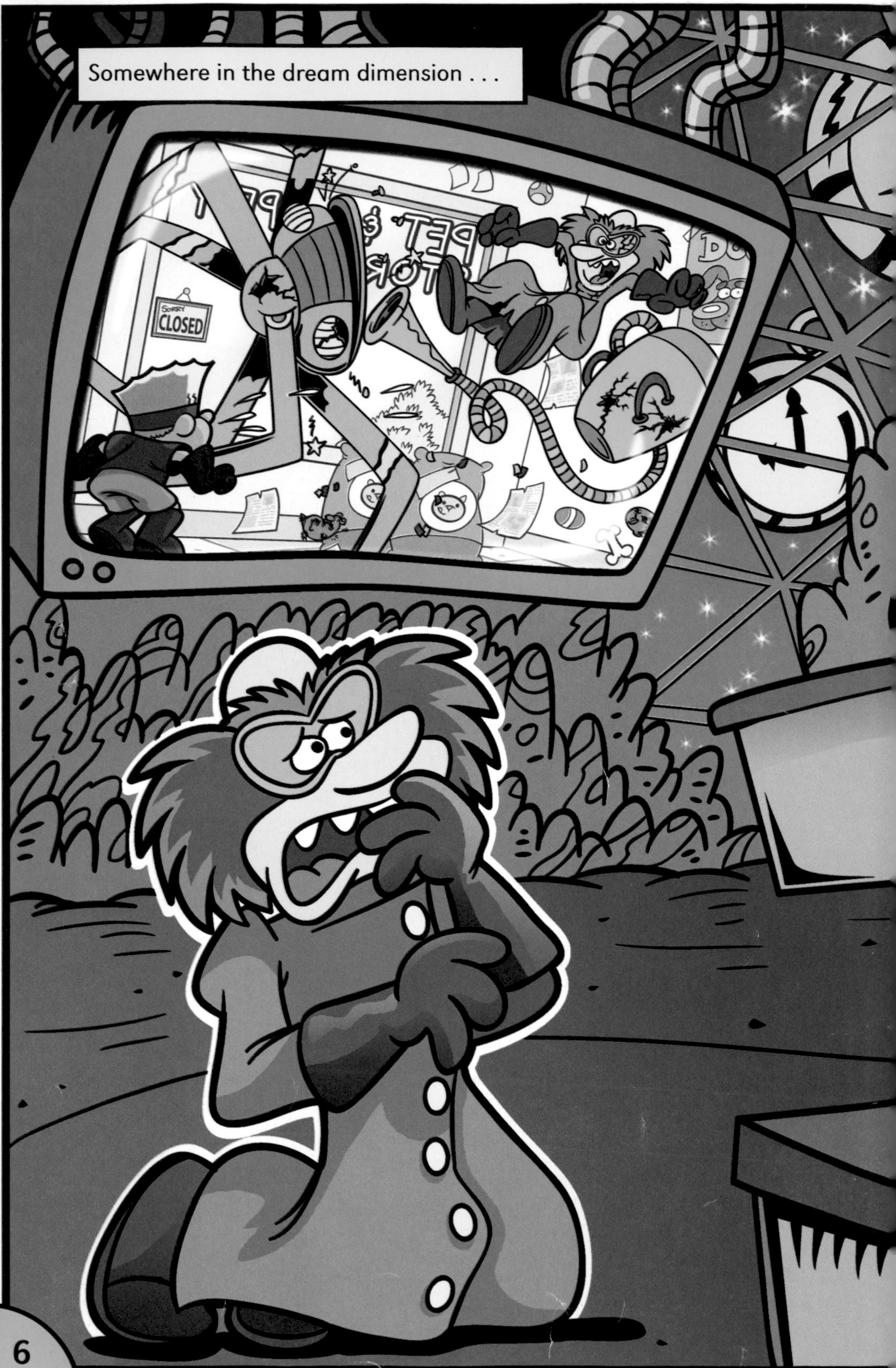
Somewhere in the dream dimension . . .
SORRY
CLOSED
PET

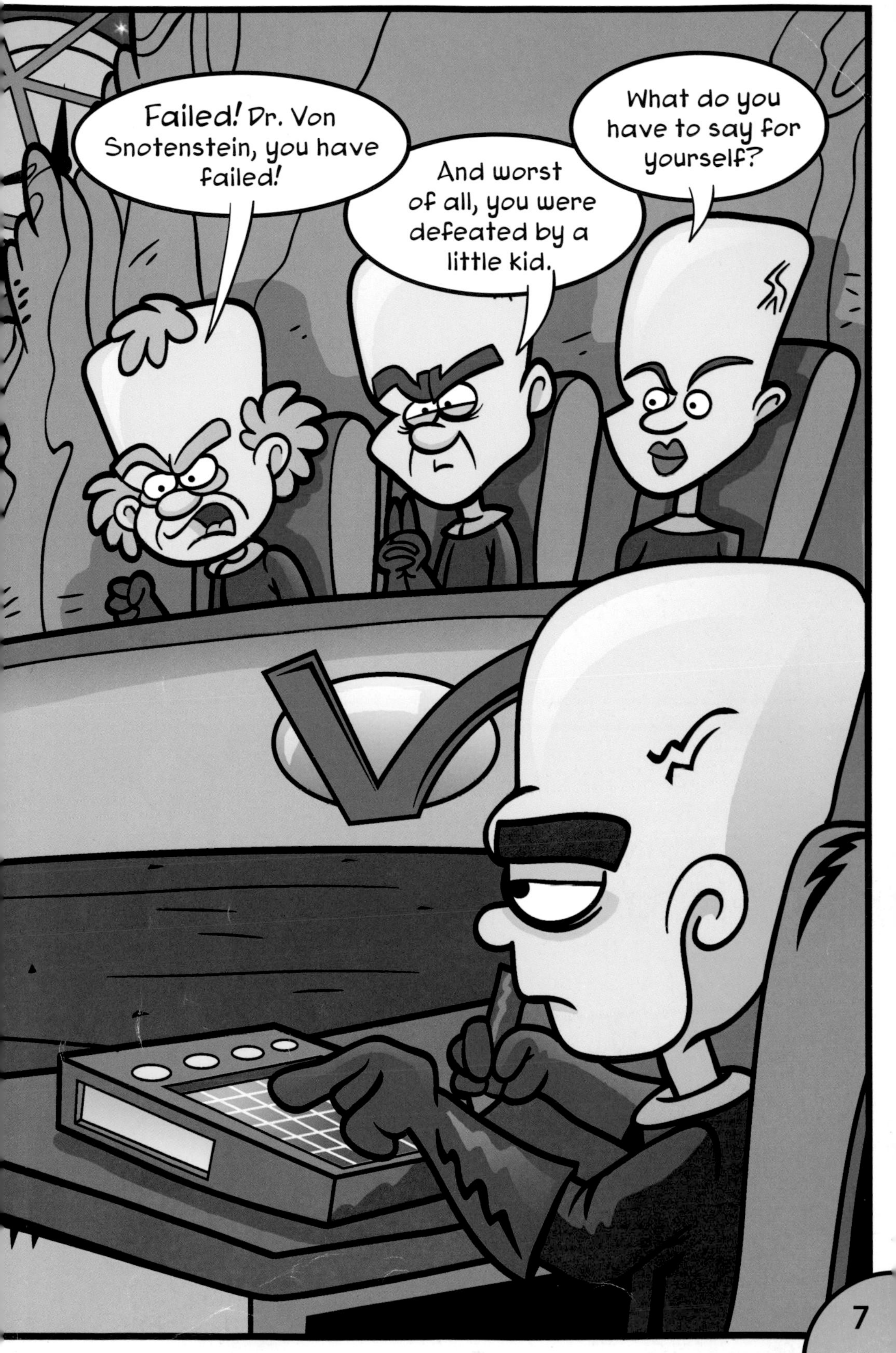
Failed! Dr. Von Snotenstein, you have failed!
And worst of all, you were defeated by a little kid.
What do you have to say for yourself?

My plan to give earthlings a cold that could only be cured by my "Dr. Von Cold B Gone" medicine was, uh, delayed by Jimmy Sniffles.

But I have a new plan! One that will get rid of the nosey nuisance once and for all!

Behold! This tube contains a single hair from the super nose of Jimmy Sniffles.

Ewww! What are you going to do with that?

Something very scientific and very evil!

8

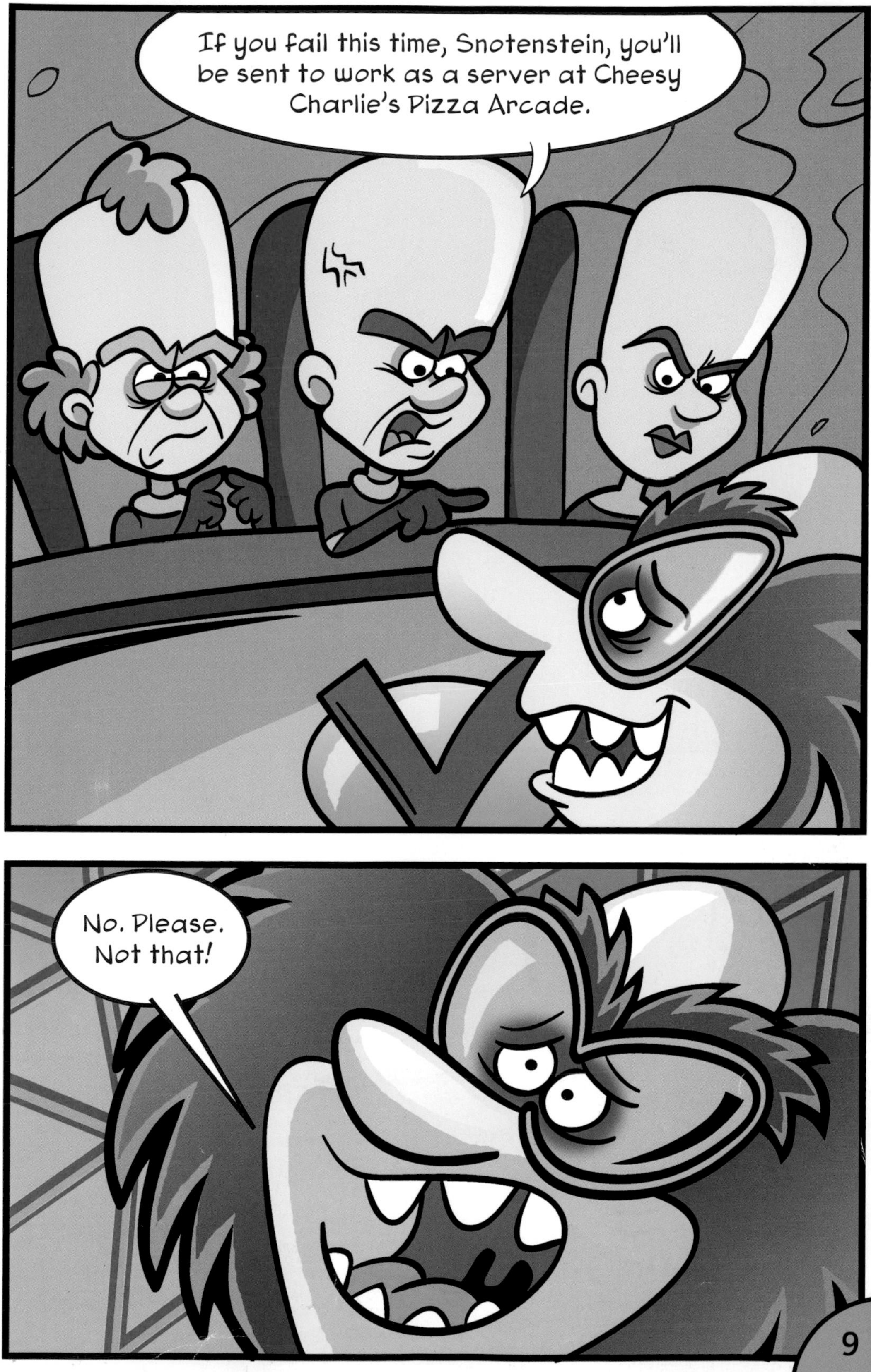
If you fail this time, Snotenstein, you'll be sent to work as a server at Cheesy Charlie's Pizza Arcade.
No. Please. Not that!

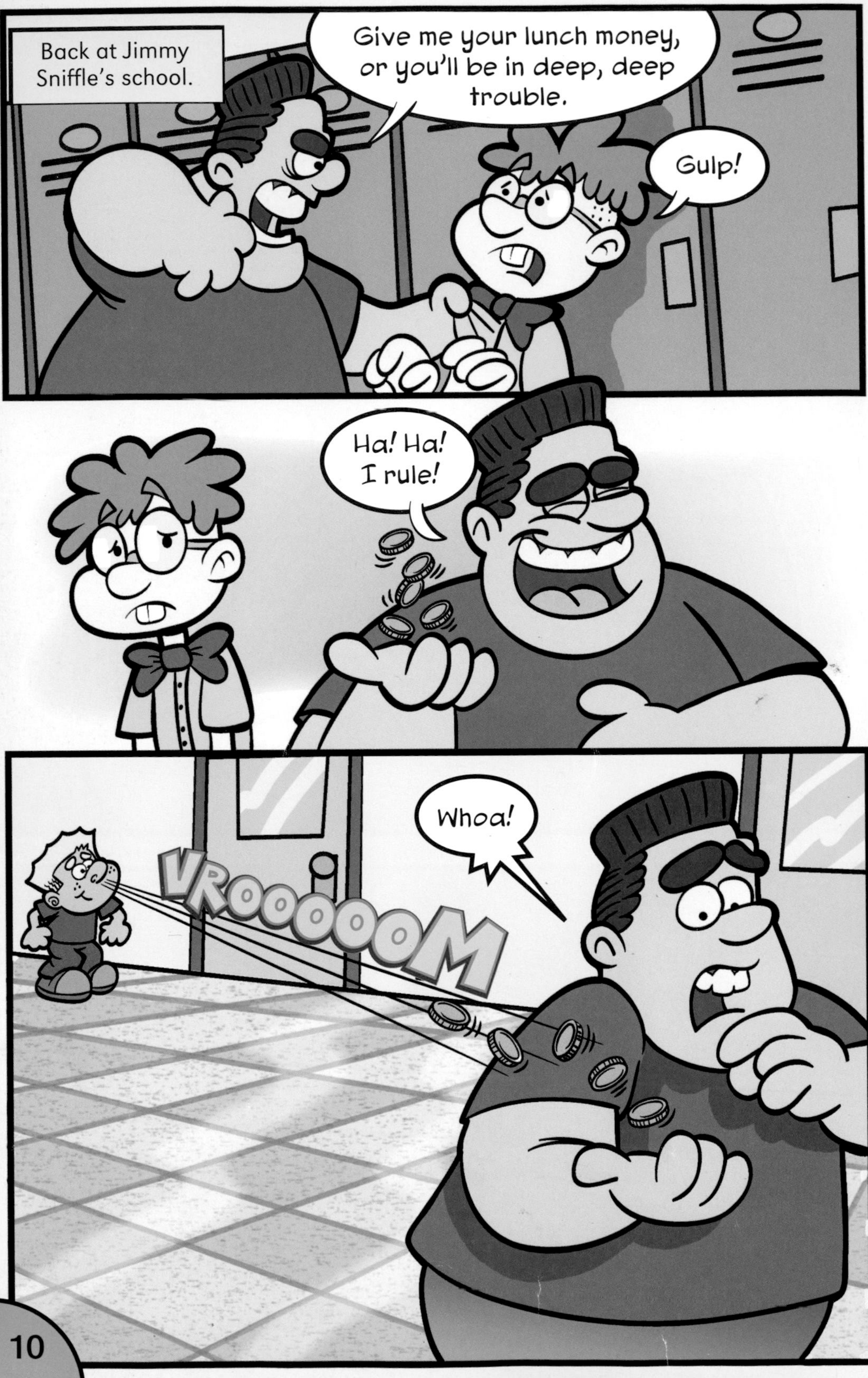
Back at Jimmy Sniffle's school.
Give me your lunch money, or you'll be in deep, deep trouble.
Gulp!
Ha! Ha! I rule!
Whoa!
VROOOOOOM

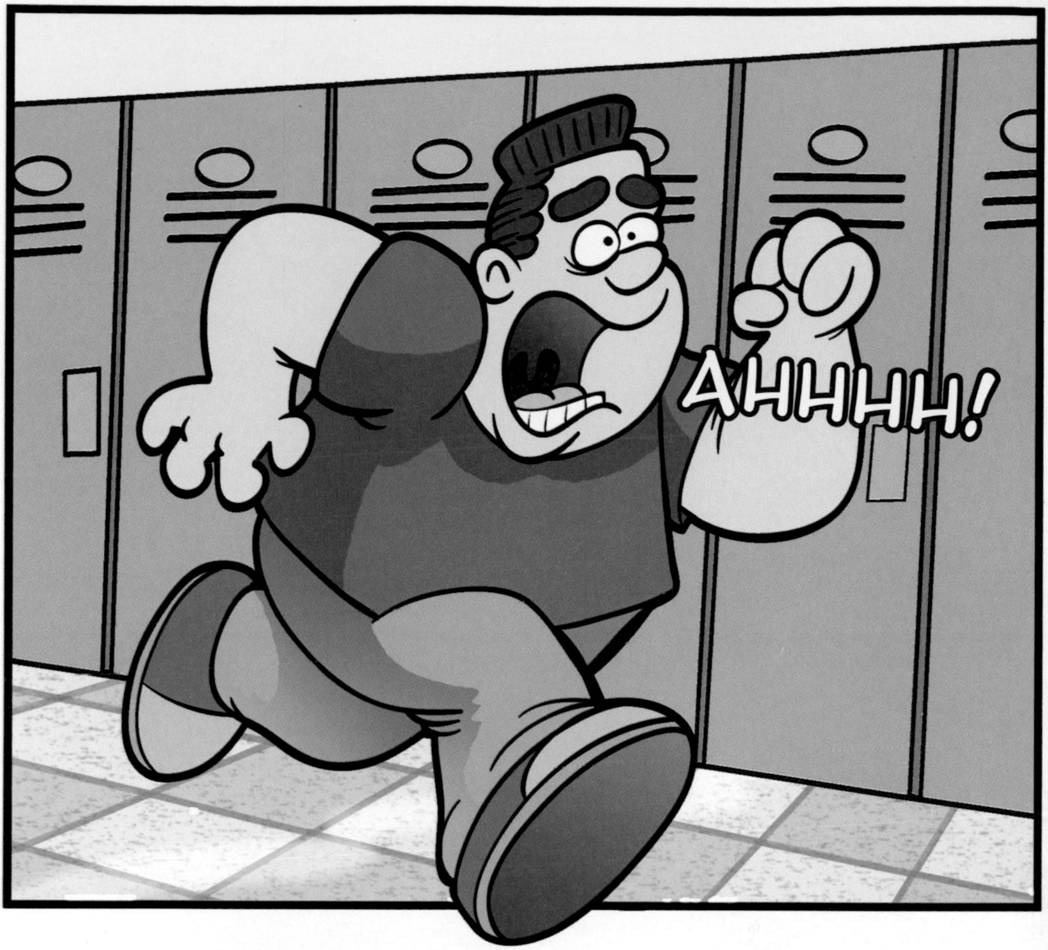
AHHHH!

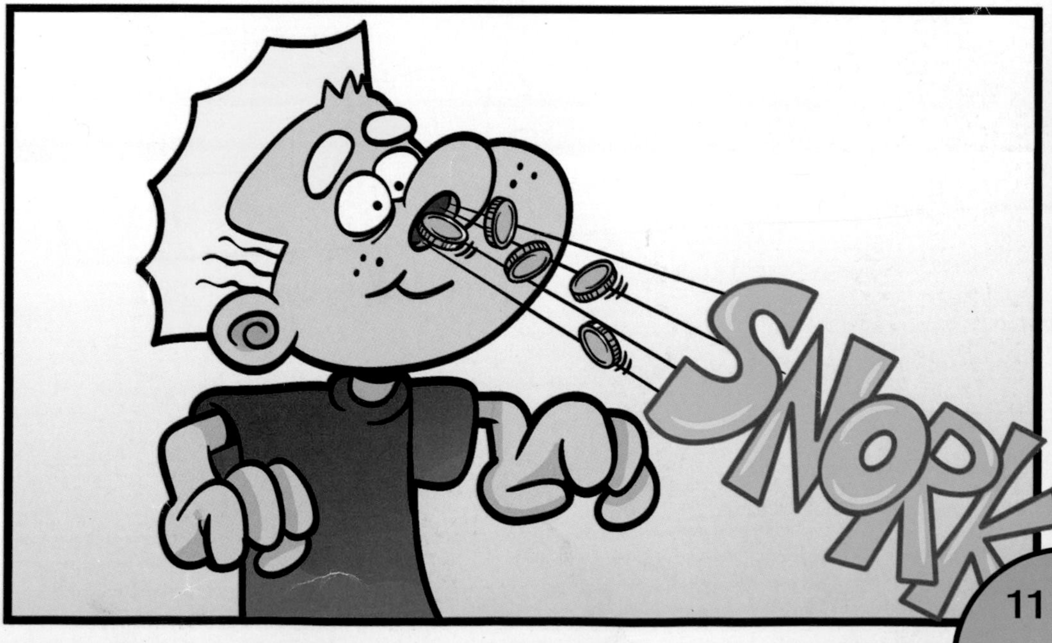
SNORK!

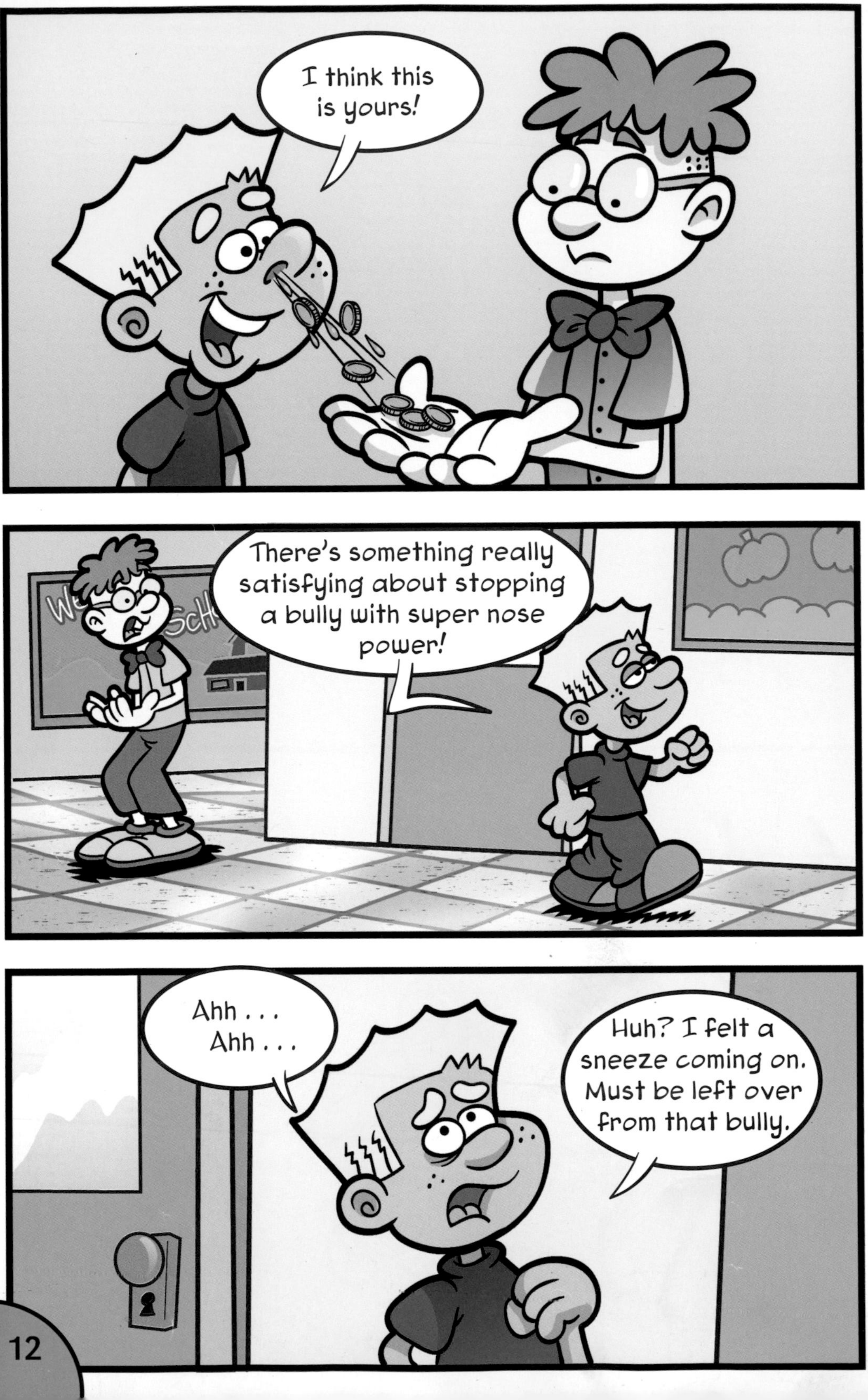
I think this is yours!
There's something really satisfying about stopping a bully with super nose power!
Ahh . . . Ahh . . .
Huh? I felt a sneeze coming on. Must be left over from that bully.

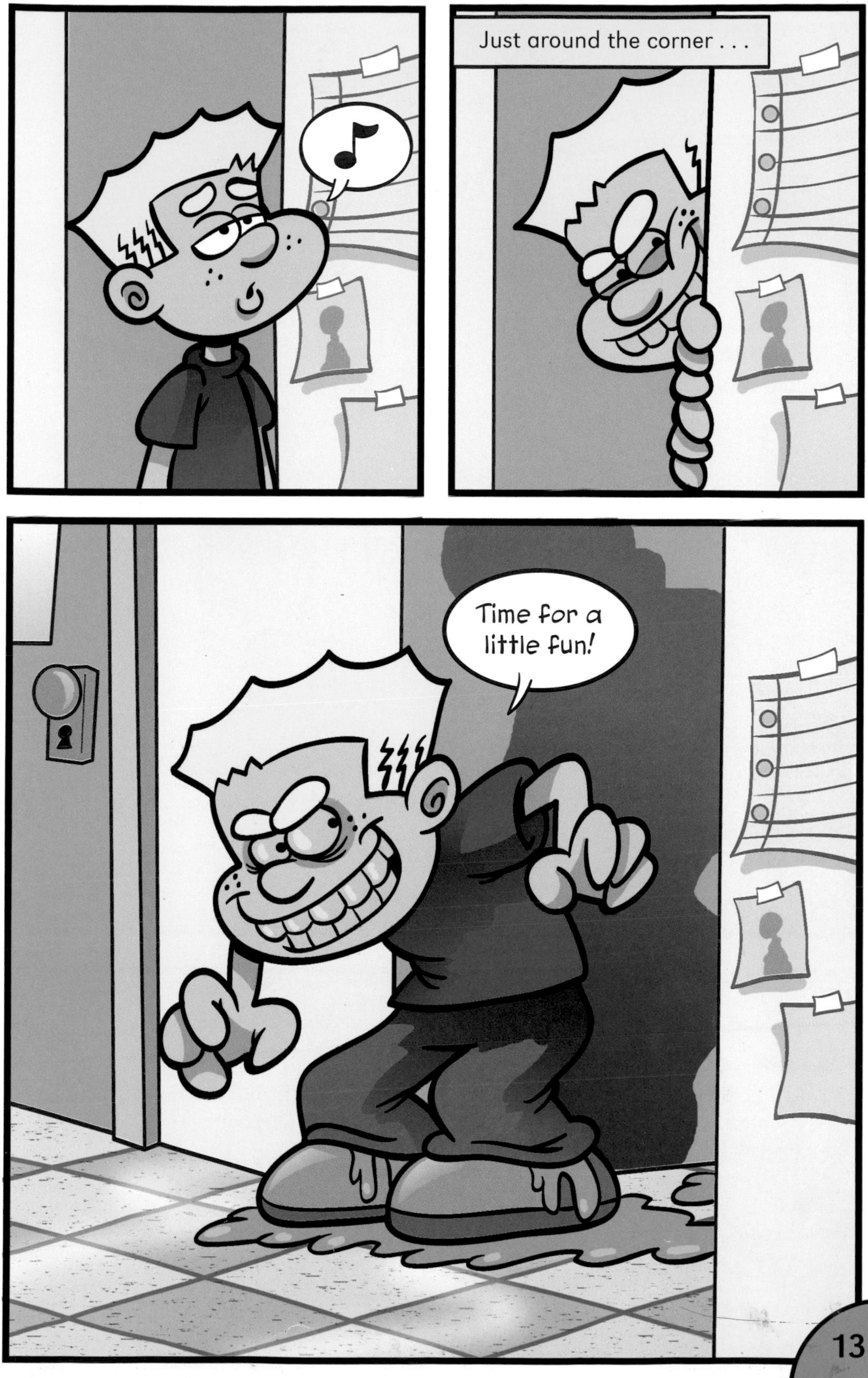
Just around the corner . . .
Time for a little fun!

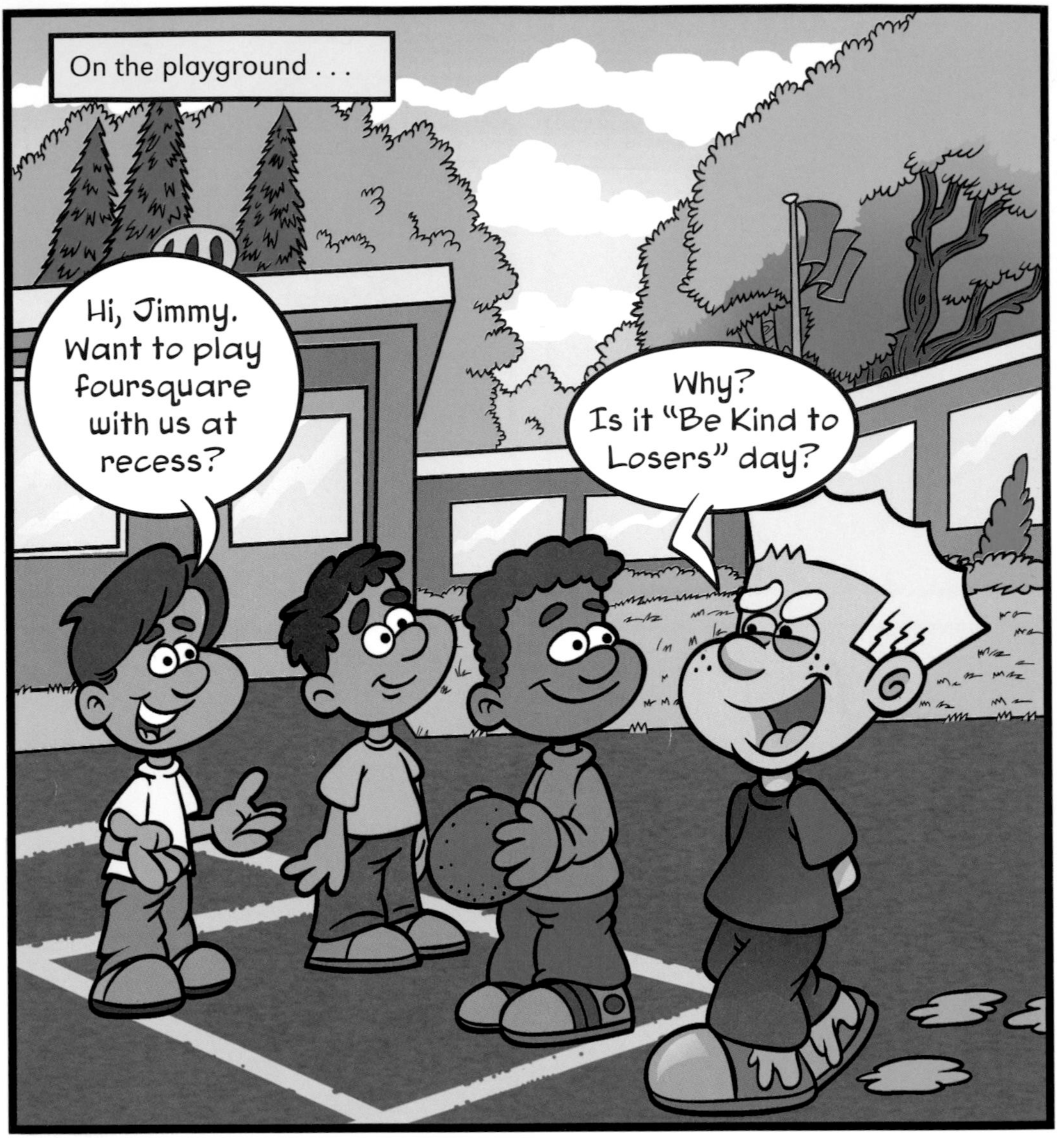
On the playground . . .
Hi, Jimmy. Want to play foursquare with us at recess?
Why? Is it "Be Kind to Losers" day?

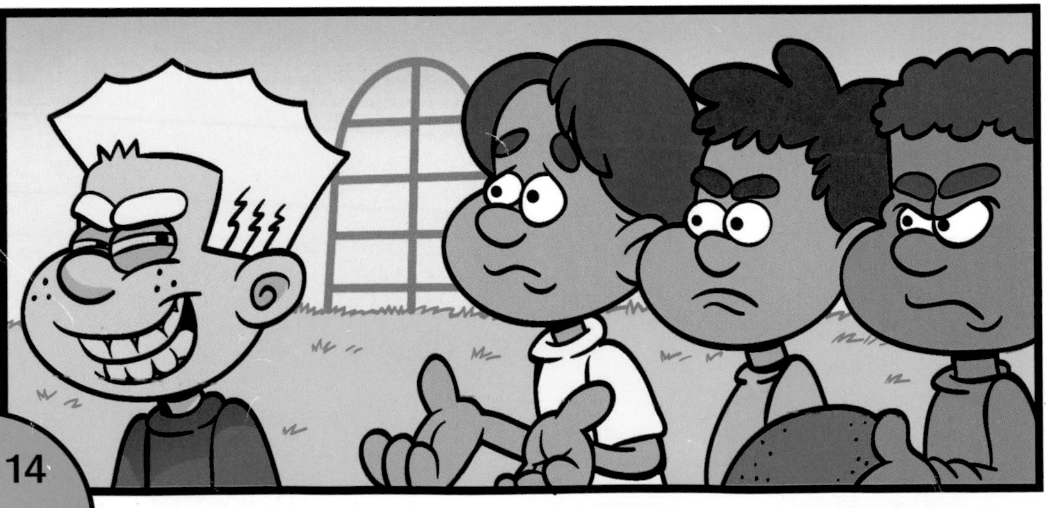

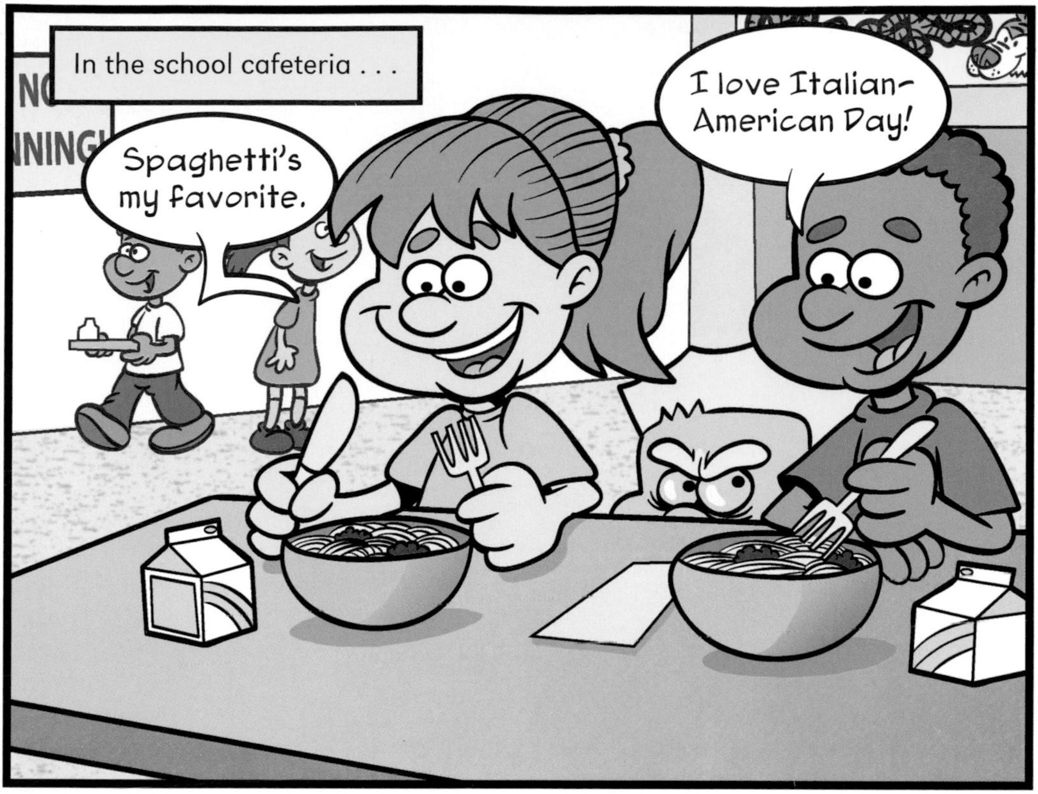
In the school cafeteria . . .
Spaghetti's my favorite.
I love Italian-American Day!

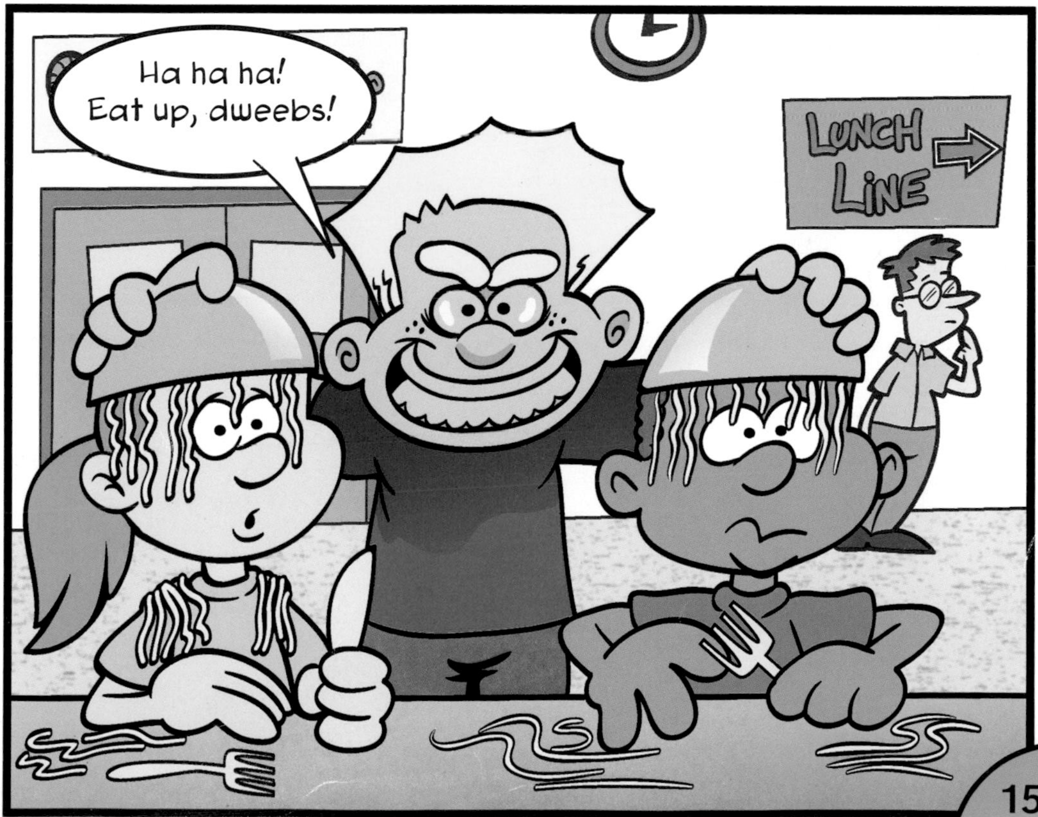
Ha ha ha! Eat up, dweebs!
LUNCH LINE

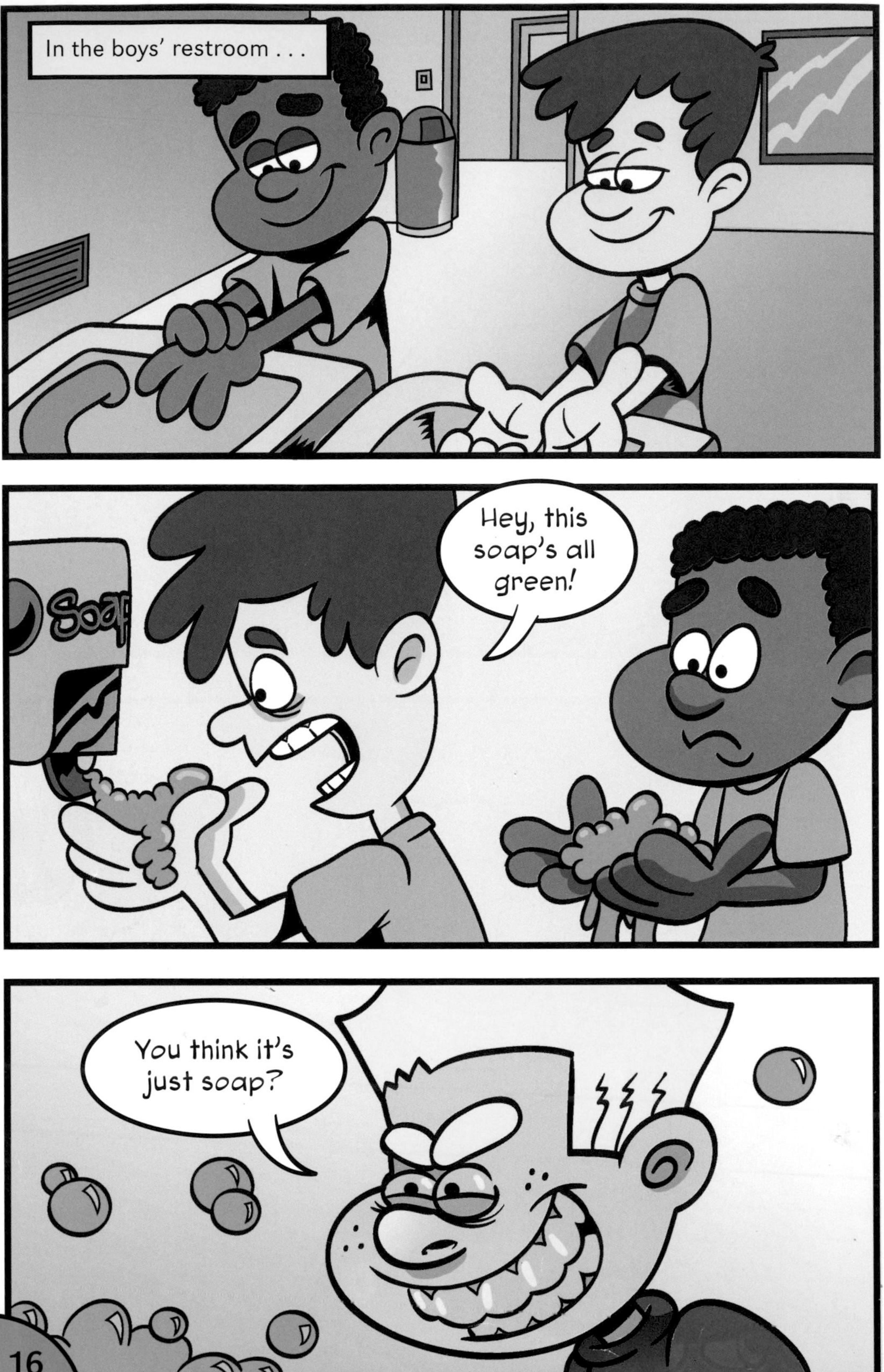
In the boys' restroom . . .
Hey, this soap's all green!
Soap
You think it's just soap?

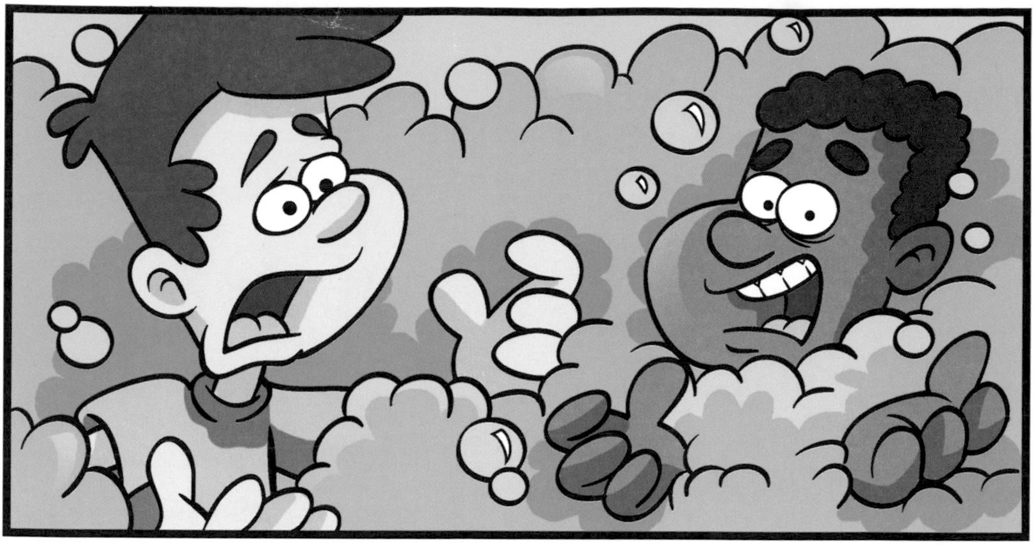

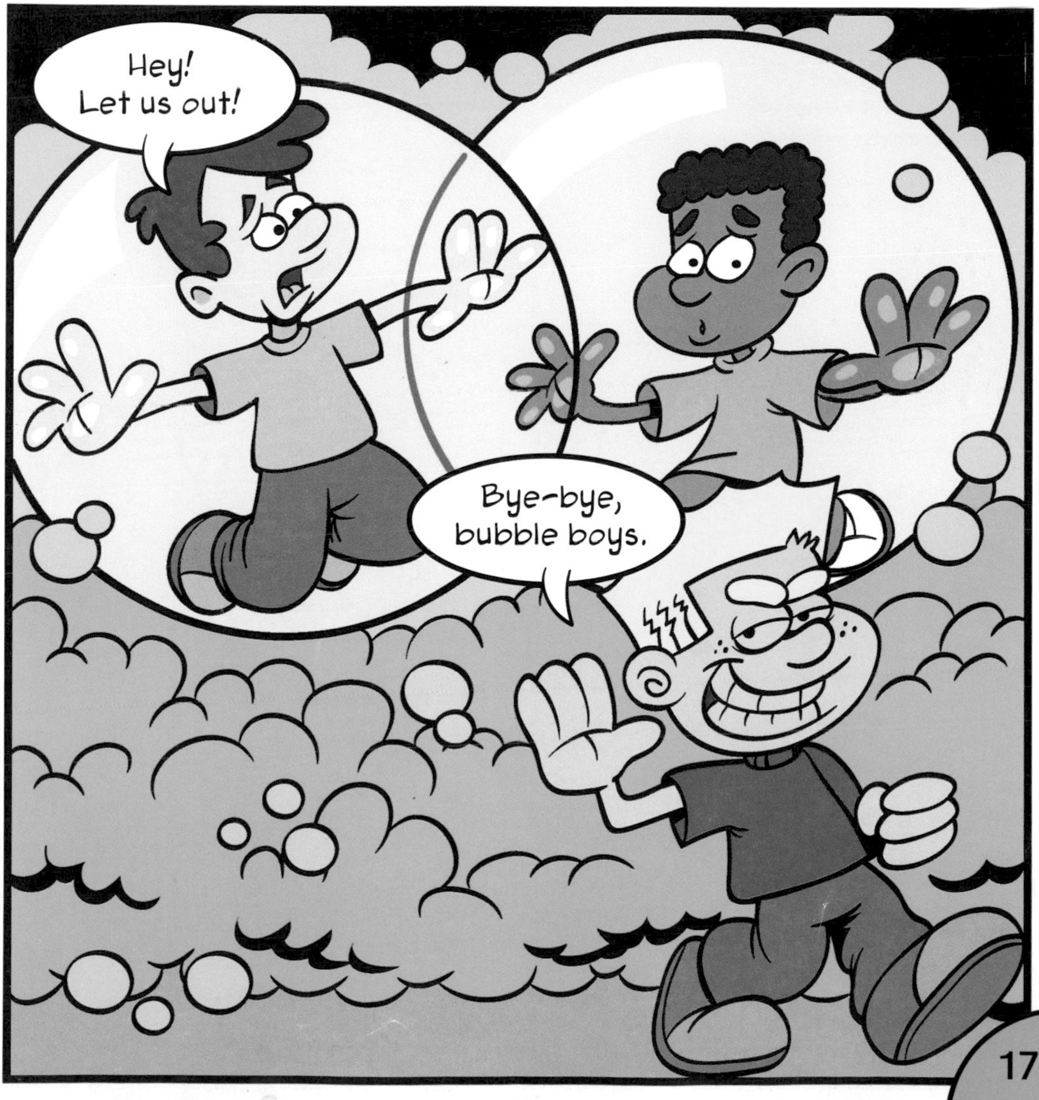
Hey!
Let us out!
Bye-bye,
bubble boys.

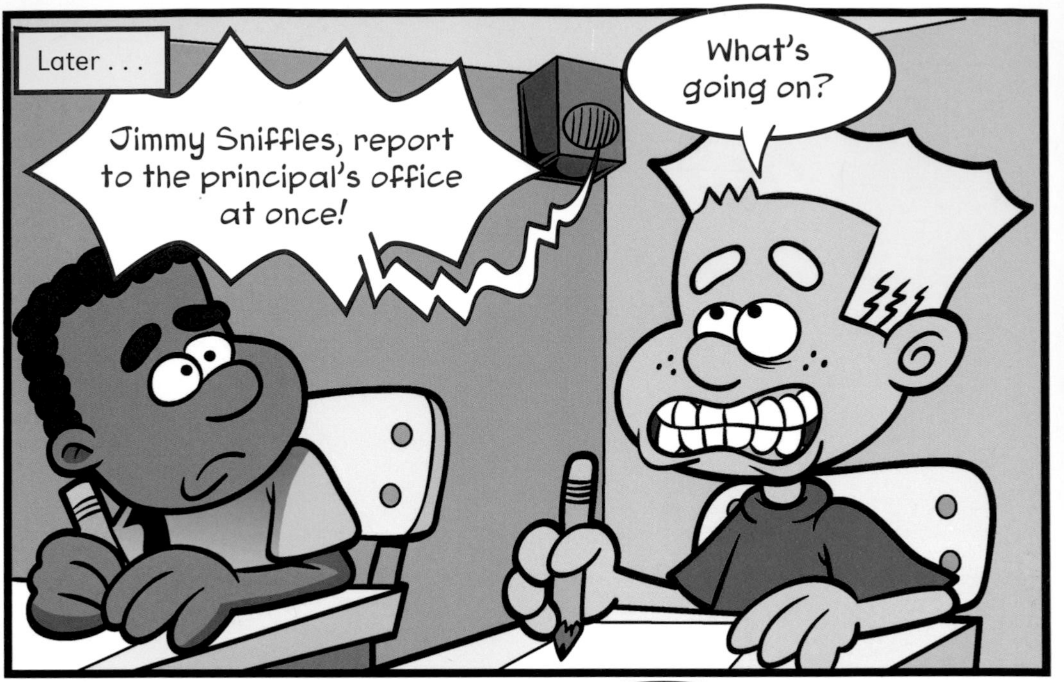
Later . . .
Jimmy Sniffles, report to the principal's office at once!
What's going on?

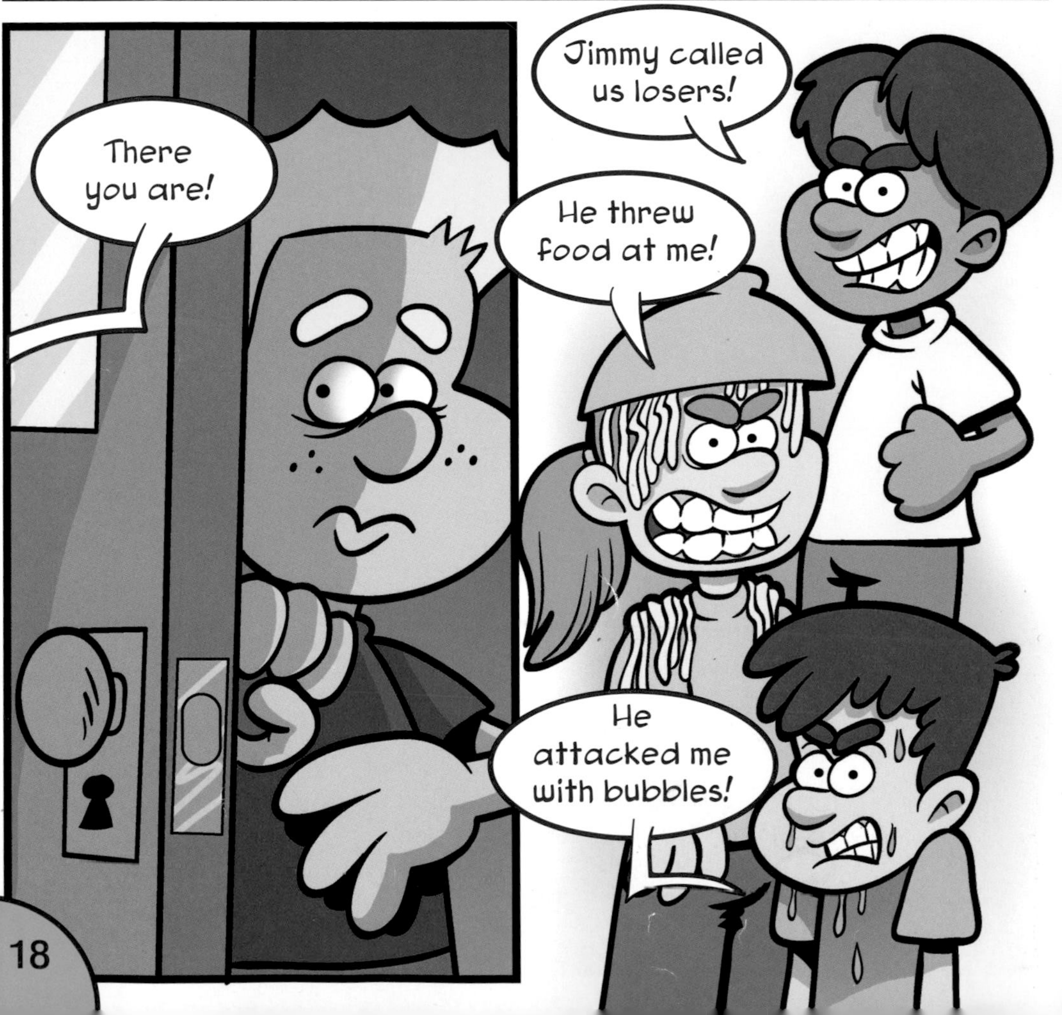
There you are!
Jimmy called us losers!
He threw food at me!
He attacked me with bubbles!

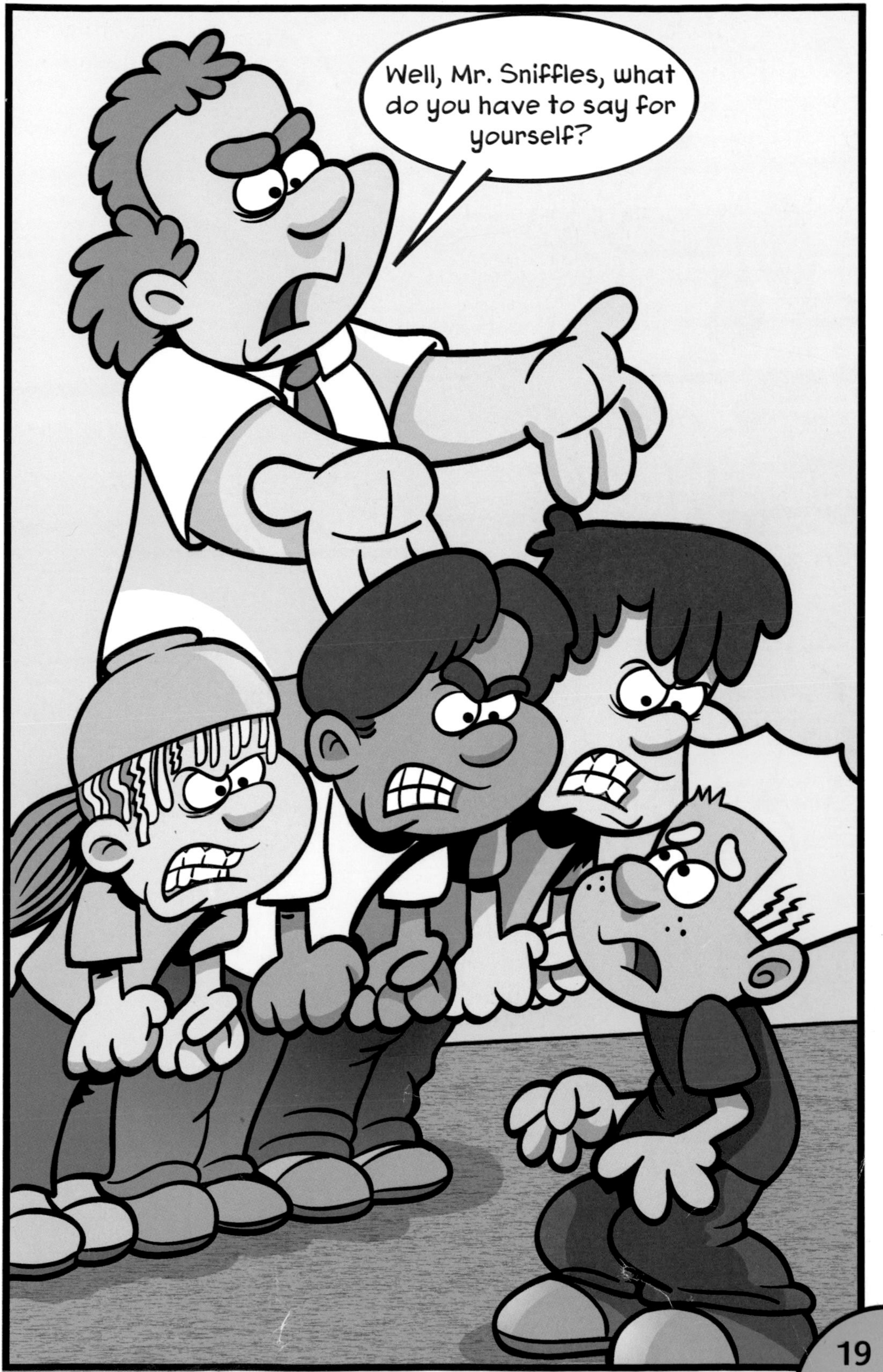
Well, Mr. Sniffles, what do you have to say for yourself?

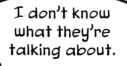

I don't know what they're talking about.

I'm disappointed in you, Jimmy. Acting up is bad enough. But lying about it is worse. Maybe some detention will improve your attitude!

Detention? But . . . but . . .

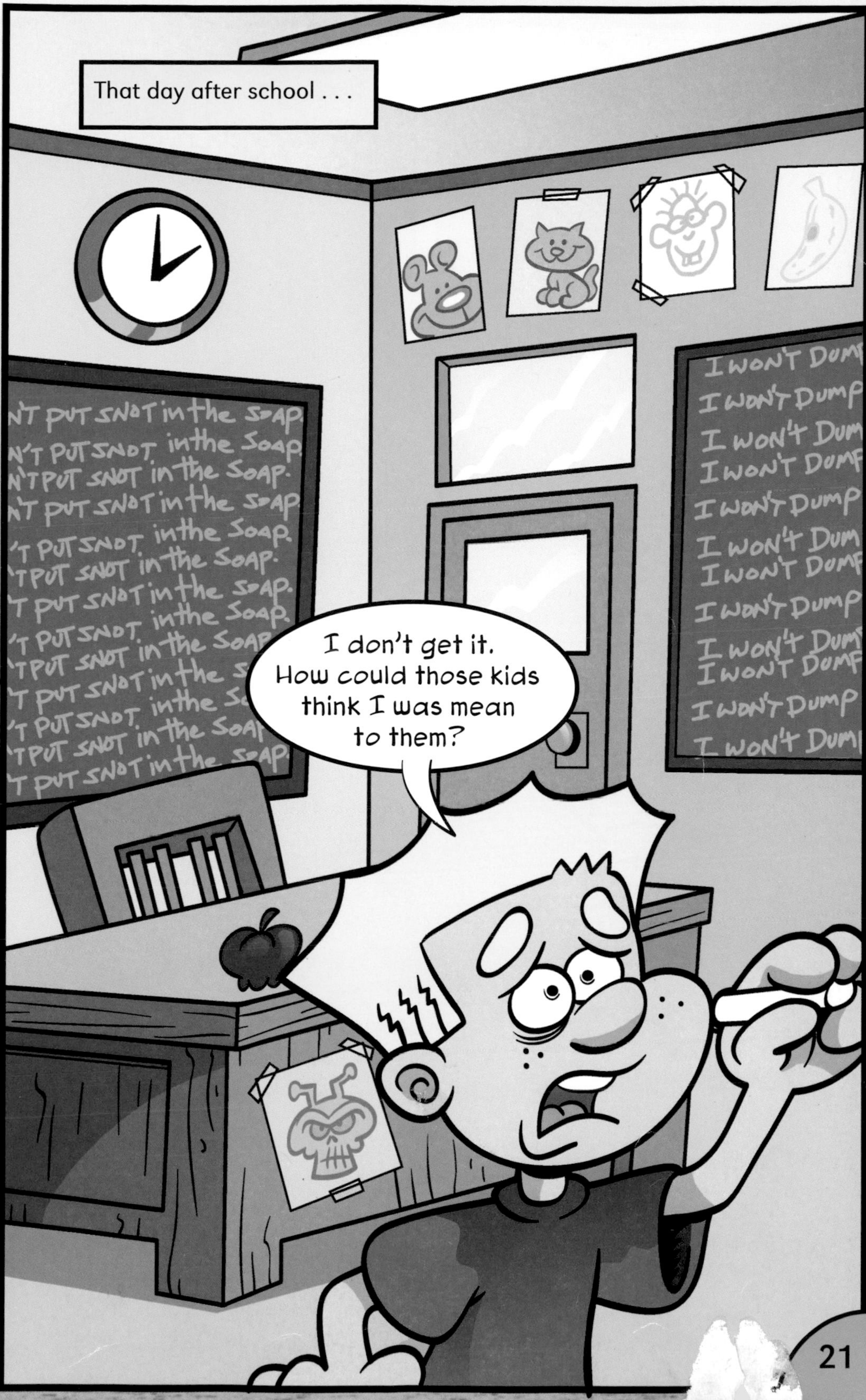
That day after school . . .
I don't get it. How could those kids think I was mean to them?

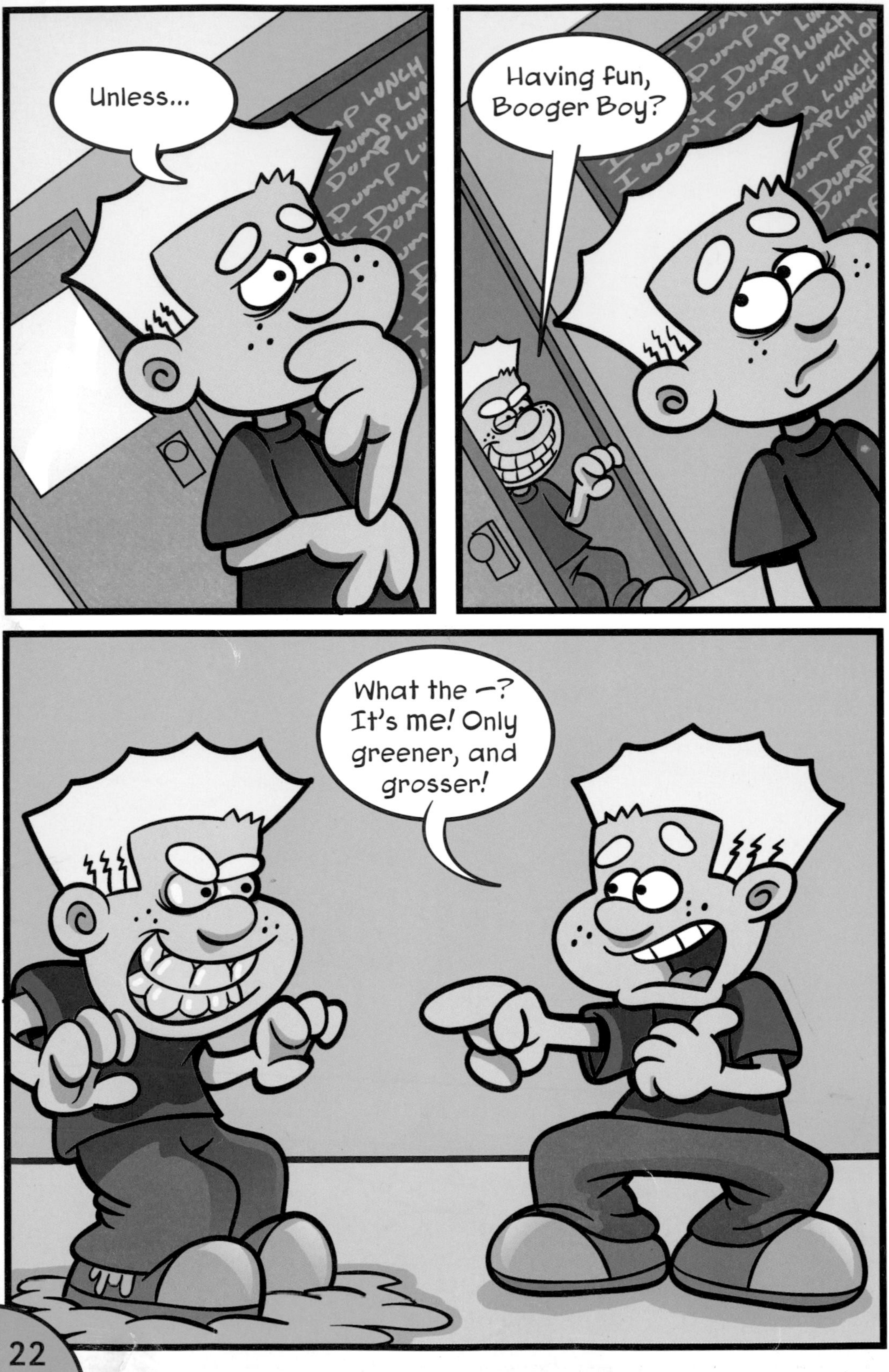
Unless...
Having fun, Booger Boy?
I WON'T DUMP LUNCH
What the —? It's me! Only greener, and grosser!

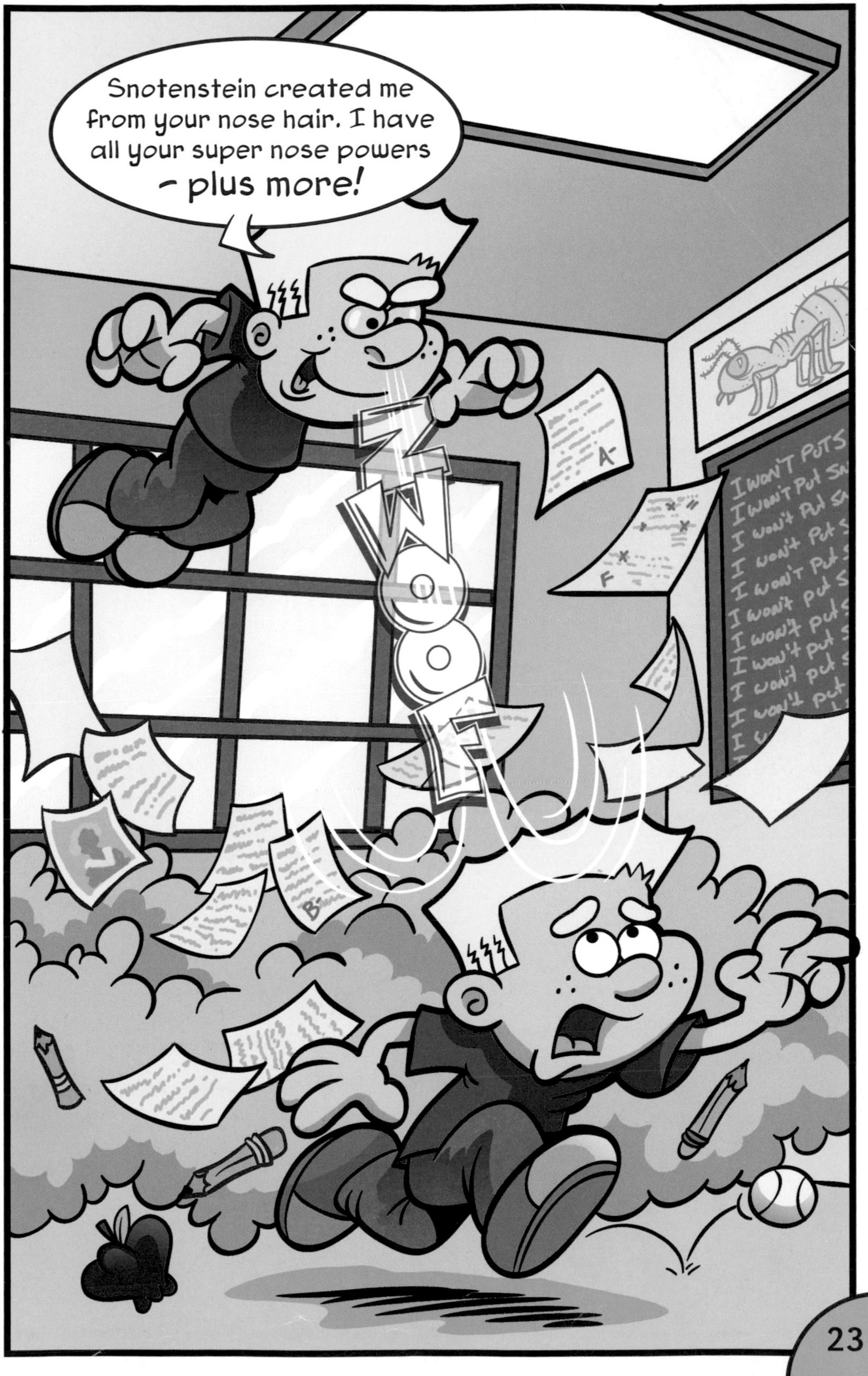
Snotenstein created me from your nose hair. I have all your super nose powers – plus more!
ZWOOF

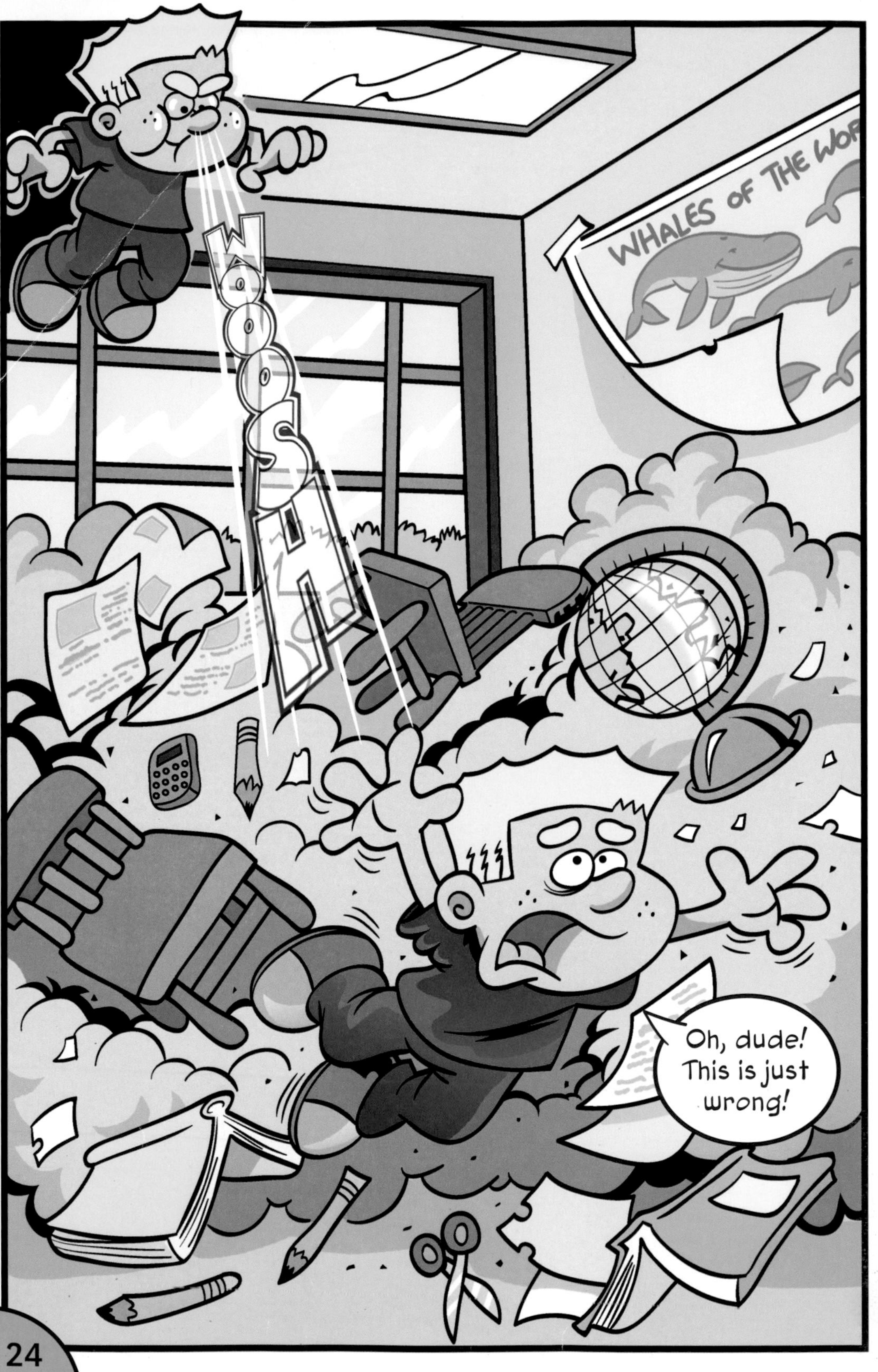
WHALES OF THE WOR
WOOOSH
Oh, dude! This is just wrong!

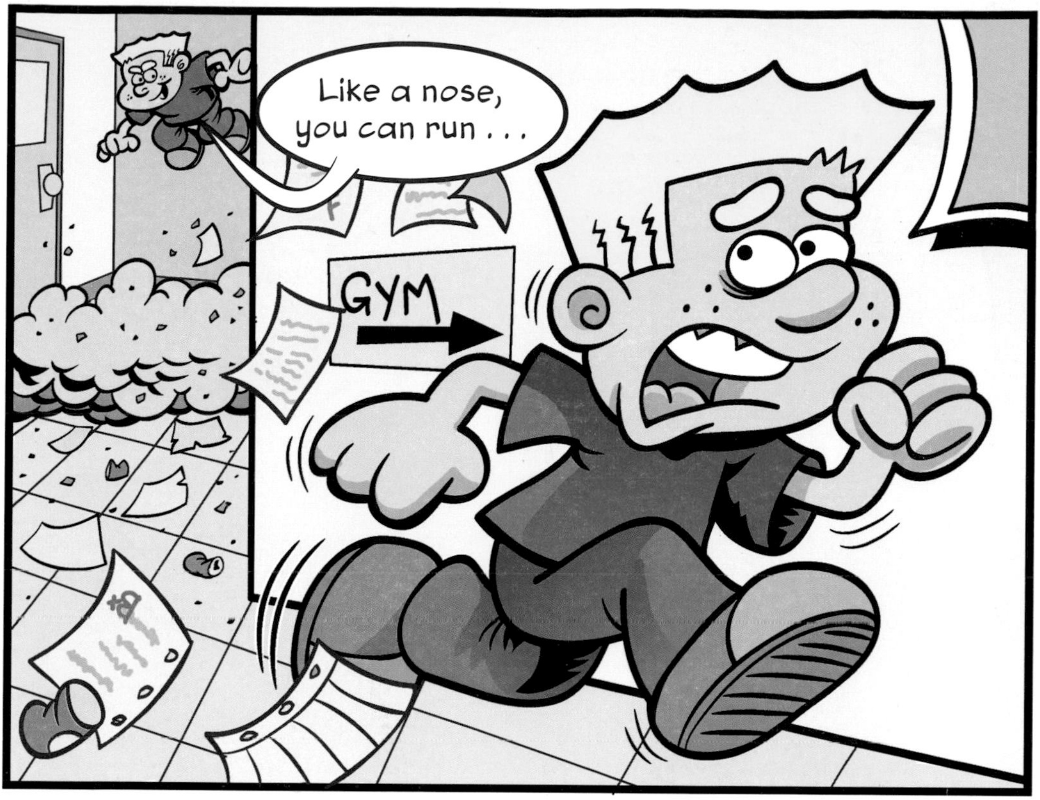

Like a nose, you can run . . .
GYM

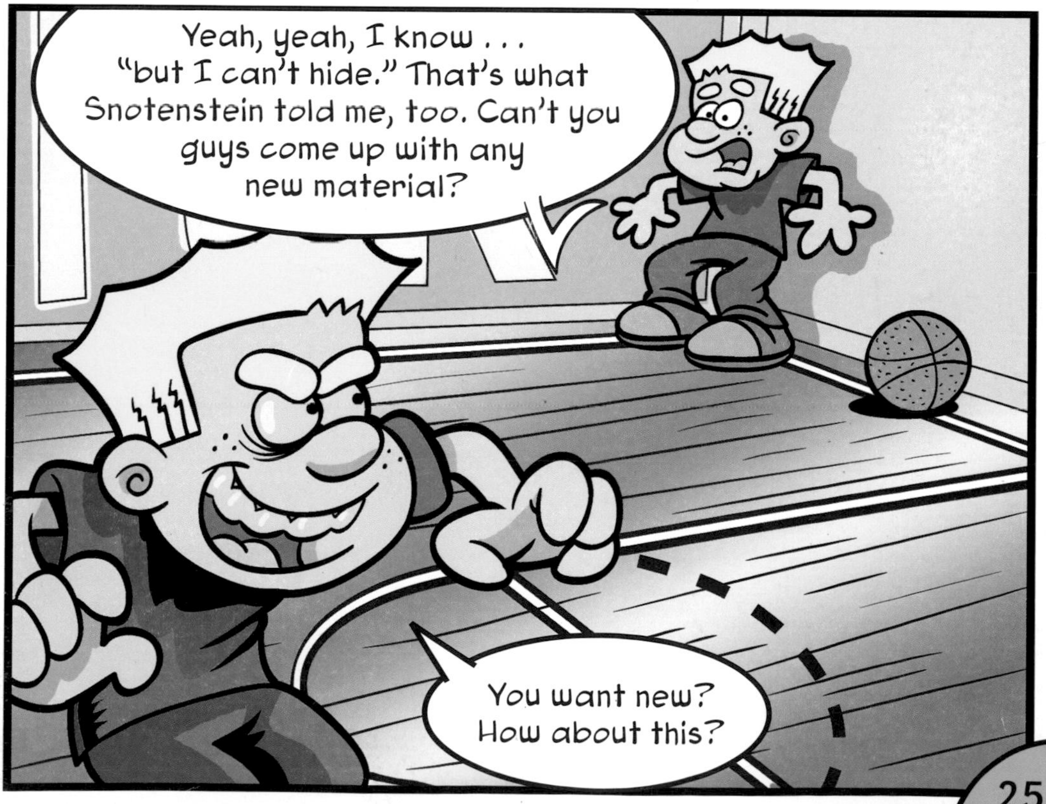

Yeah, yeah, I know . . . "but I can't hide." That's what Snotenstein told me, too. Can't you guys come up with any new material?
You want new? How about this?

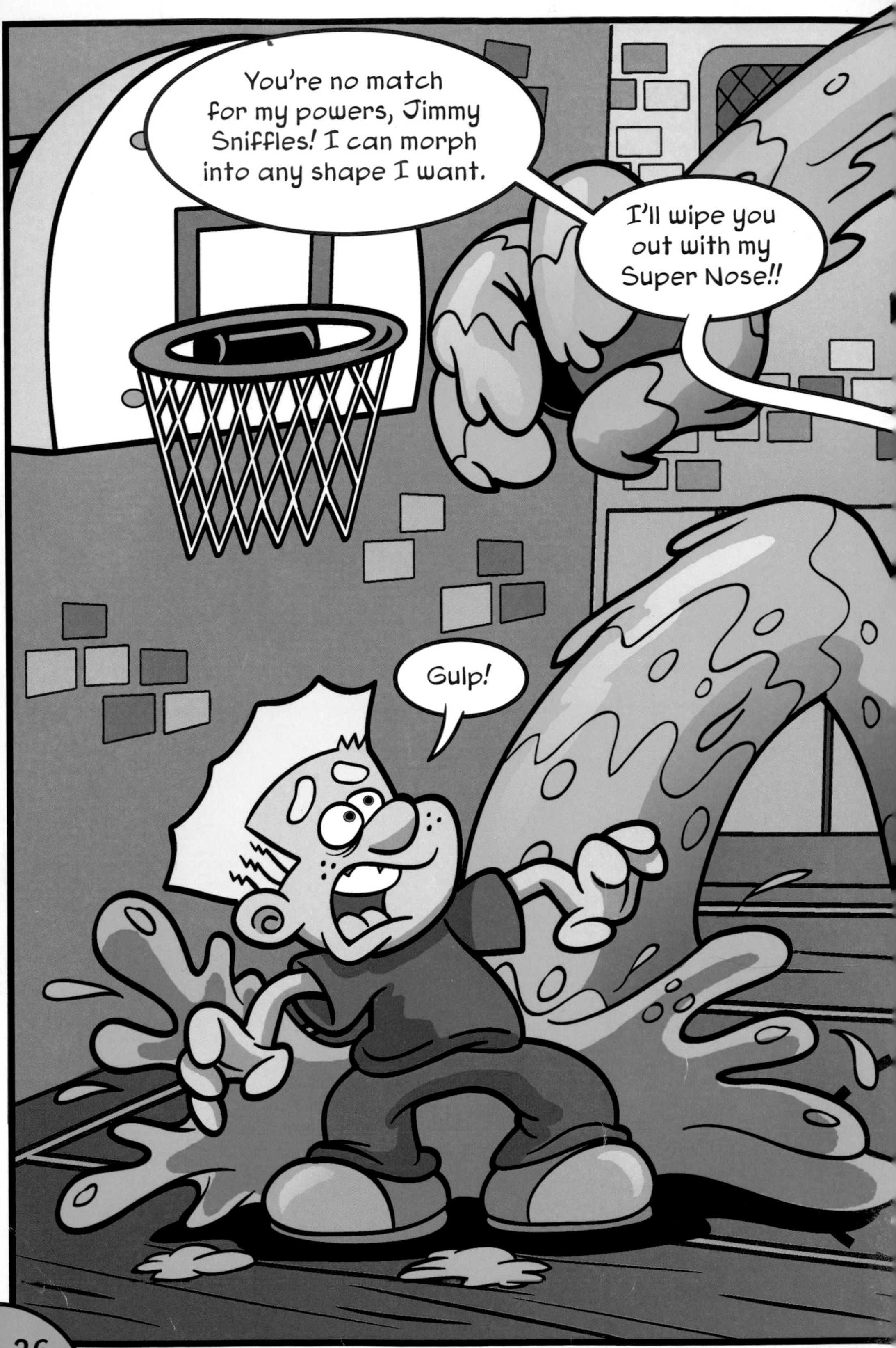
You're no match for my powers, Jimmy Sniffles! I can morph into any shape I want.
I'll wipe you out with my Super Nose!!
Gulp!

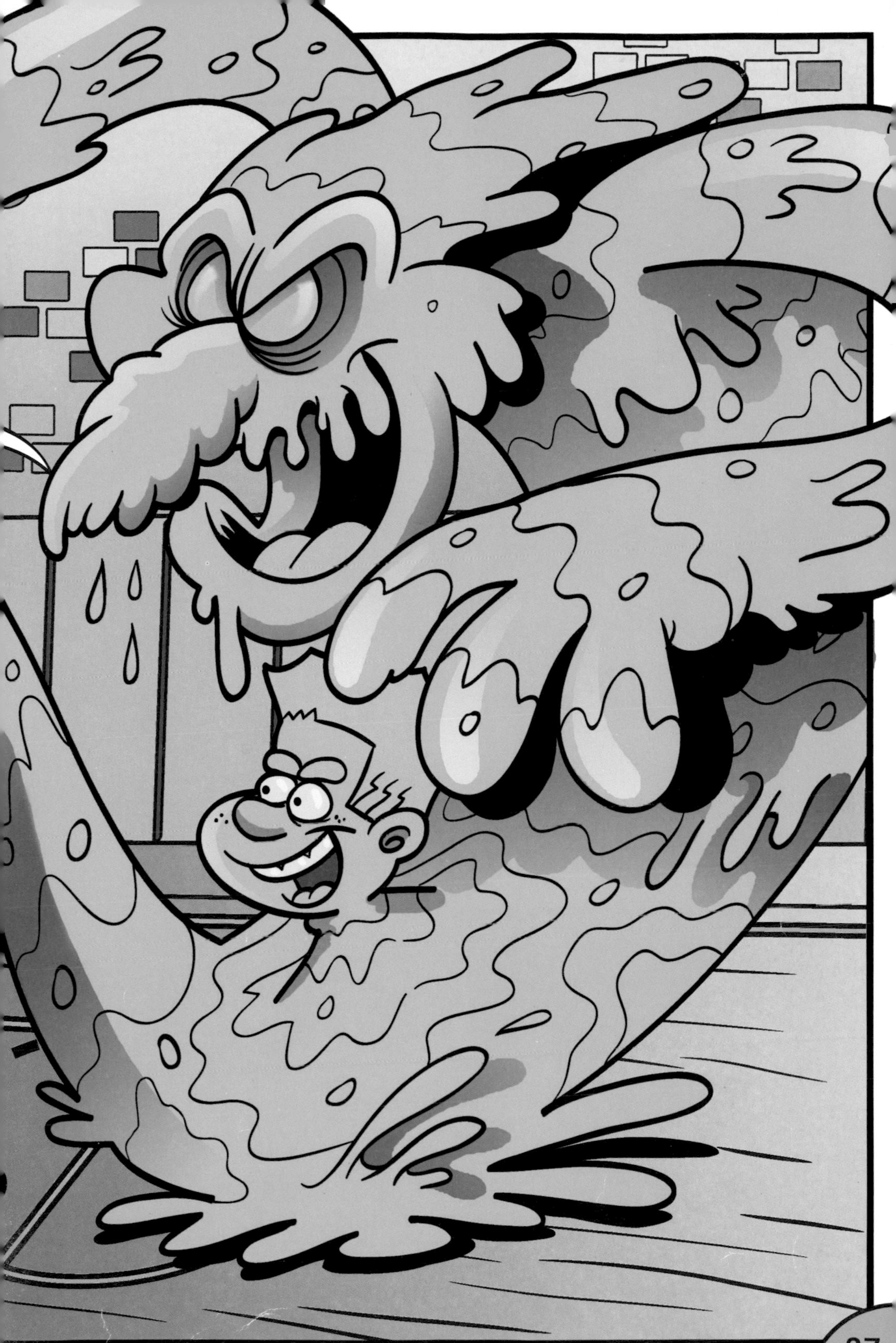

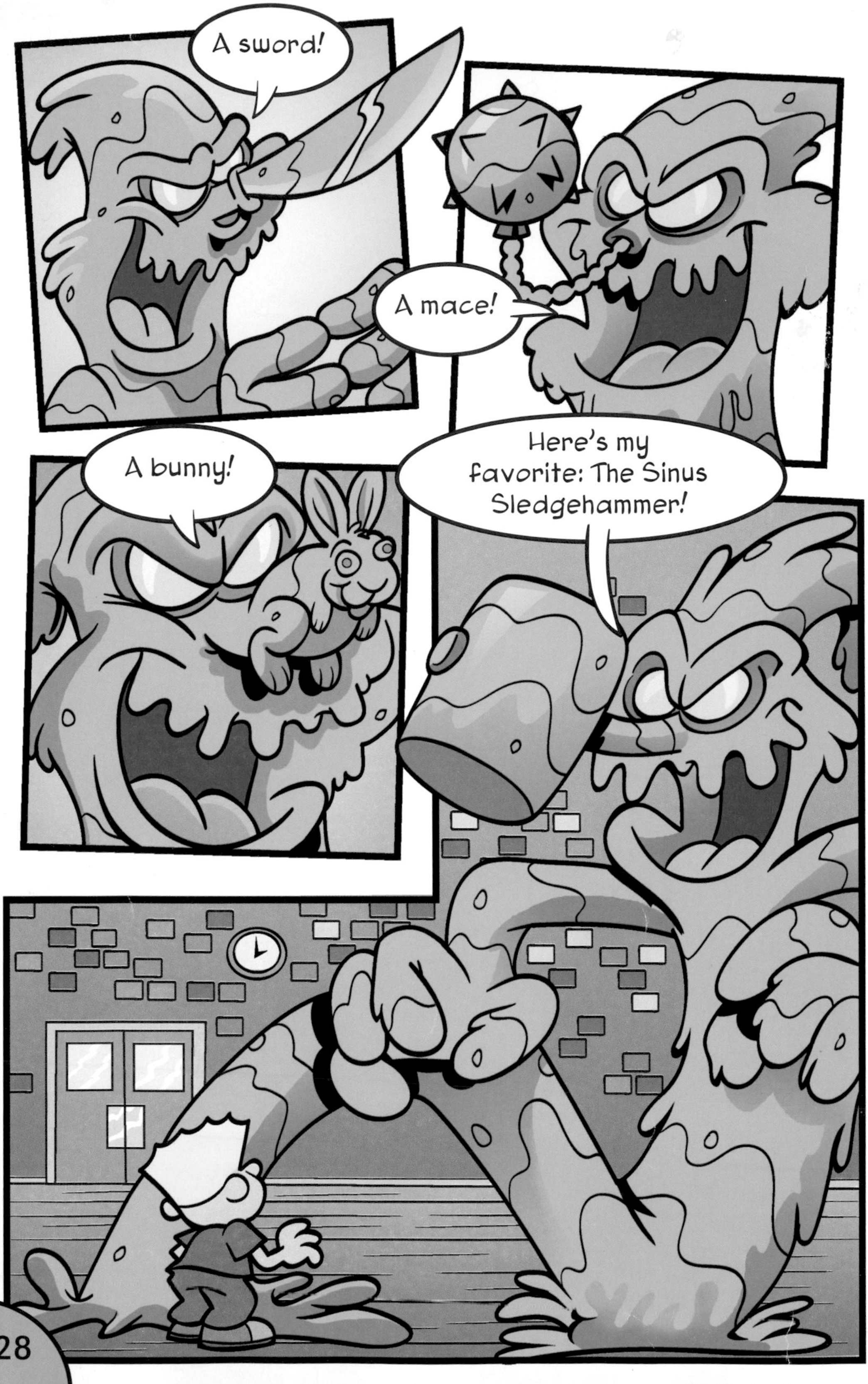
A sword!
A mace!
A bunny!
Here's my favorite: The Sinus Sledgehammer!

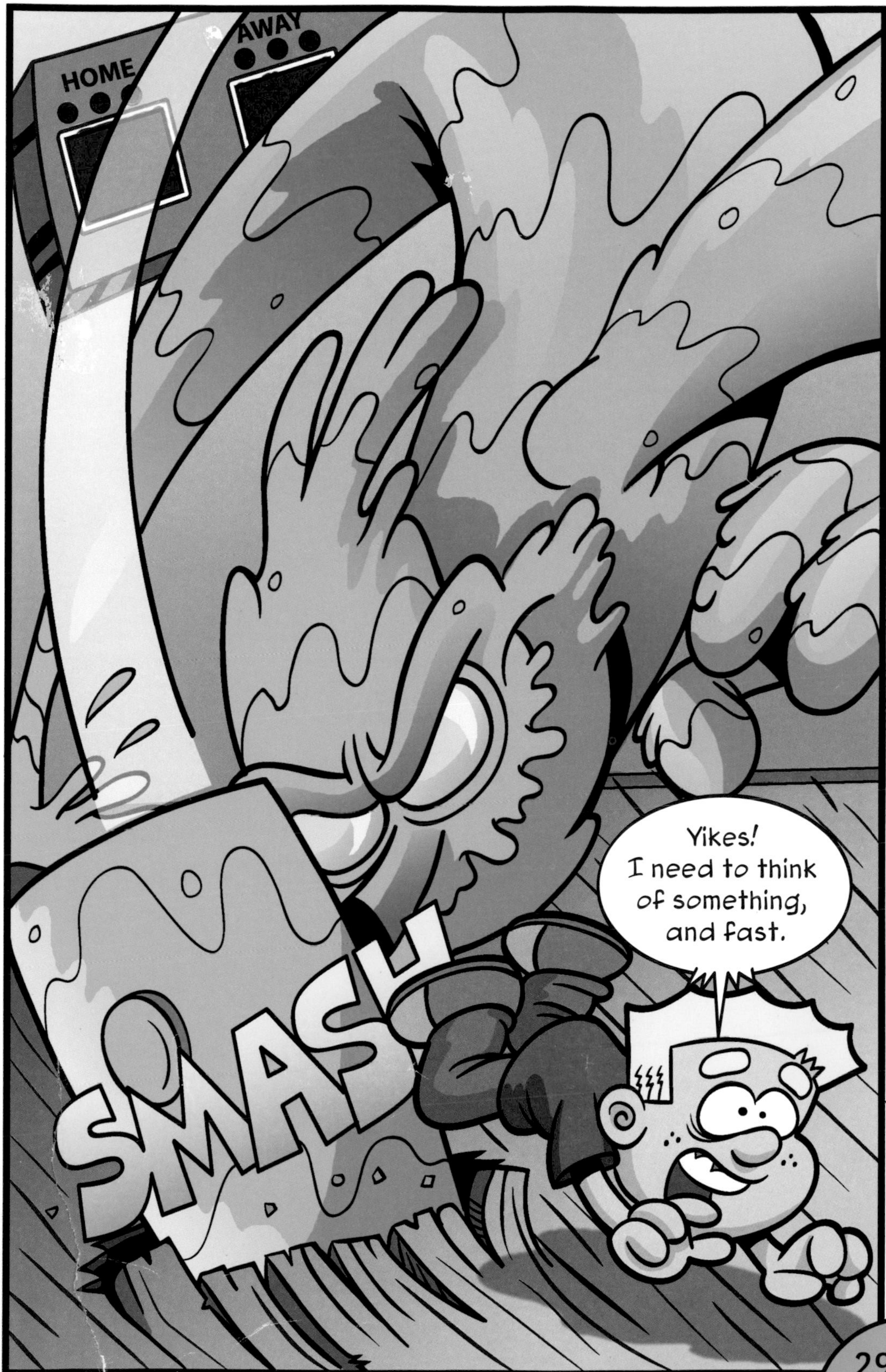
HOME
AWAY
Yikes! I need to think of something, and fast.
SMASH

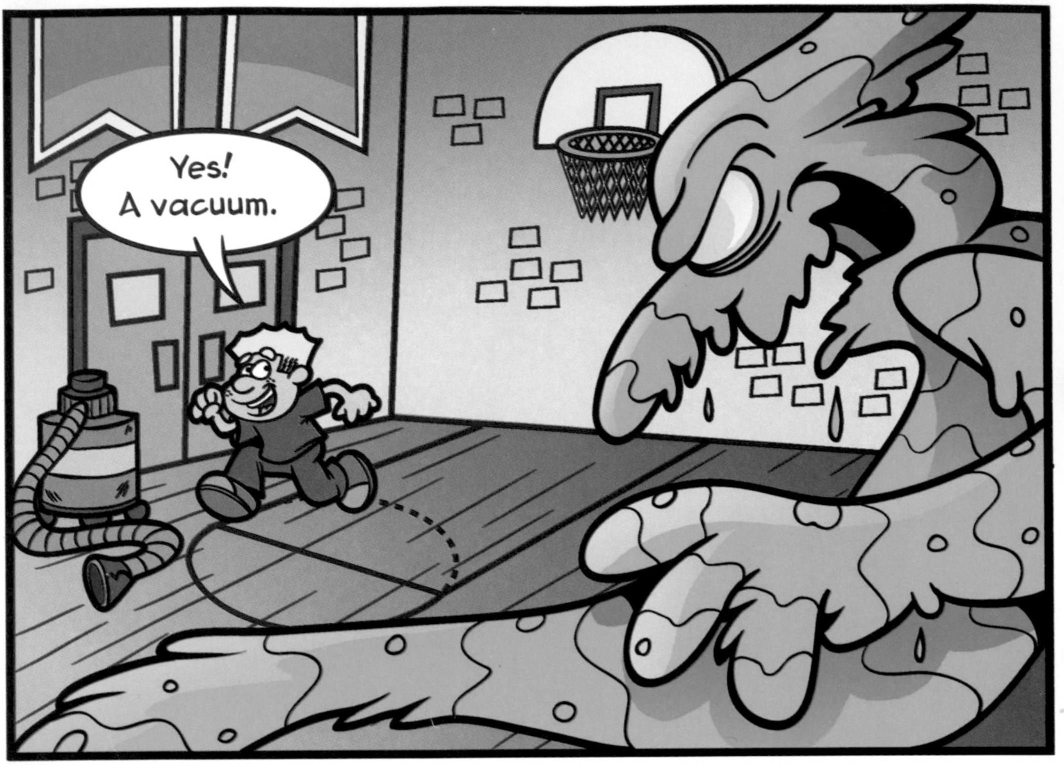
Yes!
A vacuum.

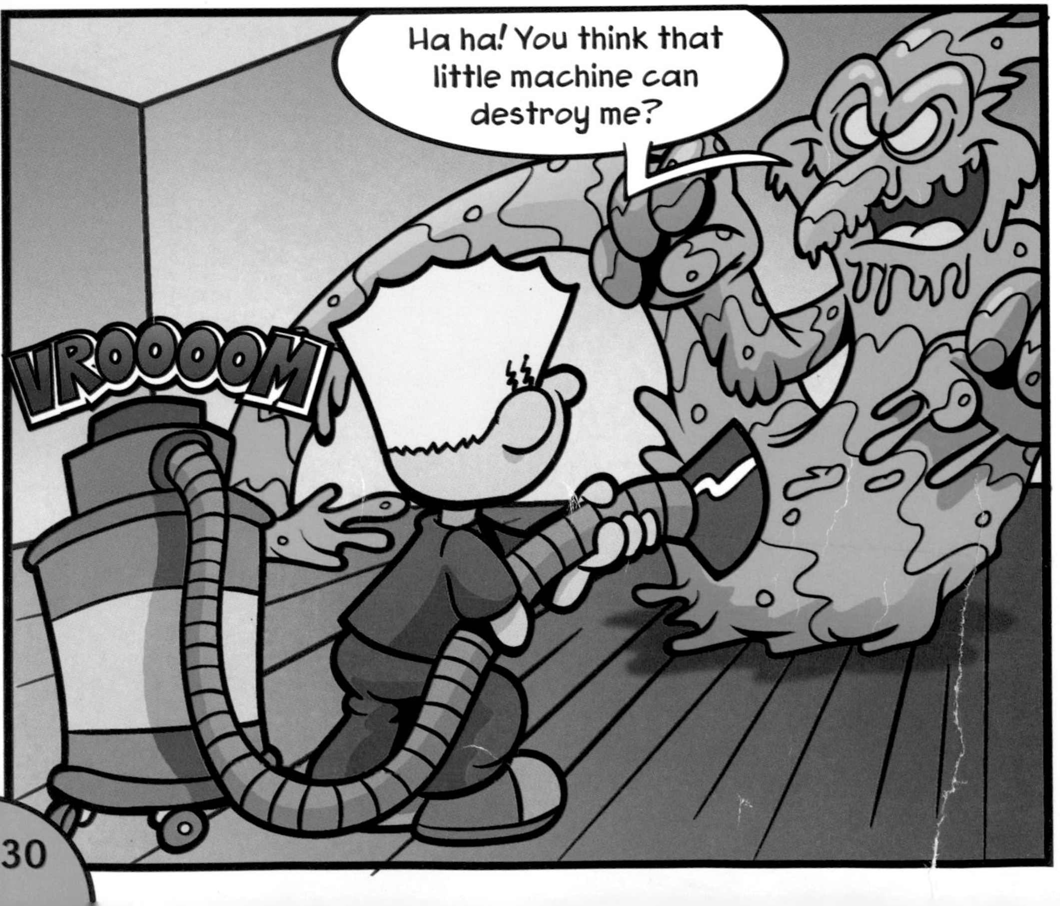
Ha ha! You think that little machine can destroy me?
VROOOOM

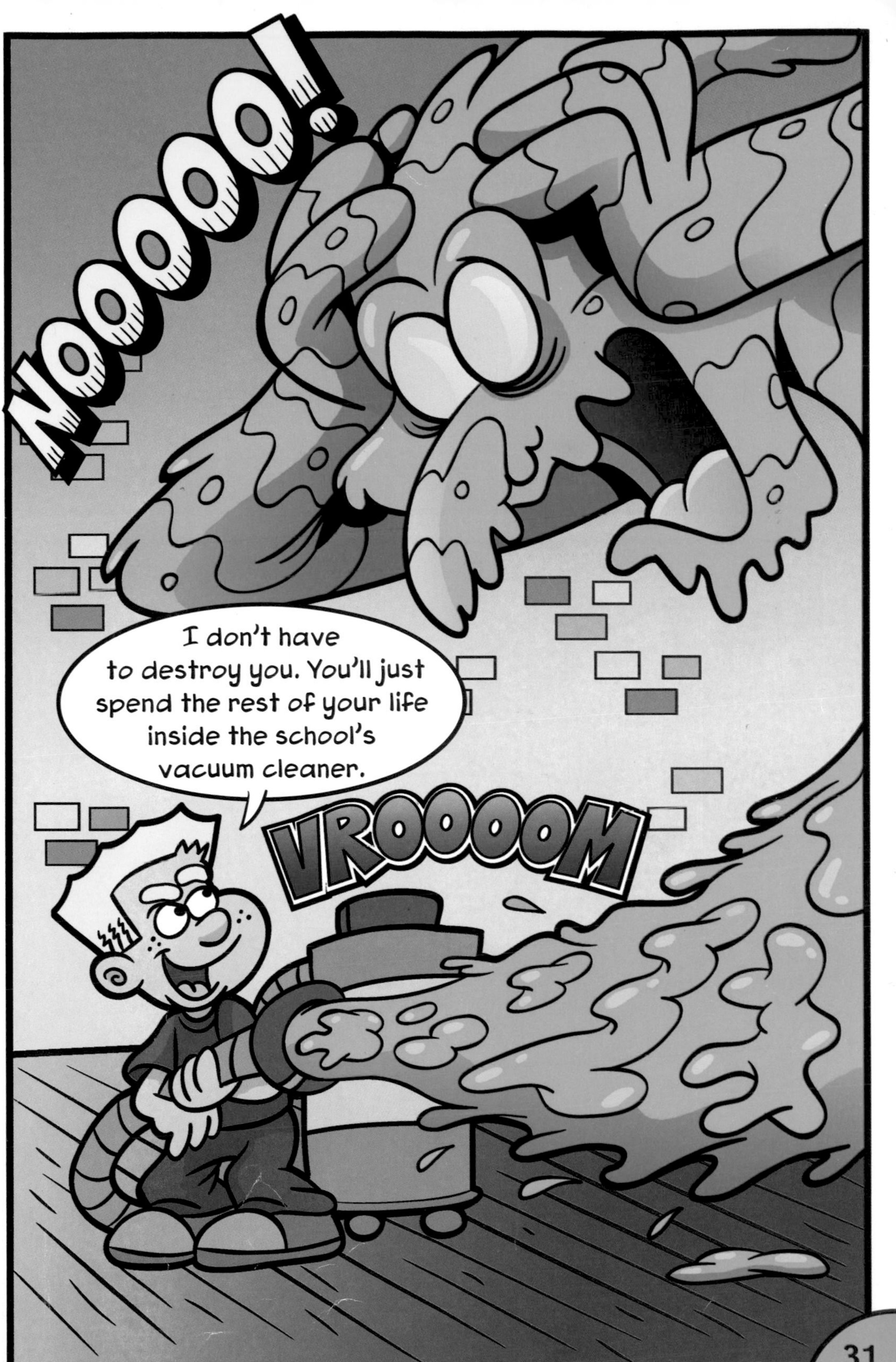
NOOOOO!
I don't have to destroy you. You'll just spend the rest of your life inside the school's vacuum cleaner.
VROOOOM

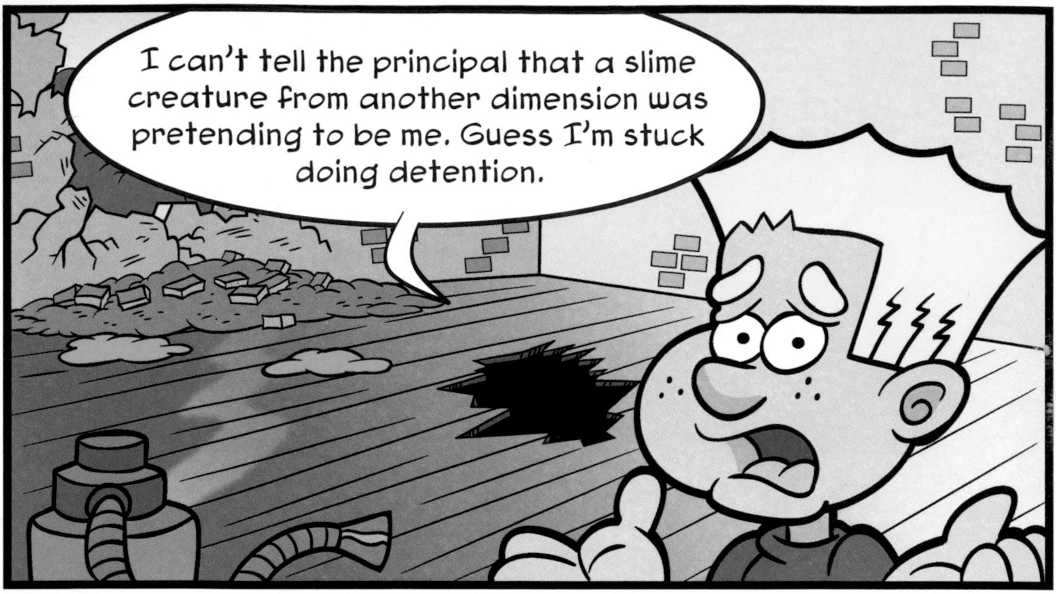
I can't tell the principal that a slime creature from another dimension was pretending to be me. Guess I'm stuck doing detention.

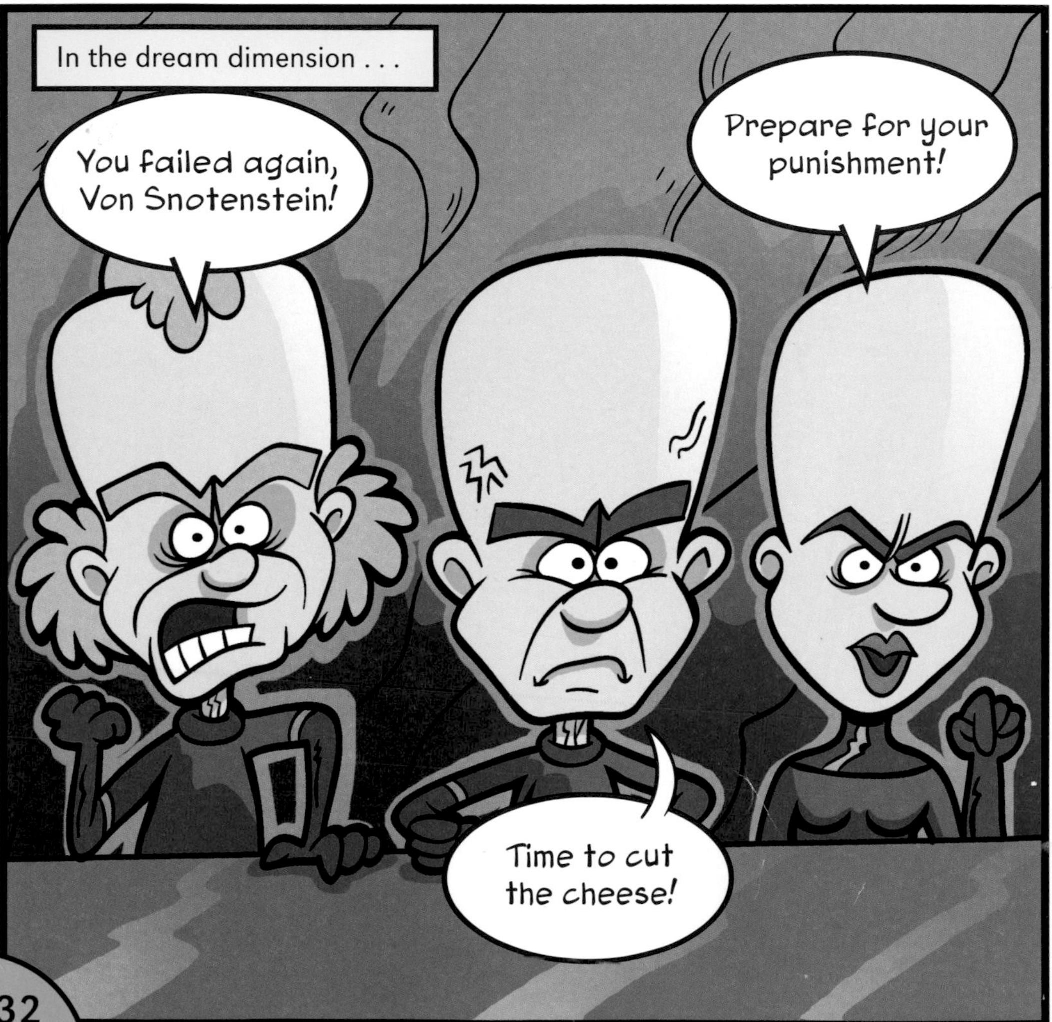
In the dream dimension . . .
You failed again, Von Snotenstein!
Prepare for your punishment!
Time to cut the cheese!

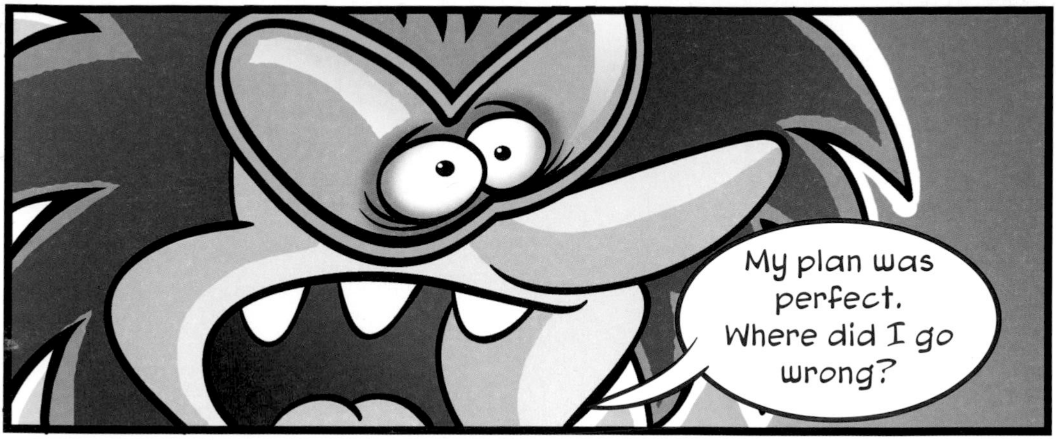
My plan was perfect. Where did I go wrong?

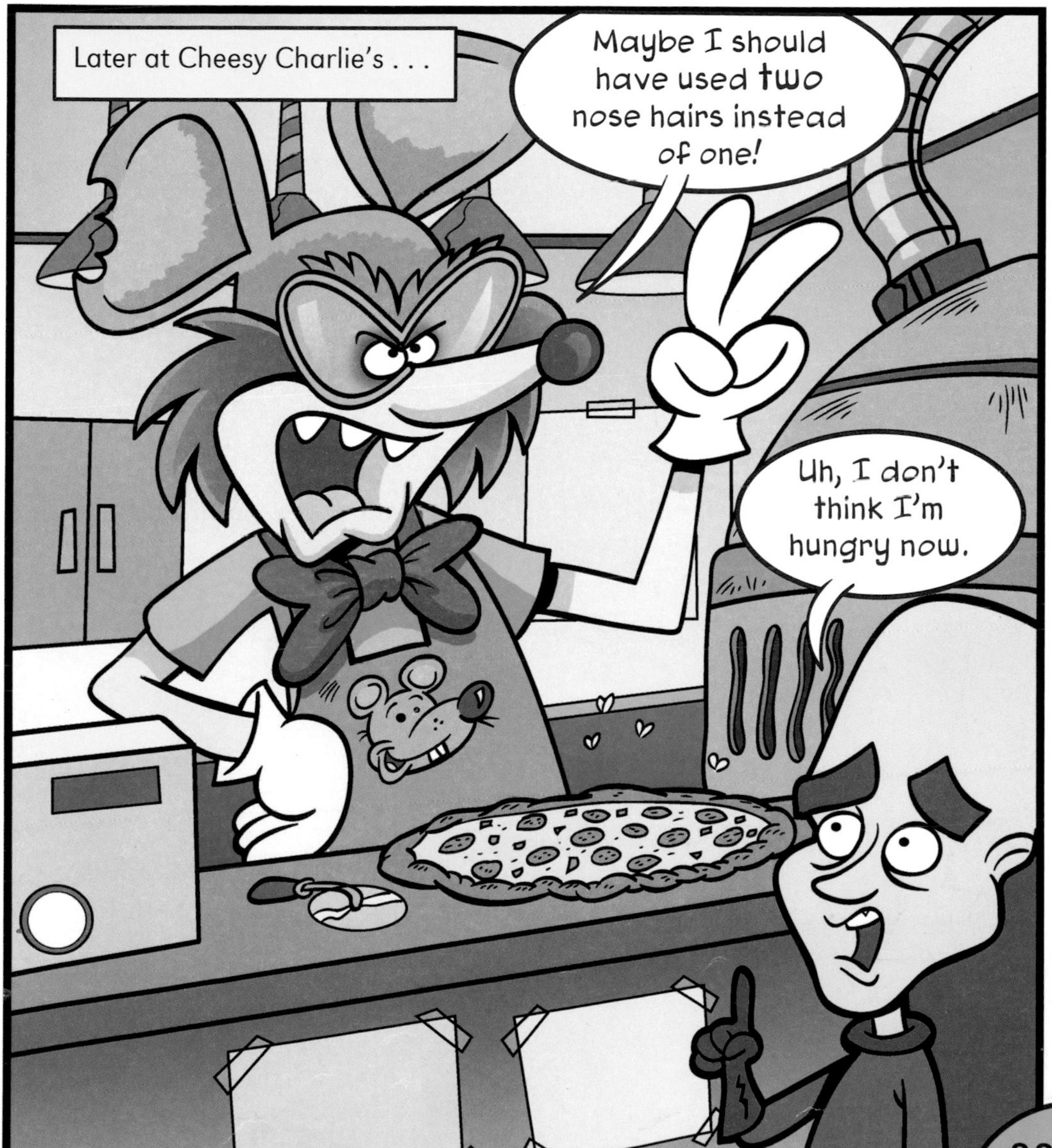
Later at Cheesy Charlie's . . .
Maybe I should have used two nose hairs instead of one!
Uh, I don't think I'm hungry now.

ABOUT THE AUTHOR

Born in 1962 in Denver, Colorado, Scott Nickel works
by day at Paws, Inc., Jim Davis's famous Garfield
studio, and he freelances by night. Burning the
midnight oil, Scott has created hundreds of humorous
greeting cards and written several children's books,
short fiction for *Boys' Life* magazine, comic strips,
and lots of really funny knock-knock jokes. He was
raised in Southern California, but in 1995 Scott
moved to Indiana, where he currently lives with his
wife, two sons, six cats, and several sea monkeys.

ABOUT THE ILLUSTRATOR

Steve Harpster has loved drawing funny cartoons,
mean monsters, and goofy gadgets since he was able
to pick up a pencil. In first grade, instead of writing
a report about a dog-sled story set in Alaska, Steve
made a comic book about it. He was worried the
teacher might not like it, but she hung it up for all
the kids in the class to see. "It taught me to take a
chance and try something different," says Steve.
Steve landed a job drawing funny pictures for books.
He used to be an animator for Disney. Now, Steve
lives in Columbus, Ohio, with his wonderful wife, Karen,
and their sheepdog, Doodle.

GLOSSARY

arcade (ar-KAYD)—a fun place in a store or shopping mall where you can play video games and funny sport games, and eat snacks. It's also a great place to give an evil villain detention.

detention (duh-TEN-shin)—a punishment for a student where they have to stay late after school. It can also mean other kinds of punishment, like coming to school early or working at a pizza arcade.

dimension (duh-MEN-shun)—an environment or surrounding where things live and move

morph (morf)—to change shape or turn into something else

nuisance (NOO-sunss)—a pest, a pain, a bother. A flea is a nuisance to a dog. A super hero is a nuisance to a villain.

sinus (SY-nis)—one of the small, hollow spaces in your head that are connected to your nose

THE TRUTH ABOUT TWINS

There are two kinds of twins, fraternal and identical.
Fraternal twins are born at the same time, but look
different from each other. Identical twins look
exactly alike.

Do twins have the same fingerprints as each other?
No! They might have some of the same patterns on
their fingertips, but they have many more differences.

The country of Nigeria in Africa has more twins than anywhere else in the world. One birth in every 22 is twins. The Nigerians think it is because they eat so many yams.

In the United States, there are more twins born in Massachusetts and Connecticut than in any other state. Maybe it has something to do with all those double letters in their names! Weird.

The talented Cirque Du Soleil circus likes to hire twins for their shows. They have had as many as 9 sets of twins performing in one show!

The world's most famous twins were Chang and Eng Bunker who were brothers from Siam (now known as Thailand). The two boys, born in 1811, were joined together at the chest. For a time, other conjoined twins were also known as "Siamese twins."

DISCUSSION QUESTIONS

1. If you don't have a twin, would you like one? Would you like to be around someone who looks and acts just like you? Why or why not? If you **are** a twin, what is it like? What would life be like if you did **not** have a twin?

2. The evil Jimmy can turn his nose into anything! If you had that power, what would you turn your nose into and why?

3. Many kids would love to work at a place like Cheesy Charlie's Pizza Arcade. Why do you think Doctor von Snotenstein hates it so much?

WRITING PROMPTS

1. Who are those strange little people who tell Dr. von Snotenstein what he can and can't do? Are they aliens? Are they powerful? Do they like Jimmy Sniffles? Describe where you think they come from and what kind of lives they have.

2. The monster that Jimmy finally defeats is scared of being trapped in the vacuum cleaner. Inside will be all kinds of things sucked up from a school lunchroom. Yikes! Describe what the monster will find inside that disgusting vacuum bag.

3. After Jimmy defeats the evil twin creature, he needs to go back and explain to his principal what really happened. Will his principal believe him? Should Jimmy apologize to the students who were hurt by the evil Jimmy? Write down what you think happens after the story ends.

More cheese!

INTERNET SITES

Do you want to know more about subjects related to this book? Or are you interested in learning about other topics? Then check out FactHound, a fun, easy way to find Internet sites.

Our investigative staff has already sniffed out great sites for you!

Here's how to use FactHound:

1. Visit www.facthound.com

2. Select your grade level.

3. To learn more about subjects related to this book, type in the book's ISBN number: 1598893149.

4. Click the **Fetch It** button.

FactHound will fetch the best Internet sites for you!

A WALL OF SEPARATION?

Enduring Questions in American Political Life
Series Editor: Wilson Carey McWilliams, Rutgers University

This series explores the political, social, and cultural issues that originated during the founding of the American nation but are still heatedly debated today. Each book offers teachers and students a concise but comprehensive summary of the issue's evolution, along with the crucial documents spanning the range of American history. In addition, *Enduring Questions in American Political Life* provides insightful contemporary perspectives that illuminate the enduring relevance and future prospects of important issues on the American political landscape.

The Choice of the People? Debating the Electoral College
Judith A. Best, foreword by Thomas E. Cronin
A Wall of Separation? Debating the Public Role of Religion
Mary C. Segers and Ted G. Jelen, introduction by Clarke E. Cochran
A Republic of Parties? Debating the Two-Party System
Theodore J. Lowi and Joseph Romance, introduction by Gerald M. Pomper

A WALL OF SEPARATION?

Debating the Public Role
of Religion

Mary C. Segers
and Ted G. Jelen

Introduction by Clarke E. Cochran

ROWMAN & LITTLEFIELD PUBLISHERS, INC.
Lanham • Boulder • New York • Oxford

ROWMAN & LITTLEFIELD PUBLISHERS, INC.

Published in the United States of America
by Rowman & Littlefield Publishers, Inc.
4720 Boston Way, Lanham, Maryland 20706

12 Hid's Copse Road
Cumnor Hill, Oxford OX2 9JJ, England

British Library Cataloguing in Publication Information Available

Library of Congress Cataloging-in-Publication Data

Segers, Mary C.
    A wall of separation? : debating the public role of religion /
Mary C. Segers and Ted G. Jelen.
        p.   cm. — (Enduring questions in American political life)
    Includes bibliographical references and index.
    ISBN 0-8476-8387-7 (alk. paper). — ISBN 0-8476-8388-5 (alk.
paper)
    1. United States—Religion.   2. Church and state—United States.
3. Religion and politics—United States.   I. Jelen, Ted G.
II. Title.   III. Series.
BL2525.S44   1998
322'.1'0973—dc21   98-23173
                                                             CIP

Printed in the United States of America

⊗ ™ The paper used in this publication meets the minimum requirements of
American National Standard for Information Sciences—Permanence of Paper for
Printed Library Materials, ANSI Z39.48—1984.

Mary Segers dedicates this to Jerry.
Ted Jelen dedicates this to Marty.

Contents

Introduction

Clarke E. Cochran

What is going on here? A civil discussion, a tolerant debate on religion and politics? Is it possible to discuss church and state in America without coming to blows or parting in stony silence? Apparently so, given the evidence before us.

"Religious minimalist" meets "moderate accommodationist." Ted Jelen and Mary Segers provide a model debate. Their essays address the deepest and most contentious questions of religion and politics, of church and state. Each takes a firm stance and does not waver; yet they treat the other's position with respect. What can we learn from this encounter?

Are there special reasons to limit religion's role in political discourse? Are there distinctive contributions that religion can make to political discourse? Jelen puts forth a "yes" to the first question and a "no" to the second. His clear, straightforward position is strongly separationist. Segers's position is less straightforward. She extends a *qualified* "no" and a *qualified* "yes" to the same questions, respectively. Recognizing the dangers in the dance of church and state, she cannot favor close contact between the two. Nonetheless, the dance is essential to American democracy; so the partners must be kept together.[1]

I want to place these essays in a particular context, to address the topics from a different angle, and to point out important concepts and issues implicit in the text. The context consists of four overarching topics: (1) religion in American political and cultural history; (2) the constitutional law of church and state; (3) the dangers to both religion and political life of "excessive entanglement"; and (4) the manner in which religion and politics will interact.

Religion in American Political and Cultural History

It is not surprising that Mary Segers covers this topic most completely. Whatever one might think in the abstract about the desirability of religious commit-

ment in political life, the concrete facts of American history demonstrate that the issue was settled generations ago. Like it or not, Americans are a religious people. Religion has played a major part in the chief developments of our history—from the exploration and settlement of the New World to the Revolutionary War, the Civil War and the debates over slavery, to Prohibition, social protest movements in the nineteenth and twentieth centuries (including the civil rights and the anti–Vietnam War movements), and to the very shape of American culture.[2] The Puritan legacy runs through our cultural veins, underscoring the experience of salvation, hard work, human sinfulness, and the importance of the individual conscience in its relation to God. Evangelical Protestantism suffuses our system of beliefs and is deeply embedded in social service agencies for health and welfare. Catholic schools and hospitals are significant economic, political, and cultural forces in major cities and small towns across the nation. Jews, Seventh-Day Adventists, Mormons, Jehovah's Witnesses, and other groups play a conspicuous role in domestic and foreign policy legislation and in court decisions affecting church and state. In short, Segers rightly emphasizes that, from a certain point of view, the question is not *whether* religion will have a voice in politics. It has; it does; and it will. The question is *the kind of voice* that is most appropriate.

American history has known skepticism about the mixing of religion and politics, as Segers recognizes. Both religious figures, such as Roger Williams, and secular leaders, such as Thomas Jefferson, acknowledged the danger of the mixture to the freedom of religion itself and to the health of government. Though we celebrate religio-political movements of the past, we do not forget other less admirable ones. Religious motivation inspired the abolition movement against slavery in the first half of the nineteenth century, but slave masters used the Bible to support the institution. Religion may indeed underpin the public and private moral order essential to social health, but the same moral crusade that begot Prohibition also produced extreme social disorder.

The contemporary manifestations of the complex historical interweaving of religion and political life in America are the related topics of "civil religion" and "culture war." Although there is considerable disagreement over the meaning and existence of an American civil religion, the issue to which the concept points is both real and important.[3] We may think of civil religion as the foundational beliefs and the civic rituals that provide a larger meaning to national life. American civil religion manifests belief in the special blessings of America, its moral destiny, and commitment to freedom, democracy, and opportunity for all. This religion has its sacred symbols and holidays—the flag, Independence Day, Thanksgiving, and presidential inaugurations. Segers and Jelen consider the "utility" of religion to a democratic society; they discuss the "legitimacy" of American political institutions and the role of religion in affirming that legitimacy and thus inculcating obedience to lawful

authority. Such themes implicitly invoke the idea of an American civil religion. Realizing that a civil *religion* is at stake in controversies such as whether the act of burning the American flag is constitutionally protected or whether group prayer should be allowed in the public schools allows one to understand their emotional—indeed, their spiritual—intensity. When one realizes that, for many, the flag is a *sacred* symbol and school prayer is *essential* for the secular health of the nation, then one can understand the forces at work and the emotions unleashed by Supreme Court cases and political campaign slogans that tap these spiritual wells. This realization produces significant questions. Does American society require civil religion for survival? If a society does not require a civil religious foundation, what is the emotional and symbolic "glue" that holds it together? Can an American civil religion be an entirely secular creed, or must it draw on the theology and symbolism of Christian faith? Jelen asserts the possibility of a secular creedal foundation, while Segers denies it.

Civil religion suggests insights into contemporary "culture wars."[4] The term refers to the deeply passionate and politically intense debates regarding such issues as abortion, gay rights, and violent and sexually explicit content in television, movies, and music, and on the Internet. The emotional spillover from these issues has made elections tests of the strength of "traditional family values" or tolerance and acceptance of "alternative lifestyles." The ardent feelings that these issues generate are not a function solely of their intrinsic importance, significant though that is; the stakes are higher. Will the sources of social authority and the foundations of American culture rest on firm moral ground following the religious traditions of Western civilization, or will authority and moral order lie with individual moral choices and with progressive forces of cultural change?

I raise these issues not to predict the ultimate victors in the culture wars, nor to suggest who should win. Instead, I introduce them to suggest that the references to American political and cultural history running through this text are more than a series of examples to buttress a separationist or an accommodationist position on religion and politics. The unique importance of the contemporary debate over the public role of religion is that it draws us into the heart of the American identity. Is our nation merely an accidental assembly of essentially disconnected individuals, or is there a crucial bond of principle and commitment that makes Americans "e pluribus unum"? If it is the latter, what contribution do religious traditions, symbols, beliefs, and values make to the *unum*? Is America a secular society, in which pride of place goes to those who can master the arguments and the language of science, technology, and personal liberation, or is there a special need for the public square to be clothed in ultimate principles?[5]

Constitutional Law of Church and State

Despite our being a society in which, according to Alexis de Tocqueville, every political question ultimately becomes a legal one, constitutional issues are far less central than the considerations of American identity. Therefore, the most important issues today debate the value—or lack thereof—of religion for American democracy. Jelen and Segers rightly conclude that Supreme Court decisions and all the stuff of constitutional law do not settle the right and proper relationship between religion and politics. The constitutional law of church and state is only a small part of the territory, whose larger reaches include the relationship between religion and civil society discussed earlier. The First Amendment's free exercise and establishment clauses do play a vital role in defining the institutional, or structural, relationships in this field. These clauses cover such matters as whether churches can receive exemptions from property taxes on their places of worship, whether church-run schools may receive financial assistance from state governments, and whether government may regulate the evangelistic activities of the Jehovah's Witnesses. Although these issues are important, they do not address whether presidential candidates can rightly appeal to values held by Catholics, or whether evangelical Christians or orthodox Jews should consult their religious beliefs when they favor or oppose legislative proposals.

Despite my statements minimizing the importance of the legal dimension of public religion, the framework of the U.S. Constitution does loom large in some of the most central issues of religion and politics today. This prominence of the law is partially a result of the American tendency to rely on the courts to settle the most contentious disagreements. This tendency is a product of a political system that prefers to avoid highly emotionally charged issues, as well as a result of American culture's preoccupation with rights, which it believes ultimately can be defined by judges. We have come to see some of the most important religio-political issues of our time through legal lenses.

Are religious beliefs and practices constitutionally special, or are they merely one kind of commitment, on a par with career choices, political ideologies, and sexual practices? For a time, religion seemed to be different. The Supreme Court had interpreted the free exercise clause in such a way as to require government to produce "compelling" reasons for imposing burdens on the religious practices of individuals or groups.[6] This legal doctrine furnished a strong foundation for the independent life and public action of religious groups of all kinds. It implied that religion itself possesses some unique properties that make it important in both public and private life.

The 1990s, however, gave birth to Supreme Court decisions that minimized the importance of the free exercise clause in a way that fits Jelen's "religious minimalism." They placed religious motivations for action on a level with any other incentive. In the test for free exercise violations established in the *Smith*

case, the Court allows governmentwide latitude in regulating religious practices, so long as it does not single out religion.[7] That is, religion receives no special protection because, implicitly, it makes no special contribution to public life. Moreover, even when the Court has protected religion, as in the University of Virginia case involving funding for a religious newspaper, the Court's decision owed more to free speech and free press considerations than to any unique religious freedom.[8] In 1993, Congress and the president tried to return religion's special status when they enacted the Religious Freedom Restoration Act, which the Supreme Court declared unconstitutional in the 1997 *Boerne* case.[9]

These legal maneuvers are not a matter of arcane constitutionalism. They reflect and in turn influence the civil religion and culture wars themes addressed earlier. The essays in this book recognize and focus on this fact; they do not allow the complexities of constitutional interpretation to overwhelm the most fundamental issues of politics and culture: whether religious belief and practice offer any singular gift to public life that would justify specific protection. Jelen answers "no"; Segers answers "yes."

One other contemporary constitutional controversy, especially pertinent to the establishment clause of the First Amendment, deserves mention at this point, as it also engages the question of whether religion is a benefit or danger to American public life. This controversy disputes whether religious social service organizations (for example, adoption agencies, child care centers, homeless shelters, drug and alcohol rehabilitation programs, and family counseling services) should be eligible to receive government grants to support their services and, if so, under what conditions. The 1996 federal welfare reform legislation contains so-called charitable choice provisions that support such faith-based providers receiving funds. The legislation also attempts to protect their religious identity and sense of religious mission as they deliver public services. The proposed Religious Equality Amendment under debate in Congress proposes the same measures for a wide variety of government programs.

Narrowly, these measures seek to influence the Supreme Court's interpretation of the establishment clause. From the perspective of this book, however, their importance goes even deeper. If religion, as Segers argues, does make a valuable contribution to American public life, then it is vital to ensure that faith-based social service organizations have the public support and the public funds they need to carry out their missions. If, however, as Jelen maintains, public religion is a danger to social life, then it would be a grave mistake to fund religious organizations with public monies, no matter how noble their intentions to serve the public and to help the poor, the homeless, and other citizens in need. The essays in this volume encourage us to think more deeply about such recent legislative and constitutional issues bearing on religion.

The Dangers of "Excessive Entanglement"

Both Ted Jelen and Mary Segers are aware of the dangers of too close an embrace between religion and politics. "Excessive entanglement" represents the Supreme Court's third test for violation of the establishment clause (the "Lemon test"),[10] but the phrase is useful as a general metaphor. Inappropriate, frequent, or intimate interpenetration of the institutions of religion and government is harmful. The dangers are familiar and both authors generate similar lists of potential problems: Religion breeds intolerance of the deepest values of fellow citizens. It introduces incivility into the democratic dialogue. Religious believers are so committed to the right and justice of their views that they will pursue "good" results without paying attention to democratic procedures. Democracy requires compromise, but those convinced of their cause's divine justice cannot compromise with persons or positions they see as evil. Religion is divisive.[11] American democracy requires overcoming differences to create a common nation, yet religion emphasizes our deepest differences of conviction.

Jelen believes that these dangers are so lethal and unavoidable that we need to isolate religion from public life, confining it to private belief and worship. The passions that religion evokes provide distinct reasons why we should limit its scope of influence. Segers believes that we can minimize the potential for harm if we attend to the question of *how* religion and politics interact, not *whether* they should.

One arresting aspect of the list of dangers is that it emphasizes the hazards that religious faith poses to democracy. Does government—democracy in particular—pose a corresponding set of dangers to religion? Our authors do not neglect this question, but neither do they emphasize it. Yet excessive entanglement is as bad for religion as it is for government. Both the compromise and the power associated with politics can corrupt. Religious leaders may be tempted to surrender essential beliefs in order to retain powerful political positions. Those same positions may enable the officeholder to coerce persons of different religious persuasions. The financial benefits of political power can sap religious purity.[12] Pride is the first religious sin. Recognition and favors granted by government officials inflate the pride of those already convinced that God is on their side.

Three additional points should be made. First, Segers's arguments regarding the utility of religion to democratic politics undermine religion at the same time that they favor it. This is an important paradox. To argue that religion enhances democracy by promoting moral behavior, facilitating community, inculcating respect for law, and advancing rights is to build up religion by making it valuable to democratic society. Yet these arguments potentially minimize religion by making it merely useful. This is the dark side of civil religion. Adherents of a particular faith hold to it out of conviction that the faith

is right, not because that faith is useful for a particular political society. The more its proponents underscore the utility of religion, the more difficult it is to recognize faith's claims to truth and rightness independent of political culture. The utility of religion is one version of civil religion, a version that makes Christian faith, for example, the servant of political and social order, rather than the judge of the value of all things—including government—under God.

Second, it is important to use examples with care. The abortion debate often becomes the primary source for examples of religion's danger to democratic politics. There are good reasons for this. Abortion *is* one of the central moral issues of our time, and it is one of great religious and political importance. Moreover, abortion politics is an abundant source of instances of intolerance, incivility, and the danger of violence. Yet it is not a good model for the day-to-day role of religion in public life. Catholic hospitals accepting public funds to care for the indigent and advocating national health insurance, or Jewish leaders lobbying on foreign policy, are more typical. Focusing on abortion all too often allows a few very large trees to obscure the rest of the forest.

Third, passionate moral intensity is not always wrong in politics, whether its source is religion or some other deeply held value. Abortion politics raises moral passions, and religious groups, such as the Catholic bishops and the Christian Coalition, are often accused of improper intervention in politics, mixing church with the business of state. Yet, the prophetic mode of political and religious discourse should not be ruled out of order. Jesse Jackson's rhetoric on race is certainly no less prophetic or passionate than the Catholic bishops' rhetoric on abortion. The issues are different, but the *manner* of his approach and his use of the church to advance the cause are not fundamentally different from the Catholic bishops'. Indeed, as political scientist Allen Hertzke has argued, the proper parallel for Jesse Jackson is not the coolness of Mario Cuomo, but the heat of the Christian Coalition's Pat Robertson.[13] Similarly, Jelen takes religious persons to task for advocating legislation against recognition of homosexual marriage, but would he make the same argument against religious leaders in the vanguard of the campaign for the Civil Rights Acts of 1964, 1965, and 1968 or for a nuclear freeze in the middle 1980s? Why is it undemocratic for religious groups to use the political process to oppose marriage rights for homosexuals, when the Hawaiian court decisions establishing such rights can hardly be deemed a model of popular political deliberation?

Not *Whether* but *How* to Interact

The considerations in the previous three sections produce implications for the role of religion in political discourse. If the nature of American civil religion and of American political culture themselves are up for grabs, then religious

voices of all kinds will join the conversation. If the structural relationships between church and state are being rethought as a result of new approaches to the delivery of social services, then churches and other religious organizations must be involved in the debate. If passionate intensity is both a danger and an inevitability in political discourse, then fervent religious voices will be heard. Therefore, the principal issue in religion and politics is not *whether* religion will appear in public, but *how* it will make its appearance. If this conclusion is correct, then Mary Segers is right to focus her argument on the impossibility of separating religion from political judgment. At the same time, Ted Jelen is correct to keep reminding us of the singular hazards of mixing religious discourse with democratic public life.

This being the case, our debaters actually agree in many areas. Both give top priority to democratic deliberation. That is, each portrays democracy as a conversation among persons and groups committed to democracy itself and to a public unity that transcends particular policy differences. Democracy, using this model, is a conversation in which each side listens to the other, presents its arguments in language accessible to all participants, and accepts the results of majority rule and other democratic decision procedures. All of this occurs under the rule of law and overarching values enshrined in the Constitution. This model of democracy demands certain qualities from political actors. They must respect the legitimacy of their opponents' presence and respect their right to offer policy proposals. They must tolerate beliefs and practices that diverge from their own, even those they find deeply offensive to their own values. Political actors must also be willing to use arguments and ideas that everyone can understand and at least potentially accept, otherwise they will never be able to persuade anyone. Finally, all must be willing to compromise rather than to insist that their way is the only way.

Both Jelen and Segers accept this noble sketch of democratic deliberation. Their disagreement is over the ability of religious interests and organizations to be responsible political actors on these terms. For Jelen, religious groups are—mostly—too intolerant and uncivil to participate; moreover, they are more committed to the truth of their causes than to compromise and the give-and-take of democratic dialogue. Most essentially, however, religion cannot be both true to itself and its unique theological vocabulary and faithful to democratic arguments made in publicly accessible language, even those made by secular political actors. Segers, on the other hand, shows that religious organizations not only can meet these conditions, but have done so historically and in the present.

Two questions might arise regarding this argument. First, accepting the picture of democracy that it builds upon, can religious voices indeed offer public sanction for their place at the political table? I think so. Second, is this model of respectful debate really the way democracy works? Not always. If not, what are the implications for religion in public?

Regarding the first question, religious voices can quite legitimately and without violating their own special identities participate fully in the deliberation that is characteristic of democracy. Because I have written explicitly about this topic elsewhere, I shall not develop the argument in detail here.[14] I suggest five conditions that religious groups should fulfill in order to take part effectively in the kind of democratic discourse that both Segers and Jelen accept as a model.

- Religious groups that wish to have a political voice should themselves use principles of democratic discourse internally. (Not all religious groups wish to have a political voice; nor should they be required to.) Using principles of democratic discourse does not mean that they must be organized democratically—a condition impossible for the Roman Catholic or the Episcopal churches, for example, to fulfill—but it means that their own internal civil debates can validate their willingness to engage in democratic political discussion. Political actors will not take particularly seriously monolithic communities without internal freedom that seek a place at a pluralistic table. The noisy debate characterizing most churches these days suggests that (sometimes raucous) internal debate is a feature of modern life for most religious organizations.
- Religious groups that take part in democratic debate need not abandon their specific theological vocabularies for an impossible neutral moral language of public discussion. Such groups, however, must develop a specific politico-theological vocabulary that applies essentially religious concepts to the specific context of democratic political life. It is not enough, for example, to speak about the requirements for eternal salvation. Instead, debaters must articulate precise ideas of the relationship between politics and eternal life. Does political order help or hinder the search for eternity? How? Catholic natural law language and Dutch Reformed orders of creation language, for example, both meet this requirement.
- Religious communities should avoid the temptations of civil religion when they appear in public. This point is an extension of one made earlier. Even if civil religion is in some sense good for a political community, churches should not associate too closely with it. It leads them away from their own distinct identities toward a merger with the identity of the nation, and it appeals more to pride and power than to specifically religious motivations. The distinct politico-religious vocabularies advocated in the preceding point counter the vocabulary of civil religion to which churches might otherwise be tempted.
- Religious communities that aim to be taken seriously in democratic dialogue must do their homework. They must learn the lingo and the empirical data pertinent to the policy arenas they wish to address. It is not enough for them to make moral pronouncements about health care or crime or immigration. Religious communities also must learn the facts and the concepts employed by policy experts and policymakers active in these arenas. This process takes time, willingness to read economic reports and policy journals as well as theological tracts, and a humble wish to learn. That religious communities are capable of these requirements is evident in the frequency with which religious figures

appear as witnesses in congressional hearings, participants in policy roundta-
bles, and commentators in secular periodicals across a wide range of religious
traditions and policy arenas. The service activities of faith-based social service
providers give them authority to speak to policy questions that touch their min-
istries.[15]

* Finally, religious groups wishing to enter public policy deliberation must employ internally the principles that they advocate in public. For example, religious groups that encourage raising the minimum wage cannot be taken seriously unless they pay fair wages to their employees. Religious voices enhance
their legitimacy and credibility in public if they live according to their own
values in private.

Obviously, these five conditions suggest a rather high standard for religious
groups to meet should they wish to take part in democratic politics. These
requirements, however, are not legal ones; nor are they the the minimum. They
are normative standards—goals for which religious groups can aim. Moreover,
the standards of democratic discourse that Segers and Jelen outline *are* high.
Ordinary secular politics often fails to exhibit the qualities of tolerance, respect, open argument, and calm deliberation that the model requires. Power,
money, and favoritism frequently overcome the calmly formed judgments of
citizens and policy experts. Democracy itself is as much aspiration as reality.

Political scientists who deal with normative questions, such as the proper
relation between religion and politics, often forget that power is central to
political life. Democratic politics as ideal deliberation takes us only so far.
American politics is as much messy argument as tolerant, informed deliberation, as much power as persuasion. Similarly, religion can be as grubby as any
other institution or interest. It is unreasonable to expect model participation
from religious groups, if such is not expected from any other part of the political or cultural spectrum. Religious groups have interests to defend and causes
to advance, as much as do other groups. We should not deny them a place at
the bargaining table any more than we should the Chamber of Commerce or
Handgun Control Incorporated.

Moreover, the raw passion of some religious voices is not necessarily a
violation of democratic norms, if these norms allow for prophetic as well as
moderate voices in the mix of policy debate. Calm, respectful, compromise is
a perfectly appropriate goal for most political issues. Health care politics and
abortion politics, however, involve matters of life and death, of justice and
injustice. It is unrealistic to expect that immoderate passion, incivility, and
appeals to fundamental principles of right and wrong will not be part of the
debate. For example, the immoderate, prophetic religious voices in the antislavery and the civil rights movements did not violate democratic norms. We
need to avoid stating those norms in an unrealistically restrictive fashion. We
also must not exclude immoderate, prophetic voices from public debates about
drug addiction, family decay, abortion, or homelessness. What is the appro-

priate metaphor for democratic debate—the Sunday tea, the graduate seminar, the sports bar on Super Bowl Sunday? Each in its own way replicates a feature of democratic politics. Religion has its legitimate parallels to each such democratic trait.

Conclusion

The great virtue of the materials in this book is that they touch on all of these issues. Both religion and politics are a messy business, invoking both high ideals and prideful power-seeking, lofty rhetoric and questionable motives. Their union is dangerous to political liberty and to religious purity; their separation impossible and imprudent. The vital goal is to keep the arguments alive, despite the occasional raised voices and broken crockery. This collection does so in fine fashion. Read on, and lend your voice to the frustrating and irresistible democratic argument.

Notes

1. This means that Jelen's position anchors the "separationist" end of the most typical interpretative spectrum. Segers's position is near the middle. The "nonpreferentialist" end of the spectrum is not represented. This comment does not imply that the "truth appears in the middle," and that, therefore, Segers has the best of the argument. (In the spirit of honest debate that characterizes this book, I should disclose that my own position on these matters lies closer to Segers's.) On matters of religion and politics, it is not at all clear that the truth lies in the middle or, indeed, that the idea of a spectrum with clear ends and a middle is helpful, despite the fact that such a model dominates church-state discussion.

2. See, for example, Sydney E. Ahlstrom, *A Religious History of the American People*, 2 volumes (New Haven, Conn.: Yale University Press, 1975); Cushing Strout, *The New Heavens and New Earth: Political Religion in America* (New York: Harper Torchbooks, 1974); and Mark A. Noll, ed., *Religion and American Politics: From the Colonial Period to the Present* (New York: Oxford University Press, 1990).

3. The best collection of materials remains Russell E. Richey and Donald G. Jones, eds., *American Civil Religion* (New York: Harper & Row, 1974).

4. The concept was popularized for the contemporary American scene by James Davison Hunter's *Culture Wars: The Struggle to Define America* (New York: Basic Books, 1991).

5. The image comes from Richard John Neuhaus, *The Naked Public Square: Religion and Democracy in America* (Grand Rapids, Mich.: Eerdmans, 1984).

6. *Sherbert v. Verner,* 374 U.S. 398 (1963). This and other important church-state cases and their implications are conveniently presented in Ronald B. Flowers, *That Godless Court? Supreme Court Decisions on Church-State Relationships* (Louisville, Ky.: Westminster John Knox Press, 1994).

7. *Employment Division, Department of Human Resources of Oregon v. Smith,* 494 U.S. 872 (1990).

8. *Rosenberger v. Rector,* 115 S. Ct. 2510 (1995).

9. *City of Boerne v. P. F. Flores,* 65 LW 4612 (1997).

10. *Lemon v. Kurtzman,* 403 U.S. 602 (1971).

11. We should not forget, however, that the secular opponents of religion can be just as intolerant and uncivil in their rejection of the supposed ignorance, superstition, and incivility of believers. See Stephen L. Carter, *The Culture of Disbelief: How American Law and Politics Trivialize Religious Devotion* (New York: Basic Books, 1993).

12. Religious leaders hardly need the help of government to fall into these sins. Indeed, government/church alliances simply magnify the dangers already inherent in religious power itself.

13. Allen D. Hertzke, *Echoes of Discontent: Jesse Jackson, Pat Robertson, and the Resurgence of Populism* (Washington, D.C.: CQ Press, 1993).

14. Clarke E. Cochran, "Religious Traditions and Health Care Policy: Potential for Democratic Discourse?" *Journal of Church and State* 39 (Winter 1997): 15–35, in which I develop the argument for religious voices in the specific context of debates over health care policy.

15. For example, see the collection edited by Stanley W. Carlson-Thies and James W. Skillen, *Welfare in America: Christian Perspectives on a Policy in Crisis* (Grand Rapids, Mich.: Eerdmans, 1996).

Part One

Debating the Public Role of Religion

1

In Defense of Religious Minimalism

Ted G. Jelen

As values to be articulated in public discourse, we should regard religious faiths and religious beliefs with a good deal of suspicion. The nature of political deliberation and discourse is such that religion is something of a dangerous stranger to democratic politics. In this essay, I make two general arguments. First, I suggest that democratic political life is based on certain values and practices, which religion has the potential to undermine. Second, I attempt to show that religious involvement in the public sphere may have negative consequences for the practice of religion in general, and for Christianity in particular. Thus, for the sake of both politics and religion, religious values are best compartmentalized into a private sphere of activity.

Before I beginning, I should express some caveats. I do not deal with the truth or falsity of religious beliefs in this work. Indeed, as I suggest later in this essay, discussion of such matters may lie beyond the range of acceptable political discourse, and, in any event, is well beyond the scope of the present inquiry. Here, I examine the political effects of religion, and in so doing pose two key questions: Does religion undermine values important to the practice of democratic politics? Does political involvement undermine values important to the practice of religion? In addressing the latter question, I offer no new insights, but rely upon the discernment of scholars who have analyzed the nature of religious belief, and upon judgments commonly expressed by religious leaders. Of course, highly religious readers may regard my decision to set aside the truth claims offered by religion as begging the most important question, and ignoring the key issue in debating the public role of religion. I have no defense against such a charge, but simply regard such an inquiry as outside the compass of this project.

Moreover, this essay is not a work of constitutional legal theory. Although the religion clauses of the First Amendment provide the starting point for my

analysis, and this essay has some implications for constitutional interpretation, I do not pretend to have discerned the "correct" meaning of the constitutional status of religion. I do not address the history of the enactment of the First Amendment, nor do I present the intentions of the framers of the Constitution. While I do occasionally refer to Supreme Court decisions, I only intend these references to be illustrations; they are not the basis for the main thrust of my arguments. In the final section, I make some suggestions as to how one should read the religion clauses of the Constitution, but I base these comments on the primarily ethical arguments that precede that section and not on any systematic form of constitutional exegesis.

A Framework for Analyzing Religion and Politics

The political and legal controversy concerning the public role of religion is based on the following section of the First Amendment of the U.S. Constitution: "Congress shall make no law respecting an establishment of religion, or prohibiting the free exercise thereof. . . ." A great deal of scholarly controversy surrounds the precise meaning of these constitutional clauses, called the "establishment clause" and "free exercise clause," respectively. The spare language of these sixteen words has confused as much as it has enlightened.[1]

At some risk of oversimplification, one can argue that the establishment clause engenders two general positions: "accommodationism" and "separationism."[2] Accommodationism generally entails the belief that people should interpret the establishment clause quite narrowly, and that this provision of the Constitution merely proscribes preferential treatment of particular religions by government. This reading of the establishment clause is often termed "nonpreferentialism." Under a nonpreferentialist understanding, government may not single out Catholicism, Methodism, or Islam for special consideration. However, government is permitted to offer general assistance to religion, in a spirit of what has been termed "benevolent neutrality."[3] No constitutional violation occurs, from an accommodationist standpoint, if government aids all religions impartially. Such government policies as providing financial aid to parochial schools, providing tuition tax credits for private education, and allowing nonsectarian school prayer are all considered constitutionally permissible, provided such opportunities apply equally to all religions. Government is required to be neutral between religions, but is not required to be neutral between religion and irreligion.

Underlying the accommodationist view of the First Amendment is the assumption that religion has on balance benevolent effects on the social and political life of the nation, and that religion is generally an important source of common morality and social cohesion.[4] The assumption (which I will dis-

cuss more fully later) is that Americans for the most part agree on the essentials of religion and especially religiously based morality.

By contrast, separationists tend to argue that religion is a fertile source of social and political conflict. Separationism assumes that religious differences pose special problems for democratic politics. The political volatility of religion is thought to come from two sources. First, religion makes "ultimate" demands on its adherents, which are not typically amenable to compromise. Religion deals with questions about the nature of the universe, as well as the meaning and purpose of life, which are difficult to negotiate. Second, religious beliefs are difficult to verify empirically, and so may be difficult to alter through discussion and competition. Religion is therefore thought to provide political discourse on a subject that is of great importance to believers, and on which it is difficult to agree.[5]

Religious citizens may well be tempted to forgo the essentials of democratic civility and procedures, and act on their belief in a "higher" (divine) law. From the standpoint of a separationist, therefore, religion is a dangerous element in democratic politics and is best confined to the private sphere.

Constitutionally, separationism entails a broad view of the establishment clause. In this account, government may not offer assistance to religion in any form. As Justice Hugo Black wrote in *Everson v. Board of Education of Ewing Township* (1947):

> The "establishment of religion" clause of the First Amendment means at least this: Neither a state nor the Federal government can set up a church. Neither can pass laws which aid one religion, aid all religions, or prefer one religion over another. . . . No tax in any amount, large or small, can be levied to support any religious activities or institutions, whatever they may be called, or whatever form they may adopt to teach or practice religion. . . . In the words of Jefferson, the clause against establishment of religion by law was intended to erect "a wall of separation between church and state."[6]

Separationists tend to emphasize the potential divisiveness of religious issues, and so would limit drastically government's ability to offer assistance to religion. Government, from a separationist standpoint, may not officially encourage religious belief. While some have suggested that separationists are necessarily hostile to religion, others have intimated that authentic religion does not require government assistance, and that such assistance may violate the free exercise clause.[7]

At this writing, the state of the law generally lies in a separationist direction. The broadest operative precedent in this area is *Lemon v. Kurtzman* (1971) in which the U.S. Supreme Court has placed substantial limits on the power of government at any level to offer assistance to religion. According to Justice Warren Burger's majority opinion in *Lemon,* government assistance to reli-

gious bodies is permissible only if such assistance meets all three of the following conditions:

- The policy must have a primarily secular purpose.
- The policy must have a primarily secular effect.
- The policy must not result in "excessive entanglement" between government and religion.[8]

The Lemon test has proven to be a rather demanding one from the standpoint of those who favor government encouragement of religion. Under the Lemon test, the Supreme Court has struck down state legislation that would have required teaching creationism as an alternative to evolution (*Edwards v. Aguillard,* 1987), as well as measures providing for a "moment of silence" in public schools (*Wallace v. Jaffree,* 1985). For present purposes, the lack of nonpreferential language in *Lemon* is of most direct interest. Under this ruling, the scope of particular policies is simply irrelevant to their constitutionality. Policies that favor religion in general but have primarily religious purposes or effects, are no more constitutionally permissible than those that would single out particular religions.[9] Thus, contemporary constitutional law has accepted one of the central tenets of separationism.

A growing body of jurisprudence, and, therefore, scholarly commentary, has been devoted to the interpretation of the free exercise clause. While there is general agreement that adherents of denominations within a Judeo-Christian tradition are entitled to worship privately, there is disagreement as to whether the religious practice of members of unpopular religious minorities are entitled to such protection, and whether religious practice merits special governmental protection.[10]

To oversimplify once again, two broad interpretations of the free exercise clause prevail: a "libertarian" understanding, and a "communalist" reading of this section of the First Amendment.[11] Libertarian analysts argue that religious belief and practice deserve special consideration on the part of government. Under most circumstances, the ultimate demands that religions impose on their adherents constitute an area in which governmental authority is illegitimate, and in which religious obligations would trump the requirements of citizenship. At the very least, government officials seeking to restrict religious liberty would be required to show compelling reasons why the restrictions are necessary.

By contrast, a communalist understanding of the free exercise clause would simply require that government refrain from discriminating against particular religions, or against religion in general, when making public policy. Government may not, from a communalist standpoint, single out religious practice in making laws. However, a communalist would argue that religious principles do not invalidate or modify the obligation to obey religiously neutral, secular

laws. (The Supreme Court makes this argument in *Employment Division, Department of Human Resources of Oregon v. Smith* [1990].) Religion does not provide an exception to the general obligation to obey the law. To illustrate, consider the question of whether members of unconventional religious groups, such as the Hare Krishnas, have the right to solicit donations or proselytize potential recruits in public places such as airports. A libertarian view of the free exercise clause would permit such solicitation, even if the airport authorities had enacted a general "no solicitation" policy. Religious representatives would have prerogatives that salespeople and political activists would not, due to the special protection that the First Amendment is thought to afford religion. On the other hand, a communalist would likely argue that, as long as the airport proscription on solicitation did not specifically single out religious proselytizing, no reason exists to exempt religious groups from the general prohibition. While a "no religious soliciting" policy probably would be unconstitutional, a general "no soliciting" policy would not.[12]

Of course, a communalist reading of the free exercise clause would modify substantially the notion that religious belief and practice constitute inalienable rights. Nevertheless, such an understanding is quite compatible with the assumptions underlying an accommodationist interpretation of the establishment clause. If religion's most important public purpose is to enhance common morality and social integration, there is no reason why the—otherwise illegal—actions of unpopular religious minorities should be afforded special constitutional protection. Moreover, one way in which citizens might exercise freely their religious beliefs is by acting on their religious values in political life. If a communalist understanding of religious free exercise is accompanied by an accommodationist interpretation of the establishment clause, it follows directly that members of religious organizations should be free to attempt to enact their preferences into public policy. Religion is a value system, like many others, and consequently there is no reason why religious beliefs should be singled out for special treatment. The actual practice of free exercise jurisprudence has undergone a fundamental change in recent years. For most of the post–World War II period, Supreme Court rulings in the area of religious free exercise have had a decidedly libertarian cast.[13] Thomas Robbins has suggested that the Court has employed a three-part test for free exercise claims, which he terms the "Sherbert-Yoder" test.[14] These criteria were derived from the cases of *Sherbert v. Verner* (1963) and *Wisconsin v. Yoder* (1972).

The first part of the Sherbert-Yoder test imposed a very high standard for government regulation of religious practice. In order to justify a restriction of religious freedom, government must show that "it has a compelling interest which justifies the abridgment of the . . . right to free exercise of religion."[15] In practice, this has meant that government must show that the proposed restriction is essential to the achievement of some central government objec-

tive.[16] If government meets this hurdle, the burden shifts to the claimant of free exercise rights, who must show that the practice the government contemplates restricting is central to the religious tradition under consideration, and that the regulation in question would pose a "substantial infringement" on religious practice.[17] Finally, under the Sherbert-Yoder test, courts have traditionally considered whether the proposed regulation of religious practice is the least restrictive alternative available to government. Here, the burden of proof shifts back to government, who must show that there is no other less intrusive alternative available.

The Rehnquist court rather abruptly limited the deference that the Supreme Court showed to free exercise claims under the Sherbert-Yoder test. In *Employment Division v. Smith* (1990), Justice Antonin Scalia, in ruling that a religious ritual involving the hallucinogenic drug peyote was not protected by the free exercise clause, took an explicitly communalist position. Scalia argued that the First Amendment does not protect actions prohibited by a state's criminal code unless the state legislature explicitly makes such an exception.[18] Leaving the scope of the free exercise clause to the legislature, of course, substantially qualifies the status of religious free exercise as a right, which presumably would lie beyond the reach of legislatures and popular majorities.[19]

The meaning of the free exercise clause was elaborated further in *Church of the Lukumi Babalu Aye, Inc. v. City of Hialeah* (1993). In this case, the Court overturned a local ordinance that banned religious animal sacrifice. The Hialeah ordinance specifically identified religious sacrifice as the proscribed practice: a prohibition that seemed to be aimed at the Santeria religion. One might infer, based on the Court's ruling in *Smith,* that if the city of Hialeah had passed a general ordinance banning animal slaughter within its borders, such a measure might well be constitutional. Moreover, the *Smith* opinion suggests that the Santerians would not be allowed an exemption from such a general, nondiscriminatory ordinance.[20]

This brief analysis of the establishment and free exercise clauses permits the development of a typology of possible positions on church-state relations, which is depicted in figure 1.[21] The position represented in the upper left quadrant of figure 1, termed "Christian preferentialist," refers to an accommodationist position on the establishment clause, along with a communalist position on the free exercise clause. People assuming this combination of positions might regard the United States as a "Christian nation" and might believe that mainstream religions are entitled to a good deal of deference in the public sphere. Adherents of minority or unorthodox religions, however, are not entitled to the same consideration, and, indeed, may only be entitled to protection from discriminatory legislation under the free exercise clause.

Accommodationists who take a libertarian view of the free exercise clause (the lower left quadrant) are termed "religious nonpreferentialists." Such citi-

FIGURE 1
A Typology of Church-State Positions

Establishment Clause

		Accommodationist	Separationist
Free Exercise	Communalist	Christian preferentialist	religious minimalist
	Libertarian	religious nonpreferentialist	religious free marketeer

zens might be regarded as "indiscriminately pro-religious," since they might seek to maximize the role of religion in the public sphere, and to protect a broad version of the free exercise rights of religious minorities.

Conversely, "separationist-communalists" (the upper right quadrant) might be termed "religious minimalists"; unlike the nonpreferentialists, such people would seek to construe the establishment clause quite broadly (and thus to proscribe government endorsements of religion over irreligion) and to limit sharply the scope of the free exercise clause.

Finally, "religious free marketeers" are "separationist-libertarians". These people appear to seek to minimize the role of government (unlike minimalists, who endeavor to de-emphasize the public role of religion). Free marketeers might view government attempts to endorse or promote religion with a good deal of skepticism but are quite solicitous of the prerogatives of religious minorities. Government may not, from this perspective, either encourage or discourage religious belief and practice.[22]

My intention in the balance of this essay is to defend the position of religious minimalism. I shall argue that the effects of religion on political life are such that we should not encourage expression of religious values in public discourse nor entitle such expression to special constitutional protection. I would remind the reader that, although the analysis of constitutional law provides the structure within which the public role of religion is debated, this essay does not have constitutional law as its primary focus. Rather, I will emphasize ethical arguments, supported where possible by reference to empirical evidence.

Many observers, including my coauthor, Mary C. Segers, have sought to illuminate the "correct" meaning of the religion clauses of the First Amendment by appealing to the historical record. We are told that it is possible to discern the "authentic" purposes of the framers if we simply understand their goals and motivations.

For two reasons, I do not regard historical exegesis as particularly helpful

in settling the political role of religion in the contemporary United States. First, the historical record is incomplete and extremely controversial. An enormous scholarly literature has emerged on the framers' "original intent," without having resolved any of the outstanding issues.[23] It is not clear, for example, which framers one has in mind when making particular claims, or which version of any given figure's thought is to be considered authoritative. Evidence indicates, for instance, that James Madison changed his mind at least once on the meaning of the establishment clause; in his "Detached Memoradum," written after his retirement from public life, Madison expressed regret for apparently accommodationist acts performed during his presidency.[24]

Certain observers have also produced evidence for a "separationist" understanding of the framers' motives. Some have suggested that "multiple establishment" was a familiar practice in some states, and that the common understanding of the concept of religious establishment was not limited to a single, government-sponsored denomination.[25] Finally, Leonard Levy has argued that three versions of the establishment clause, all of which contained explicitly nonpreferentialist language, were put before the U.S. Senate, which rejected all three.[26] Thus, a determination of the "real" intentions of the framers is probably a fruitless exercise. The motives of the people who had a hand in formulating and approving the religion clauses of the First Amendment vary across time and by individual. Given the incorrigibly political nature of the adoption of the Bill of Rights, the historical record appears to provide ample evidence for accommodationists and separationists alike.

Second, even if one were to grant that an authoritative reading of the framers' intentions was possible, it is not clear that such an understanding should be operative over two centuries later. The framers, and members of the first U.S. Congress, were not omniscient, but were writing in particular social and historical circumstances that do not obtain today. For example, Barry Alan Shain has argued that the individualist understanding of the origins of the American political system is a "myth," and that the various actors associated with the founding of the American republic had a much more communal, accommodationist (to use an anachronism) understanding of the rights and obligations of citizenship.[27] However, Shain's analysis is based on the strong probability that there existed much less religious diversity in the United States in the late eighteenth century than can be found in the late twentieth century. Indeed, the subtitle of Shain's book *(The Protestant Origins of American Political Thought)* suggests a narrow range of variation of religious belief in the United States at the time of its founding.[28] Much of contemporary America is non-Protestant (indeed, non-Christian), and it is difficult to see why such fully American, but religiously pluralistic, citizens should accept a Protestant conception of citizenship as binding.

Segers also argues that many important political movements in American history, such as the abolitionist, temperance, and civil rights movements, have

had important religious roots. Segers is clearly correct in this matter, but in taking these historical facts as the basis for an accommodationist understanding of the political role of religion, she makes two important assumptions: First, Segers's argument assumes that political religion in the United States generally has been a force for good, and second, it assumes that the movements in question were much less likely to have occurred but for the effects of religious belief.

With respect to the first assumption, the political legacy of American religion has been ambiguous at best. For example, both proponents and opponents of slavery used religious arguments and biblical invocations. Also, many religious organizations supported the McCarthyite movement of the 1950s,[29] and evangelical Protestant churches were among the most strenuous opponents of civil rights for African-Americans in the mid-twentieth century.[30] Religion clearly is a formidable force in American culture, including American politics. Whether that force is used for good or bad ends depends on the circumstances under which religiously based political activism occurs, and, indeed, on the values of the observer.

The second assumption raises more difficult issues, and reflects the core of the accommodationist-separationist debate. Historical counterfactuals are notoriously difficult, and ultimately futile, but one might reasonably ask whether it is *necessarily* the case that the abolitionist, antiwar, or civil rights movements could not have occurred but for the activity of religious belief and religious activists. Many apologists for an active political role for religion appear to be generally skeptical about alternative, secular bases for morality and ethics,[31] but it seems at least possible that one could be morally offended by slavery, discrimination, or abortion without invoking religious beliefs or passion. Religion is one of several bases for ethical decisions available to democratic citizens and varies in importance from person to person. For example, Laura Grindstaff has shown that antiabortion rhetoric has become more "secular" (specifically, more "scientific") and perhaps more effective over time.[32] At bottom, many accommodationists appear to believe that religion is a superior basis for morality than its alternatives (an issue discussed in more detail later). It is difficult to make such an assertion without making claims for the *content* of particular beliefs. To make content-based claims is to undermine the interreligious neutrality that underlies most accommodationists readings of the First Amendment. If indeed, religion is a valuable political resource because of its effects, some religions (those most likely to produce desirable secular effects) may well be "more equal" than others.

Thus, I regard history as an uncertain and ambiguous guide to assessing the proper role of religion in American politics. Determining religious principles' appropriate place in the political system should be based on the consequences of the assertion of religious values in the practice of democratic politics. It is to that task that I now turn.

Democracy and Deliberation

As the twentieth century draws to a close, the values of liberal democracy seem ascendant on the world stage. Indeed, Francis Fukuyama has written of the "end of history," in which liberal democratic principles are no longer seriously contested anywhere.[33] However, even as the symbol "democracy" becomes more popular, we become increasingly confused about the meaning of the concept. For example, James Fishkin has argued that contemporary democratic theory varies along at least three dimensions (Madisonian-Majoritarian, direct-representative, and deliberative-nondeliberative), and little consensus exists concerning which combination of these characteristics is most authentically "democratic."[34]

For the purposes of this essay, I wish to offer a comparison along one dimension: the extent to which democracy is properly understood as involving public, reasoned deliberation. I wish to distinguish between "protective" and "developmental" democracy, and to suggest that the latter is usually superior to the former. That is, democratic institutions and practices should be designed to serve education, as well as protective functions.

The notion that members of the mass public are generally politically unsophisticated and uncommitted to civic values has a long and distinguished pedigree. Indeed one can trace at least as far back as Aristophanes, the ancient Greek playwright, the idea that we can attribute the intellectually impoverished and morally degrading aspects of much democratic discourse to cognitive and moral deficiencies on the part of ordinary citizens.[35] The central question for democratic theory is not whether members of the public are unqualified to engage in self-governance, but whether such characteristics are *necessary* qualities of mass publics.[36] That is, is citizen incompetence a fact of political life, around which political leaders must operate, or can ordinary people be educated to become more sophisticated, unselfish citizens? James Madison (often termed "the father of the Constitution") is frequently described as holding the former view. It seems appropriate to regard Madison as a proponent of the "protective" view of popular government. In his classic *Federalist #10,* Madison expresses a deeply pessimistic view of human nature, which forms the basis for much of his political thinking:

> As long as the reason of man continues fallible, and he is at liberty to exercise it, different opinions will be formed. As long as the connection subsists between his reason and his self-love, his opinions and his passions will have a reciprocal influence on each other and the former will be objects to which the latter will attach themselves. . . . From [this] ensues a division of the society into different interests and parties. The latent causes of faction are thus sown into the nature of man.[37]

Madison is suggesting that conflict, owing to differences in self-interest, is an irreducible element of civil society. Madison's political philosophy—perhaps

especially his suspicion of majority rule—can be attributed to his belief that the sources of political conflict are intrinsic to human nature, and perhaps we can never alter them.[38] Conflict is a problem to be managed, since the sources of conflict cannot be ameliorated. The purpose of politics in this view is the protection of the interests of individual people from one another, since no one can be reliably trusted to transcend their narrow interests.

By contrast, another democratic tradition exists, one which we can consider "developmental." The core assumption of the developmental approach to democracy is that the incompetence of the mass public is not intrinsic to human nature, but that ordinary citizens are educable. Moreover, it is often argued that an important source of civic education is political participation itself. That is, citizens who are active participants in politics acquire knowledge about public affairs, as well as a sense of common interests with their fellow citizens.[39] One of the most prominent theorists of developmental democracy is John Stuart Mill. In his *Considerations on Representative Government,*[40] Mill argues that the development of individual character is one of the most important payoffs of popular government, and the most compelling reason to prefer participatory forms of government to any other. In his introduction to Alexis de Tocqueville's *Democracy in America,* Mill elaborates on this theme:

> The private money-getting occupation of almost everyone is more or less a mechanical routine; it brings but few of his facilities into action, while its exclusive pursuit tends to fasten his attention and interest exclusively upon himself, and upon his family as an appendage of himself; making him indifferent to the public, to the more generous objects and the nobler interests, and, in his inordinate regard for his personal comforts, selfish and cowardly. Balance these tendencies by contrary ones; give him something to do for the public, whether as a vestryman, a juryman, or an elector; and, in that degree, his ideas and feelings are taken out of this narrow circle. He becomes acquainted with more varied business, and a larger range of consideration. He is made to feel that besides the interests which separate him from his fellow-citizens, he has interests which connect him with them; that not only is the common weal his weal, but that it partly depends on his exertions.[41]

This somewhat lengthy passage illustrates the nature of developmental democratic theory rather nicely. The benefits of political participation are both cognitive ("he becomes acquainted with more varied business") and moral ("the common [weal] is his weal, [it] depends on his exertions"). Participation in public affairs is valuable from this standpoint because such participation produces better citizens.

My theoretical point of departure is to assume that the developmental model of democracy is substantially correct. While the "participation hypothesis"[42] has occasioned a great deal of controversy,[43] it seems quite reasonable to suppose that participation in public affairs could improve the capabilities and

characters of ordinary citizens. This hypothesis has received impressive empirical support as well, most recently from Sidney Verba, Kay Scholzman, and Henry Brady.[44] Political participation causes active citizens to engage in a public deliberation, in which they are exposed to new ideas and perspectives. While such public deliberation carries no guarantee that common interests will be found, such democratic dialogue makes the discovery of "the public weal" much more likely.[45]

The foregoing analysis contains an important implication. Democracy, understood in its developmental sense, is ultimately a persuasive system.[46] Authoritative political judgments must be justified, and not simply imposed by public officials. From this, it follows that democratic dialogue is only likely to be useful to the extent that citizens are allowed to insert their own characters and interests into the public deliberation. "Persuasion" is an empty exercise if citizens cannot compare alternative policy justifications to their own preferences. This implies that democratic citizens are perhaps entitled to two important prerogatives: autonomy and self-determination. By autonomy, I mean that citizens are entitled to make their own independent judgments about matters affecting them, free from coercion or intimidation. By self-determination, I refer to the ability of citizens to participate actively in the formation of their own characters. Self-determining citizens are allowed to choose among life circumstances that may influence their independent judgments. For example, self-determining citizens are allowed to choose whom to marry, to choose between religions (or between religion and irreligion), and to choose among the various available communications media. Indeed, I would assert that the value of self-determination is the principle underlying the various rights enumerated in the First Amendment. A common feature of the rights of free expression, religious freedom, and freedom of association is the empowering of citizens to select those influences on which they will base their political (or nonpolitical) values.

Thus, democracy, understood in its developmental sense, provides conditions within which public deliberation can be conducted. In the next section, I examine more closely the nature of public deliberation.

The Nature of Public Discourse

Many of my students, and, indeed, many Americans, make a sharp distinction between "facts" and "opinions," or between "facts" and "values." We view facts as relatively certain, epistemologically accredited statements of "real" states of affairs, while we think of "opinions," or "values" as subjective expressions of preferences. We generally regard the difference as one of verification: We can certify factual statements in some manner as "true" or "false," while we can make no such final adjudication in the realm of opinion.

Many philosophers have argued that innumerable problems are inherent in the fact-value distinction. I will call attention to only one: the existence of an intermediate category, which I would term "judgments." Provisionally, I would define judgments as evaluative statements for which justifications can and should be offered. While judgments do involve expressions of "better" or "worse," they are not simply preferences. Rather, the evaluative components of judgments involve some sort of cognitive basis.

To illustrate, as I write this, I am approaching my forty-sixth birthday. Thus, the statement, "Ted Jelen is 86 years old" is a factual claim, although a false one. The incorrect report of my age is not controversial, since such a claim can be easily verified or falsified. Conversely, it is my (sincerely held) opinion that I am married to the most beautiful woman in the world. While I am absolutely convinced of the "truth" of this statement, I have no means of convincing people who might be disinclined to agree with me. The latter statement is simply an expression of taste or prejudice, for which we lack any means of finding agreement among people who might dissent. "Opinion," in its purest sense, is thus ultimately—and necessarily—a private matter.

Consider, however, this intermediate case. In the 1996 presidential election, I cast a vote for Bill Clinton. Indeed, as a political scientist, I often seek out political conversation, and I devoted a great deal of, usually futile, effort to the task of convincing others that "Bill Clinton will make a better president than either Robert Dole or Ross Perot." Such a statement resembles an opinion, in that it is clearly evaluative. However, it differs from the opinion about my wife's beauty, in that I could be, and was, often challenged to produce reasons to support the assertion about Clinton, or to refute reasons why such a judgment might be inappropriate. In other words, judgments, unlike opinions, require justifications, or what Stephen Toulmin has called "warrants."[47] Were I to justify my support for Clinton's candidacy by saying that "I simply like him better," or "That's just my opinion," I would be guilty of privatizing a public choice, and presumably would not be very persuasive.

Judgments can, of course, be quite private and personal. A friend's decision to smoke tobacco in areas in which bystanders would not be affected, might be justified by a combination of tastes ("I really enjoy the flavor and aroma"), judgments about one's capabilities ("I wish I'd never started, but now I just can't quit"), and judgments about risks ("This probably won't do me any harm"). One might certainly criticize the decision to smoke and would likely do so (at least in part) on the basis of scientific judgments about the health risks associated with tobacco. However, such a conversation assumes that both parties will share a general assessment of the validity of scientific findings. The discourse stops if the smoker, for example, asserts that "scientific studies linking smoking to health problems are fraudulent; scientists simply falsify their results to retain their funding." Faced with the difficult, if not impossible, task of establishing a negative ("scientists typically do not falsify"), one

might quite reasonably terminate the conversation at that point. Moreover, a conversation on the merits of smoking also assumes agreement on certain value judgments, such as a belief that long life is preferable to early death, or that good health is preferable to illness. The smoker would stop an attempt to persuade her to quit smoking in its tracks if she asserted that she continues to smoke because "I'm really trying to commit suicide incrementally." In the unlikely event that one really preferred death to life, or illness to health, no basis exists for criticism, or, indeed, for conversation.

We can generalize this point. Judgments, unlike opinions, require warrants or justifications. Justifications will typically consist of combinations of irreducible value judgments (e.g., "living is preferable to dying"), and plausible factual assertions (e.g., "the evidence linking smoking to health problems is really pretty compelling"). If two or more people are to share judgments, they must at some level agree on what sorts of values and factual claims would count as warrants. The purpose of much communication between people who disagree is to find such "common ground," which, in principle, can serve as the basis of agreement. This is not to say that the discovery of commonly shared justifications is in any way easy. Anyone who has made an important decision in conjunction with a spouse, friend, or family member can attest to the difficulty of finding consensus. Not only is it the case that no group of people will share completely a set of value or factual justifications, but members of a given community will weight competing justifications differently. A Republican friend and I might agree that: (1) A second Clinton administration would create more jobs than a Dole administration, and (2) More abortions would be performed during Clinton's second term than during a Dole presidency. Nevertheless, even if we agreed that more jobs were preferable to fewer, and that abortion should be discouraged, we might disagree as to which candidate should be elected, because we place different values on full employment and the protection of "the unborn."

When common ground appears elusive as a basis for shared judgments, a frequent response is for people to "agree to disagree." In the case of an election, two people will generally accept the autonomy of each other's voting decisions, and end the conversation by canceling out one another's vote. With respect to a smoker who is unpersuaded by accounts of the health hazards associated with smoking, one must simply accept the (apparently irrational) decision to continue to use tobacco. In such a position, I might insist that the smoker refrain from smoking in my presence, and, if I felt strongly enough about the issue, I might discontinue my association with that person.[48] In many instances, it will be impossible to discern common bases for agreement on particular judgments, and a belief in individual autonomy may be a solution for such situations.

Having said that, one must note that, for a certain class of judgments, the option of agreeing to differ is simply not viable. The category of judgments

to which I will refer as "political" involve questions of public policy made by public authorities, and is characterized by at least two salient characteristics. First, political judgments are public, in that they apply to all persons in particular jurisdictions, whether the individuals affected accept the justifications for public policies or not. Thus, I am not free to disregard or to nullify acts of public authorities with whom I may disagree quite strenuously. In most cases (setting aside instances of civil disobedience or other controversial exceptions), the law applies to everyone, whether individuals agree with the law in question or not. The obligations of citizenship are not typically optional. Second, political judgments are authoritative, in that the coercive power of the state is placed in the service of the enforcement of public policies. Governmental laws or policies (when the term "government" is drawn rather narrowly to include formal governmental institutions) differ fundamentally from other judgments, in that such policies may be, and ultimately are, enforced with physical coercion.

It would seem to follow from this that we should be meticulous about the range of acceptable justifications for political judgments. Unless we agree with the position taken by Thrasymachus in the *Republic*[49] that justice is simply the interest of the stronger party, a respect for the autonomy and dignity of fellow citizens requires that their beliefs, values, and judgments be taken seriously in the formulation of public policy. Indeed, democratic policy deliberation would appear to demand nothing less.

One important criterion for the public justification of public policy is that of public accessibility.[50] If we are to express judgments about the desirability of certain public policies, we must offer justifications for them. The requirement of public accessibility simply, but not easily, entails that those justifications be cast in ". . . a manner intelligible or comprehensible to those who speak a different religious or moral language—to the point of translating one's position into a shared, or 'mediating,' language."[51] In other words, the justification of public judgments involves attempts to persuade those with whom we might differ. In order to engage in such a conversation or dialogue, one must attempt to find common premises on which one might base persuasion or agreement. To do otherwise is simply to assert the superiority of one's own position and perspective, and such a strategy is incompatible with notions of democracy as self governance.

It is perhaps important to note that the requirement of public accessibility applies only to the justification of policy preferences, rather than to their motivation. As Alexander Hamilton put it in *Federalist #1,* "My motives must remain in the depository of my own breast. My arguments will be open to all, and may be judged by all."[52] The inspiration for a public judgment may come from anywhere, as long as the reasons given seek to find shared premises on which possible agreement might be based.

To illustrate this point, during his Senate confirmation hearings as Secretary of the Interior in 1981, James Watt took the position that the United States had overinvested in public lands, and that, in his view, many such lands should be made available for private investment. When asked whether such a policy would not deprive future generations of public land use, Watt replied that he was not certain how many future generations there might be. Watt suggested that, since a number of prophecies in the Book of Revelation seemed to be coming to pass, it appeared as though the end of the world, as foretold in the Bible, might well be at hand. Therefore, it was not necessary to husband natural resources for future generations.

The requirement of public accessibility suggests that Watt's response is inadequate. James Watt, as an American citizen entitled to the free exercise of religion, is certainly entitled to believe in a premillennialist eschatology, and to base his policy preferences on such beliefs. However, since premillennialism is not generally shared across the American population, Watt's invocation of such theology is not a legitimate justification for his proposed policy. Watt, in essence, suggested that those who did not share his application of biblical principles to the politics of ecology were not full participants in the public deliberation, since the political judgment would depend on premises which such citizens do not share. Rather than seeking to persuade his fellow citizens of the wisdom of his judgment, Watt asserted an authoritative pronouncement, accessible only to those who held similar religious beliefs. The foregoing analysis suggests that determining what would count as a publicly accessible justification is essentially a matter of social construction. Ultimately, publicly accessible warrants are those shared by all or most participants in a conversation. This means that distinguishing between accessible, and, therefore, potentially acceptable, justifications and unacceptable justifications depends crucially on the identity and characteristics of the "public" in question.

Kent Greenawalt offers the following illustration of the social nature of public accessibility.[53] Consider the factual question of whether Jesus Christ bodily rose from the dead. Among many religious traditions, including the one in which I was raised, such an issue is simply not controversial. Indeed, acceptance of this assertion may be a condition of membership in a religious community. In such a community, the common ground is the general acceptance of the divine inspiration of Scripture.

However, if the conversation includes both people who hold orthodox Christian beliefs and agnostics who accept the Bible as a reasonably accurate, but not authoritative, historical source, justifications for the assertion "Christ rose from the dead" might involve the text of the New Testament, as well as analyses of the motives and dispositions of the actors in the Gospel. One might argue that the Apostles were so demoralized that acceptance of a resurrection claim would have required an extraordinary event, or it might be argued that the Romans (who presumably had a stake in debunking resurrection claims)

would have produced Jesus' body if they had been able to do so. In this latter, more ecumenical, conversation, publicly accessible justifications include the basic historical accuracy of the Scriptures, although not their divine inspiration, and conventional, "folk psychology" accounts of human motivation. If, however, the intended audience includes people who are genuinely skeptical about the veracity of the Bible as history, no such conversation is possible. Counterfactual claims about the dispositions of the Apostles, or the motives of the Romans, depend in the last analysis on descriptions of particular situations or contexts. If participants in a public discussion are not prepared to accept such descriptions, it follows that they will be unable to reach an agreement.

Thus, if we take democracy to be a genuinely deliberative process, justifications for public, and publicly enforceable, judgments must be publicly accessible. Public accessibility is essentially context dependent, in that the content of publicly accessible warrants depends on the beliefs and values of members of the "public." If we understand democracy to involve self-government, the legitimate basis for government is up to the "self" that is to be governed.

Religion and Public Accessibility

The preceding analysis suggests the following question: Are religious justifications publicly accessible? Many analysts have argued that, not only do religious justifications meet the requirement of public accessibility, but they are among the only warrants that do so. That is, religion provides a uniquely valuable basis for public deliberation, and a moral and intellectual basis within which political life can be conducted. Religious beliefs and values are thought to be so generally held that they provide the "common ground" on which shared moral and political judgments can be based. Moreover, the transcendent nature of religious beliefs renders them extremely powerful as sources of political cohesion. Peter Berger has suggested that shared religious convictions provide a "sacred canopy" under which we can conduct social and political life. Barry Alan Shain and Robert Booth Fowler have made similar arguments.[54] Fowler's "unconventional partners" discussion appears to depend crucially on the existence of widely shared religious beliefs.

Although the idea that a moral or religious consensus exists in the United States is a very old one, the exact content of this general agreement is not clear. A genuine societal consensus is likely, by definition, to be rather loosely articulated. Why, after all, would we debate issues on which all or most of us agree?

Some have argued that the content of an American consensus is based on ethics or morality, rather than on specifically theological beliefs. A century

and a half ago, Alexis de Tocqueville made the following observation about the political effects of American religion:

> The sects that exist in the United States are innumerable. They all differ in respect to the worship which is due the Creator; but they all agree in respect to the duties which are due from man to man. . . . Moreover, all the sects of the United States are comprised within the great unity of Christianity and Christian morality is everywhere the same. . . . Christianity, therefore, reigns without obstacle, by universal consent; the consequence is . . . that every principle of the moral world is fixed and determinate, although the political world is abandoned to the debates and experiments of men.[55]

In this passage, Tocqueville argues that the apparent diversity of American religion is, for practical purposes, illusory. Differences between denominations, according to Tocqueville, revolve around the relationship between humanity and God (the so-called First Table of the Ten Commandments). Ethics and morality (the "Second Table") are matters of consensus. Tocqueville regards religion as one of the factors that mitigate against the "tyranny of the majority," by placing certain issues out of bounds with respect to political debate. "The political world" exists within borders established by the Christian consensus.

More recently, Jerry Falwell has suggested that it is morality, rather than religion per se, that constitutes the content of the American consensus. The very concept of a "Moral Majority" (the name of Falwell's political organization in the 1980s) suggests that there exist widely shared, but clearly not universal, beliefs on moral issues. Falwell is quite clear that the nature of such a moral majority is ethical, rather than religious:

> Today, Moral Majority, Inc., is made up of millions of Americans, including 72,000 ministers, priests, and rabbis, who are deeply concerned about the moral decline of our nation, the traditional family, and the moral values on which our nation was built. We are Catholics, Jews, Protestants, Mormons, Fundamentalists—blacks and whites—farmers, housewives, businessmen and businesswomen. We are Americans from all walks of life united by one central concern: to serve as a special interest group providing a voice for a return to moral sanity in these United States of America. Moral Majority is a political organization and is not based on theological considerations.[56]

The claims of ecumenical membership in Moral Majority seem somewhat exaggerated. Most Moral Majority members were white, and members of independent Baptist churches.[57] Nevertheless, Falwell's core claim is that it is moral, rather than religious, values that define the dominant social culture in the United States. Falwell's list of the religious groups that form the potential constituency for Moral Majority suggests that a genuinely religious consensus

does not, and cannot, exist in this country. However, Falwell does suggest that there is widespread agreement about the moral consequences of religious beliefs.

A. James Reichley advances a contrasting argument. In his *Religion in American Public Life,* Reichley examines seven different ethical systems, including humanism, authoritarianism, personalism, and idealism. In an elegant theoretical analysis, Reichley argues that only "theist-humanism" is adequate to the task of providing a public basis for political life. Reichley concludes that:

> Theist-humanism solves the problem of balancing individual rights against social authority by rooting both in God's transcendent purpose, which is concerned for the welfare of each human soul. This does not, of course, provide a formula for settling all, or even most, or even any social problems. But it does create a body of shared values through which problems can be mediated.[58]

Although Reichley appears to agree with Tocqueville on the consensual nature of religious values, Reichley offers a different account of the content of such general agreement. While Tocqueville locates the consensus at the level of application ("the duties which are due from man to man"), Reichley appears to situate the American consensus at the somewhat more abstract level of theology. The analysis suggests that shared religious values do not provide specific guidance for particular issues, but that such values impose a general, transcendent framework. Reichley's argument depends crucially on a God with rather specific characteristics: transcendent, yet caring for each human soul. Alternative conceptions of God, such as Calvin's judgmental God who would predetermine the eternal fate of his creations,[59] or the Enlightenment "watchmaker" God (a passive creator who does not seek to intervene in human affairs), are not really compatible with Reichley's vision.

Richard John Neuhaus offers a similar, theological, description of an American religious consensus. In his classic work, *The Naked Public Square,* Neuhaus writes:

> Politics derives its directions from the ethos, from the cultural sensibilities that are the context of political action. The cultural context is shaped by our moral judgments and intuitions about how the world is and how it ought to be. Again, for the great majority of Americans, such moral judgments and intuitions are inseparable from religious belief.[60]

While Neuhaus's argument is not as directly theological as Reichley's, the thrust of the two positions is quite similar. Religious belief has moral and political consequences, which are generally beneficial for society. We cannot do without some sort of common ground in the course of public deliberation, and that common ground has roots that are essentially theological.

Whether the content of an American consensus is primarily religious or ethical, the notion that religious, or religiously derived, values provide a publicly accessible basis for public deliberation is based crucially on an empirical claim: That at some level, there exists in American society general agreement about the range of acceptable beliefs and behaviors. Apologists for an accommodationist understanding of church-state relations typically argue that some set of religiously based values are widely shared among the American public. Such general agreement is thought to make political dialogue possible, by limiting the range of politically permissible alternatives.

The problem with such an argument is that such publicly accessible agreement on religiously based values simply does not exist in the United States. Indeed, the diversity of religious and moral values in the United States suggests that when such values enter the public sphere, they are much more likely to be sources of contention than sources of social cohesion. First, a theological consensus does not exist in the United States, and perhaps never did. Although it is commonplace to argue that the United States is a Judeo-Christian nation, with a common religious heritage, the area of agreement is narrow indeed. Historically, religious beliefs have quite frequently divided the political values of Americans. For example, doctrinally conservative Protestants have often exhibited high levels of anti-Catholicism and anti-Semitism. Indeed, the Catholic Church has been characterized by some Protestants as the "Whore of Babylon" (a symbol from the Book of Revelation) or the "Harlot of Rome."[61]

In his recent book, *Politically Incorrect,* Ralph Reed (former executive director of the Christian Coalition) devotes a great deal of attention to the historical problems of anti-Catholicism, and the contemporary possibilities for evangelical-Catholic cooperation:

> Perhaps most encouraging is a new spirit of ecumenism that permeates the profamily community. . . . The union of Roman Catholics and conservative Protestants could have a greater impact on American politics than any coalition since African-Americans and Jews came together during the civil rights movement. From the rumblings of the Reformation to the nativist rantings of the Know Nothings, Protestants and Catholics have eyed one another suspiciously across a chasm of painful history. Differences on some theological issues remain. But the darkness of the culture has become so pervasive that those of like mind and common faith feel compelled to join together in unity.[62]

This passage suggests that Protestant-Catholic antipathy is a historical problem, which must be, and can be, overcome. Nevertheless, recent evidence suggests that Catholics have been slow to mobilize into the Christian Right. Catholics remain among the most Democratic of white Christians, and white Catholic Republicans have not shifted based on their position on moral or lifestyle issues.[63] Moreover, apart from interest groups concerned specifically

with the issue of abortion, Catholics contribute relatively little support to Christian Right organizations such as the Christian Coalition or Focus on the Family.[64] Clearly, an evangelical-Catholic coalition would be quite formidable, although the obstacles to such cooperation would be quite imposing as well. Theological divisions between Catholics and Protestants are not the only source of religious division in the United States. Research on the "old" New Christian Right (the Moral Majority, Pat Robertson's 1988 presidential campaign) has suggested that Christian right support was badly fragmented by the effects of religious particularism. Particularism, defined as a belief in the superiority of one's own religious tradition, has made interdenominational cooperation between conservative Protestants difficult.[65] For example, despite general agreement on *political* issues with Pat Robertson, Jerry Falwell endorsed Episcopalian George Bush for president in 1988. Among the differences between Falwell and Robertson was Robertson's charismatic brand of Christianity, with its emphasis on spiritual gifts (faith healing, speaking in tongues, etc.). Not only did candidate Robertson failed to mobilize Roman Catholics (an important constituency for the Christian Right), he failed to attract support beyond a very narrow group of charismatic and pentecostal Protestants.[66] Thus, specifically theological differences (not political or moral differences) have had profound political consequences. As Kent Greenawalt puts it:

> In a very religious but extremely tolerant society, public airing of particular religious views might work well, but in actuality such discourse promotes a sense of separation between the speaker and those who do not share his religious convictions and is likely to produce both religious and political divisiveness.[67]

Of course, religious particularism is not a necessary characteristic of religious belief. Reed's *Politically Incorrect* is, in part, an exhortation to conservative Christians to put aside theological differences to achieve political or cultural ends. Recent research into support for the Christian Coalition has shown that it has a somewhat more ecumenical base of support than did earlier Christian Right figures or organizations.[68] Such interdenominational success may be attributable to strategic actions taken by Reed and others, and may also be attributable to the effects of the Clinton presidency. Clinton's early public support for gay rights and reproductive freedom appears to have had the effect of providing a common foe for culturally conservative Christians. Thus, it seems quite possible that religious divisions can be overcome, and that it is possible to discern broad areas of agreement between religious traditions with a history of hostile relations. To the extent that religiously motivated political activity seems desirable, sophisticated leaders might well suppress potentially divisive theological differences.

However, it is also possible that the roots of religious division are deeper

than contemporary political circumstances might suggest. In a recent book, Roger Finke and Rodney Stark have suggested that a comparison between religious denominations and firms in a free market economy might be quite useful. In *The Churching of America, 1776–1990*, Finke and Stark argue that religious devotion and participation on the part of laypeople is increased by religious pluralism, and by competition between denominations.[69] In their analysis, lay members of congregations can be regarded as consumers of religious goods. Such consumers will expend resources (time, money, devotion) to the extent that religious producers (denominations) satisfy consumer preferences. In religiously competitive markets, denominations have strong incentives to adapt their messages to the preferences of the laity. By contrast, in situations in which one denomination has a practical monopoly, as in the case of a legally established church, or in communities with little religious diversity, religious producers have little reason to accommodate the preferences of the laity. Since consumers have the ability to choose whether to engage in formal religious activity, as well as the capacity to choose between denominations, it follows that the aggregate level of organized religious activity (church membership, attendance, etc.) is a function of the level of religious competition and pluralism within a given community. Indeed, it is often argued that the religious vitality of the United States, in contrast to other industrialized nations, is in large part attributable to the country's religious diversity, which in turn results from the legal separation of church and state.[70]

Clearly, the analogy between religion and economics is controversial and has occasioned an enormous amount of scholarly literature.[71] To the extent that the comparison is valid, it is possible that the increases in religious competition may increase religious particularism. If in fact denominations must compete among themselves for lay members, it may follow that clergy must engage in what market researchers call "product differentiation." That is, clergy may have an incentive to distinguish their specific denomination from others, by making doctrinal or theological differences as clear as possible. It is probably rational for religious leaders to provide reasons why people should attend one particular church rather than another. Moreover, such distinctions are most likely to occur among churches that are similar to one another.[72] Thus, clerical messages to the laity can be expected to increase, rather than suppress, perceptions of interdenominational differences in theology.

All of this suggests, of course, that the logic of religious recruitment tends toward disaggregation. The same forces that occasion relatively high levels of religious activity (denominational competition) also seem likely to result in religious particularism. To the extent that church members emphasize the doctrinal distinctiveness of their denominations, it is unlikely that religious belief can serve as a common ground from which one can draw publicly accessible justifications. With respect to religious beliefs, I would argue that an inherent tension exists between the political imperatives of religion (tending toward

aggregation) and theological religious imperatives (tending toward disaggregation).

An example may make this point more clearly. Reichley has argued that the Prohibition movement of the early twentieth century resulted from a strong religious coalition of Protestant progressives and conservatives.[73] It should be noted at the outset that the Prohibition movement did not represent a societal consensus, since the ecumenical Protestant coalition was organized as a nativist movement against practices common among Roman Catholic immigrants. Nevertheless, progressive or liberal Protestants were able to argue that the antialcohol crusade was an obvious extension of the "Social Gospel," which was a theological movement designed to adapt the Scriptures to modern conditions.[74] Adherents of the Social Gospel argued that alcohol was among the horrors of modern urban life that Christians were obligated to combat. Conversely, Protestant "fundamentalists" (so called because of their desire to return to the "fundamentals" of an inerrant Bible) were not willing to "adapt" the inerrant Word of God in any way. Such doctrinally conservative Protestants were nonetheless able to find specific scriptural injunctions, mostly from the Book of Leviticus, against drinking alcohol. Thus, with respect to the Eighteenth Amendment to the Constitution, Protestants of diverse theological orientations were able to make a common cause to advance a common ethical objective.

However, the progressive-fundamentalist coalition that had been so successful in advancing Prohibition splintered during the Scopes "Monkey Trial." At issue was the teaching of evolution in the public schools. This question divided the progressives, who wished to accommodate the Scriptures to the insights of modern science, and the fundamentalists, who sought to preserve the authority of the Bible against "modernist heresy." The evolution question brought to the forefront doctrinal differences that had been effectively suppressed during the antialcohol crusade.[75]

The general point is that religious doctrine in the United States typically has been a source of division, rather than cohesion. Thus, religious beliefs, in and of themselves, would seem to be poor candidates for the publicly accessible justifications demanded by democratic political discourse. Indeed, recent research in the sociology of religion has suggested that the very act of church attendance may make the problem of particularism even more severe.[76]

If religion itself is not a plausible candidate for publicly accessible justifications, it may be that the application of religious doctrine might fare somewhat better. Is there not, then, an ethical consensus in the United States that might serve as the common ground on which democratic discourse depends? Is it not possible that Tocqueville was correct, and (to paraphrase him) that there is general agreement on the duties owed "from person to person"? Conceivably, the issue of Prohibition might be more typical than that of evolution. If that is the case, it may not matter that the theological justification for ethical

or moral practices might differ from individual to individual or across religious traditions.

Perhaps unfortunately, it appears no more likely that a moral consensus exists in the United States than a religious one. Once we get past murder, theft, and rape (which perhaps could be proscribed on secular grounds as well), it is difficult to discern the content of a common American morality. Indeed, we find that many moral issues are contested within American Christianity, and even within specific denominations.

A few illustrations should make this point quite clearly. The role of women is debated within both Protestantism and Catholicism.[77] While support for "feminism" in its various forms differs across denominational families, substantial support for gender equality proliferates, even among conservative evangelical Christians.[78] Leaders in a number of different denominations have debated the issue of female ordination; this debate has included some of the more conservative, evangelical groups.

Even among extremely religious—and highly doctrinally conservative—Christians, the belief that sexual relations outside of marriage are immoral has eroded considerably. Indeed, leaders of one mainline denomination have advanced the concept of "justice-love." This idea suggests that the important moral variable in a sexual liaison is the power relationship between the participants.[79] Whether an intimate physical relationship is "exploitive" or "mutually supportive" is considered more important than the gender or marital status of the people involved.

While there is probably a societal consensus that murder is morally wrong, some applications of this ethical principle remain contested. The issue of abortion is almost a caricature of a contested political issue. Clearly, no general agreement exists on the morality of abortion, the humanity of the fetus, or the appropriate procedural requirements surrounding the abortion decision. Moreover, the center of gravity of public opinion on this issue most decidedly lies in the pro-choice direction, even among adherents of Roman Catholic or evangelical Protestant churches.[80] That is, while members of certain denominations are more likely to take pro-life positions than those outside those denominations, pro-choice Catholics or evangelicals outnumber their pro-life religious counterparts.

Gambling, once illegal virtually everywhere, is now widely accepted throughout the country, and government-sponsored lotteries now provide a large share of educational funding in a number of states. Moreover, while widespread support may exist for the principles of the free-enterprise system, recent research has suggested that such support for capitalism is lower among members of evangelical denominations.[81] Despite the pronouncements of some evangelical leaders (Falwell, Robertson, Reed), lay evangelicals are moderately supportive of generous social welfare policies, and some are skeptical of the philosophical roots of American capitalism.[82]

Finally, and perhaps most importantly, there no longer exists a societal consensus on the immorality of homosexuality. Again, while differences abound between denominations, and between people with differing levels of religiosity, homosexual rights are fiercely debated in contemporary politics. In some mainline denominations, the issue of gay ordination has been argued, and some congregations have selected openly gay men and women as ministers.[83] Quite recently, the Central Conference of American Rabbis (a Reform organization) endorsed civil marriage for homosexuals, and voted to oppose government efforts to bar such marriages.[84] Thus, disagreements over the rights of homosexuals, and over the morality of homosexuality, are not differences between the orthodox and the secular. Rather, these issues are contested vigorously within diverse communities of faith.

Thus, there are very few moral issues on which general agreement exists in the United States. Further, it seems clear that the major cultural value that inhibits general social condemnation of abortion, extramarital sex, or homosexuality is the value placed on Lockean individualism.[85] For many Americans, issues of personal morality occupy a nearly sovereign "private sphere," within which they think government intervention is illegitimate. As the value of individualism is virtually unchallenged in American politics,[86] the emergence (or reemergence) of a moral consensus seems likely to be elusive.[87] Thus, religion is unlikely to serve as the basis of publicly accessible political justifications for public policies in the United States. Whether we consider the effects of religious principles, or the moral consequences of religious beliefs, neither appears to be a plausible candidate for the common ground on which democratic political discourse might depend.[88]

We should perhaps note, if only in passing, that this particular characterization does not depend on whether the political role of religion is "priestly" or "prophetic."[89] If religion is to serve a political role as legitimator or social critic, people must have shared religious or moral premises from which they can argue. Indeed, if one wishes to criticize prevailing political practices from a religious perspective—as have such diverse exemplars as Martin Luther King, Jr., and Randall Terry—one must appeal to some common sense of values. Prophets are only effective to the extent that their criticism strikes a responsive chord with the citizens whose practice is the object of the prophets' commentary.

Religion as a Source of Political Dysfunction

Thus far, I have simply argued that religious beliefs are inadequate warrants or justifications for political ideas in a religiously diverse polity. This centrifugal property is by no means unique to religion. After all, race, region, ethnicity, or even science have failed to produce consensus on many important ques-

tions, and no one argues that these considerations should be left out of political discourse. To single out religion for special treatment in public discourse would seem to be discriminatory and would place religiously motivated citizens at a disadvantage.[90] Nonreligious citizens would be permitted to use the full range of arguments available to them, but believers would be proscribed from using certain of their arguments; indeed, perhaps their most deeply held and clearly articulated beliefs would be considered suspect. Are there, then, special reasons why we should limit the role of religion in political discourse?

This question brings to mind the analysis offered by Kent Greenawalt. In his elegant *Religious Convictions and Political Choice,* Greenawalt argues that those who would make religiously based arguments about matters of public policy should defer to publicly accessible reasons when such reasons are available.[91] Greenawalt concedes that religion is unlikely to serve as a publicly accessible justification in a religiously diverse society such as the United States. In most cases, religious justifications will be superseded by science, politics, or common elements of American culture. However, Greenawalt suggests that in many instances, publicly accessible warrants do not yield specific solutions or limit the range of intellectually permissible alternatives. In such situations, there is no reason to exclude religious beliefs from public deliberation:

> if commonly shared moral perspectives and forms of reason provide no evidently correct perspective, it is hard to understand why a liberal democrat should eschew his deeply held religious premises in favor of some alternative assumptions that also lie beyond public reasons and can yield a starting point . . . everyone must reach beyond commonly accessible reasons to decide many social issues and . . . religious bases for such decisions should not be disfavored in comparison with other possible bases.[92]

Greenawalt uses the examples of abortion, animal rights, and environmentalism to illustrate cases that have not had common frames of reference in the United States. He suggests that such issues constitute "borderline cases," in which commonly held perspectives are vague or nonexistent. Presumably, most Americans would agree that a fetus has some moral standing, and that the decision to abort is of greater moral gravity than deciding to undergo other forms of surgery. However, probably few would consider a fetus to hold the same rights as a born human, even among those who would argue that life begins at the moment of conception. Similarly, animals are entitled to some moral consideration, and not many people would oppose, on principle, anti-cruelty laws. Nevertheless, the decision to euthanize a dog is probably less morally questionable than a similar decision with respect to a human, and few would grant animals the same respect accorded humans. However, drawing distinctions between such "borderline" beings as animals or a fetus and hu-

mans is quite difficult, and Greenawalt argues that we should not exclude religious perspectives and arguments from such public discussions. The problem with such a religiously neutral viewpoint, in my view, is that religion threatens to undermine the process of public deliberation, and situations in which no substantive publicly accessible justifications exist for particular public policies exacerbate this tendency. Obviously, many public issues go unsettled in the sense of producing a consensus for or against a particular outcome. Although I enjoy political discussions with my students and my friends, I recognize that most of these types of conversations are ultimately futile. For example, despite my considerable skills of persuasion, I was unable to convince my Republican friends that four more years of a Clinton administration would be preferable to the election of Robert Dole. While such discussions may be stimulating and enjoyable, they rarely result in agreement.

If such an argument cannot be settled, neither can its public aspect be postponed or privatized. While individual citizens may agree to differ, someone had to be inaugurated as president on January 20, 1997. We may agree to respect the autonomy of one another's preferences, but a public, authoritative decision must be made. In order to make such necessary decisions and have them generally accepted, we must locate other sources of common ground. In democratic regimes such as the United States, publicly accessible common ground is typically grounded in respect for procedures, or what John Rawls has termed "Constitutional essentials."[93] That is, even as citizens disagree about the appropriate substantive outcomes of public decisions, they can, and should, agree on the processes by which such decisions are reached and enforced. Thus, my Republican friend and I may continue to disagree as to whether Bill Clinton or Bob Dole would make the better president, but we can probably agree that the candidate who receives a majority of the electoral vote is legally entitled to assume the office. Indeed, if Dole, or anyone else, had received 270 or more electoral votes in 1996, I would anticipate that Bill Clinton would have relinquished his office voluntarily. Indeed, it is arguably an important characteristic of the American political culture that our commitment to constitutional essentials takes precedence over our commitments to particular electoral or policy outcomes.[94]

A problem with religious belief is that such theological values often supersede commitments to constitutional essentials. There is, to be sure, little religious resistance to democratic procedures as such. I am aware of no religious movement that advocates the abolition of our bicameral legislature, the separation of powers, or elections as a means of recruitment of public officials.[95] However, the constitutional essentials of American politics are not limited to procedures, but include substantive prerogatives on the part of ordinary citizens. It is my contention that religious values are suspect participants in public deliberation because religion often undermines and subverts such prerogatives.

Two examples should clarify this point. In addition to the establishment and

free exercise clauses, the First Amendment to the Constitution guarantees the right of free speech and a free press. While the precise contours of free expression remain contested in American jurisprudence,[96] there appears to be general agreement as to the rationale that underlies these sections of the First Amendment. The free expression and circulation of ideas has an educative function, and to provide the robust, informative debate necessary for self-governance.[97] If citizens are to make intelligent choices among alternative candidates or policies, they must be informed by the public interplay of competing ideas and perspectives.

A great deal of research has suggested that certain religious beliefs, and religiosity generally, are negatively related to support for the free expression presumably guaranteed by the First Amendment.[98] Enormous controversy prevails over whether intolerance is intrinsic to or a necessary consequence of religious commitment.[99] Nevertheless, the empirical evidence relating religious values to intolerance and incivility is quite impressive. Regarding the incivility of Christian fundamentalists, Green et al. write:

> At least three times in this century, however, fundamentalists have burst into the public square with a vigorous and uncivil challenge to the political establishment. . . . fundamentalists are goaded into policies by sharp deviations from traditional morality that are accepted, or worse yet, endorsed and promoted by public authorities. Such a moral imperative provokes an angry reaction. Not only does it distract from otherworldly concerns, it threatens the well-being of humanity on a cosmic scale. . . . fundamentalist challenges to the modern world are "defensive offensives" . . . designed to stave off moral calamity until the Lord's work on earth is completed. *Thus the very motivation for political action reduces the civility of their politics.*[100]

This passage, which comes at the end of an empirical analysis demonstrating fundamentalist activists' relative lack of political tolerance for the First Amendment rights of nonconformists, is quite revealing. Fundamentalist political activism is depicted as being contingent on public support for certain rather narrowly drawn theological and moral perspectives. Since such support is not forthcoming—indeed, the support for moral alternatives is the principal motivation for political participation—support for the constitutionally essential value of free expression is withheld, and even challenged. Particular—and perhaps particularistic—religious beliefs are shown to undermine support for an important aspect of the process of public deliberation. Further, the basis of this undermining is the belief in a "higher value" (God's work on earth), which is thought to trump the value of democratic civility. In this passage, fundamentalists are depicted as placing certain desired policy outcomes above commitment to the process by which policy is made.

The problem of incivility is not limited to fundamentalist or evangelical Christians. Recently, the Bishop of the Lincoln, Nebraska, Catholic diocese,

threatened to excommunicate Catholics who belong to any of twelve organized groups. The threat of excommunication—the most serious religious sanction the Catholic Church can impose—may be applied to members of a number of pro-life groups, as well as to members of organizations that publicly favor the ordination of women and those with affiliations with the Masons.[101] Again, if the right of free association is a constitutionally protected right, the actions of Bishop Bruskewitz constitute a religiously based threat to the prerogatives of democratic citizenship. Such a policy, if enacted, would limit substantially Catholic citizens' access to public deliberation.

Moreover, the constitutionally subversive potential of religion is not limited to issues of free expression. If the American constitutional order is ultimately based on the value of self-governance, it follows that individual citizens must be granted a certain level of personal autonomy and self-determination. To some extent, of course, individual preferences are the consequence of life histories and circumstances. If citizens are to exhibit the autonomy necessary for self-governance, they must be granted some control over their individual biographies and circumstances. For example, the ability of competent adult citizens to choose their occupations, educational levels, spouses, and places of residence are fundamental to the goals of democratic self-governance.

To illustrate, consider the issue of "gay marriage." At this writing, the Supreme Court of the state of Hawaii has declared that marriages between members of the same sex must be legally recognized. Under most circumstances, acts of state governments are to be honored in other states, under the "full faith and credit clause" of the Constitution (Article IV, section 1). For example, a heterosexual couple married in Illinois are entitled to the same legal rights as other married couples if they should move to Texas. Constitutionally, the government of Texas is required to recognize the legality of a marriage performed in Illinois, even if the laws governing marriage are different in Illinois than in Texas.

Presumably, the full faith and credit clause of the Constitution could mean that state governments are required to recognize marriages between members of the same sex, if the gay couple were legally married in Hawaii. The possibility that same-sex marriages could be made legal everywhere in the United States has galvanized a great deal of political activity on the part of religious interest groups such as the Christian Coalition and the Catholic Alliance.[102] In response to this activity, numerous states have passed laws nullifying the legality of such marriages within their borders. Congress recently passed the Defense of Marriage Act, which would prevent gay couples from claiming legal rights under the full faith and credit clause. Regardless of how one might view gay marriages, the response of Congress and state legislatures to the events in Hawaii pose at least two major problems. Legally, the acts of state governments, and the Defense of Marriage Act, are of dubious constitutionality. The full faith and credit clause does not appear to grant either Congress

or state governments the right to make substantive exceptions to the provision.[103] One might well argue that, if nonrecognition of gay marriages outside of Hawaii is the desired outcome, the proper way to proceed is through a constitutional amendment, rather than through an ordinary act of the legislature. The Defense of Marriage Act might illustrate a willingness to compromise constitutional procedure for the sake of a religiously motivated policy goal.

Second, even setting aside legal considerations, the Defense of Marriage Act would seem to violate normative principles of developmental democracy. The decision whether to marry, and whom to marry, is a fundamental, self-determining action.[104] The act of entering into a legally enforceable, monogamous relationship is based on certain character traits and has implications for the future development of one's character and political interests. To the extent that opposition to gay marriage has a religious basis—as it clearly does—religious values detract from the autonomy on which democratic citizenship is based. Commitment to a political outcome, for some, apparently supersedes commitment to the process by which political outcomes are determined. Thus, the invocation of religious values may undermine the most important publicly accessible justification for public policy available to democratic governments: the legitimacy of the process under which public deliberation is conducted, and, indeed, under which individual preferences are formed, and public decisions are ultimately made.

Consequently, religion is potentially incompatible with democratic public deliberation for two reasons. First, contemporary religious belief and practice fails to provide a publicly accessible set of justifications for political decisions. This is the case regardless of whether attention is focused on the content of religious beliefs themselves, or on the ethical or behavioral consequences of such beliefs. This apparent lack of consensus on religious or moral values is not simply the result of a rise in secularism but is grounded in alternative religious visions of justice and virtue. Second, the authority that religion exerts over its adherents threatens the most basic common ground on which democratic governance depends: a widely shared, common commitment to the procedures and constitutional essentials that form the framework within which we conduct politics. If religious values are allowed to trump civil political processes, they can undermine the common ground on which policy judgments can be justified publicly.

This argument does not depend on any form of the "secularization thesis," in which religion is thought to be increasingly irrelevant to the concerns of citizens of advanced industrial democracies.[105] For example, Ronald Inglehart has suggested that, in Western culture, religion is not becoming irrelevant in any but the most formal, institutional sense.[106] Religion, in Inglehart's account, has become less institutionalized and more individualized but is perhaps no less important to the believer. However, this sort of "privatization"

of religion—if such a phenomenon is in fact occurring—precisely undermines religion's authority as a source of *public* justification for *political* judgments. Even if Inglehart's "culture shift" hypothesis is an imperfect match with an older version of "secularization theory," the political implications of the former are perhaps as profound as those of the latter.

The Political Contamination of Religion

Up to this point, I have argued that religion has the potential to undermine democratic politics. In this section, I offer a different, but complementary, thesis; namely, that participation in democratic politics can undermine authentic religious belief and practice.

Earlier, I argued that it is unlikely that any American consensus would include agreement on religious beliefs or values. Suppose for the moment that my earlier arguments are incorrect. I propose that, if such a consensus were to exist, it would threaten authentic religious belief and practice.

In a polity containing a genuine religious consensus, there would be a strong risk of idolatry, or the legitimation of contemporary political structures in religious terms.[107] A consensual religion would have a priestly function, in which religion serves to promote support for prevailing practices, rather than a prophetic social function, wherein religion serves as a social critic.[108] In this type of culture, religion may lack an independent basis from which to criticize prevailing social practices. A politically consensual religion might well be capable of identifying and sanctioning socially deviant behavior but may not be equipped to challenge the established norms of the culture. Since humanity defines and actualizes the culture, including politics, such institutions are, according to most versions of Christianity with which I am familiar, sinful, incomplete, and corrupt.

Further, the notion that the United States is a Christian nation, or adheres to a Judeo-Christian tradition, risks identifying national success or prosperity with divine favor. As Jerry Falwell has written:

The rise and fall of nations confirms the Scripture that says "Be not deceived; God is not mocked; Whatsoever a man soweth, that shall he also reap" (Galatians 6:7). Psalm 9:17 admonishes, "The wicked shall be turned to hell, and all the nations that forget God." America will be no exception. If she forgets God, she too will face his wrath and judgement like every other nation in the history of humanity. But we have the promise in Psalm 33:12, which declares, "Blessed is the nation whose God is the LORD." When a nation's ways please the Lord, that nation is blessed with supernatural help.[109]

Taken literally, this passage suggests that it is possible to determine the degree to which the United States is in divine favor by the extent to which our situa-

tion is peaceful and prosperous. Falwell also suggests that God judges nations collectively, rather than on the basis of individual grace or desert. To the extent that such sentiments are widely shared, individual religious or moral decisions lack their private autonomous character and can be criticized as jeopardizing a common enterprise. In other words, a consensus around religious values can be legitimately enforced, if such communal divine judgments are taken seriously. At one level, of course, such enforcement would violate the political requisite for autonomy and individual self-determination discussed earlier. Perhaps more seriously, such ideas carry a threat to certain religious values. If religious beliefs are valid only to the extent that they are chosen freely, to make the profession of such values a public matter would promote hypocrisy, and delegitimate authentic, if unconventional, religious conviction.[110]

Problems also abound if one does not assume the existence of a religious or moral consensus in the United States. In recent years, a number of analysts have argued that American society has been divided into two groups: a secular or humanist elite, which has disproportionate control over the means of communications, and a more religious mass public (a moral majority?). Indeed, the rhetoric of the Christian Right is often characterized by dualism.[111] Perhaps the most thorough analysis of American politics from this dualistic perspective is James Davison Hunter's *Culture Wars: The Struggle to Define America.*[112] In this ambitious work, Hunter argues that contemporary American culture is divided into proponents of orthodoxy and progressivism. This division pits religious conservatives of all stripes against secularists and religious modernists. Such a cleavage in society displaces previously salient differences between religious denominations or social classes.[113]

Hunter argues that there does not exist much potential for public dialogue between the Progressives and the Orthodox, since both have relatively complete and mutually incompatible worldviews. The common ground on which democratic deliberation depends simply does not exist in a dualistic, religiously mobilized society, as indicated by the marital metaphor of a culture "war." Thus, the first casualty in the culture war is likely to be political civility.[114]

The lack of tolerance and civility on both sides in a religiously dualistic polity may be endemic to this type of social environment. Protagonists in a culture war may have little reason to respect their opponents' motives, values, or goals. This tendency to demonize one's adversaries may be exacerbated on the side of the orthodox, since Christianity provides a relatively complete theory of false consciousness: original sin. Since all humankind is sinful and corrupt as the result of the Fall in the Garden of Eden, secular perspectives that deemphasize the need for God, or for divine grace, are easily explainable. Indeed, such beliefs are represented in the Fall itself, since the serpent's argument to Eve was precisely that eating from the Tree of Knowledge of Good

and Evil would render God superfluous ("Ye shall be as Gods"; Genesis 3:5). Such false consciousness might be most easily ascribed to those who have consciously resisted the redeeming effects of God's grace, by inhabiting a secular, or modernist, worldview. If one can explain—apparently irrational— behavior of one's opponents from within one's own belief system, one does not need to take seriously the content of the arguments advanced by such people.[115]

From a religious standpoint, the risk this argument entails is the sin of pride. A division of society into saints and sinners might produce feelings of moral superiority over those on the progressive side of the culture war. Most versions of orthodox Christianity with which I am familiar involve the belief that all of humanity is sinful, and that attempting to provide gradations of relative sinfulness is ultimately futile. Glenn Tinder reminds us that even our judgments about right and wrong, and about the "correct" meaning of the Scriptures, are necessarily corrupt, limited, and therefore flawed. Even for the orthodox—or perhaps especially for the orthodox—salvation is a quest, which may proscribe passing judgment on the behavior of others. Such forbearance may well be incompatible with the political mobilization of religious beliefs.

Finally, some descriptions of American politics allow for candid acknowledgement of the diversity of American religion. Under theories of pluralism, the stability and civility of the American political order is preserved by the interplay of competing groups.[116] Indeed, when such a perspective is applied to religious groups, the existence of multiple religious voices in American politics could possibly avoid some of the more serious problems with religion in consensual or dualistic theories. When multiple theological perspectives are presented in the public sphere, little danger of idolatry exists, since the illusion of societal consensus is unlikely to be plausible. Similarly, the temptation of pride is reduced when religious viewpoints are pitted against one another, as well as against secularism. A pluralistic religious polity would perhaps demand no special treatment for religion, but simply a place at the table in public deliberations.[117] Particular religious outlooks would be in a position to articulate, but not perhaps to aggregate, religious values. Such voices, which by definition would not constitute political majorities, might serve as prophetic voices of social criticism, without threatening to dominate the political dialogue.

Several analysts have analyzed the proper, normative role of religion in pluralistic societies, such as the United States. A common theme in such analyses is that, if religious perspectives are to have a legitimate place in the public square, their proponents must abide by the rules of democratic discourse. As noted earlier, Kent Greenawalt has argued that religious viewpoints should defer to publicly accessible justifications for policy choices when such justifications exist. Greenawalt would confine the articulation of religious values to the portion of the public sphere in which such warrants are not available; as

an empirical matter, Greenawalt takes this religiously legitimate space to be rather large.[118] Similarly, Michael Perry has endorsed a concept of "ecumenical political dialogue," in which religion might well play an essential role. Perry has argued that religious arguments in the public sphere must meet the criteria of public accessibility, public intelligibility, and be offered in the spirit of pluralism and fallibilism. The requisite of pluralism entails the belief that moral understandings can be enhanced by confrontations with alternative positions, while the requirement of fallibilism demands that religious perspectives be advanced with a sense of self-critical rationality. That is, the believer must be prepared to alter his or her viewpoints in response to participation in public dialogue.[119]

Perry's analysis has much in common with that offered by Clarke Cochran. In his sophisticated work, *Religion in Private and Public Life,* Cochran argues that religion and politics should be separated by a clear, yet permeable border. Both the private and public spheres have characteristic strengths and weaknesses.[120] For example, a purely private religion might well degenerate into an extremely individualistic, subjective belief system (e.g., Bellah et al.'s famous example of "Sheilaism,")[121] or to an unself-conscious fanaticism.[122] Conversely, an excessively public religion might either come to dominate the secular aspects of political life, or become so accommodating that it loses its distinctive social function. Cochran suggests that the challenge of contemporary politics is to "combine the passion of religion with the civil tolerance of democratic pluralism."[123] Authentic religion and authentic democracy both require that religion and politics interact through a discernable, yet permeable, border.[124] Religion and politics exist in a state of tension, which, understood properly, can enrich both spheres of human activity.

Finally, Glenn Tinder's *The Political Meaning of Christianity* suggests that democratic civility is a religiously required attitude, if Christianity is properly understood. Tinder argues that the fallen nature of humanity renders politics both necessary and difficult.[125] As James Madison argued in *Federalist #51,* "if men were angels, no government would be necessary."[126] Tinder would also have us take the possibility of redemption, through God's sanctifying grace, quite seriously. A fallen human nature makes politics necessary and limits our ability to eliminate injustice. However, the prospect of salvation requires the attempt to eliminate particular injustices on our part.

Tinder's analysis of the question of political tolerance illustrates his general point quite nicely. Tinder argues, in a manner similar to John Stuart Mill's argument in *On Liberty,* that to seek to repress the opinions of others is to assume an unwarranted infallibility. A proper appreciation of our fallen state, Tinder suggests, requires that we forgo such an assumption, and further requires that we not proscribe the expression of certain viewpoints or judgments. If we take sin seriously as a condition, rather than as a set of discrete acts, we must regard our attempts to understand and codify religious doctrine

as ultimately flawed and incomplete. Tinder points out that the Gospels are cast in a narrative form. Even if we take the Gospels to be inerrant—a contested assumption within American Christianity—it does not follow that our interpretations of the Gospel message are inerrant as well. An appreciation of our moral and intellectual limits precludes prejudging the content of the belief systems of others. Thus, for Tinder, tolerance and civility are not only compatible with Christianity, they are demanded by Christian theology.

What the analyses of Greenawalt, Perry, Cochran, and Tinder have in common is the sense that religion is entitled to a place at the table of public discourse as long as religious believers, in some important sense, "mind their manners," and refrain from pressing their cases too stridently. Democratic deliberation assumes certain ground rules—public accessibility, fallibilism, etc.—which must be observed if the expression of religious viewpoints is to be compatible with democratic civility.

Indeed, some empirical evidence suggests that participation in the public sphere has generally positive effects on religious citizens, when these effects are viewed from the perspective of democratic civility. Grindstaff has shown that pro-life rhetoric has, over time, become less specifically religious, and more secular and scientific.[127] As religious citizens have participated in the public dialogue over abortion, they have accommodated their messages to the requirements of democratic deliberation—if one assumes that science is more publicly accessible than particular religious insights. Similarly, Wilcox et al. have shown that Moral Majority members who are active in organizational activities are less authoritarian and dogmatic than their more passive comembers, and that activists have higher levels of self-esteem as well.[128] Allen Hertzke has suggested that certain religious leaders, specifically Jesse Jackson and Pat Robertson, may have occasioned a revival of the spirit of populism in American politics.[129] Moreover, Verba et al. have shown that active participation in church activities leads to the development of political skills that can be used in the public sphere.[130] Thus, substantial empirical evidence supports Cochran's argument that the religious and political spheres of activity can sometimes interact to the benefit of both.

However, these analyses pose two distinct problems for the practice of religion. The first of these is relativism, or the belief that multiple perspectives are to some extent valid approximations of the truth. The risk is that religious denominations or traditions that derive their distinctiveness from the authority of divine revelation may endanger their distinctive theological missions in the pursuit of political goals.

For example, in the American Catholic Bishop's Pastoral Letter, *Economic Justice for All,* the bishops place a high value on ecumenism, as well as on the argumentative, rather than the authoritative, aspects of their position:

> we do not claim to make these prudential judgments with the same kind of authority that marks our declaration of principle. But we feel obliged to teach by

example how Christians can undertake concrete analysis and make specific judgments on economic issues.[131]

The self-conscious limitation of religious authority, as well as the appeal to teach by example, would certainly be consistent with the demands of democratic civility. The bishops simply sought to enter the public conversation concerning the economy, rather than dictate to the consciences of Roman Catholics. However, one might legitimately raise the question of whether such concessions violate the unique theological position of the Catholic Church. Under one version of Catholic theology, the Church is not on the same level as the Chamber of Commerce or the National Rifle Association, but rather regards itself as the earthly manifestation of God's Kingdom, with the power to compel individual consciences. It is instructive, for example, to contrast the Bishops' civil, deferential tone on issues of economics or foreign policy[132] with much more authoritative Catholic pronouncements on the issue of abortion.[133] If economic issues do have important moral or spiritual components—and they clearly do—is not an organization like the Catholic Church incumbent to use its authority to achieve justice? Is not deference to the demands of secular public deliberation an abdication of religious responsibility?

The general point is that religion is usually based on some form of divine revelation, which may or may not occur in accordance with the secular requirements of democratic discourse or deliberation. For religious perspectives to accommodate such secular demands may risk diluting or subverting the essentially supernatural nature of religious insights.

Segers's use of Mario Cuomo and Jesse Jackson as exemplars of the positive ways in which religion and politics can interact illustrates this problem quite well. In adapting the presentation of their religious beliefs to their public roles as political leaders, Jackson and Cuomo have clearly met the qualifications for political civility, tolerance, and public accessibility. However, in so doing, the former governor of New York and one of the de facto leaders of contemporary African Americans may have purchased political respectability at the substantial price of having subverted their religious principles. Jesse Jackson appears to have discovered that a pro-choice position is perhaps a necessary credential for being a serious participant in the national Democratic Party, and has thus modified his initial reaction to *Roe v. Wade*. Similarly, Mario Cuomo's distinction between his private and public roles was certainly eloquent but did little to discourage the practice of abortion in New York during his three terms as governor. If indeed opposition to abortion is a position mandated by Cuomo's Catholicism, or Jackson's evangelical Protestantism, both leaders have seriously compromised their religious principles for the sake of active political participation.

Second, the various requirements suggested by Greenawalt, Perry, Cochran, and Tinder incur the risk of discrimination.[134] If attitudes of public accessibil-

ity, fallibilism, or pluralism are the price of admission to the public conversation, members of some religious traditions can pay much more easily than others. Religious citizens who, because of the content of their religious beliefs, regard the toleration of certain viewpoints as harmful or pernicious, or who regard modern science as a symptom of, rather than a solution to, problems associated with modernity, are by implication excluded from democratic deliberation. If we are to believe empirical researchers who monitor changes in religious attitudes and affiliations,[135] the growth of theologically conservative churches suggests that the religious values that deserve expression in the public sphere may apply to a shrinking percentage of the religious population.

For example, it is instructive to consider possible religious reactions to Dean Hamer and Peter Copeland's recent book, *The Science of Desire*.[136] Hamer and Copeland present evidence based on findings from biology and social science to suggest that a genetic basis for male homosexuality might exist. This finding, if accepted, might force devout citizens from a variety of religious traditions to accept the possibility that a benevolent and omnipotent God deliberately created homosexuals, and that homosexuality is a primarily ascriptive characteristic. That is, being gay may be quite similar to being black or female. The requirements of fallibilism and pluralism would seem to demand that religious citizens take such a possibility seriously, despite obvious implications for the authority of scriptural proscriptions on homosexuality. The attitude of pluralism would require that Hamer and Copeland receive a respectful hearing, while the stance of fallibilism would call for believers to leave open the possibility that scientific evidence might entail a reconsideration of the authority of the Bible. Moreover, because religious insights are contested in the United States, the requirement that counterarguments be cast in publicly accessible terms would mean that religiously based proscriptions on homosexuality be cast in scientific terms; this requirement appears to rule out appeals to divine or scriptural authority.

Of course, citizens with religious scruples against homosexuality are not defenseless in the face of scientific evidence. One is perfectly free to attempt to refute Hamer and Copeland's work, which is certainly not definitive from a scientific standpoint, on its own terms, by criticizing their methodology, inferences, or other procedures. However, if one's religious convictions involve epistemological, as well as ontological or ethical, commitments, such a strategy is precluded.[137] Particular religions can and do put forth their own theories of knowledge, based on some form of divine revelation. Some religiously based arguments are admissible; others are not. It may, for example, be possible to critique *The Science of Desire* on Thomistic, natural law grounds, since such insights are considered by the Catholic Church to be accessible to the unaided reason, but such a strategy would appear to put a Catholic, rationalist heuristic above an evangelical, scriptural argument.

From the standpoint of the requisites of pluralist democracy, then, some

religious perspectives are more equal than others. Adherents of religious traditions that are theologically orthodox and/or particularistic, are permitted to participate in the public dialogue, provided that the participant abandons the unique and defining characteristics of his or her religious commitment.

Thus, religiously motivated participation in politics carries certain risks for the practice of religion, as well as for democratic politics. The nature of the risk depends crucially on the circumstances under which religious political activity is contemplated. When a religious tradition is invoked from a position of apparent strength, as in the case of consensus or dualistic descriptions of American politics, the possibility exists that the transcendence of the divine will be compromised by close identification with the sinful and the fallible. To put the matter as simply as possible, religion may be corrupted by close identification with the secular world of politics. The authority of religious belief may come to legitimate practices and institutions that are, ultimately, all too human. Devout, politically mobilized citizens may render unto God what is in fact Caesar's. Conversely, when religion is invoked from a position of political weakness, religiously motivated citizens, concerned with achieving political influence, could come to accommodate their religious principles to the secular demands of politics. They may be rendering unto Caesar that which is God's.

Constitutional Implications

At this point, it is important to be clear on what I am not advocating in this essay. I am not suggesting that religious beliefs have no value, nor that we should ignore or suppress them as a source of political judgments. People receive their initial ideas from a variety of sources, and there is no reason to exclude religious values from the setting of personal political agendas. Nor am I suggesting that we suppress the expression of religious ideas. Even if religious minimalism did not allow for a good deal of latitude in the free exercise of religion, the free speech and press clauses of the First Amendment would certainly apply to religious expression. A communalist view of the free exercise clause requires that religious expression and practice not be singled out for government regulation.

My analysis does suggest that, as citizens, we should be extremely careful about accepting religious values as justifications for political judgments. Religion does not provide a set of publicly accessible warrants for political dialogue in contemporary politics, and religious values threaten to undermine a general consensus on the procedures and processes of American politics. This essay has not focused on issues of constitutional law, although the religion clauses of the First Amendment do set the context in which the political role of religion is debated. It would take too long to produce an analysis of the

"correct" meaning of the establishment or free exercise clauses. Nevertheless, the preceding sections do suggest an ethical or normative approach to the constitutional issues involved in church-state relations. This approach would focus primarily on the establishment clause, as do most separationist analyses.[138] Recall that an assumption underlying the accommodationist interpretation of the establishment clause is that religion serves as a source of common morality and social cohesion. Accommodationists tend to believe that religious beliefs and values are widely shared, and provide an ethical context within which politics can be conducted. The thrust of my arguments in the section on religion and public accessibility is that such an assumption is simply false. Once we get beyond proscriptions on murder or theft, which presumably can be justified rather easily on nonreligious grounds, the content of a moral or religious consensus becomes extremely elusive. Therefore, the social and political benefits of "benevolent neutrality" between religions are tenuous, and perhaps not worth the risk to democratic civility described in the section on religion as a source of political dysfunction.

Moreover, the lack of theological or ethical consensus in the United States makes the very notion of religious neutrality or nonpreferentialism problematic. If the argument in the section on public accessibility is in any way correct, it is difficult to see how any substantive policy can benefit religion in general, without providing disproportionate rewards to particular religions. To take a simple example, suppose an accommodationist view of tuition tax vouchers were to prevail, and such assistance to private education were not held to violate the establishment clause. Clearly, certain denominations with elaborate educational institutions, such as Catholicism, would receive the lion's share of such a windfall. If one assumes that Catholicism is just one manifestation of a generally shared Judeo-Christian culture, presumably such an outcome would not be a problem from an accommodationist standpoint. If the tenets of Catholicism are the object of religious or political controversy, however, such disproportionate aid to this particular denomination could well violate the accommodationist requirement of neutrality. Similarly, if these vouchers were shared among established Christian denominations, the result might be discrimination against adherents of non-Christian religions, especially if a high percentage of such adherents are recent immigrants with few opportunities to establish educational institutions of their own. In sum, the religious and moral diversity of American culture renders the formulation of genuinely religiously neutral public policies extremely difficult. Those who advocate benevolent neutrality assume an extremely stringent burden of proof to establish that apparently neutral policies are not in fact discriminatory.

This broad view of the establishment clause has implications for the free exercise clause as well. Religious minimalism entails the requirement that the free exercise clause be interpreted quite narrowly, and apply only to overt discrimination against religious belief or practice. If government generally

permits religiously motivated exceptions to otherwise valid laws, it violates even an accommodationist interpretation of the establishment clause, by favoring one religion over another.

Jesse Choper has provided an intriguing example of this last point.[139] During the most recent period of American history in which there existed a military draft, one could claim an exemption from military service for religious purposes, by convincing a local draft board that one's religious principles proscribed the taking of human life under any circumstances. Depending on the nature of one's faith, as a conscientious objector one could attain the status of a noncombatant in the military, or could substitute civilian duty for military service. For members of some denominations (e.g., Mennonites, Quakers), in many jurisdictions, such exemptions from combat duty were virtually automatic, while adherents of other traditions faced a much higher burden of proof. Choper argues that extending the right of religious free exercise to religiously based draft exemptions violated the establishment clause. If one assumes that exemption from involuntary military service has value—as it clearly does—government, by granting such exemptions, is favoring Mennonites or Quakers over adherents of other faiths. Again, even an accommodationist reading of the establishment clause suggests that government may not discriminate in favor of particular religions. Similarly, this analysis suggests that the Court in fact ruled correctly in *Employment Division v. Smith,* in which native Americans were denied a religious exception to a state law banning the use of hallucinogenic drugs. If one assumes that the use of peyote is desirable for religious or hedonistic purposes, to grant native Americans a religiously based exemption is to discriminate in favor of such religions, and against adherents of more commonly held traditions.[140]

Thus, the analysis I present in this essay suggests that the potential mischief that religion can cause in public life creates a presumption in favor of a broad reading of the establishment clause. Given the threats religious belief pose to democratic political discourse, we should regard with suspicion the use of religious justifications in the public sphere. Moreover, this analysis further suggests that, in cases in which the establishment and free exercise clauses appear to conflict, the establishment clause should be given priority. Religious free exercise should be protected only to the extent that such religious prerogatives do not run the risk of violating the establishment clause.

Conclusion

The roles of democratic citizen and religious believer both impose obligations on individuals. Despite the apparent clarity of Jesus' admonition to "render unto Caesar," the jurisdictions of God and Caesar overlap to a substantial degree. It might well occur that an individual believer would decide that the

demands of discipleship supersede those of citizenship, and that, as a matter of conscience, religious principles have priority over political ones. However, I hope to have shown that the active inclusion of religious values into political discourse carries some risk for democratic politics, and vice versa. Religion can, under certain circumstances, undermine the publicly accessible warrants on which political dialogue depends. It is unreasonable to require democratic government to collaborate in challenging and limiting its own legitimacy.

Notes

1. The precise wording of the First Amendment refers only to Congress, and, perhaps by extension, to the federal government. In the twentieth century, the Bill of Rights has been applied to the actions of state and local governments through the doctrine of "incorporation." See Leonard W. Levy, *The Establishment Clause* (New York: Macmillan, 1986) and Fred W. Friendly and Martha J. H. Elliot, *The Constitution: That Delicate Balance* (New York: Random House, 1984). For a general overview, see Ted G. Jelen and Clyde Wilcox, *Public Attitudes toward Church and State* (Armonk, N.Y.: M. E. Sharpe, 1995).

2. See Robert L. Cord, *Separation of Church and State: Historical Fact and Current Fiction* (New York: Lambeth Press, 1982); Gerard V. Bradley, *Church-State Relationships in America* (Westport, Conn.: Greenwood, 1987); and Russell Kirk, ed., *The Assault on Religion* (Lanham, Md.: University Press of America, 1986).

3. See Stephen V. Monsma, *Positive Neutrality: Letting Religious Freedom Ring* (Westport, Conn.: Praeger, 1993); and Kenneth D. Wald, *Religion and Politics in the United States,* 2d ed. (Washington, D.C.: CQ Press, 1992).

4. Peter Berger, *The Sacred Canopy: Elements of a Sociological Theory of Religion* (New York: Doubleday, 1967); A. James Reichley, *Religion in American Public Life* (Washington, D.C.: Brookings, 1985); and Richard John Neuhaus, *The Naked Public Square* (Grand Rapids, Mich.: Eerdmans, 1984).

5. Leo Pfeffer, *Church, State and Freedom* (Boston: Beacon Press, 1967); Levy, *The Establishment Clause.*

6. Cord, *Separation of Church and State,* 18 (emphasis added). In *Everson,* the Court upheld a measure authorizing reimbursement of transportation costs to parents whose children attended parochial schools.

7. See Jelen and Wilcox, *Public Attitudes toward Church and State.* For an account of Jefferson's thinking on church-state relations, see Garry Wills, *Under God* (New York: Simon and Schuster, 1990).

8. Jelen and Wilcox, *Public Attitudes toward Church and State;* Wald, *Religion and Politics in the United States.*

9. In recent years, the Court appears to have moved very cautiously in an accommodationist direction on establishment clause issues, without directly overturning the *Lemon* precedent. See Melvin I. Urofsky, "Church and State: The Religion Clauses," in *The Bill of Rights in Modern America,* ed. D. J. Bedenhamer and J. W. Ely (Bloomington: Indiana University Press, 1993), 57–71.

10. Richard A. Brisbin, "The Rehnquist Court and the Free Exercise of Religion" *Journal of Church and State* 34 (1992): 57–76.

11. Reichley, *Religion in American Public Life.*

12. I confine my attention here to the *religious* constitutional issues raised by this example. It may be that a general "no soliciting" policy would be unconstitutional under the free speech clause of the First Amendment. However, no particular religious issue is raised by the free expression question, and I thus ignore the free speech issue here.

13. Frank Way and Barbara Burt, "Religious Marginality and the Free Exercise Clause," *American Political Science Review* 77 (1983): 654–65.

14. Thomas Robbins, "The Intensification of Church-State Conflict in the United States," *Social Compass* 40 (1993): 505–27.

15. Leo Pfeffer, "The Current State of Law in the United States and the Separationist Agenda," *The Annals* 446 (December 1979): 1–9.

16. Wald, *Religion and Politics in the United States.*

17. Jelen and Wilcox, *Public Attitudes toward Church and State.*

18. David G. Savage, *Turning Right: The Making of the Rehnquist Supreme Court* (New York: John Wiley and Sons, 1993).

19. In 1993, Congress, responding to the Court's ruling in *Smith,* passed a measure termed the Religious Freedom Restoration Act, which would have restored the compelling state interest standard. This act was overturned in 1997 in the case of *City of Boerne v. Flores.*

20. Jelen and Wilcox, *Public Attitudes toward Church and State,* 27.

21. Jelen and Wilcox, *Public Attitudes toward Church and State,* 25.

22. For an elaboration of this typology, as well as an account of its empirical adequacy, see Jelen and Wilcox, *Public Attitudes toward Church and State.* Interestingly, we found that the most irreligious category in this typology are the free marketeers. Minimalists, rather than being irreligious or secular, tended to be doctrinally conservative Christians (Baptists being the largest category) who opposed religious involvement in politics for theological, rather than political, reasons.

23. For an overview, see Jelen and Wilcox, *Public Attitudes toward Church and State.*

24. See Wills, *Under God;* and Elizabeth Fleet, ed., "Madison's 'Detached Memoranda,' " *William and Mary Quarterly* 3 (1946): 535–62.

25. Leonard W. Levy, *Original Intent and the Framers' Constitution* (New York: Macmillan, 1988); and Levy, *The Establishment Clause.*

26. Leonard W. Levy, *The Establishment Clause;* see also James W. Wood, *The First Freedom: Religion and the Bill of Rights* (Waco, Tex.: J. M. Dawson Institute of Church-State Relations, Baylor University, 1990).

27. Barry Alan Shain, *The Myth of American Individualism: The Protestant Origins of American Political Thought* (Princeton, N.J.: Princeton University Press, 1994).

28. The historical record on this particular point is not as clear as might be supposed. It has been suggested that religious adherence in the early history of the United States, and in colonial times, was much lower than had previously been supposed. See Roger Finke and Rodney Stark, *The Churching of America, 1776–1990* (New Brunswick, N.J.: Rutgers University Press, 1992).

29. See William Martin, *With God on Our Side: The Rise of the Religious Right in America* (New York: Broadway Books, 1996).

30. Ralph Reed, *Politically Incorrect: The Emerging Faith Factor in American Politics* (Dallas: Word, 1994).

31. See especially Reichley, *Religion in American Public Life.*

32. Laura Grindstaff, "Abortion and the Popular Press: Mapping Media Discourse from *Roe* to *Webster*" in *Abortion Politics in the United States and Canada: Studies in Public Opinion,* ed. Ted G. Jelen and Marthe A. Chandler (Westport, Conn.: Praeger, 1994), 57–88.

33. Francis Fukuyama, *The End of History and the Last Man* (New York: Free Press, 1992).

34. James S. Fishkin, *Democracy and Deliberation: New Directions for Democratic Reform* (New Haven, Conn.: Yale University Press, 1991).

35. Aristophanes, "The Knights," in *Five Comedies* (New York: Fine Edition Press, 1948).

36. The literature on citizen competence in the United States is voluminous. For a superlative overview, see Herbert B. Asher, *Presidential Elections in American Politics: Candidates and Elections Since 1952,* 5th ed. (Pacific Grove, Calif.: Brooks-Cole, 1992).

37. Alexander Hamilton, James Madison, and John Jay, *The Federalist* (New York: Modern Library, 1937).

38. See Fishkin, *Democracy and Deliberation.*

39. See Peter Bachrach, *The Theory of Democratic Elitism: A Critique* (Boston: Little, Brown, 1967), and Carole Pateman, *Participation and Democratic Theory* (London: Cambridge University Press, 1970).

40. John Stuart Mill, *Considerations on Representative Government* (London: Oxford University Press, 1975).

41. John Stuart Mill, "De Tocqueville on Democracy in America," in *Collected Works of John Stuart Mill* (21 volumes) ed. J. M. Robinson (Toronto: University of Toronto Press, 1977).

42. Pateman, *Participation and Democratic Theory.*

43. See Ted G. Jelen, *Human Knowledge and Democratic Theory: An Analysis of Participatory Democracy* (Ph.D. dissertation, Ohio State University, 1979).

44. Sidney Verba, Kay Lehman Scholzman, and Henry E. Brady, *Voice and Equality: Civic Voluntarism in American Politics* (Cambridge, Mass.: Harvard University Press, 1995).

45. Of course, some may regard the hypothesis that political participation leads to intellectual and moral improvement as quite controversial. Such an assumption may contradict a central tenet of Judaism and Christianity; namely, that humanity is *essentially* corrupt, due to the Fall in the Garden of Eden, and that authentic human improvement in the face of our fallen nature is futile without some sort of divine agency. See especially Glenn Tinder, *The Political Meaning of Christianity* (Baton Rouge: Louisiana State University Press, 1989).

46. Ronald Thiemann, *Religion in Public Life: A Dilemma for Democracy* (Washington, D.C.: Georgetown University Press, 1996).

47. Stephen Toulmin, *The Uses of Argument* (London: Cambridge University Press, 1974).

48. John Stuart Mill, *On Liberty* (London: Oxford University Press, 1975).

49. Richard W. Sterling and William C. Scott, trans., *Plato: The Republic* (New York: W. W. Norton, 1985).

50. Kent Greenawalt, *Religious Convictions and Political Choice* (New York: Oxford University Press, 1988); Greenawalt, "Grounds for Political Judgment: The Status of Personal Experience and the Autonomy and Generality of Principles of Restraint," *San Diego Law Review* 30 (1993): 674–75; Michael J. Perry, *Love and Power: The Role of Religion and Morality in American Politics* (New York: Oxford University Press, 1991); and Robert Audi, "Separation of Church and State and the Obligations of Citizenship," *Philosophy and Public Affairs* 18 (1989), 258–96.

51. Perry, *Love and Power,* 106.

52. Hamilton, et al., *The Federalist,* 6.

53. Greenawalt, "Grounds for Political Judgment."

54. Robert Booth Fowler, *Unconventional Partners: Religion and Liberal Culture in the United States* (Grand Rapids, Mich.: Eerdmans, 1989); Peter Berger, *The Sacred Canopy;* and Barry Alan Shain, *The Myth of American Individualism.*

55. Alexis de Tocqueville, *Democracy in America,* 2 vols., ed. Phillips Bradley (New York: Vintage Books, 1945), 314–15.

56. Jerry Falwell, "An Agenda for the 1980s," in *Piety and Politics: Evangelicals and Fundamentalists Confront the Modern World,* ed. Richard J. Neuhaus and Michael Cromartie (Washington, D.C.: Ethics and Public Policy Center, 1987), 113.

57. Clyde Wilcox, *God's Warriors: The Christian Right in the Twentieth Century* (Baltimore: Johns Hopkins University Press, 1992); Clyde Wilcox, Ted G. Jelen, and Sharon Linzey, "Reluctant Warriors: Premillennialism and Politics in the Moral Majority," *Journal for the Scientific Study of Religion* 30 (1991), 245–58.

58. Reichley, *Religion in American Public Life,* 52.

59. See Max Weber, *The Protestant Ethic and the Spirit of Capitalism,* trans. Talcott Parsons (London: G. Allen and Unwin, 1930).

60. Neuhaus, *The Naked Public Square.*

61. Wilcox, *God's Warriors.*

62. Reed, *Politically Incorrect,* 13–14.

63. Ted G. Jelen, "Religion and Public Opinion in the 1990s: An Empirical Overview," in *Understanding Public Opinion,* ed. Barbara Norrander and Clyde Wilcox (Washington, D.C.: CQ Press, 1996), 55–68.

64. Clyde Wilcox, Mark J. Rozell, and Roland Gunn, "Religious Coalitions in the Christian Right: The Decline of Religious Particularism," *Social Science Quarterly* 77 (1996): 543–58; and John C. Green, "Pat Robertson and the Latest Crusade: Religious Resources and the 1988 Presidential Campaign," *Social Science Quarterly* 74 (1995): 157–68.

65. Rodney Stark and Charles Y. Glock, *American Piety: The Nature of Religious Commitment* (Berkeley: University of California Press, 1968).

66. Green, "Pat Robertson and the Latest Crusade"; Jelen, *The Political Mobilization of Religious Beliefs* (Westport, Conn.: Praeger, 1991).

67. Greenawalt, *Religious Convictions and Political Choice,* 219.

68. Mark J. Rozell and Clyde Wilcox, *Second Coming: The New Christian Right in Virginia Politics* (Baltimore: Johns Hopkins University Press, 1996); Wilcox, Rozell, and Gunn, "Religious Coalitions in the Christian Right."

69. Finke and Stark, *The Churching of America.*

70. Wald, *Religion and Politics in the United States;* R. Stephen Warner, "Work in Progress toward a New Paradigm for the Sociological Study of Religion in the United States," *American Journal of Sociology* 94 (1992): 1044–93.

71. For an overview, see Warner, "Work in Progress."

72. Ted G. Jelen, *The Political World of the Clergy* (Westport, Conn.: Praeger, 1993).

73. See Reichley, *Religion in American Public Life.*

74. See Wald, *Religion and Politics in the United States.*

75. Reichley, *Religion in American Public Life;* Wills, *Under God.*

76. Moreover, this argument does not take into account the increasing religious diversity that exists in the United States as the result of immigration. A growing percentage of U.S. residents and citizens are adherents of Buddhism, Confucianism, Islam, Hinduism, or other religions from outside the Judeo-Christian tradition. To the extent that religious diversity inhibits social and political cohesion, such qualitative increases in diversity would exacerbate this tendency.

77. Ted G. Jelen, "Helpmeets and Weaker Vessels: Gender Role Stereotypes and Attitudes toward Female Ordination," *Social Science Quarterly* 70 (1989): 575–85; Clyde Wilcox and Ted G. Jelen, "The Effects of Employment and Religion on Women's Feminist Attitudes," *International Journal for the Psychology of Religion* 1 (1991): 161–71.

78. Clyde Wilcox, "Feminism and Anti-Feminism among Evangelical Women," *Western Political Quarterly* 42 (1989): 147–60; Clyde Wilcox and Elizabeth Adell Cook, "Evangelical Women and Feminism: Some Additional Evidence," *Women and Politics* 9 (1989): 27–49.

79. Richard N. Ostling, "What Does God Really Think about Sex?" *Time* (June 24, 1991): 48–50.

80. Elizabeth Adell Cook, Ted G. Jelen, and Clyde Wilcox, *Between Two Absolutes: Public Opinion and the Politics of Abortion* (Boulder, Colo.: Westview, 1992).

81. Stephen Hart, *What Does the Lord Require? How American Christians Think about Economic Justice* (New Brunswick, N.J.: Rutgers University Press, 1992); Laurence R. Iannaconne, "Heirs to the Protestant Ethic? The Economics of American Fundamentalism," in *Fundamentalisms and the State,* ed. Martin R. Marty and R. Scott Appleby (Chicago: University of Chicago Press, 1993), 342–66.

82. Joseph B. Tamney, Ronald Burton, and Stephen D. Johnson, "Fundamentalism and Economic Restructuring," in *Religion and Political Behavior in the United States,* ed. Ted G. Jelen (New York: Praeger, 1989), 67–82.

83. Mike Dorning, "Episcopal Heresy Trial Tests Gay Clergy Issue," *Chicago Tribune* (February 28, 1996): 1:4.

84. David W. Dunlap, "Reform Rabbis Vote to Back Gay Marriage," *New York Times* (March 28, 1996). According to the same article, this move was opposed by several prominent Orthodox Jewish leaders.

85. James R. Bowers, *Pro-Choice and Anti-Abortion: Constitutional Theory and Public Policy* (Westport, Conn.: Praeger, 1994); Herbert J. Gans, *Middle American Individualism* (New York: Free Press, 1988).

86. See especially Louis Hartz, *The Liberal Tradition in America* (New York: Harcourt, Brace and World, 1955).

87. I leave to others two interesting questions raised by this analysis. First, it is not clear to what extent the lack of a moral consensus in the United States is a recent phenomenon. According to accounts in the popular culture, a prevailing moral consensus was shattered by the events and social trends of the 1960s. However, the recent work of Roger Finke and Rodney Stark suggests that, for many periods of American history (most notably the colonial period), religious observance was quite low. Therefore, the possibility exists that the apparent consensus of earlier historical periods may well have been illusory and might have resulted from the marginalization of many citizens, including large numbers of "the unchurched." See Roger Finke and Rodney Stark, *The Churching of America, 1776–1990*. Second, some observers have suggested that American individualism has religious, specifically, Christian, roots. If so, it may be that American religion has undermined its own authority. See Fowler, *Unconventional Partners;* and Jelen, *The Political World of the Clergy.*

88. Richard Rorty, "Religion as Conversation-Stopper," *Common Knowledge* 3 (1994): 1–6.

89. For an elaboration of this distinction, see David C. Leege, "Religion and Politics in Theoretical Perspective," in *Rediscovering the Religious Factor in American Politics,* ed. David C. Leege and Lyman A. Kellstedt (Armonk, N.Y.: M. E. Sharpe, 1993), 3–25.

90. Perry, *Love and Power.*

91. Greenawalt, *Religious Convictions and Political Choice.*

92. Greenawalt, *Religious Convictions and Political Choice,* 113.

93. John Rawls, *Political Liberalism* (New York: Columbia University Press, 1993), 227.

94. This is not to suggest that constitutional principles or procedures are unassailable, or not subject to criticism. It is to say that the Constitution itself provides means for constitutional changes, and that opponents of the Electoral College, or of any other constitutional requirement, must undergo the amendment process if the Electoral College seems unwise or unfair. For someone to refuse to accept the legitimacy of an Electoral College winner without such a constitutional amendment is to undermine the basis of the American regime.

95. Of course, certain religiously motivated individuals have engaged in such acts as violence against abortion clinics and providers. This sort of activity certainly suggests an impatience with the procedural aspects of American democracy. However, the case against a public role for religion is not based on such unusual violent activity. The perpetrators of such acts are not typical of religious citizens generally, nor is the resort to violence unique to religious activists in the United States. See Dallas Blanchard, *The Anti-Abortion Movement and the Rise of the Religious Right: From Polite to Firey Protest* (New York: Twayne, 1994); Dallas Blanchard and Terry J. Prewitt, *Religious Violence and Abortion: The Gideon Project* (Gainesville: University Press of Florida, 1993); and Carol J. C. Maxwell, "Introduction: Beyond Polemics and toward Healing," in *Perspectives on the Politics of Abortion,* ed. Ted. G. Jelen (Westport, Conn.: Praeger, 1995), 1–20.

96. See especially Lee C. Bollinger, *The Tolerant Society* (New York: Oxford University Press, 1986).

97. L. Kent Sezer, "The Constitutional Underpinnings of the Abortion Debate," in

Perspectives on the Politics of Abortion, ed. Ted G. Jelen (Westport, Conn.: Praeger, 1995), 131–76; L. Kent Sezer and Ted G. Jelen, "Pornography, Feminism, and the First Amendment," paper presented at the annual meeting of the Northeastern Political Science Association, Philadelphia, Penn., 1985.

98. John L. Sullivan, James Pierson, and George E. Marcus, *Political Tolerance and American Democracy* (Chicago: University of Chicago Press, 1982); Samuel Stouffer, *Communism, Conformity, and Civil Liberties* (Gloucester, Mass.: Peter Smith, 1955); Clyde Wilcox and Ted G. Jelen, "Evangelicals and Political Tolerance," *American Politics Quarterly* 18 (1990): 25–46; Ted G. Jelen and Clyde Wilcox, "Denominational Preference and the Dimensions of Political Tolerance," *Sociological Analysis* 51 (1990): 69–80; Herbert McClosky and Alida Brill, *Dimensions of Tolerance: What Americans Believe about Civil Liberties* (New York: Russell Sage, 1983); and John C. Green, James L. Guth, Lyman A. Kellstedt, and Corwin E. Smidt, "Uncivil Challenges: Support for Civil Liberties among Religious Activists," *Journal of Political Science* 22 (1994): 25–49.

99. For an excellent overview of this issue, see Tinder, *The Political Meaning of Christianity.*

100. Green, et al., "Uncivil Challenges," 44 (emphasis added).

101. "Bishop Threatens Excommunication," *Chicago Tribune* (March 28, 1996): 1:10.

102. Clyde Wilcox, *Onward, Christian Soldiers? The Religious Right in American Politics* (Boulder, Colo.: Westview, 1996).

103. The Full Faith and Credit Clause also States that ". . . the Congress may by general laws prescribe the Manner in which such Acts, Records, and Proceedings shall be proved, and the Effect thereof." This aspect of the Full Faith and Credit provision would seem to grant Congress jurisdiction over the *administration* of interstate cooperation, but not over the *content* of such regulations. For a contrary view, see Ken I. Kersch, "Full Faith and Credit for Same-Sex Marriages," *Political Science Quarterly* 112 (1997): 117–36.

104. See especially Sezer, "The Constitutional Underpinnings of the Abortion Debate."

105. See Jose Casanova, *Public Religions in the Modern World* (Chicago: University of Chicago Press, 1994).

106. Ronald Inglehart, *Culture Shift in Advanced Industrial Society* (Princeton, N.J.: Princeton University Press, 1990).

107. This problem bears some resemblance to Robert Bellah's account of "civil religion." However, such a discussion is beyond the scope of the present inquiry and may not be directly relevant. Christianson and Wimberly have suggested that civil religious beliefs are not strongly related to other religious variables and can exist in the absence of other, more conventional, variants of religion. See Robert Bellah, "Civil Religion in America," in *Religion in America,* ed. W. McLoughlin and Robert Bellah (Boston: Houghton-Mifflin, 1968), 3–23; and J. A. Christenson and R. C. Wimberly, "Who Is Civil Religious?" *Sociological Analysis* 39 (1979): 77–83.

108. See Leege, "Religion and Politics in Theoretical Perspective."

109. Jerry Falwell, *Listen, America!* (Garden City, N.Y.: Doubleday, 1980), 24.

110. See especially Wills, *Under God.*

111. See Blanchard and Prewitt, *Religious Violence and Abortion.*

112. James Davison Hunter, *Culture Wars: The Struggle to Define America* (New York: Basic Books, 1991).

113. See also Ted G. Jelen, "Religion and the American Political Culture: Alternative Models of Citizenship and Discipleship," *Sociology of Religion* 56 (1995): 271–84.

114. In case the point is missed, Hunter has published a subsequent book with a similar theme, with a more prosaic title. See James Davison Hunter, *Before the Shooting Begins* (New York: Free Press, 1994).

115. It is perhaps worth noting that the tendency to disparage the motives and competence of one's opponents is fully reciprocal and well represented on the side of the Progressives as well. An extensive literature attempts to "explain" religious orthodoxy or religiously based political activism by positing psychological or sociological deficiencies on the part of such believers and activists. For overviews and critiques of this literature, see Kenneth D. Wald, Dennis E. Owen, and Samuel S. Hill, "Habits of the Mind: The Problem of Authority in the New Christian Right," in *Religion and Political Behavior in the United States,* ed. Ted G. Jelen (New York: Praeger, 1989), 93–108; Wilcox, *God's Warriors;* and Wilcox, Linzey, and Jelen, "Reluctant Warriors."

116. Arthur Bentley, *The Process of Government* (Chicago: University of Chicago Press, 1980); Robert A. Dahl, *Who Governs? Democracy and Power in an American City* (New Haven, Conn.: Yale University Press, 1961); and David Truman, *The Governmental Process* (New York: Knopf, 1971).

117. See Reed, *Politically Incorrect.*

118. Greenawalt, *Religious Convictions and Political Choice.*

119. Perry, *Love and Power.*

120. Clarke Cochran, *Religion in Private and Public Life* (New York: Routledge, 1990).

121. Robert Bellah et al., *Habits of the Heart: Individualism and Commitment in American Life* (Berkeley: University of California Press, 1985).

122. Blanchard and Prewitt, *Abortion and Religious Violence.*

123. Cochran, *Religion in Private and Public Life,* 168.

124. See also Ted G. Jelen, "Religion and Democratic Citizenship: A Review Essay," *Polity* 23 (1991): 471–81.

125. Tinder, *The Political Meaning of Christianity.*

126. Hamilton, et al. *The Federalist,* 337.

127. Grindstaff, "Abortion and the Popular Press."

128. Clyde Wilcox, Ted G. Jelen, and Sharon Linzey, "Rethinking the Reasonableness of the Religious Right," *Review of Religious Research* 36 (1995): 263–76.

129. Allen Hertzke, *Echoes of Discontent: Jesse Jackson, Pat Robertson, and the Resurgence of Populism* (Washington, D.C.: CQ Press, 1993).

130. Verba, Scholzman, and Brady, *Voice and Equality.*

131. National Conference of Catholic Bishops, *Economic Justice for All* (Washington, D.C.: United States Catholic Conference, 1986), 11. For a thorough analysis of the issues raised by this pastoral letter, see Jeremy Waldron, "Religious Contributions in Public Deliberation," *San Diego Law Review* 30 (1993): 817–48.

132. National Conference of Catholic Bishops, *The Challenge of Peace: God's Promise and Our Response* (Washington, D.C.: United States Catholic Conference, 1983).

133. See especially Mary C. Segers, "The Catholic Church as a Political Actor," in *Perspectives on the Politics of Abortion,* ed. Ted G. Jelen (Westport, Conn.: Praeger, 1995), 87–130; and Patricia Fauser et al. "Conclusion: Perspectives on the Politics of Abortion," in *Perspectives on the Politics of Abortion,* 177–99.

134. David M. Smolin, "Regulating Religious and Cultural Conflict in a Postmodern America: A Response to Professor Perry," *Iowa Law Review* 76 (1992): 1067–104; and Sanford Levinson, "Religious Language and the Public Square," *Harvard Law Review* 105 (1992): 2061–79.

135. See Laurence Iannaccone, "Why Strict Churches Are Strong," *American Journal of Sociology* (1994): 1180–1211; Roger Finke and Rodney Stark, *The Churching of America;* and Wade Clark Roof and William McKinney, *American Mainline Religion* (New Brunswick, N.J.: Rutgers University Press, 1987).

136. Dean Hamer and Peter Copeland, *The Science of Desire: The Search for the Gay Gene and the Biology of Behavior* (New York: Simon and Schuster, 1994).

137. For example, in Genesis 3:5, the serpent convinces Eve to eat from the Tree of Knowledge of Good and Evil by telling her that "ye shall be as Gods." I have frequently had occasion to reflect on this passage when considering the accomplishments of modern science, particularly in the field of genetics. An argument could be made that the serpent's persuasive speech is a prophecy, which is on the verge of being fulfilled. Science might thus be viewed, from certain religious standpoints, as the result of a strong, prideful temptation on the part of humanity.

138. See Ted G. Jelen and Clyde Wilcox, *Public Attitudes toward Church and State.*

139. Jesse Choper, *Securing Religious Liberty* (Chicago: University of Chicago Press, 1995).

140. Readers who are of the "baby boom" generation, which came to maturity during the 1960s and 1970s, might find this an interesting discussion topic.

2

In Defense of Religious Freedom

Mary C. Segers

The United States of America is "a nation with the soul of a church."

G. K. Chesterton, *What Is America?*

"Religion is the first of their political institutions."

Alexis de Tocqueville, *Democracy in America*

The most fundamental beliefs a person holds are his or her religious beliefs. For many people, religion is the root of civilization and culture. It is a spiritual anchor in life; it provides an explanation and a justification for death. Religion often speaks to our need to find meaning in life and to the deepest human aspirations for peace, harmony, community, and spiritual sustenance. At the same time, religion supplies moral vision and undergirds ethical values such as goodness, justice, fairness, and equality. Given these profound aspects of religiosity, how can religion be divorced from politics? Is it possible or even desirable to segregate religious beliefs and aspirations from our political discourse?

While religion has brought comfort and security to many people, it has brought pain, suffering, and death to others—to Arabs and Jews in the Middle East; to Catholics and Protestants in Northern Ireland; to Hindus and Muslims in India; and to Serbs, Croats, and Bosnians in the Balkans. Religion can be divisive and can contribute to sectarian strife and civil war. Religion can be dangerous precisely because it gives priority to spiritual aspirations over worldly concerns, encouraging us to prefer God to Caesar. Political scientists and those who are concerned with the welfare of society worry about this potential of religion to trump politics. Thus, some argue that religion does not belong in politics and should be privatized whenever possible.[1]

I have presented here two conflicting views of the relation between religion and politics, one positive and the other negative. For much of U.S. history,

53

American thinkers and political leaders have wondered whether religion could support the American experiment in democracy and have worried about the divisive potential of religious belief. They attempted to control and manage the relationship between religion and politics by enshrining in the U.S. Constitution the religion clauses of the First Amendment: "Congress shall make no law respecting an establishment of religion, or prohibiting the free exercise thereof." But the Constitution does not say what a religion is, nor does it define controversial terms such as "free exercise" or "establishment of religion."

Our constitutional attempt to manage the relationship between the secular and the sacred raises as many questions as it answers. We must turn to history in order to understand the meaning of these religion clauses. When we do that, we discover some interesting facts about America's past and present.

We Americans are a curious people. We have one of the highest rates of religious affiliation and church attendance in the world, yet our constitution emphasizes a strict separation of church and state and forbids the use of religion as a litmus test for public office. Some observers think these two facts about America are related—that we can be free to worship according to conscience *because* government steers clear of organized religion.

At the same time, we must remember that church-state relations are not the same as the complex linkage between religion and politics that has shaped American history. Religious communities have influenced politics and public policy in the past and in the present. We need to explore this relationship between religion and politics in America in order to understand the origin of our commitment to tolerance and religious freedom.

My approach in this essay is to stress the historical and political role religion has played in American society and culture, not to provide one more constitutional analysis of Supreme Court religion cases. After all, the phrase "wall of separation" is not a constitutional law phrase (it appears nowhere in the U.S. Constitution) but a historical metaphor traceable to Thomas Jefferson, third president of the United States, and to Roger Williams, founder of the colony of Rhode Island. I will argue for a very permeable wall of separation between religion and politics. I support a moderate accommodationist view of religion in American public life—with due respect for a fundamental commitment to liberal, democratic values.

My coauthor, Ted G. Jelen, makes a striking claim in his essay. He argues that religion is a source of political dysfunction in a liberal democracy. He explains this dysfunction in two ways. First, religion threatens to undermine the process of public deliberation because of the tendency of religious activists to be uncivil, intolerant, and disrespectful of nonbelievers' First Amendment rights to freedom of speech, press, expression, and assembly. Second, because of its appeal to divine authority, religion undermines or subverts the substantive prerogatives of democratic citizenship—namely, the autonomy and self-determination necessary for democratic self-governance. These are serious

arguments that suggest that religion and democracy are fundamentally incompatible.

Needless to say, I strongly disagree with these views. Contrary to what Jelen maintains, I argue that religion promotes and enhances democracy in the United States. Churches and temples are often the primary or sole voluntary organization to which some people belong. To the extent that such religious institutions contribute to public debate and participate in the democratic process and to the extent that they articulate the views of church members, they facilitate the political representation of otherwise alienated individuals. A recent example of this in American politics is the fact that the Religious Right as a political movement has given hitherto unrepresented citizens a voice in the political process. And for years, Christian socialists and other members of the religious left have articulated the interests of the poor, the unorganized, and the marginalized.

While religion can be inimical to democracy, as Jelen shows, religious values can also enhance and support liberal democratic institutions and ideas such as human rights, equality, political community, tolerance, and respect for the law. Moreover, many political thinkers, among them Machiavelli and Rousseau, have argued that religion can be useful in educating a virtuous citizenry, a body politic of civic-minded persons that is the basic prerequisite of a democratic republic. Religious values can be the source of public morality; indeed, we need to carefully examine the relationship between religion, morality, and public policy in a pluralistic society. In the history of the United States, religious traditions have often been fertile sources of constructive political action. The antislavery, temperance, women's suffrage, civil rights, and 1960s antiwar movements were all at least partly inspired and motivated by religious values and religious commitment. Thus, before we confine religion to the arena of private life, we need to examine the many ways in which, historically, religion has contributed to American public life.

In order to discuss what role religion should play in public life in the United States, I raise the following questions (which are topical subdivisions of this essay):

1. What role has religion played historically in American public life?
2. What role did the Founders think religion should play in public life?
3. What role does religion play in contemporary American society and culture?
4. What is the proper role of religious convictions in American public life?

Before addressing these questions, however, I want to comment on Jelen's "religious minimalist" position and the schema he develops for analyzing constitutional perspectives on church-state relations in the United States.

A Framework for Analyzing Religion and Politics

As mentioned earlier, Jelen suggests that religion and democracy are essentially incompatible in fundamental ways. Moreover, he argues that if religion poses real dangers to the political process, politics itself threatens to undermine religion. By conflating religion with established culture, the political involvement of churches poses the danger of idolatry or the legitimation of contemporary political structures in religious terms. Furthermore, empirical evidence suggests a loss of civility among believers who are politically active. In culture wars over social values and public policies, such religious activists tend to demonize political adversaries and fail to show the elemental respect that suggests that they take their opponents' views seriously. Given these dangers and the risks posed by the intermingling of religion and politics in the United States, churches and governing agencies arc wise to avoid unnecessary entanglement. Governments should neither endorse nor promote the expression of religious values in politics and public policy. For their part, churches should refrain from becoming heavily invested in political advocacy lest they lose sight of their authentic spiritual mission.

Jelen thus concludes that although religious activists may express religious ideas in public deliberation, the general citizenry should be extremely wary about accepting religious values as justifications for political judgments. In general, religion is a dangerous thing in a democracy, and, in particular, religious values threaten to undermine a general consensus on the procedures and processes of American politics. Thus, Jelen defends "religious minimalism"—that is, he wants to minimize the public role of religion and to grant few religious exemptions to our civic duty to obey otherwise valid laws.

This means that he wants to protect government from the encroachment of churches and to guard against the use of religion to justify disobeying existing laws. In any conflict between religion and politics or church and state, government prevails. At bottom, Jelen seems to mistrust religion and to view it as a potentially negative, divisive force in society. I have a more positive view of religion and think there can be greater cooperation between religious and political institutions.

Given the framework of this book as a clash of opposing viewpoints, it might be supposed that I support religious maximalism in opposition to Ted Jelen's espousal of religious minimalism. I do not think I want to defend religious maximalism, whatever that might mean. But I do want to criticize religious minimalism as being unfair to believers. According to Jelen's analysis, religious minimalists interpret the establishment clause quite broadly to prohibit almost all governmental endorsement of, or aid to, religion. They also want to limit sharply the scope of the free exercise clause. But why would a good liberal such as my colleague Ted Jelen want to limit the free exercise rights of religious minorities such as Mormons, Muslims, Christian Scientists,

Jehovah's Witnesses, and members of the Native American Church? I am puzzled why a committed liberal democrat would want to constrain the religious freedom of individual Americans and minority churches, because I understand liberal democracy to be a philosophy and a form of government that strongly emphasizes individual rights and the values of freedom, respect, and tolerance.

My view of the religion clause of the First Amendment—"Congress shall make no law respecting an establishment of religion, or prohibiting the free exercise thereof"—is that there is one clause with two provisions: nonestablishment and free exercise. I argue that the institutional church-state separation mandated by the nonestablishment provision is a means of protecting the free exercise of religion by American citizens. Nonestablishment is a means to, and a guarantor of, religious freedom and freedom of conscience.

Of course, no liberty is absolute in American political and constitutional thought. There are always outer limits to our liberties, and we can understand if churches that practice snake-handling, for example, as part of their worship services are regulated by state and local governments in the interests of public safety. Yet it seems that a strong emphasis on religious liberty characterizes American history, politics, and culture. Thus, I adopt a historical perspective rather than a constitutional analysis in the first part of this essay. We cannot interpret the Constitution apart from our knowledge of its historical context and the American political culture. An analysis of America's religious history shows a high priority given to freedom of religion and freedom of conscience.

It is tempting to try to locate my position in Jelen's matrix or analytical framework. However, I may not be able to fit my views into any of the four categories—Christian preferentialist, religious minimalist, religious nonpreferentialist, or religious free marketeer. For one thing, the interdependence and interpenetration of religion and politics is too complex to admit of such simple categorization. Furthermore, I agree with separationists on some points and with accommodationists on others. For example, I do not subscribe to the

FIGURE 1
A Typology of Church-State Positions

Establishment Clause

	Accommodationist	Separationist
Communalist	Christian preferentialist	religious minimalist
Libertarian	religious nonpreferentialist	religious free marketeer

Free Exercise

strict, absolute separation of church and state—the notion that government may not offer assistance to religion in any form. American history and experience indicate that, as a society, we reject this idea. There are many ways in which government acknowledges and aids religion in contemporary society. Nor do I think that religion has no public role to play in society and should be confined to private life.

On the other hand, I do share the separationist concern regarding religion's potential to be a sectarian, divisive force. Again, the lessons of history are telling, whether they are lessons from the French religious wars of the sixteenth century, from our colonial history in Massachusetts and Virginia, or from Northern Ireland today. We must also recognize that religious citizens may be tempted to forgo the essentials of democratic civility and act on their own belief in certitude or in a higher divine law—act, that is, to impose their religious values upon dissenters and nonbelievers through coercive policies. (In the latter portion of this essay, I address this question of civility, tolerance, and respect in a democratic society.) At the same time, we must recognize that the intolerant, uncivil behavior of some religious believers is no reason to exclude all religious people from public deliberation—just as we did not, in the past, exclude all anticommunist citizens because some of them ran roughshod over the civil liberties of others.

I agree with James Madison that authentic religion does not *require* governmental assistance.[2] On the other hand, government may aid religions in a nonpreferential manner. In fact, as Stephen Monsma shows, government in the United States aids religion all the time and in many different ways.[3] Government may offer general assistance to religion in a spirit of what has been termed "benevolent neutrality." From an accommodationist perspective, there is no constitutional violation if government aids all religion impartially. Such nondiscriminatory aid embodies principles of strict neutrality and does not constitute governmental "endorsement" of religion. Indeed, it is beyond the competence and authority of government to endorse religion.

Taking the four categories of Jelen's church-state framework, I would not fit into the category of "Christian preferentialists," those who seek to maximize the role of religion in public life. For example, the approach of those who argue that "the United States is a Christian nation" connotes a kind of arrogant triumphalism and religious imperialism because of their willingness to use political power to impose their religious values on others. The category of "religious minimalist" is also an inappropriate description of my views. The desire of minimalists to reduce the public role of religion seems misguided, and they fail to give serious weight to certain believers' need to be exempted from the duty to obey otherwise valid laws. "Religious free marketeers" is a third category that seems inappropriate for me; while these people are quite solicitous of the prerogatives of religious minorities, they seek to reduce the role of government, a goal that seems fantastic and unrealistic in

contemporary American society. There is an enormous degree of interdependence between government and churches already, a situation that is unlikely to be reversed. For example, the government imposes fire and safety regulations on churches. Churches help society and the government carry out necessary tasks, including schooling, care of the sick and elderly, child care, and assistance to the poor and homeless. We need to recognize existing institutional cooperation between religion and government in addressing social problems. The fourth category of "religious nonpreferentialists" does this because they favor strict impartiality in government assistance to all groups in society (including religious and nonprofit groups). Religious nonpreferentialists do not necessarily seek to maximize the role of religion in the public sphere; they are simply interested in fairness and impartiality among all groups. They also seek to defend the right of religious believers to contribute their moral insights to the democratic process.

Thus, if I had to identify myself using Jelen's categories, I conceivably could be described as a religious nonpreferentialist. Such a view is accommodationist and libertarian, in the sense that it seeks to protect the free exercise rights of religious minorities such as members of the Native American Church, Santeria believers, Mormons, and Christian Scientists. However, I would dispute Jelen's characterization of these religious nonpreferentialists as believers who "seek to maximize the role of religion in the public sphere." Such religion-sympathizers may be concerned less with maximizing the role of religion and more with protecting the right of religious believers to contribute their moral and political insights to the democratic process.

What Role Has Religion Historically Played in American Public Life?

It is important that we understand the historical role of religion in American politics and culture. I suggest three reasons why this perspective is so essential: First, it is important that we understand this because it is part of our collective identity. Just as an individual derives continuity and identity from his childhood and formative years, so, too, our nation has been shaped by its history and culture. And if we examine U.S. history, we see how formative religion has been in the American experience. Second, I will discuss events and trends in American culture that suggest how deeply intertwined religion and politics are. I assume that knowledge of our history should convince us how difficult it would be to segregate religion from American public life. Third, we will not really understand contemporary American politics and the activities of groups such as the Christian Coalition, Operation Rescue, the Moral Majority, Sojourners, the National Right to Life Committee, or the

American Civil Liberties Union unless we are aware of America's religious history.

If we turn now to the question of what role religion has played historically in American public life, we find that the United States is among the most religious countries on earth and, at the same time, among the most secular. The vast majority of Americans claim to be believers. Church attendance is astonishingly high, especially when this country is compared with other advanced industrial societies. Religion in America today is thriving, activist, and diverse.

This description of the religious character of contemporary American society is a fairly accurate description of American history as well. As Stephen Carter notes, deep religiosity has always been a facet of the American character, and its importance has grown consistently throughout the nation's history.[4]

That Americans are a religious people was evident at the time of the first European settlements. Many colonists such as the Pilgrims and the Puritans came to this country in search of religious freedom—that is, freedom to practice their beliefs without being persecuted by the government. Needless to say, such freedom did not necessarily mean a willingness to tolerate other religious traditions. As William Lee Miller has written, "Those [Puritan] forefathers came to institute religious liberty, at most, *for themselves* and were in their turn intolerant of others."[5] Yet the unintended consequence of their theological commitments was to advance the cause of religious liberty. As Miller states, "the English and colonial Puritans, for all their zealous narrowness and for all their participation in intolerant episodes, still promulgated principles that sometimes led by implication beyond their own behavior: Every man his own priest; justification by faith; the Bible as the sole authority; the gathered, congregational, nonhierarchical, internally democratic church."[6] These religious ideas had unintended social and political results, setting in motion currents of religious and political liberty, equality, justice, and democratic organization.

In order to understand the close relationship between religion and politics in American history, we review here some examples of this intimate connection. These include (1) the Puritan legacy; (2) nineteenth- and twentieth-century social protest movements; (3) the peculiar mix of religion and politics made possible by the expanded role of the federal government in health and welfare in the twentieth century; and (4) the deep historical and cultural roots of contemporary Protestant evangelicals and fundamentalists.

The Puritan Legacy

Historically, Americans owe a great deal to the Puritans of Massachusetts, whose powerful vision of the Massachusetts Bay Colony as "a shining city on a hill" and "the new Jerusalem" exercised disproportionate influence in

America for 150 years before the Revolutionary War. Rooted in Calvinist Reformed theology, the Puritans derived their name from their desire to *purify* England's Anglican Church of "papist" traces of Roman Catholicism and of other unbiblical, worldly, corrupt influences. In England the struggle between Anglicans and Puritans dominated seventeenth-century religious and political thought. Inevitably, this struggle spilled over into the colonial New World, with Anglicans colonizing Virginia and Puritans (known as Separatists and Independents, or Congregationalists) settling in Plymouth and Boston in Massachusetts.

The Puritan legacy helped to shape American culture and politics. They bequeathed to the nation the idea of self-government, strong civic institutions, a sense of national mission or providential destiny, a reformist zeal, and a sense of sin to temper that zeal, which led Americans to fear concentrated governmental power.[7]

While Puritan settlements began their history as intolerant, exclusive theocracies, their covenant theology and congregational church structure helped to nurture self-government in the New World. The Puritans in Massachusetts interpreted the Bible to authorize what we call a Congregational polity, which had two particular features. Each congregation or church was founded on an explicit and verbal covenant with God and with the members of the community bound together. The community was not defined by geography or by neighborhood (it was not a parish). Instead, the Puritans defined the true church by belief and experience—it should be composed only of the redeemed, or "visible saints." As the historian Perry Miller wrote, "Congregationalism required that membership be severely limited to the 'visible' saints, to those openly examined before the assembled church, who could make a convincing 'relation' of their spiritual experience, and who could demonstrate their ability to swear to the covenant."[8] If membership was exclusive and restrictive, it also implied the idea of a purely voluntary church and it placed power in each congregation and the people in it.

The second principle of Congregationalism followed from this: all churches were autonomous and equal in status, and there existed above them no hierarchy of ecclesiastical superiors such as bishops or presbyters. Each church was independent and self-governing. Over time, these ideas about church polity or organization filtered into political thought and contributed to the idea of self-governing communities in America.

The Massachusetts Puritans also took seriously the metaphor of exodus in the Hebrew Bible, the exodus of Jews from slavery in Egypt to the Promised Land in Israel. The Puritans saw themselves as leaving the corruption of the Old World and traveling across the sea to the New Israel in America. The New World was a promised land in which these faithful Christians could build a holy commonwealth. They saw this task as divinely ordained. Through these courageous Puritan settlers, the nation inherited a sense of providential destiny

as part of its self-definition. Periodically, throughout American history, we Americans have invoked, for example, a sense of "manifest destiny" to justify westward expansion to the Pacific coast and beyond. In the early twentieth century, Woodrow Wilson called upon America's sense of special mission to "make the world safe for democracy." President John Kennedy's Peace Corps and President Bill Clinton's efforts to station troops in troubled areas such as Bosnia and Haiti are perhaps other examples of the nation's sense of mission. This, too, is part of the Puritan legacy in American history.

A sense of human fragility, weakness, and sinfulness is a third aspect of the Puritan contribution to American culture and religion. Puritan theology was Calvinist in inspiration and therefore tinged with notions of predestination, original sin, and human depravity. At some level, human beings were all "sinners in the hands of an angry God." Such religious realism carried over into politics and contributed to the American fear of concentrating governmental power. As Fowler and Hertzke have noted, "If leaders are as tempted by sin as others, then precautions against abuse must be built into the system."[9] In the *Federalist Papers,* James Madison wrote that under the new federal constitution drawn up in 1787, "ambition must be made to check ambition," and a new governmental structure must be erected that will divide power and rely upon a system of checks and balances to reduce the potential for tyranny.[10] The political realism and distrust of human nature underlying Madison's cautions are in part attributable to the sense of evil and sinfulness inherited from the Puritans.

Finally, the Puritans of Massachusetts had a strong sense of reforming zeal that also influenced American religion and culture. Religious revivals— invitations to reject worldliness and sinfulness and to embrace the straight and narrow path of godliness—have been part and parcel of American history from the Great Awakening of the 1740s to the Second Great Awakening of the early nineteenth century and evangelical camp meetings in the late nineteenth and early twentieth centuries. The revival of the Religious Right in the last quarter of the twentieth century—associated with Jerry Falwell, Pat Robertson, Jimmy Swaggart, and a host of other televangelists—is but the latest example of this enduring tendency in American culture. The zeal for moral reform associated with such revivals has carried over into American politics, as illustrated in the antislavery and temperance movements and even in directly political reform movements associated with progressivism, women's suffrage, civil rights, and peace movements in the late nineteenth and twentieth centuries. As Fowler and Hertzke remark, when figures such as Pat Robertson and Jesse Jackson (both of whom ran for president in 1988) prophesy against the evils of society and equate their political struggles with God's cause, they are exemplifying the American Puritan tradition.[11]

Of course, the fact that religion was influential in American politics in the past does not necessarily mean that it should influence contemporary politics.

However, historical tradition and a people's desire for continuity with the past suggest that it is very difficult for Americans to compartmentalize religious belief and separate it from politics. I argue that they should not do this, partly because religious traditions have often been fertile sources of constructive political action in American history.

The Religious Bases of Major Social Reform Movements

Historically, most churches have not shunned political involvement in the United States. The antislavery, temperance, women's suffrage, civil rights, and 1960s antiwar movements were all at least partly inspired and motivated by religious commitment. And churches and synagogues actively participated in such movements. Even the controversial abortion issue finds church leaders and religious lobbies on both sides—with the Clergy Consultation Service (a 1960s referral network) and the Religious Coalition for Reproductive Rights on the pro-choice side, and the American Catholic bishops and conservative evangelical leaders on the pro-life side.

This cross-fertilization of religion and politics is nothing new in American society. Inevitably, as religiously committed citizens struggled to discern the real-life implications of their religious principles, they sought to bridge the gap between belief and practice. In the nineteenth century, Baptists, Methodists, and other evangelicals established schools, hospitals, and orphanages, and they reformed prisons and created temperance and abolitionist societies. Quakers were very active in the antislavery movement and in the creation of penitentiaries where criminals could reform their lives. In the latter part of the nineteenth century, Frances Willard, the committed Methodist leader of the Women's Christian Temperance Union, led the WCTU in the crusade against alcohol as well as in movements for women's suffrage and educational reform. Again, in the 1890s, Elizabeth Cady Stanton and other suffragists, realizing the power of organized religion as an obstacle to women's suffrage, published *The Woman's Bible,* in which they reinterpreted Christian scriptures to advance ideas of gender equality. Protestant evangelicals were prominent in the nineteenth-century temperance movement and in the twentieth-century Anti-Saloon League, which played a major role in passing the Eighteenth Amendment, banning the sale and production of intoxicating beverages. In all these ways, religiously committed citizens sought to reform corrupt society. These moral reformers were not deterred by notions that religion is a private matter between the believer and her God. Instead, they drew inspiration from religious principles to work toward social improvement.

The same could be said of the civil rights activists of the 1950s and 1960s. Black churches were major sources of political mobilization in the cause of racial justice. Mainline Protestant denominations such as the Episcopal, Lutheran, Presbyterian, and Methodist Churches organized strong, effective pub-

lic support for passage of the historic 1964 Civil Rights Act and the 1965 Voting Rights Act. Clergy and laity from Protestant, Catholic, and Jewish traditions were prominent in the protests against the Vietnam War. The nuclear freeze movement of the 1980s relied upon local churches across the country for ideological, organizational, and logistical support. Even second-stage feminism benefited from the committed activism of Protestant and Jewish clergy, scholars, and students in seminaries and theological schools.

Given these examples of religious-political activism in nineteenth- and twentieth-century American history, we need to critically scrutinize claims that religion and politics do not mix and that religion should be privatized and kept separate from the sphere of public life. It does not make sense to urge religious believers to suppress deep religious beliefs and aspirations that are sources of committed political and social action. As citizens in a democracy, they will perhaps inevitably draw upon religious and moral traditions in efforts to shape public opinion and policy. It could also be argued—from a utilitarian standpoint—that American society has gained historically and will continue to benefit from the work of political and social activists, many of whom derive their commitment from religious sources.

The Welfare State and the Mix of Religion and Politics

Still another reason it is so difficult to compartmentalize and segregate religion from public life has to do with the overlap of government agencies and church institutions in rendering similar services in advanced industrial societies. As American society changed from a laissez-faire, minimalist government in the nineteenth century to an interventionist, welfare state in the twentieth century, the roles and functions of religious and political institutions expanded to meet new social needs. Since churches operate a host of hospitals, schools, charitable organizations, and social service agencies, they are often affected by government. In the nineteenth century, issues important to churches and religiously committed people, such as education, child welfare, temperance, and prison reform, were state and local matters and not part of the federal government's jurisdiction. However, the growing federalization of economic and social life in twentieth-century America has greatly expanded the role of the federal government, a development that has had enormous implications for church-state relations.[12] Religious institutions engaged in social service must take into account the taxing and regulatory powers and codes of the federal government on matters such as employment discrimination, health insurance, social security deductions, and a host of other matters. They must monitor policy developments in Washington. Inevitably, they must represent their concerns to political authorities in the federal government. This has resulted in an enormous increase of religious lobbies or advocacy groups in the nation's capital since the Second World War.[13] These developments have

brought religion and politics closer together in public life, making it increasingly difficult to maintain a solid, impregnable wall of separation between church and state.

Evangelical Aspects of American Religious Tradition

A fourth reason it is so difficult to segregate religion from public life relates to the evangelical dimension of Protestant Christianity in the United States. Today, nearly 40 percent of Americans define themselves as born-again evangelicals. Evangelical religion is deeply rooted in American culture. Evangelical Christianity is the branch of Protestantism that accepts the orthodox tenets of the Christian faith as contained in the Bible. Evangelicals stress the absolute authority of scripture, which, in their view, provides the key to personal salvation. To evangelicals, the gospels contain the good news of salvation, which Christians have a duty to communicate to others. Evangelical Protestantism thus emphasizes preaching and teaching in an effort to convert others to Christianity. Typically, such proselytizing is designed to bring about an adult conversion experience in which one is "born again" to a new life free from sin and corruption. Evangelicals define this born-again experience as a decisive election by the believer of Jesus Christ as one's personal savior.[14] Such a transforming conversion experience is what President Jimmy Carter, a Southern Baptist, referred to in his 1976 presidential campaign when he described himself as "a born-again Christian."

Born-again Christians recognize this experience as an adult initiation into the Christian religion (in contrast to infant baptism in the Lutheran and Roman Catholic traditions). Once a believer has been called by God and has received the amazing grace of Christian conversion, he or she will want to share this experience with others. By word and example, an evangelical Christian is duty-bound to proselytize and convert nonbelievers. Many American Protestant missionaries had their roots in evangelical churches.

Evangelical Christianity is associated with Baptist, Methodist, Pentecostal, and Holiness Churches, with religious revivals and camp meetings, with powerful forms of personal piety, and with emotionally appealing hymns and church music (including the gospel music featured in many African American churches). It is also associated with exhortations to godly living, exemplified in moral crusades against alcohol, tobacco, dancing, gambling, and sexual promiscuity.

Evangelical Christianity was the dominant strain of Protestantism in the United States in the nineteenth and early twentieth centuries and it reemerged as a major religious and political force in the late 1970s. As a religious worldview, it is voluntarist and activist: one must "stand up and be counted for the Lord" and work hard to convert others to godly living as exemplified in the Christian gospels.

Evangelicals actually include a rather diverse group of Protestant Christians in the United States. This pluralism can be traced historically to a split in the late nineteenth century between liberal, mainline Protestants and conservative evangelicals. The split occurred in response to two intellectual developments: the use of historical scholarship to interpret the Bible and new developments in modern science, particularly Charles Darwin's theory of evolution. Whereas liberal Christianity was receptive to new forms of biblical criticism, evangelicals thought religious belief was threatened by the "higher criticism" associated with biblical scholarship in Europe. Similarly, while liberal Protestantism could adapt to new theories of human evolution, conservative evangelicals insisted upon a literal interpretation of the biblical account of the creation of man. Evangelicals held the Genesis story of the creation of Adam and Eve to be literal, not metaphorical, truth.

For some evangelicals, this insistence on literal truth led to an emphasis on the inerrancy of the scriptures. Whatever the Bible said was regarded as strictly true, because God's revelation in scripture could not possibly be false. Evangelicals who adopted this approach to biblical interpretation were concerned about the implicit relativism of new developments in scientific and historical scholarship and responded by insisting that the fundamental teachings of Christianity were absolutely true and universally valid. Their strict interpretation of the Bible led them to define certain key doctrines as factually true: the virgin birth of Jesus, the saving grace of Christ's death by crucifixion as atonement for sin, and the physical resurrection of Christ from the dead. By the early decades of the twentieth century, members of this branch of American Protestantism became known as *fundamentalists* because of their commitment to scriptural inerrancy and to the literal truth of basic Christian beliefs. Of the approximately 40 million evangelicals in the United States today, fundamentalists number from twelve to fifteen million. Fundamentalism is thus a subset of evangelicalism in the United States.[15]

Some scholars of religion detect fundamentalist tendencies in other religions besides Christianity. Indeed, they see fundamentalism in the late twentieth century as a global phenomenon, a pattern that has emerged in all the major world religions during the last twenty-five years. It is discernible in some branches of Islam in Egypt and Iran, in some segments of Judaism in Israel, and in Hinduism in India—as well as in American Protestant Christianity. According to this view, religious fundamentalists share in common a certain style of religio-political activism. They are militant separatists who typically constitute a minority within their religious tradition. They see themselves as upholding "the truth faith," the authentic teachings of Christianity or Islam, for example. They tend to reject modernity, relativism, liberal theology, and historical approaches to the interpretation of sacred texts. Finally, they tend to be absolutists who are unwilling to compromise religious beliefs in the face of the evil and sinfulness of the modern world.[16]

We must remain aware of this broader definition of fundamentalism as a distinctive tendency present in many world religions at the end of the twentieth century; however, we are mainly concerned here with fundamentalism as that branch of evangelical Protestantism in American society that emphasizes biblical literalism (scriptural inerrancy) and moralism regarding human behavior.

Of course, evangelical Protestants in the United States include other groups besides fundamentalists. Randall Balmer uses the word *evangelical* to refer broadly to conservative Protestants—including fundamentalists, evangelicals, pentecostals, and charismatics—who insist on some sort of spiritual rebirth as a criterion for entering the kingdom of heaven and who often impose exacting behavioral standards on the faithful.[17] For our purposes, many evangelicals in late twentieth-century America tend to be conservative, both theologically and politically. They include groups such as the Christian Coalition (founded by Pat Robertson and led by executive director Ralph Reed and by his successor Randy Tate); the now defunct Moral Majority (a political action committee led by Jerry Falwell in the 1980s); Concerned Women of America (a women's interest group founded and led by Beverly LaHaye); Focus on the Family (this group, led by James Dobson, emphasizes proper family life); the Family Research Council (a Washington think tank led by Gary Bauer); and the large number of televangelists (Jimmy Swaggart, Pat Robertson, Jerry Falwell, and, in the 1980s, Jim and Tammy Bakker) who regularly preach to national TV audiences. Together these groups comprise what has come to be called the Christian Right or the Religious Right in contemporary American politics.

It is important to realize that some evangelicals may be theologically conservative yet politically liberal. A noteworthy example is former President Jimmy Carter, a Southern Baptist and self-described "born-again Christian," whose understanding of Christian faith led him to espouse fairly liberal positions in environmental politics and in foreign affairs. Carter emphasized biblical stewardship of God's creation as a framework for protecting the environment and sought to advance human rights and peace in foreign policy. Since leaving the White House, he has continued to emphasize peacemaking and has been very active in Habitat for Humanity, a community organization that mobilizes volunteers to construct inexpensive housing for low-income families.[18]

Other examples of evangelicals who are theologically conservative yet politically liberal include Evangelicals for Social Action (ESA), a group founded by Ronald Sider in the 1970s that is concerned with poverty, racism, discrimination, and injustice in society. The radical group Sojourners, headquartered in Washington, D.C., and led by Jim Wallis, is very active on peace and justice issues. The Evangelical Women's Caucus (EWC) is a group of evangelical feminists who interpret scripture as supporting gender equality and equity; they seek to counter conservatives who rely on the Bible to confirm traditionalist views of the role of women as wives and mothers.[19] These groups illustrate an important point about evangelical Christianity in the United States, a

point emphasized by Charles Dunn in his *American Political Theology,* namely, that persons with common theological assumptions may nevertheless differ in the political conclusions they draw from shared theological premises. We shall see that this same phenomenon occurs among American Catholics as well. In short, religious commitments do not automatically dictate political positions.

Generally speaking, however, in the last quarter of the twentieth century, evangelical Protestantism has been largely associated with conservative politics in the United States. We therefore need to understand more about the agenda of the Christian Right in order to consider the proper role of religion in contemporary American politics. Conservative evangelicals and fundamentalists are deeply disturbed by what they regard as corrupting tendencies in American society: a high divorce rate, drug abuse, sexual permissiveness, and juvenile and adult crime. Accordingly, they emphasize moral reform, "family values," the restoration of prayer in public schools, support for parental choice in education (which translates into endorsement of school vouchers for direct aid to Christian schools), and support for the teaching of "creationism" (the biblical account of creation) as an alternative to evolutionary theory. Members of the Christian Right strongly oppose legalized abortion, pornography, and gay rights legislation (such as antidiscrimination ordinances and laws permitting gay and lesbian marriage).

In general, the Christian Right in America wants the nation's laws and policies to reflect the values, beliefs, and principles of America's Christian majority. They note that a majority (85 percent) of Americans are in fact Christian, and they conclude that the nation's laws and policies should reflect the beliefs of the majority (as is the case in Ireland and Israel). Like the Puritans of colonial times, these Christian political activists contend that "It is the business of politics to ensure for men [*sic*] the freedom to do their duty. Every man's first duty is to win salvation. This is a way of saying that there are things that matter more than mere politics and should precede them in importance. Good politics, like good economics, depend on good morals. Good morals depend on religion."[20]

It is important to note that even if Christians did not constitute a majority of the American population, this would not deter Protestant evangelicals from using politics to translate their religious and moral views into public policy. That is, a positive political role for religion does not depend on the existence of a religious majority such as the 85 percent of Americans who call themselves Christians. Christians, Muslims, or Jews do not lose their citizenship rights to bring their religiously based moral judgments to bear in public deliberation simply because they are members of a religious minority. In a pluralist democracy, religious freedom means that believers have a right to participate in the political process whether they belong to the majority or a minority.

The Christian Right thus echoes a strong theme in American history—the

notion held by Protestants in the early nineteenth century that Americans should be about the business of establishing "a complete Christian commonwealth." Robert T. Handy has analyzed this idea in *A Christian America: Protestant Hopes and Historical Realities*. He notes that although Protestants accepted the idea that there was to be no established church in the United States, they still "looked for a Christian America and worked toward that end. It was to be won not by the use of laws and public monies that had marked establishment but wholly by methods of persuasion. Voluntary rather than governmental means were to be depended upon, for it had come to be believed that they would achieve the desired end. . . ."[21] It is in this sense that the Religious Right, which believes it has a moral duty to restore a Christian America, reechoes an old idea in American history, an idea that stems from the Puritan legacy of colonial Massachusetts. Whether twentieth-century America can constitutionally reflect the religion of the majority is a major challenge posed by conservative evangelicals. It has provoked all sorts of Americans to raise questions about the wall of separation between church and state and the deeper relationship between religion and politics. My point here is that there is nothing astonishingly new about the intent of the conservative political agenda. As I have tried to show in this section of my essay, the driving ideas of conservative evangelicals and fundamentalists have deep roots in American history and culture.

What Role Did the Founders Think Religion Should Play in Public Life?

Those who think religion has subversive tendencies and should be segregated from public life typically appeal to the religion clauses of the Constitution and the Bill of Rights. They contend that the establishment and free exercise clauses of the First Amendment erect a "wall of separation" between religion and public life. We need, therefore, to understand the intentions of the Framers when they fashioned these religion clauses. And since the phrase "a wall of separation between church and state" appears nowhere in the Constitution, we need to know something about the origin of this metaphor and how it crept into our political lexicon.

The Intentions of the Framers

The Framers were not pious men, but they were not hostile to religion either. They saw the need for religion in society as a support for morality and for republican virtues of patriotism, love of country, courage, honesty, public spiritedness, and a concern for the common good. (They were not unaware of the writings of thinkers such as Machiavelli and Rousseau on the utility of

religion for public order.) What motivated the Founders in dealing with religion was a recognition of religious diversity in the colonies/states and a fear of sectarian strife. According to A. James Reichley, "Their common objective was to secure the moral guidance and support of religion for the republic, while escaping the political repression and social conflict with which religion had often been associated throughout history and specifically in the public life of the former colonies."[22]

We might characterize the Framers as deeply ambivalent about the relationships between religion and politics and between church and state. They wanted religion to be a positive force supporting and nourishing a moral citizenry. Yet they realized that in a pluralistic culture, sectarian divisiveness was a threat to be avoided. Some were influenced by Enlightenment ideas (Madison and Jefferson, for example); they favored religious liberty and feared governmental persecution of people who were not religiously orthodox. Others (for example, Baptists and Presbyterians) drew upon traditions of dissenting Protestantism to support religious freedom.[23] Still others favored the maintenance of established churches, directly supported by public funds, in their own states because they believed in the socially beneficial effects of religion (these included George Washington, John Adams, Patrick Henry, and John Marshall). They were opposed by men such as Jefferson and Madison; the latter led the successful attempt to disestablish the Anglican Church in Virginia. From these diverse views about the role of religion in public life, there emerged a consensus: "All agreed that there could be no established national church in a country already so culturally various and intellectually diverse as the new United States."[24] At the same time, states could continue to have established churches; in 1789 there were established churches in five states, including Connecticut and Massachusetts. (The last of the state religious establishments was finally terminated when Massachusetts disestablished the Congregational Church in 1833.) Finally, in Article VI, the Constitution prohibited religious tests for federal public office, although some states continued to have such requirements (North Carolina retained its religious test for office until 1835).[25]

The Framers were, of course, aware of the history of religious establishment in the American colonies. Religious establishment meant having one official church in a nation or state, usually the religion of the majority. Political rights and privileges would be awarded only to members of that church. Dissenters (those who did not belong to the established church) were minorities who were persecuted, harassed, or, at best, barely tolerated. As Martin Marty has remarked, the established church was in a "winner-take-all" situation.

It is important to realize that religious establishment was the pattern that the Western world took for granted for 1,400 years or so. Many colonists, like their European ancestors, thought that religion—an established church—was essential to morality. Nine of the original thirteen colonies had established churches; Rhode Island, New Jersey, Delaware, and Pennsylvania did not.

New Englanders were so used to established churches that they really questioned whether Rhode Island, without an official religion, could be taken seriously as a state, a moral and political community. They called it "Rogues' Island" and referred to it as a "latrina," a dump for the refuse of humanity—immoral men and women.

The Framers also had firsthand experience of religious establishment. In colonial Virginia, and even in the state of Virginia after 1783, one had to be Anglican to be elected to the state legislature, one had to be married in the Anglican Church even if one were not Anglican, and one had to attend the Anglican Church once a month under penalty of being fined. In Virginia in the 1780s, Madison and others fought against religious establishment on the grounds that religion did not need the support of government to thrive and that government meddling did not advance the cause of religion. The arguments of Madison in "A Memorial and Remonstrance on the Religious Rights of Man" (1784) and of Jefferson in "Virginia Statute of Religious Liberty" (written in 1779, adopted in 1786) were powerful weapons against the idea of religious establishment.[26] Madison, in particular, argued that individuals had a natural right to religious freedom; that government was not competent to judge religious truth; that Christianity did not need the support of government to thrive; and that religious establishment brought in its wake a host of negative consequences, such as indolence and hypocrisy. Madison was deeply impressed with the injustice faced by non-Anglican churches in Virginia, and he showed genuine concern for the religious freedom of these other believers.

In arguing against an established church in Virginia, Jefferson and Madison echoed an important theme in colonial thought. Indeed, it could be said that Americans have always had a healthy skepticism about mixing religion and politics. Church-state entanglement evokes fears of religious establishment, of preferring one official religion over all others and endowing that favored religious group with special privileges. From colonial times, the phrase "a wall of separation" was used to express such reservations about the relationship between the sacred and the secular in American public life. Although this phrase does not appear in the Constitution, it is commonly thought to be there, and it is routinely invoked whenever citizens think religion and politics are becoming too enmeshed. But where did this metaphor originate, and what could it possibly mean?

While the phrase is commonly attributed to Thomas Jefferson, it was first used 158 years earlier by Roger Williams in colonial Rhode Island. Since Williams's use of this celebrated metaphor is different from Jefferson's, it is worth examining.

Williams and Jefferson on the "Wall of Separation"

Roger Williams was a seventeenth-century Puritan who took the notion of religious dissent to new conclusions. He left England in 1630 and in 1631 was

welcomed to the Massachusetts Bay Colony as a minister. Opposing his first church assignment, Williams chose instead to live in the colony of Plymouth for two years. Later, he became minister to a church in Salem, Massachusetts. By 1635 his unorthodox ideas had so provoked the Puritan establishment in Boston that he was banished from the Massachusetts Bay Colony. Williams then traveled south and founded Providence, Rhode Island, in 1636.[27]

Williams's relationship with Boston's Puritan divines was troubled from the start. He did not think the Puritans had sufficiently freed themselves from the taint of Anglicanism and he therefore moved quickly to a separatist view, advocating a complete break with the Church of England. He also was disturbed by theocratic tendencies among the Puritan leaders in Boston. Williams challenged the idea of a Puritan theocracy in which church and state were fused and insisted that the church had to be separated from the state. In founding Providence, he fashioned a policy of religious toleration that extended to Quakers, Baptists, and other dissenters (although not to Catholics or Jews).

It is important to note that Williams's arguments for religious liberty and for church-state separation were grounded in theology. He argued that religious persecution by church and civil authorities in Boston contradicted Christ's teachings, since Christianity was a religion of love, not a religion of coercion. Furthermore, religious persecution and conflict undermined civil peace and engendered hypocrisy among those coerced by civil authority to profess orthodox beliefs. To protect religious freedom, Williams spoke of a "wall of separation between the garden of the church and the wilderness of the world." Williams first used this phrase in reply to John Cotton, a leading proponent in Massachusetts of a Puritan orthodoxy that sought the fusion of religion and government.[28]

Note that Williams spoke of a "wall of separation" from the perspective of the church. Separation was designed primarily to keep the faithful cultivating God's garden, free from the corrupting influence of the world and of civil government. Moreover, Williams held that civil power is incapable of making people virtuous Christians. The state exists to maintain peace, law and order, and public morality. Government need not be a Christian theocracy to carry out such secular functions, for statecraft is a practical skill, unrelated to Christian faith.

Williams thus made a religious argument for a radical kind of church-state separation. His primary objective was to protect the church from the taint of worldly corruption. At the same time, he did not believe that religious liberty exempted church members from the performance of civic duties. In a January 1655 letter to the town of Providence, Williams, responding to religious followers who objected to being called into the militia to defend the colony against the Indians, rejected any claim of religious or conscientious exemption. To Williams, religious liberty meant freedom to worship as one believes, not freedom from civic or public duties.[29]

On religious grounds, then, Williams sought a radical separation between church and state. For him, the wall of separation was to insulate the garden of the church from the wilderness of worldly affairs. As A. James Reichley has noted, this was "a substantially different intention than that which Thomas Jefferson later conveyed through the same metaphor."[30]

If Roger Williams represents the argument for religious freedom from the perspective of dissenting Protestantism, Thomas Jefferson argued for religious liberty from the tradition of rational Enlightenment. In "Notes on Virginia" (1781–1782) and in "Virginia Statute of Religious Liberty" (1779), Jefferson wrote that religious liberty was one of the natural rights of mankind. Jefferson was opposed to any government-sponsored religion and favored disestablishment of the Anglican Church in Virginia. His arguments have the ring of classical liberalism: To coerce belief is to make dissenters into hypocrites. Truth can stand by itself and does not need the support of government. To subject religious belief to state coercion in order to achieve uniformity is not useful; on the contrary, religious diversity is valuable because the different religions censor and monitor each other. The only effective protection against error is reason and free inquiry, not force or coercion. Moreover, subjecting religious beliefs to political coercion is to entrust to fallible human beings the role of inquisitor. Jefferson's views are summarized in this celebrated passage from "Notes on Virginia": "The rights of conscience we never submitted [to rulers], we could not submit. We are answerable for them to our God. The legitimate powers of government extend to such acts only as are injurious to others. But it does me no injury for my neighbor to say there are twenty gods, or no God. It neither picks my pocket nor breaks my leg."[31]

In the struggle to disestablish the Anglican Church in Virginia, Jefferson and Madison had as unlikely allies Baptists, Presbyterians, and other dissenters. Later, during his 1800 presidential campaign, Jefferson was again supported by dissenting Protestants while Adams and the Federalists were backed by Anglicans, Congregationalists, and other proponents of religious establishment. As president, Jefferson supported a group of Danbury Baptists who were struggling to live with an established Congregational Church in Connecticut. His January 1, 1802, letter to these Baptists invokes the famous image of a wall of separation between church and state.

Believing with you that religion is a matter which lies solely between man and his God, that he owes account to none other for his faith or his worship, that the legislative powers of government reach actions only, and not opinions, I contemplate with sovereign reverence that act of the whole American people which declared that their legislature should "make no law respecting an establishment of religion, or prohibiting the free exercise thereof," thus building a wall of separation between Church and State. Adhering to this expression of the supreme will of the nation in behalf of the rights of conscience, I shall see with sincere

satisfaction the progress of those sentiments which tend to restore to man all his natural rights, convinced he has no natural rights in opposition to his social duties.[32]

Note the differences between Williams's and Jefferson's use of the "wall of separation" metaphor. Whereas Williams approached the subject of church-state relations from the church's side of the wall, Jefferson addressed the matter primarily from the government's side of the wall. Williams wanted to insulate the church from worldly corruption; Jefferson was perhaps more concerned with the harmful influences of religion upon civil government. Jefferson spoke from the perspective of politics and sought to ensure the freedom of public governmental institutions from the excesses of religious enthusiasm.

It is Jefferson's celebrated use of the "wall of separation" metaphor that was later picked up by the Supreme Court in two major opinions. In *Reynolds v. United States* (1879), Chief Justice Waite ruled against the Mormon practice of polygamy. The Chief Justice quoted Jefferson's letter to the Danbury Baptists, thus giving official Court recognition to the use of this expression. Again, in *Everson v. Board of Education of Ewing Township* (1947), the Court considered the issue of aid to church-related schools (specifically, municipal reimbursement of the costs of bus transportation to parochial schools in Ewing Township, New Jersey). Justice Hugo Black, writing for the Court majority, described the establishment clause as follows:

> The "establishment of religion" clause of the First Amendment means at least this: Neither a state nor the Federal Government can set up a church. Neither can pass laws which aid one religion, aid all religions, or prefer one religion over another. Neither can force nor influence a person to go to or to remain away from church against his will or force him to profess a belief or disbelief in any religion. No person can be punished for entertaining or professing religious beliefs or disbeliefs, for church attendance or non-attendance. No tax in any amount, large or small, can be levied to support any religious activities or institutions, whatever they may be called, or whatever form they may adopt to teach or practice religion. Neither a state nor the Federal Government can, openly or secretly, participate in the affairs of any religious organizations or groups and vice versa. In the words of Jefferson, the clause against establishment of religion by law was intended to erect "a wall of separation between Church and State."[33]

Thus, it is Jefferson's use of the wall metaphor that has found its way into modern Supreme Court jurisprudence. Jefferson sought to keep religion from dominating politics. His conception of church-state separation is still used by those favoring strict separation to justify denial of all aid to religions or churches. However, it is at least conceivable, and perhaps even possible, that had the Supreme Court interpreted the wall metaphor à la Roger Williams to protect religious liberty from state secularism, it might have reached judicial

conclusions more amenable to accommodationists—those who believe the First Amendment permits aid to religion so long as it is administered in a nonpreferential manner.

The reflections of both Williams and Jefferson remind us that maintaining a wall of separation between church and state is a delicate balancing act. Historically, however, Williams's view came first. As Stephen Carter has noted, the metaphorical wall of separation "originated in an effort to protect religion from the state, not the state from religion."[34] Carter restates for a contemporary audience this alternative view of church-state separation (Jefferson's is the dominant, or strict separationist, view, while Williams's view of the wall metaphor may be called the alternative view). In his 1993 book, *The Culture of Disbelief,* Carter contends that in contemporary American society, the regulatory ubiquity of the modern welfare state threatens the independence of religion more than religious fanaticism endangers the body politic. He argues, therefore, that public agencies should do more to accommodate religious believers. He worries that recent Supreme Court decisions have transformed the Constitution's establishment clause from a guardian of religious liberty into a guarantor of public secularism. The wall of separation, he argues, has to have a few doors in it. "The purpose of church-state separation is not the shielding of the secular world from too strong a religious influence; the principle task of the separation of church and state is to secure religious liberty." Carter's reading of constitutional history and theory on church-state separation is consistent with the views of Roger Williams.[35]

Carter's argument is that, to be consistent with the Founders' vision, the Constitution's religion clauses should be used to avoid tyranny—that is, to sustain and nurture religions as independent centers of power, as democratic intermediaries. I shall consider Carter's claim that religious institutions promote democracy at a later point in this essay.

To summarize these reflections on the Founders' intentions in fashioning the religion clauses of the First Amendment, I note that the Framers were ambivalent about religion. If they sought to enjoy the beneficial effects of civic virtues taught by religions, they also wanted to avoid the divisive effects of sectarian strife in civil society, and they thought that the way to achieve these ends was to avoid establishing any official religion at the federal level of government. Their metaphor for church-state relations implied a "wall of separation" between the garden of the church and the wilderness of the world. Yet metaphorical meaning can be notoriously opaque and difficult to discern. We need to ask how high the wall of separation is and whether there are any cracks in the wall.

The Wall Metaphor and the Meaning of Church-State Separation

What does "separation of church and state" mean in practice? Does it mean that clergy cannot serve in Congress? Congressman Robert Drinan (D-MA)

was a Jesuit priest, Congressman William Gray (D-PA) was a pastor of a large congregation of black parishioners in Philadelphia, and Senator John Danforth (R-MO) was an Episcopalian priest. Does church-state separation mean that President Clinton cannot host a meeting of one hundred ecumenical religious leaders at the White House (as he did on August 30, 1993)? Does it mean that President Reagan acted unconstitutionally when he appointed an ambassador to the Vatican in 1983?

Obviously, there is continuing debate over just exactly what measures are constitutional. The Constitution does prohibit religious tests for public office, which means that clergy are not barred from serving in Congress as elected representatives of the people. The president can solicit advice from many different leaders and citizens in carrying out the duties of his office. Sending an American ambassador to the Vatican was out of the question throughout much of U.S. history and has only become politically acceptable in the last quarter of the twentieth century.

Paul Weber reminds us that vigorous debate over the meaning of the First Amendment religion clauses continues partly because enormous social changes have occurred since the Framers wrote the Constitution and because "the Founders did not write the First Amendment with either the clairvoyance or the specificity that would make it easy to apply their principles to problems arising in today's church-state relations."[36] Weber contends that of the different varieties of church-state separation that exist in the modern world, perhaps only one type obtains in the United States, namely, structural separation of church and state. The characteristics of structural separation are independent clerical and civil offices; separate organizations for government and religion; separate systems of law (for example, civil law in the United States is not Islamic Sharia, Jewish law, or Roman Catholic canon law); independent ownership of property; and the absence of any officially designated church or religion. The idea behind structural separation is that there is an institutional division between church associations and government agencies. Jefferson, Madison, and most of the Framers accepted the need for a structural separation of church and state, and it is this institutional arrangement that distinguishes most Western systems from the organic systems existent in Iran and Saudi Arabia.

Beyond this institutional separation, however, the United States does not have anything approaching absolute church-state separation—a view that would hold that no financial aid of any type should flow from government to the churches or vice versa. Throughout American history, enormous amounts of aid, both direct and indirect, have been distributed in both directions. Aid from government to religion includes funds for schoolbooks, bus transportation, sign language interpreters, and tax exemptions. These forms of aid are regarded as constitutional in the United States.

If "absolute separation" does not accurately describe church-state relations

in the United States, neither does what Weber calls "transvaluing separation." This variety of church-state separation would deny aid to religious organizations and would work to secularize the political culture of the nation. Secularization means that government and society reject as politically illegitimate the use of any religious symbols or appeals to religious values, motivations, or policy objectives in the political arena. This type of separation existed under the constitution and law of the former Soviet Union—under Soviet rule, churches in Russia were simply destroyed—but it has never existed in the United States. Neither Thomas Jefferson nor the U.S. Supreme Court has accepted this conception of church-state relations. According to Weber, "Jefferson's desire to provide access to the University of Virginia for neighboring schools of divinity is prima facie evidence that he did not favor this type of separation."[37] And the Supreme Court, in *Lemon v. Kurtzman* (1971), rejected the idea of total separation. The Court noted that "Some relationship between government and religious organizations is inevitable. Fire inspections, building and zoning regulations, and state requirements under compulsory school-attendance laws are examples of necessary and permissible contacts. . . ."[38]

Finally, the notion of complete secularization has never taken hold in the United States. American political culture is rife with religious symbolism. Our coins bear the motto "In God we trust." We pledge allegiance to the flag and "to one nation, under God, with liberty and justice for all." We appoint congressional chaplains and pay them federal salaries to open sessions of Congress by invoking the Almighty in prayer. It simply is not the custom in the United States to reject as politically illegitimate the use of religious symbols or appeals to religious values and motivations. In fact, the contrary is true: religion is still a vital force in American culture, society, and politics.

To conclude, I shall say that in the United States, we do indeed have a structural separation between church institutions and government agencies. Yet we do not separate religion and politics in any precise way; the two are intertwined, both historically and in contemporary society. In other words, we have never really had what Jelen calls "religious minimalism" in American culture and politics. Churches have always been actively involved in public affairs, and government has always aided and accommodated religion. It is virtually impossible to separate religion and politics in the United States, but the close connection between them raises central questions about how to maintain liberal democracy in a religiously diverse society. I will now turn to these issues.

What Role Does Religion Play in Contemporary American Society and Culture?

Thus far, we have explored the significant role religion has played historically in American public life. Clearly, religious traditions have often been fertile

sources of constructive political action in American history. Moreover, historical tradition and the desire for continuity with the past suggest that it is very difficult for Americans to compartmentalize religious belief and separate it from politics. To urge Americans to privatize religion and remove it from the public square would be, in a sense, analogous to telling an individual to suppress all memory of his family of origin, his ancestry, his history. Our desire for continuity with the past makes it difficult to ignore the powerful legacy of religion in American history and culture.

At the same time, the historical significance of American religion does not necessarily mean that religion should influence contemporary politics. The argument for the normative role of religion in American public life is as much influenced by data about contemporary religiosity as it is by historical arguments about the critical role religion played in the past. Evidence regarding religious participation in the United States points to a high degree of religious belief among present-day Americans. In light of this, efforts to exclude religion from public life would appear to be futile. Perhaps citizens in a democracy will inevitably draw upon religious and moral traditions in their efforts to shape public opinion and policy. It seems senseless to urge believers to suppress deep religious beliefs and aspirations that are sources of committed political and social action. To exile religious voices from the public square in this manner is undemocratic.

Ultimately, I must consider how religion functions in an American society that is committed to liberal democracy. To do this, I will briefly review the statistics on American religious participation and the diversity of American religious expression. (After all, one justification for liberal democracy concerns the pluralism of American religion and culture.) I will then discuss the much debated relationship between religion and democracy in the United States, in order to better evaluate Jelen's argument that religion subverts democratic governance.

Religious Beliefs and Participation in America

Statistics show that the contemporary United States is clearly a believing society. The vitality of religion persists, as does the diversity of religious expression. Approximately 94 percent of Americans profess a belief in God or a universal spirit; 90 percent have a religious preference; and a majority say that religion is very important in their lives. Some 70 percent of Americans express belief in life after death; 65 percent believe in the Devil; and over 40 percent of Americans say they pray daily. The majority of Americans are churchgoers, and some 40 percent say they attend in any given week. Indeed, church participation is the single most engaged-in group activity in the United States, and churches themselves are very active in society. A large share of

the charitable giving in the United States is done through churches, temples, and synagogues.[39]

In comparison with other advanced industrial societies, the United States has an astonishingly high degree of religiousness. "Americans repeatedly express far more religious faith than citizens in Great Britain, West Germany, France, and most other nations in Europe."[40] A third of the American public say they have had a powerful religious awakening that changed their lives. Some 86 percent of Americans identify themselves as Christians. Americans also invest considerable confidence in religious institutions and clergy. While the U.S. military is the most trusted institution in the nation, the public expresses more confidence in organized religion than it does in the U.S. Supreme Court, Congress, banks, public schools, television, organized labor, and big business.

Of course, whether American religious vitality actually translates into ethical conduct is another matter. According to Fowler and Hertzke, "Critics suggest that religion in America is like the proverbial prairie river, a mile wide and an inch deep. They note an obvious gap between high levels of apparent faith and considerable business dishonesty, tax fraud, sexual promiscuity, marital infidelity, family breakdown, cheating in school, crime, violence, and vulgarity in the popular culture."[41] That American religion is marked by this gap between professed faith and conduct suggests that the religious faith of many Americans may be shallow and superficial. It also indicates that the public utility of religion in American society operates independently of the truth or persuasiveness of religious belief. In other words, although Americans may not always practice what they preach, they think churches should inculcate moral values that will help to humanize capitalism, support public order, and give direction to democracy.

Pluralism and Religious Diversity

If we Americans are a religious people, we are also a people historically and constitutionally committed to religious pluralism. A bewildering diversity of religious expression continues unabated in the United States. Such pluralism existed since colonial times, but the range of religious groups has increased in the late twentieth century. People from all major world religions are represented: Protestant, Catholic, Jewish, Buddhist, Muslim, and Hindu. Within Judaism, every branch is found in America—Orthodox, Conservative, Reform, Hasidic, and secular. Baptists include black Baptists and white Baptists, fundamentalists and moderates, northern branches and southern ones. Even the Catholic Church is pluralistic, containing liberal, progressive Catholics and conservative, traditional Catholics.[42]

Fowler and Hertzke cite, as explanatory factors for this religious pluralism, a constitutional doctrine in the First Amendment religion clauses that protects

religious freedom; a relative openness to immigration (which brings in new religious groups); and a tradition of individualism that promotes the formation of new sects. Among the new religious groups that have developed in the United States since colonial times are the Mormons, Christian Scientists, Jehovah's Witnesses, and Seventh-Day Adventists.

Despite the diversity of religious expression characteristic of American culture, some scholars call attention to differential treatment of majority and minority creeds. Mainstream religions receive special privileges and protection while minority churches are granted few exemptions. Mormons, for example, were not held exempt from laws against polygamy in the nineteenth century, and members of the Native American Church, who use peyote in worship services, were not exempted from the state of Oregon's antidrug policy in the twentieth century.[43] On the other hand, some minority sects have been treated fairly, with the respect due to equals: the Old Order Amish received a religious exemption from truancy laws mandating high school attendance;[44] and in 1993 the Supreme Court struck down, on free exercise grounds, an overly broad municipal ordinance banning members of the Santeria tradition from practicing animal sacrifice in worship services.[45]

The existence of religious pluralism in the United States is a powerful argument for religious freedom and church-state separation (nonestablishment) in American society. The existence of so many creeds heightens fears of sectarian strife and creates a powerful impetus for religious tolerance. However, as Carter pointed out in *The Culture of Disbelief*, American society currently seems more intent on accepting ethnic diversity rather than religious pluralism. Although at the moment we accept various voices in the public square (blacks, Latinas, Asians, and women), we are paradoxically saying that religious voices should be excluded from public discourse. While it is all well and good to recognize multiculturalism and ethnic diversity, why exclude religious witness from the public square? In a truly democratic society, no one should be excluded from participation in public life.

The Relationship Between Religion and American Democracy

In contrast to my colleague Ted Jelen, I do not think religion necessarily subverts or undermines democratic deliberation and governance. On the contrary, I argue that religion serves to enhance democracy in the United States. Currently, this is happening in three different ways: First, religion has the positive effect of broadening political representation—something all democrats should, in principle, applaud. Second, religion promotes democratic citizenship by training people in the political abilities and civic skills necessary for effective participation. Third, religion transmits moral values without which democracy could not thrive. In this way, the churches act as powerful socializing agents and as effective barriers to political and social tyranny.

Before discussing these points, I should clarify what I mean by democracy. In the modern world, democracy is not simply majority rule or the rule of the many poor, as Aristotle defined it.[46] The type of democracy which is most important to the United States is liberal democracy, which seeks maximum political participation and majority rule, yet emphasizes fundamental respect for individual and minority rights. Liberal democracy, as it has developed in a populous and diverse society such as the United States, emphasizes protective institutions such as representative government, periodic elections that hold representatives accountable, individual constitutional rights defended through an independent judiciary, and private ownership of property to guarantee political independence. The values essential to a liberal, democratic society include personal freedom, tolerance for the rights of others, distributive justice, citizen participation in decision making, social discipline, and respect for law. In a sense, we could say that in an ideal liberal democracy, both the welfare of the individual and the common good of society are the goals.

Religion and Political Participation

How does religion enhance political participation in contemporary American society? In his study of religious interest groups in American politics, Allen Hertzke suggests that religious lobbies actually promote American democracy by providing political access to individuals and groups previously left out of the political process.[47] Hertzke argues that more Americans join churches than any other single voluntary association. Although they have a variety of reasons for doing so, their association with religious groups facilitates a kind of representation hitherto denied them by a political process inevitably skewed toward powerful, well-educated, monied interests. In this sense, churches become an alternative channel for expressing the views of many ordinary, believing Americans who might otherwise have no voice. Such political involvement by churches and religious lobbies facilitates democracy, political representation, and political participation by bringing more citizens into the political process.

Of course, Hertzke is thinking of groups such as the Christian Coalition (led until recently by Ralph Reed and founded by Pat Robertson) and other Religious Right organizations that have given voice to conservative evangelicals who had been marginalized and excluded from the political process in America throughout much of the twentieth century. Such religious lobbies provide a much-needed corrective to the distorted nature of the lobby system in the United States. In American politics, interest groups representing the affluent and the well-educated tend to have enormous political advantages. For example, because of their expertise, money, and social status, the American Medical Association and the American Bar Association have political clout out of all proportion to the size of their professional membership. Such groups

usually lobby for their own particular interests rather than on behalf of the common interest of everyone in society (however that may be defined). By contrast, religious lobbies usually urge citizens to consider the common good rather than selfish interests. Churches often articulate universal values of peace and justice as public policy goals. And churches and synagogues frequently champion the interests of the poor and the disadvantaged, those persons not usually represented by a lobby system that is biased in favor of the affluent and the well educated. To the extent, then, that churches (religious lobbies) counter the elitism of the lobby system, they contribute to democracy in American society. As Hertzke notes, "The national religious lobbies, collectively, enhance the representativeness of the modern American polity."[48] They provide a significant corrective to the American pluralist system through their role in representing non-elites and unpopular attitudes.

In addition to his work on religious lobbies, Allen Hertzke has directed our attention to religiously based populist movements in American politics. In his important analysis of the presidential candidates Jesse Jackson and Pat Robertson in the 1988 election, Hertzke described their campaigns as manifestations of a kind of "gospel populism" voiced through tightly knit churches (black congregations and conservative charismatic assemblies).[49] According to Hertzke, both candidacies were examples of the power of church-based social movements, and both candidates sounded populist themes, blending a critique of economic and cultural elites with a call for the restoration of moral values in American society. Both Jackson and Robertson criticized the excessive individualism of American liberalism and proposed a populist blend of radical economics and traditional moralism. In 1988 the gospel populism of black congregations and conservative charismatic churches filled a vacuum that had been left by the weakening of political parties, trade unions, and other traditional local political institutions.

According to Hertzke, the link between populism and religion flows in part from the character of church life in the United States. Because churches operate in an intensely competitive religious marketplace, they thrive or decline on the basis of popular support. Given this need to appeal to popular themes in order to recruit church members, it is relatively easy to see how such social protest movements as the civil rights movement of the 1950s and 1960s, the nuclear freeze movement of the 1980s, and the Religious Right movement of the 1980s and 1990s originated in churches. In terms of democratic participation, Hertzke stresses that church membership is decidedly broader than the elite membership of most political pressure groups. Religious lobbies may represent the institutional interests of churches, but church-based social protest movements tend to voice the needs and concerns of ordinary people. As Hertzke contends, there is no comparable institution in which average Americans participate in such large numbers as the church. In this way, gospel populism has contributed to greater democratic participation.

Religion, Civic Skills, and Democratic Citizenship

A second dimension of the relationship between religion and democracy in the United States concerns the way in which religion promotes democratic citizenship by training people in the civic skills necessary for effective political participation. Modern political thinkers, from Machiavelli to Rousseau, from Jefferson to John Dewey, have pondered the relationship between religion and democratic citizenship. Now two recent studies by sociologists and political scientists illustrate how churches in the United States contribute concretely to democratic participation.

The first of these is a study of six paradenominational groups in American society, which was conducted by John A. Coleman, sociologist and professor at the Jesuit School of Theology in Berkeley, California. According to Coleman, these paradenominational groups—organizations that are religious in their orientation but not affiliated with any single church or denomination—are engaged in a broad range of civic activities. These include community organizing (by the Pacific Institute for Community Organizing, or PICO), lobbying on hunger issues (Bread for the World), mobilizing volunteers to construct housing for low-income families (Habitat for Humanity), protesting war and weapons manufacturing (Pax Christi), lobbying for family-related laws and policies (Focus on the Family), and spearheading community development, education, and housing programs in African American communities.[50]

These groups blend religious motivation and practical civic voluntarism; they wed discipleship to citizenship in constructive ways. They remind us that many of the citizen-revitalization movements around the nation that have already renewed our democratic citizenship and gained a voice for ordinary Americans are linked to churches. They also indicate that, as Coleman states, "It is not just the Christian Right that translates its vision of discipleship into a more public political arena. Nor does the Christian Right represent the only faith-based political movement that is growing and having an impact."[51]

The reason such groups are linked to churches has to do with the special role of the latter in the American social landscape. "No institution in America generates as much social capital as the churches," states Coleman, using the term coined by political scientist Robert Putnam to refer to the social networks of mutuality and norms of trust that enable people to work together for common goals.[52] Putnam linked social capital to conventional political participation. While social capital is not the same as political participation, it leads to it and maximizes it. People connected to networks of communication and mutuality are more likely to vote and more likely to give time and money not only to religious causes but to secular efforts as well. By creating a climate of trust and community—social capital—churches and synagogues foster civic voluntarism.

Coleman's research confirms what political scientists Sidney Verba, Kay

Schlozman, and Henry Brady found about religious organizations' contribution to democratic potential. In *Voice and Equality,* their massive study of political participation in the United States, these scholars argue that churches offer four important resources that increase the likelihood and effectiveness of both civic and political involvement:

- They teach people transferable skills, such as how to give a speech, organize a meeting, write a memo, or raise money—skills that can then be translated back into politics.
- They provide networks of friends and neighbors from which civic activists can be recruited. People respond better to requests for help when asked by a friend rather than a stranger.
- They give people a sense of efficacy in a local setting that increases confidence in making a difference politically.
- They deliver information and cues about political issues. They also expose people to political messages in settings that are not explicitly political.[53]

Verba, Schlozman, and Brady note that other organizations besides churches teach people these political and organizational skills. People acquire such training in the workplace or nonpolitical civic organizations such as the Rotary Club. However, the workplace and other organizations have a built-in bias toward providing civic and political advantages to the affluent and well educated—to managers, not ordinary workers. "Only the religious institutions provide a counterbalance," according to Verba, Schlozman, and Brady. "They play an unusual role in the American participatory system by providing opportunities for the development of civic skills to those who otherwise would be resource poor."[54]

Both Coleman and Verba et al. cite churches and labor unions as places where ordinary blue-collar workers might acquire civic skills. Yet whereas strong unions and social democratic political parties are present in other Western democracies, they are not prominent in contemporary America. As a result, "a blue collar worker in America is more apt to be given opportunities to practice civic skills in church than in a union."[55] This is partly true because many more blue-collar workers are members of churches than are members of unions.

Verba, Schlozman, and Brady note the implications of this fact for American democracy:

> The relative equality with which opportunities for skill development are distributed in churches is a finding of potential significance for the understanding of American politics. Among the several ways in which American politics is exceptional among the world's democracies is the attenuation of the oragnizations that bring disadvantaged groups to full participation in political life elsewhere. The labor unions and political parties are weak, and there are no working class or peasant parties. Less frequently remarked is the strength of religious institutions—which contrasts with the weakness of parties and unions—and the

frequency with which Americans attend religious services. By providing opportunities for the practice of politically relevant skills, the American churches—especially the Protestant churches—may partially compensate for the weakness of institutions that ordinarily function to mobilize the disadvantaged.[56]

In short, churches and synagogues in the United States contribute to democratic potential by creating the climate of mutuality and trust that is necessary for cooperative civic ventures and by training ordinary Americans in the civic skills that are essential to political participation. In America, "the domain of equal access to opportunities to learn civic skills is the church."[57] This is especially important to the American democratic experiment because so many of the other opportunities to acquire these skills occur in settings (work, nonreligious civic organizations) oriented toward the well heeled and well educated. In this way the churches and synagogues enhance democracy in America. Or, as a Southern Baptist pastor in Pensacola, Florida, told Coleman's research team in an interview, "You take the churches out of this part of town, there's no voice for the people. You really don't have anyone else speaking for the people and with the people."[58]

Religion and Mediating Institutions of Civil Society

A third aspect of the relationship between religion and democracy in the United States concerns the role churches play as important socializing agents and as effective barriers to political and social tyranny. Religion can be a source of moral values for citizens; indeed, some scholars (A. James Reichley and, to a lesser extent, Stephen Carter) question whether democracy can flourish without support from religious values. Since both Carter and Reichley make major, though different, theoretical arguments about the importance of religion to democracy, I shall consider their arguments in detail here.

In *The Culture of Disbelief,* Carter draws upon Alexis de Tocqueville's famous observations about religion and American politics to argue that religion serves two chief functions in a democratic society: First, through education and socialization, religion shapes the moral character of citizens. Religions, according to Carter, can serve as sources of moral understanding without which any majoritarian system can deteriorate into simple tyranny. For example, by emphasizing in their basic teachings the unique dignity of each individual, Judaism and Christianity both support notions of human rights and civil liberties, which are the foundation of modern, liberal democracy and which limit the power of the state.

Second, as intermediate groups in society, churches fill the vast space between the people and their government and act as protective buffers between the state and the individual. Religions can mediate between the citizen and the apparatus of government, providing an independent moral voice. They can do

this because, as Carter puts it, "Religions live by resisting. . . . Like other intermediate institutions, religions that command the devotion of their members actually promote freedom and reduce the likelihood of democratic tyranny by splitting the allegiance of citizens and pressing on their members points of view that are often radically different from the preferences of the state."[59]

Note that Carter here recapitulates an age-old theme about Western religion—namely, that the advent of Christianity into the Graeco-Roman world introduced a new concept of divided loyalties, or allegiances to God and to Caesar. Once this occurred, the political order could no longer command the total allegiance of the citizen. Allegiance to God could trump loyalty to Caesar and to Caesar's laws.[60]

Carter thus stresses the prophetic role of religion in society. He sees that religions are sources of moral understanding that can lead citizens to effectively criticize existing institutional arrangements and policies. He thinks that the principal value of religion to a democratic polity is its ability to preach resistance. As he writes, "Democracy is best served when the religious are able to act as independent moral voices interposed between the citizen and the state: . . . our tendency to try to wall religion out of public debate makes that role a harder one to play."[61]

Carter does not fear the subversive potential of religion but accepts that religions are autonomous communities of resistance and independent sources of meaning. He acknowledges that "A religion is, at heart, a way of denying the authority of the rest of the world." He thus accepts the paradox that religion can be both critical and constructive in modern democracies; as he notes, "The very aspect of religions that their critics most fear—that the religiously devout, in the name of their faith, take positions that differ from approved state policy—is one of their strengths."[62]

By contrast, A. James Reichley tends to emphasize the role of religion as legitimating, rather than challenging, existing political and social arrangements. He doubts whether democracy can flourish without support from religious values. Reichley emphasizes the public utility of religion. Appealing to the work of the framers of the U.S. Constitution, he claims that "While warning against the potentially divisive effects of religious differences on national politics, most of the Founders concluded that a republican democracy depends for moral sustenance on broad public attachment to religious values." Reichley thinks the Founders were essentially correct: "From the standpoint of the public good, the most important service churches offer to secular life in a free society is to nurture moral values that help humanize capitalism and give direction to democracy."[63]

According to Reichley, adequate secular sources for democracy have not yet been found. The political philosophies of liberalism, Marxism, libertarianism, civic humanism, or communitarianism have either failed in practice or

tend to shade off into a narrow political elitism (in which too many ordinary citizens are excluded from a conversation held primarily by intellectuals). As for moral education, churches have the edge over other institutions that shape our values today—the media, secular educational elites, Hollywood, TV, and Madison Avenue. In the United States, churches have shown that religious institutions can be very useful in the education of a virtuous citizenry.

At the same time, Reichley is wary about too much intermingling of religion and politics. He is not unmindful of the potentially debilitating effects of religion in public life. Religion can be divisive; that is, churches can incite or promote sectarian strife. Moreover, the absolutist social outlook often associated with religion tends to hamper working out the pragmatic accommodations needed by a functioning democracy. Accordingly, Reichley recommends that churches be prudent about the extent and methods of their political involvement. As he suggests:

> The religious problem for democracy . . . is how to maintain a social environment favorable to the free exercise of religion, while avoiding the hazards, for both religion and secular society, of mingling institutional religion too closely with governmental authority. These hazards—principally, violation of individual conscience, manipulation of religion by the state, and incitement of group antagonisms—can largely be overcome through reasonable and consistent application of the First Amendment, as the modern Court has done admirably with the free exercise clause but much less successfully with the establishment clause. Beyond that, politicians honoring religious freedom should forego using religion as a campaign device. And the churches, to preserve their autonomy and their integrity, should usually hold themselves some distance above the rough-and-tumble of ordinary politics, whether in election campaigns or on Capitol Hill.[64]

To summarize this section on religion in contemporary American society, I note the vitality and diversity of religious expression that obtains in the United States. Religious commitment makes it extremely difficult to privatize religion and exclude churches from public discourse. At the same time, religious pluralism makes it imperative that measures be taken to prevent religious differences from degenerating into sectarian strife. In the United States we have generally looked to the Constitution and the courts to enforce institutional church-state separation.

However, the First Amendment religion clauses say little about the intermingling of religion and politics that characterizes American history, culture, and contemporary society. Some beneficial effects of mixing religion and politics concern the ways in which religion enhances democracy in the United States. I have argued here that, in American society, religion broadens political representation, and religious lobbies provide a much-needed corrective to the bias toward wealth in the American interest group system. In addition, churches train people in the civic skills necessary for effective political partic-

ipation, they educate citizens in the moral values supportive of democracy, and they serve as mediating institutions and protective buffers between the individual and the state. In this way, churches and synagogues serve as agents of resistance to limit the potential tyranny of majoritarian democracy.

Note that sometimes these roles and functions of religion may conflict. For example, churches in the United States often play a legitimating role in society; by educating a moral citizenry, they help to sustain the American system of government. At other times, churches take on a prophetic role, criticizing existing social and political arrangements (such as racism, poverty, pornography, homelessness, crime, and militarism). Reichley stresses the legitimating function of religion whereas Carter emphasizes the prophetic role religion can play in a modern democracy.

I trust the case has been made for including the religious voice in the public square, for not excluding churches and religious institutions from the political process. However, the style and method of political participation by religious leaders, clergy, and laity must be scrutinized carefully. Here is where, as Reichley suggests, religious believers must be careful not to violate the rights of fellow citizens in a liberal democracy. It is to this subject that I now turn.

What Is the Proper Role of Religious Convictions in American Public Life?

By now it should be clear that although I favor institutional church-state separation, I do not support the privatization of religion and its exclusion from public life. Unfortunately, strict separation of church and state has become a notion used by many to say not only that state support for religion is unconstitutional but that religion itself has no legitimate place in public life. While Americans can constitutionally separate church institutions and government agencies, they have never segregated religion from politics. In American history, religious traditions have often been fertile sources of constructive political action in the form of social protest movements. Moreover, as indicated earlier, churches have enhanced and promoted the working of democracy in the United States. Finally, it is perhaps impossible for citizens to suppress the religious and moral understandings they bring to politics. Many Americans wish to connect discipleship and citizenship; they strive to integrate religious-moral values with practical civic engagement. Should believers impose gag rules on themselves and not use the language of faith when they engage in common civic pursuits? When addressing political questions, should religious citizens scrupulously abstain from faith-based language or appeals?

These considerations raise deeper questions about the proper role of religious convictions in American public life. What is the relationship between

religion, morality, and public policy? What should it be? Both citizens and lawmakers may view religion as a source of moral judgment that is relevant to public policy. Citizens, and especially public officials, must therefore address the question of the legitimacy of using the political process to impose their religious beliefs upon others who do not necessarily share their religious commitments. After all, it is only in theocracies that "God says so" or "God wills it" carries the day. A commitment to liberal democracy in a religiously diverse society means that Americans must negotiate with care the complex relation between religion, morality, and law.

This raises the further question of religious authority and religious revelation. In a pluralist society, what sources should we use for our ideas about sound law and public policy? Should such sources be wholly secular? When the vast majority of Americans draw on religious sources for their deepest moral convictions, is it not self-defeating and impractical to silence so many? Is revealed religion a principle of authority or simply a source of wisdom? What is meant by religious authority and how binding is it? What is authoritative? The Bible, the Koran, papal pronouncements and encyclicals? Some values of faith are accepted only or primarily on the basis of religious authority, while other religious values (peace, justice, compassion for the needy, hospitality toward the stranger, promoting the common good) might be said to be universal—that is, you can find them in all religions. Moreover, they appeal to everyone on secular, rational grounds. It is these values that are most important to the functioning of a liberal, democratic society.

While all citizens must carefully consider these questions, they are especially compelling for two groups of Americans, public officials and religious leaders. Politicians and clergy have special responsibilities in the matter of integrating religious-moral values and civic duties. To illustrate how two public officials have balanced religious commitment and political duty, I will discuss Jesse Jackson and Mario Cuomo as examples of political leaders who effectively translate religiously based values into policy positions.

To illustrate how religious leaders approach these same issues, I will examine the response of American Catholic cardinals and the Pope to President Clinton's veto, in April 1996, of a late-term abortion bill. My concern throughout this final section is to show the need for tolerance and restraint on the part of religious believers when they address the moral dimensions of public policy in the political arena of a pluralistic society. In a religiously diverse society, this tolerance on the part of believers toward nonbelievers is not only prudent and expedient: it is justified, at least in the case of Christianity, on theological as well as philosophical grounds. In other words, respect and tolerance are religiously rooted values as well as important elements of liberal, democratic theory. Once again, religion and democracy converge.

Jesse Jackson, Religious Language, Moral Values, and Political Discourse

Is it appropriate to use explicitly religious language in political activity? Is "God-talk" permissible, proper, or effective in public debate? Or should political engagement remain strictly secular—that is, should religious citizens scrupulously refrain from faith-based language or appeals? This sounds like a very abstract issue—until we recall that in the 1988 presidential campaign two ministers ran for president, thus illustrating the strong political involvement of committed religious activists in contemporary American politics.

Some political scientists and political philosophers have argued that religiously motivated people should practice a kind of "epistemic abstinence" in public debate, carefully expunging from their language all religious references, justifications, and appeals to religious authority. In order to show equal respect for fellow citizens who are not believers, they contend, religious citizens, when addressing issues of public policy or supporting laws that coercively bind all citizens, should abstain from appeals to faith-based or sectarian language. Instead, they should offer adequate secular reasons for supporting a particular law or policy.[65]

Several fears and concerns prompt these cautionary warnings about God-talk in the political arena. First, there is the danger of intolerance. Partly because of the nature of religion and religious commitment, religious believers run the risk of being intolerant of nonbelievers in a diverse society (although, it should be noted, they have no monopoly on intolerance—plenty of secular ideologues run this same risk). Americans in general, and democratic theorists in particular, are wary of the absolutist social outlook often associated with religion. As Reichley has written, "Practically all religions claim to embody ultimate truths about the nature of the universe and the human condition. At some level, therefore, they can hardly be tolerant of rival beliefs."[66] Reichley suggests ways in which religious institutions can avoid social intolerance.[67] Yet because of the moral absolutism often associated with religion, the danger of intolerance always exists.

Second, religious conviction can inhibit the ability or willingness to compromise on matters of law and public policy. As Reichley notes, "Injection of religion into political controversies tends to hamper working out the pragmatic accommodations needed by a functioning democracy, particularly in a socially pluralistic nation like the United States."[68] A recent example of this in American politics was the failure of campaign managers for GOP presidential candidate Bob Dole to convince the 1996 Republican Party Platform Committee, headed by pro-life congressman Henry Hyde (R-IL), to include a plank stating that the Republican Party tolerated a broad range of views on abortion policy. Dole had wanted a tolerance plank included in the Republican platform in order to appeal to moderate, pro-choice Republicans and voters. However,

such a political compromise was unacceptable to religious conservatives at the GOP convention, who insisted that the Republican Party platform could not dilute in any way its support of a constitutional amendment banning all abortions. It is this unwillingness to compromise on the part of religious believers that worries political scientists and philosophers—particularly because negotiation and compromise are essential in a diverse democracy such as the United States.

Yet a third reason that political analysts worry about God-talk in the political arena concerns the way religious believers view and treat political opponents. Religious conviction may lead a devout citizen to brand a political opponent as evil, immoral, or sinful for disagreeing with him over what sound public policy should be. In a democracy citizens learn to disagree without losing respect for one another—without, that is, consigning an opponent to eternal perdition as an evil, sinful person simply because he or she has a different policy view.

Finally, some political thinkers base their fear of religious argument on the anxiety that religion could be dangerously divisive in public. One philosopher remarks that "Conflicting secular ideas, even when firmly held, can often be blended and harmonized in the crucible of free discussion; but a clash of gods is like a meeting of an irresistible force with an immovable object."[69]

To these fears, anxieties, and concerns, religiously committed citizens reply that they cannot renounce their deepest selves, motivations, and language whenever they enter the common arena of citizenship and instead "pretend to be a kind of self they really are not." Not only is it impossible to do this, but they should not be *asked* to do this; it is neither democratic nor liberal to force religiously devout citizens to submit to gag rules before they are allowed to act as legitimate citizens. Instead of censoring their religious language, they should be allowed to make their arguments—subject, of course, to the prerogative of listeners to reject the arguments, should these be unpersuasive. Conceivably, this could work—since arguments based solely on religious authority, such as the Koran, the Bible, or a papal encyclical, would probably have little appeal or persuasiveness to nonbelievers, and this would force believers to translate their religious convictions into secular language understandable to all.

To shed light on this debate about the use of religious language in American politics, I turn to the rhetoric of Jesse Jackson, the civil rights leader, as an example of language containing the proper blend of religious commitment and political duty. An ordained Baptist minister, Jackson freely uses religious language and imagery in his political speeches. Yet, I would argue, he uses explicitly religious language in a way that is neither oppressive nor offensive to nonbelieving citizens.

Jesse Jackson's approach to politics is shaped by his roots. Although he ran for president in 1984 and again in 1988, he did not enter electoral politics

through political clubhouses or local party organizations. Jackson comes from two venerable traditions in American culture: the black church, with its singular combination of religion and political-social activism; and the civil rights movement of the 1960s, which struggled for racial justice in American society. From the black church, Jackson draws religious motivation and fundamental ideas and values; from the civil rights movement, Jackson takes the view that religious beliefs about human dignity need to permeate society, not just be affirmed in the activities of churches. Throughout his career, Jackson has consistently argued for social justice for all, regardless of race, color, creed, gender, or national origin.

In Jackson's approach to life, religion and politics are inseparably related. Religion is a source of personal motivation for him: "My religion obligates me to be political, that is, to seek to do God's will and allow the spiritual Word to become concrete justice and dwell among us. . . ." As this quote indicates, Jackson freely uses biblical language and imagery, referring, for example, in the previous passage to the beginning of the Gospel of St. John: "And the Word was made flesh and dwelt among us" (John 1:14). Moreover, Jackson's fundamental political goals are shaped by the biblical religion of the black churches. As Roger Hatch has noted, three general ideas form the core of his worldview: the dignity and worth of each individual, the interdependence and interrelation of all people and of all aspects of life, and the importance of vision.[70]

Jackson bases his idea of individual worth on the biblical notion that all human beings are made in God's image and hence have intrinsic value. His conviction that every person is God's child enables him to stress the importance of self-respect and self-esteem. This is the origin of Jackson's famous chant "I Am Somebody," which he invokes in speeches to students. As Jackson states, "[This] litany is designed to say to all of us, I may be poor, uneducated, unskilled, prematurely pregnant, on drugs, or victimized by racism—whether black, brown, red, yellow, or white—but I still count. I am somebody. I must be respected, protected, and never neglected because I am important and valuable to myself and others." By emphasizing the fundamental notion of self-respect and human dignity in this way, Jackson encourages political struggle against racism—a struggle that transforms people spiritually as well as psychologically.

Jackson's second basic idea, of human interdependence and interrelatedness, is also biblical in origin, rooted in the same fundamental notion of the parenthood of God and the kinship of all peoples. Jackson believes that although individual differences are important and must be acknowledged, in the end, all people, all institutions, and all dimensions of life are interrelated. He uses images of patchwork quilts and rainbows to convey the idea of diversity amidst unity. Interrelationships between people and between issues open up the possibility of forming progressive coalitions, which is at the center of

Jackson's approach to politics. The "Rainbow Coalition" signifies respect for individuals engaged in a common, cooperative effort.

Jackson's third fundamental idea is the notion of vision as being necessary for human fulfillment. He frequently quotes Proverbs 29:18: "Where there is no vision, the people perish." What President George Bush called "the vision thing" is, for Jackson, absolutely essential in American politics. Vision provides both goals and the hope of achieving those goals. Jackson redefines national greatness in terms of how we value and care for our people. Thus, it is not the size of our GNP or our military might that is the key to America's greatness. Rather, it is how we as a society care for the poor, the elderly, the children, the weak, and the vulnerable. This kind of vision has clear implications for government policies regarding education, health care, social security, poverty, immigration, welfare, and homelessness. For Jackson, politics must be informed by vision (as well as self-interest), and he is frank and forthright about the biblical roots of his vision of a transformed American society.

If Jackson's politics are so rooted in his religious principles, how is it that he has not often been accused of violating church-state separation and of using politics to impose his theology and religious beliefs upon everyone else? Jackson's blend of religion and politics, of discipleship and citizenship, raises the fundamental question about the role of religious convictions in American public life. Are Jackson's religious principles legitimate bases for determining public policy?

Roger Hatch suggests that the proper questions to ask about any religious or religion-based activity in the general political arena concern its *public effects*. We need to analyze how religious principles are brought to bear upon political judgments about strategy and public policy. If we examine how Jackson does this, we discover several important points. First, Jackson consistently appeals to people as fellow citizens, not as co-religionists or fellow believers, not as adherents of a common Christian religious tradition. His principles and political positions are effective insofar as they are persuasive to voters who are thinking and acting as citizens, not as fellow believers.

Second, insofar as Jackson appeals to religious principles, he appeals to them as public, not private, principles. This means that these principles are not his private possession and are not the result of a direct revelation to him from God. Other citizens can obtain them in a variety of ways. Jackson does not claim to have a special "hotline" to a God who privileges him with special insights and revelations.

Third, religious principles are open to criticism and challenge; they do not enjoy a privileged status because of their religious origin. They are legitimate insofar as they are open to reasoned argument and examination. Jackson's religious principles have no special authority in the political arena. Indeed, Jackson does not appeal to authority in his public discourse but argues ratio-

nally to elicit a consensus. Another way of saying this is to note that he does not employ religious principles to compel people to agree with him.

Fourth, because he appeals ultimately to reason as the final judge and arbiter of sound public policy, Jackson does not regard those who disagree with him as evil or satanic. His basic respect for his opponents is both principled and strategic. This is especially important, given Jackson's preferred political strategy. Since Jackson is genuinely interested in coalition politics, such tactics would undermine his efforts to build coalitions and to practice a politics of inclusion.

Jackson is, in my judgment, a good example of a political leader whose religion and politics are inseparable. Because Jackson addresses his fellow Americans as citizens and appeals to them on rational grounds; because he does not vilify his opponents as immoral, evil, or treasonous; and because he does not claim privileged access to divinity, Jackson exemplifies a political leader who legitimately draws upon his religious tradition for moral wisdom about sound public policy. Style and method are crucially important here, particularly because they embody the democratic value of basic respect for all fellow citizens, not just fellow believers. Although religion and politics are inseparably related for Jackson, he is not a theocrat but a democrat. He does not ask the theocratic question "Will God Approve?" He asks the democratic questions "Will the people approve, and is it good for the people?"

Mario Cuomo and the Relation Between Religion, Morality, and Public Policy

Former New York governor Mario Cuomo is another political leader who has negotiated reasonably safe passage through the swirling currents of church-state relations in the United States. During his twelve-year tenure as governor of New York (from 1983 to 1995), Cuomo, who is Roman Catholic, dealt with difficult moral issues such as abortion and the death penalty. Cuomo is known as an intelligent, articulate lawmaker who has often reflected upon the moral-political dilemmas confronting leaders in public life. During the 1984 presidential campaign, when controversy about the role of religion in American politics was particularly intense, Cuomo addressed the Department of Theology at the University of Notre Dame on the topic "Religious Belief and Public Morality." In this celebrated, controversial lecture, Cuomo considered the issue of abortion and his responsibilities as a Catholic public official. His address is deservedly well regarded as a pioneering discussion of the complexities of church-state relations in the United States and of what it means to be a religiously committed public official in a pluralistic society dedicated to religious freedom.[71]

As a Catholic governor, Cuomo described the dual responsibility inherent

in his position. His adherence to Roman Catholicism meant that he accepted his church's teaching on the immorality of abortion. However, his tenure as chief executive of the second largest state in the nation obligated him to create conditions under which everyone in this pluralist democracy could live with dignity and freedom. And this political duty to create conditions of harmony and tolerance for all—believers and nonbelievers—led Cuomo to embrace a position of personal opposition to abortion on moral grounds coupled with public support of abortion rights on legal grounds. It is Cuomo's "I'm-personally-opposed-in-conscience, but-I-publicly-support-legalized-abortion" view that has triggered controversy and criticism.

Cuomo's considered effort to balance religious commitment and political duty in the matter of abortion policy must be seen, of course, in the political context of the 1984 presidential election campaign. At that time, John Cardinal O'Connor, archbishop of New York, stated that the church could take disciplinary measures against Catholic lawmakers who did not use their power to translate the church's moral teaching against abortion into a public law banning all abortions. O'Connor's remarks were targeted specifically against the Democratic vice-presidential candidate Geraldine Ferraro, a Catholic congresswoman who supported abortion rights. That Ferraro was the first woman in American history to run for high national office on a major party ticket only heightened the political drama surrounding Cuomo's speech.[72]

In his Notre Dame address, Governor Cuomo made a compelling case for a Catholic lawmaker's personal moral opposition to, yet public support of, legalized abortion. To the bishop's assertion that Catholic officials have a moral obligation to challenge the legal status of abortion, Cuomo responded that there was nothing in church doctrine that required him to accept the political judgment of the bishops that the best way to combat abortion is to seek to outlaw it. Insisting that Catholics are not required to seek to have every church teaching enacted into law, Cuomo outlined a complex argument involving, first, a commitment to religious freedom, tolerance, and civic peace in a pluralist society; second, a recognition that religious belief probably cannot be translated into public policy in the absence of a broad consensus; third, a consequentialist assessment of the probable failure of antiabortion laws in reducing the incidence of abortion (it would be "Prohibition revisited," according to Cuomo); fourth, a suggestion that Catholics, who support the right to abortion in equal proportion to the rest of the population, should not use the law to compel non-Catholics to practice what Catholics themselves do not observe; and, fifth, a recommendation that pro-life and pro-choice forces should unite behind policy measures that would give women greater support and genuine choice in situations of unwanted pregnancy.

In making these arguments, Cuomo appealed to Catholic political thought, which has always acknowledged that the translation of religious values into public policy is a matter not of doctrine but of prudential judgment. The

church's traditional thinking about the state, law, and politics recognizes that not every sin need be made a crime and that prudence and calculation of the consequences of public policies are essential in a well-ordered society, particularly one of divided religious allegiance. Quoting their 1983 pastoral letter "The Challenge of Peace," Cuomo noted that the American Catholic bishops themselves recognize that "The Church's teaching authority does not carry the same force when it deals with technical solutions involving particular means as it does when it speaks of principles or ends. People may agree in abhorring an injustice, for instance, yet sincerely disagree as to what practical approach will achieve justice. Religious groups are as entitled as others to their opinion in such cases, but they should not claim that their opinions are the only ones that people of good will may hold."[73]

It is important to note that although he opposed a constitutional amendment outlawing abortion and he supported Medicaid funding, Governor Cuomo did not embrace either a religious or a political quietism on the subject of abortion policy. Instead, he suggested what might be called "a social justice agenda" (although those were not his words)—a wide range of public policies intended to enhance respect for all life and to reduce the incidence of abortion without coercing women. Advocating policies that would provide food, clothing, housing, job training, education, and medical care for poor women, Cuomo stated: "If we want to prove our regard for life in the womb, for the helpless infant—if we care about women having real choices in their lives and not being driven to abortions by a sense of helplessness and despair about the future of their child—then there is work enough for all of us. Lifetimes of it."

Both Mario Cuomo and Jesse Jackson exemplify conscientious political leaders who struggle for moral consistency in public life. They try to integrate discipleship and citizenship, to reconcile religious commitment and political duty. What can we learn from their efforts to clarify the role of religion in public life and the role of religiously based moral judgments in public debate about law and policy?

We learn, first of all, that religion need not be segregated or excluded from public life. Religion provides motivation for public service; as Jackson puts it, "My religion obligates me to be political." As for Cuomo, a speech he gave on "Catholics and the Commonweal" (in Brooklyn, N.Y., in 1988), emphasized his conviction that public service was a high, noble calling, a way of contributing to the common good of society and of fulfilling religious obligations to realize justice, care for the needy, give shelter to the homeless, and work for the welfare of all in society.[74] To the extent that religious traditions motivate people to enter public life to create conditions of harmony, peace, and prosperity, this would seem to be a positive factor (it certainly seems to be a better motivation for public service than greed or personal ambition).

Beyond motivation for public service, however, can religion contribute positively to the everyday work of politics and to the daily political debate over

substantive issues? I think that Jackson's political career shows how religious language and faith-based appeals can resonate with a people's historical traditions and can evoke a sense of continuity with the past. For example, the story of the Israelites' exodus from slavery in Egypt to the eventual freedom of the Promised Land in Israel—related in Exodus, the second book of the Hebrew Bible—has been used repeatedly in American politics by Jews, African Americans, and other civil rights advocates to set the context for, and evoke a sense of continuity with, historic, legitimate struggles for human freedom. To the extent that such biblical narrative and imagery can evoke a people's deeper vision of the kind of society they wish to be, such religious language, I would argue, has a role to play in public discourse. But the religious myths, stories, and references must have a wide resonance with many different groups in society, otherwise such references to sacred books can be narrowly sectarian and divisive. The exodus of the Jews from slavery in Egypt to the freedom of the Promised Land has wide appeal to Jews, Christians, liberation theologians, civil rights advocates, and to many nonreligious Americans who recall the history of slavery in this country. Notice, however, the use of religious language here: it functions metaphorically to provide meaning, to give voice to a people's legitimate ideals and aspirations, to articulate their vision of the type of just and free society they aspire to create.

A third lesson we can learn from Jackson's and Cuomo's use of religion, religious language, and religiously based moral convictions in public life has to do with the need to appeal to everyone in public debate and to shape the communal consensus necessary for sound public policy. These politicians teach us, I think, that the use of religious imagery in public life may be permissible, but that the use of religious doctrine or dogma to justify particular public policies may not be wise or prudent. In a religiously diverse society, the use of Catholic moral teaching to justify laws banning divorce, contraception, and abortion is exceedingly problematic because it involves giving official sanction or preference to one religious tradition's moral teachings over a host of competing, and even opposing, religious beliefs. What the writings and conduct of Jackson and Cuomo illustrate is an important political truism in American politics: that religious beliefs and teachings must be translated into rational, secular, broadly persuasive language in order to justify binding public policies. Religious-moral opposition to contraception, for example, must be reasonable and persuasive to many citizens before it can become the justification for public policies banning the sale, manufacture, and use of contraceptives.

Broadly speaking, both Cuomo and Jackson stress that religious beliefs can become part of the public morality underlying public policy, provided that they appeal to a broad communal consensus. If religious values are used to support policies that would impose restrictions on people that they find unacceptable, this simply may not work in a pluralistic democracy committed to

religious and political freedom. Although communal consensus is very important, the majority may not always be right and governments must take care not to unjustifiably and unduly coerce various religious and other minorities. Furthermore, an additional limit on the will of the majority is the duty of responsible lawmakers to make sound public policy. The chief criterion of sound public policy is not whether it accords with the will of God or even with the will of a democratic majority. It is the duty of legislators and executives to evaluate the wisdom or appropriateness of public policy by looking at the probable consequences if the legislation is enacted and enforced.

Cuomo's Notre Dame address illustrates this complex reasoning. As a Catholic public official, Cuomo finds no automatic answers in Christian theology and church teaching to the vexing public policy questions raised by the abortion issue. "There is neither an encyclical nor a catechism that spells out a political strategy for achieving legislative goals." Thus, whether a Catholic politician must use the power of his office to reinstate restrictive abortion laws is, for Cuomo, not a matter of doctrine but a matter of sound political judgment.

If abortion policy is a matter of prudent judgment, and if church teaching does not automatically dictate any political strategy, then Catholic public officials must engage in a measured attempt to balance moral truths against political realities. And one of these realities is that Catholic public officials take an oath to preserve the Constitution, which guarantees to Catholics and to all Americans religious and political freedom. Such freedom is not license; it imposes upon us duties of respect and tolerance for others and embodies an egalitarian quid pro quo. American Catholics know that "the price of seeking to force our beliefs on others is that they might someday force theirs on us."

Prudent political judgment suggests a consequentialist approach to reinstating restrictive abortion laws. Secular scholars and scholastics dating from the time of Thomas Aquinas have insisted that good lawmaking requires the presence of clear sanctions attached to law, the possibility of compliance and enforceability, and acceptance as useful by the majority of the governed. Traditional Catholic thought has always been realistic in acknowledging the possibilities and limits of lawmaking and state regulation.

Cuomo calls upon this tradition of "American Catholic realism" when he considers abortion law and policy. When he makes his judgment call, he says it would be better to enact policies that address the underlying causes of abortion than simply to outlaw abortion. Cuomo thinks we can best reduce the incidence of abortion and embody the crucial values of respect for life by using political power to pass laws and policies that get at the root causes of the high number of abortions in the United States: poverty, violence against women, and the need for child care assistance. Such generally pro-life policies also stand greater chances of being enacted than does a constitutional amendment banning abortion. In thus favoring policies that seem better designed to

achieve the goal of reducing abortions and have a better chance of being enacted, Cuomo fulfills his moral obligations as a public official to make and execute sound public policy.

To summarize, Mario Cuomo does not believe that church teaching requires him as a Catholic lawmaker to work toward the reinstatement of restrictive abortion laws. He does believe that abortion is profoundly wrong morally; moreover, he is willing to use political power to right the wrong by pressing for passage of laws and policies designed to enhance women's and children's lives and create genuine choice. He is not willing to use the coercive sanction of criminal law to right the wrong of abortion because, in his political judgment, such laws would not work and would have negative consequences. Moreover, in the absence of consensus, imposition of such laws risks violating constitutional freedoms. Cuomo concludes that "approval or rejection of legal restrictions on abortion should not be the exclusive litmus test of Catholic loyalty."

What can we learn from the efforts of Jesse Jackson and Mario Cuomo to reconcile and balance religious commitment and political duty? The conclusion seems inescapable that, in a pluralistic society, religiously derived and religiously justified moral convictions must be subject to the tests of rational argument and persuasiveness if they are to be universalized and made into public policy for all citizens. Moreover, prudent political judgments must be made in any attempt to have one's values embodied as part of our public morality. The thoughtful positions of Cuomo and Jackson on religion, morality, and public policy illustrate well these "hard truths" about the relationship between religion and politics in American society.

Let me clarify my position here in relation to Jelen's argument that, in a pluralistic liberal democracy, the use of religion as a justification for political values is impermissible. I agree with Jelen on this point. In a multicultural society such as the United States, the plain reality is that religious convictions may be articulated in the shaping of public policy, but no one will be persuaded by such convictions if they remain particularistic. We must all appeal to a common standard of reasonableness if we are to converse, persuade, and agree upon public policy. This is one of the requirements of living as citizens in a multicultural democracy.

Yet this is a very complex matter. The requirements of rationality and public accessibility that Jelen has explained so eloquently do not necessarily lead to a position of religious minimalism or strict separation. To be a consistent separationist, Jelen should favor exclusion of all possibly nonrational or irrational arguments from public debate. Religious beliefs and religiously based moral convictions are nonrational by definition; they are matters of faith, not of reason. Logically, it follows that they should be excluded from public debate. Moreover, not all secular moral principles or nonreligious ethical norms may be rational either. If this is so, then Jelen's rationality criterion would

mean these should also be barred from public discourse. Citizens should not burden each other with their own particular versions of theology, ethics, or their conceptions of the good life. Such views are matters of faith and may be nonrational, irrational, even possibly erroneous. Thus, they should not be admitted to the public square.

I disagree with this view, which seems to raise rather high barriers against using religious language in public discourse. As I argued earlier in the discussion of Jesse Jackson's use of biblical references, it seems obvious that excluding religious language and biblical imagery from public discourse would impoverish our language and deprive us of rich metaphorical allusions that convey meaning. After all, what is problematic about using religious language? We Americans used to be much more tolerant of such language—recall the many biblical allusions in the speeches of Abraham Lincoln. Those who favor the inclusion of religious language in political discourse argue that such language and imagery enriches public debate and enables people to express their deepest convictions and commitments. Surely Americans do not want to "dumb down" political discourse. As long as we use such language to communicate in an intelligent fashion, we need not bar religious metaphor and allusion from political speech. However, we had better be prepared to hear quotations from the Koran, the I Ching, and sacred Hindu writings as well as the Hebrew Bible and the New Testament.

This is my response to Jelen's argument that applying the criteria of rationality and public accessibility to religion is potentially discriminatory. I think it is—and therefore I would not bar admission to any religious voice in the public square. All views should be heard: "Let a hundred flowers bloom." The people will then decide what are appropriate justificatory arguments for sound public policy. As a democrat, I have faith in the rationality of the people to sift truth from error and to separate compelling policy reasons from weak ones.

Thus far, we have been examining how politicians and public officials integrate religious-moral values and civic duties. But the problem of reconciling religious commitment and political duty exists for clergy as well as for politicians. To see how religious leaders approach these same issues, we turn now to a case of clerical mobilization that attempted to override a recent presidential veto—specifically, the efforts of Roman Catholic and conservative evangelical clergy to organize voters to lobby Congress in 1996 in order to override President Clinton's veto of a measure banning late-term abortions. Once again, we will see the need for tolerance and restraint on the part of religious believers when they address the moral dimensions of public policy in a pluralistic society.

The American Catholic Church and Anti-Abortion Lobbying

The 1995–1996 controversy over the congressional ban of a late-term abortion procedure is a prime example of the difficulties church leaders and mem-

bers face in trying to bring moral values to bear in the shaping of public policy. In November 1995, the House of Representatives voted 288 to 139 to ban a method of late-term pregnancy termination called "intact dilation and extraction" by the medical community and its supporters and called "partial-birth abortion" by its opponents. One month later, the Senate also approved the bill 55 to 44 but included an amendment that would allow the procedure to be performed to save the life of the woman. (The Senate had rejected a broader amendment that sought to make an exception for a woman's health as well as her life.) After House and Senate versions of the bill were reconciled in conference, the House voted 286 to 129 to pass the so-called "partial-birth ban" (H.R. 1833) in March 1996, and the bill was then sent to the White House for the president's signature.[75]

On April 10, 1996, President Clinton vetoed the bill because it did not include an exception to the ban for cases in which the woman's health would be seriously harmed by carrying a pregnancy to term.[76] A month earlier Clinton had sent a letter to Capitol Hill expressing his concern about this "very disturbing" procedure. Saying that he could not "support its use on an elective basis," he nevertheless wrote of "rare and tragic" circumstances in which the procedure might be needed to save a woman's life or health, and he said that exceptions for such cases must be included in the legislation to meet the constitutional requirements set by the Supreme Court. In announcing his veto of the bill, President Clinton was joined in the Roosevelt Room of the White House by several families who had had to face situations that called for the procedure. These couples learned in late pregnancy that, for example, the fetus's brain was developing outside the skull, or that the fetus suffered from a chromosomal disorder that would probably cause it to die in the womb. Both women, in grief, had opted for the intact dilation and extraction procedure. President Clinton allowed the families with him in the Roosevelt Room to share their stories as a counter-balance to the lurid descriptions of the procedure that anti-abortion groups were then circulating.[77]

Shortly after the president's veto, the eight Roman Catholic cardinals in the United States, together with the president of the National Conference of Catholic Bishops, wrote a public letter to President Clinton strenuously protesting his veto. The three-page letter accused the president of deciding to permit a procedure "more akin to infanticide than abortion." Terming Clinton's decision "shameful" and "beyond comprehension," the cardinals pledged to do all they could in the coming months to inform people of the issue and to encourage "Catholics and other people of good will" to urge Congress to override the president's veto.[78]

The cardinals and the bishops' conference followed through systematically on this pledge to mobilize voters to urge a congressional override. Throughout the late spring, summer, and early fall of 1996, these episcopal leaders held prayer services and wrote columns in their diocesan newspapers denouncing

President Clinton's veto. Boston's Cardinal Bernard Law, who heads the NCCB pro-life committee, appeared on David Brinkley's *ABC Sunday Morning News* program to urge that "every effort should be made to override this veto." ABC correspondent Cokie Roberts then asked Cardinal Law: "Are you saying that Catholics should not vote for politicians who voted against this ban or for the president who vetoed it?" Cardinal Law replied: "Well, I can only speak for myself. I think Catholics will vote . . . the way they want to vote. But it does seem to me that the basic right to life, which is so imperiled by a procedure such as this, would certainly cause one to think very, very carefully before voting for someone who would be supportive of permissiveness with regard to this procedure."[79]

On several occasions, Cardinal John O'Connor of New York urged people to contact members of Congress and urge them to override President Clinton's veto. He also urged Roman Catholics to return to the traditional practice of not eating meat on Fridays as a protest if Congress failed to override.[80] The bishops' conference then distributed millions of pre-printed postcards at Sunday Mass services throughout the summer. Parishioners were urged to send these postcards to their congressmen, urging them to override Clinton's veto of H.R. 1833. Sermons were preached and church members were exhorted to lobby Congress. One week before the vote, eight U.S. cardinals were among more than seventy prelates and hundreds of Catholics who held a prayer service on the steps of the U.S. Capitol. All in all, the American Catholic bishops led a massive political campaign during a presidential election year to achieve congressional override of the president's veto.[81]

For its part, the Christian Coalition's Catholic Alliance took as its first major initiative the task of promoting a grassroots effort to override the veto. The Catholic Alliance is an effort to mobilize Catholic voters under the Christian Coalition's mostly evangelical Protestant and conservative umbrella by emphasizing solidarity with the Catholic hierarchy's position on abortion. Proclaiming solidarity with Pope John Paul II and American Catholic bishops, the Catholic Alliance circulated postcards and petitions to Congress and solicited funds from Catholics to support their nationwide drive to override the Clinton veto. In particular, they targeted "several Catholic members of our U.S. Senate [who] think they have a clearer insight on God's law and His gift of life than Holy Mother Church." The targeted senators included: Ted Kennedy (D-MA), John Kerry (D-MA), Patty Murray (D-WA), Chris Dodd (D-CT), Tom Daschle (D-SD), Barbara Mikulski (D-MD), Tom Harkin (D-IOWA), Patrick Leahy (D-VT), and Carol Moseley-Braun (D-IL).

On September 19, 1996, the House of Representatives voted 285 to 137 to overturn Clinton's veto of this late-term abortion procedure. However, a week later (September 26), the Senate failed to get the two-thirds vote needed for override, thereby sustaining the president's veto.[82] Thus, despite an exhaustive effort to mobilize political pressure against "partial-birth abortion," the

American Catholic hierarchy and the Christian Coalition's Catholic Alliance were not successful. Leaders of the Christian Coalition vowed retribution at the polls in the November 1996 presidential elections.

What can we learn from this unusual case of political intervention by a significant number of clerical and episcopal leaders? The first thing we might consider is that perhaps such political mobilizations led by church leaders are not all that uncommon in American politics. African American churches, for example, have often invited political leaders such as the Rev. Jesse Jackson or former Congressman William Gray (also a clergyman) to address moral-political issues from the pulpit. Political and religious concerns have been closely intertwined in black congregations partly because, for many years, blacks were denied other avenues of access to the political process. African Americans often faced discrimination by political party organizations or interest groups. Frequently, black churches were the only community organizations where African Americans could congregate and mobilize to speak out against injustice and discrimination.

The unusual situation of black churches, black clergy, and black political activists was not typical, however, of other churches. White Protestants and Roman Catholics did have access to political party organizations and pressure groups and could run for office in primaries and general elections. Historically, as we have already noted, religiously minded citizens have used the political process to convey their message about the need for moral reform in American society. Whether abolitionists or prohibitionists, ordinary Americans have formed social protest movements as a means of bringing religiously based moral judgments to bear in political debates about sound public policy. As I have argued earlier, American citizens cannot, and should not be expected to, separate their religious-moral beliefs from their participation in public policy debates.

However, it is one thing for ordinary, believing citizens to address the moral dimensions of policy issues—and quite another for clerical leaders to do so. Clergy and bishops occupy positions of authority within their denominations and speak with special religious authority from the pulpit. This is especially true within hierarchically structured churches such as the Roman Catholic Church. Catholics regard their bishops and priests as officially appointed teachers of religious doctrine and moral principles and accord their judgments a certain degree of respect and deference. Problems arise, however, when bishops and clergy use the pulpit to suggest which *political* judgments citizens should make. While lay Catholics owe their religious leaders respectful consideration, they do not and cannot, as citizens in a democracy, abdicate their responsibility to make their own prudential political judgments about candidates and issues. Bishops and priests who ignore these political realities act to undermine principles of democratic governance and civic participation. In using the privileges and trappings of religious authority to influence political

decision making, clergy fail to show proper respect for the political autonomy of their parishioners, who are, after all, their political equals in a liberal democracy.

It is morally and politically risky for church leaders to blur the distinction between religious and political authority. The first risk that clergy run is to be perceived as more politically powerful than they actually are. The old adage about whether "the generals have any troops" still pertains to the situation of church leaders who take specific political positions and claim to speak for the faithful. Claims to deliver the Catholic vote are, for example, risky since Catholic lay people do not always, or even usually, follow the lead of their bishops and priests. The NCCB's claim to represent and speak for Catholics in Washington or to represent the official Catholic position on a particular policy issue may be legitimately questioned when lay Catholics do not follow their leaders' suggestions on how to vote or lobby. The risk the bishops run here is that their failure to deliver the Catholic vote will mean that politicians and officeholders can then ignore the hierarchy's moral message because the bishops have no political clout in terms of votes.

A second risk religious leaders take in conducting massive political campaigns to, for example, secure a congressional override of a presidential veto is that their churches will be perceived by the general public to be simply institutional interest groups like all the other special interests that dot the American political landscape. The danger here is that the deeper spiritual and moral contribution churches can make to American culture will be lost sight of. Churches, it seems to me, are more than mere interest groups and political action committees. They have a special duty to attend to the common good and to universal values of peace and justice. By engaging so directly in the political process, churches risk undermining their distinctively religious mission to witness to transcendent values and to a spiritual realm of interiority that, in my judgment, American society sorely needs. In other words, the political activities of churches and clergy could ultimately be self-defeating.

Politicizing Church Services to Mobilize Catholic Voters

If Catholic churchmen should respect the constitutional obligations of Catholic lawmakers, they should also respect the citizen rights of Catholic voters. Concretely, this means that bishops and clergy should not use the pulpit to issue voting instructions or otherwise exert coercive pressure on Catholic voters. Catholics do not go to Mass in order to be politically mobilized. Using church services as centers for grassroots mobilization and using sermon time as an occasion for distributing postcards to mail to Congress is, some would argue, an improper politicization of the sacred liturgy.

The use of Sunday Masses to organize a postcard drive for the congressional override of President Clinton's veto of the "partial-birth abortion" ban

is merely the latest example of this tactic. In 1993 and 1994, postcards were distributed nationwide to parishioners during the Catholic Mass, urging them to lobby Congress to oppose inclusion of abortion coverage in a national health plan. Another example of such political mobilization occurred during the 1989 gubernatorial election campaign in New Jersey. On Respect Life Sunday (October 1, 1989), Catholics in three New Jersey dioceses were asked during Mass to sign pledge cards authorizing pro-life commissions to use the resulting list of names (called a "Life Roll") to lobby for pro-life legislation.[83]

Politicizing the liturgy in this manner is questionable from an ecclesiological perspective. The Catholic Mass is an inappropriate forum for conducting political mobilization campaigns. It could be argued that using sermon time to exhort a captive audience of congregants to sign political pledge cards is coercive of conscience and disrespectful to Catholic citizens who have a right and a duty to make their own judgments about sound public policy. Within the church, bishops are moral teachers, but in a pluralist democracy members of the hierarchy do not necessarily have either the competence or the right to tell citizens how to vote or what policies to support.

Furthermore, such political mobilizations are imprudent and improper because they suggest that there is a single policy position that all Catholics should adopt. As Governor Cuomo noted, there are no automatic answers in Christian theology and Catholic teaching to the vexing questions of public policy raised by the abortion issue. Abortion policy must balance the conflicting claims of different interests (believers, agnostics, and atheists) as well as the competing values of freedom, order, equity, justice, and privacy. There is no single Catholic solution to this *policy* dilemma just as there is no single Jewish or no single Methodist answer.

Bishops are religious and moral teachers, but they do not have, by virtue of their office, any special expertise in public policy. They must therefore recognize that they have no special competence in the politics of a liberal democratic society. They may be good managers and diocesan administrators, and they may be experts in internal church politics, but little in their seminary training or clerical experience in a hierarchically structured, authoritative teaching institution has prepared them for civic participation in a democratic polity. As citizens, clerical and lay Catholics are equals. The bishops have no special expertise in public policymaking that would give them the authority to tell Catholic lawmakers how to do their jobs. Nor do the clergy have any special knowledge or insight that would confer upon them the right to tell Catholic citizens how to vote. On those occasions when bishops and priests have taken Catholic politicians to task over the abortion issue or used the pulpit to issue voting instructions, they have exceeded their legitimate authority as church leaders. Such clerical intervention is inappropriate in a democratic society. Not only do the bishops risk losing their tax exemption by such partisan actions; they also betray insufficient awareness of the meaning of

church-state separation and of the tension American Catholics feel between a hierarchical church and a democratic government.

To summarize: In 1996, Roman Catholic bishops and priests in the United States conducted a massive political campaign to secure a congressional override of President Clinton's veto of the ban on "partial-birth abortions." This occurred during a presidential election campaign in which President Clinton's opponent, former Senator Robert Dole, denounced Clinton's veto. The Catholic bishops' campaign for a congressional override thus appeared to be very partisan during an election year in which the Catholic vote was touted as the crucial swing vote. It also opened the bishops' conference to the charge that they were, once again, focusing on a single issue—abortion—to the exclusion of other important political issues (e.g., immigration, health care, education, welfare reform, and tax cuts). The bishops did make statements about these other issues during the 1996 campaign, but no other issue triggered such a massive mobilization and postcard drive by Catholic Church leaders as did the campaign against "partial-birth abortion." Aside from the fact that this campaign was unsuccessful, it in effect conveyed the message that, when it comes to abortion, Catholic leaders are willing to be partisan and single-issue in their politics. Moreover, they are willing to politicize the Sunday liturgy and to use their clerical authority to tell parishioners how to lobby Congress to shape public policy. All of this suggests to me that the commitment of Catholic clergy to the spirit of the First Amendment religion clauses, to church-state separation, to nonpartisanship in presidential elections—and, above all, to respect for parishioners as democratic equals—is perhaps weak and tenuous.

To reiterate, religious leaders may use the pulpit to teach theology and morality, but their religious authority brings with it no special expertise in politics and no extraordinary competence in making prudential political judgments. In fact, in a liberal democracy, just the opposite is true; as citizens, church leaders and members are democratic equals, which means that each must respect the political autonomy of his or her fellow citizens.

As citizens, church leaders do have the right to contribute to public policy debate and to try to influence the political process. However, bishops and clergy cannot impose minoritarian or sectarian positions on others in our pluralistic democracy, but must use the persuasive power of rational argument to influence public opinion and fashion a consensus, say, against elective abortion.

Clergy may also use the power of example to convey their abhorrence of abortion as immoral. That is, the Catholic Church, by conducting programs of assistance for involuntarily pregnant women and their families, can provide practical alternatives to abortion and can also exemplify the commitment to charity that is the hallmark of Catholic Christianity. The Church can teach

by example rather than by passing coercive civil and criminal laws banning abortion.

In a pluralist society committed to religious freedom and church-state separation, religiously devout citizens must exercise tolerance and restraint in addressing the moral dimensions of public policy. They should be wary of establishing religion. As A. J. Reichley wrote, "Politicians honoring religious freedom should forgo using religion as a campaign device. And the churches, to preserve their autonomy and their integrity, should usually hold themselves some distance above the rough-and-tumble of ordinary politics, whether in election campaigns or on Capitol Hill."[84]

Conclusion

In the history of American culture and politics, we have never really had what Jelen calls "religious minimalism." Churches have been actively involved in public affairs, and government has always aided and accommodated religion, even if only indirectly. We Americans have found it virtually impossible to separate religion and politics. Even during the past fifty years of Supreme Court jurisprudence, when the Court was guided for the most part by a strict separationist conception of church-state relations, government has continued to aid religious groups in many social service activities for the benefit of the public good. In my judgment, religious minimalism fails to reflect accurately these realities of American history and politics.

I also reject religious minimalism because it provides insufficient protection for the free exercise rights of religious citizens. In a genuinely liberal democracy, believers have the right to participate in the political process and to bring to bear their religiously derived moral principles in democratic deliberation about sound public policy. Instead of erecting a high wall of separation, a people's democracy must accord believers a place at the table and be prepared to take their arguments seriously.

At the same time, I agree with Jelen that religious proponents must argue intelligibly in their effort to persuade nonbelievers of the wisdom of their policy recommendations. Religious language should not be excluded automatically from public debate by appeal to some mythological "wall of separation." However, appeals to theological doctrines cannot, by themselves, justify public policies in a society constitutionally committed to church-state separation. The civic rights of believers entitle them to an equal say in the political process, but believers themselves must be prepared to translate their religious convictions into the rational arguments that are necessary to create a public policy consensus.

Finally, I do not find Jelen's argument convincing, that religion subverts democratic governance. On the contrary, in this essay I have tried to show the

ways in which religion enhances democracy in the United States. In American society, religion broadens political representation, and religious lobbies provide a much-needed corrective to the bias toward wealth in the American interest group system. In addition, churches train people in the civic skills necessary for effective political participation, educate citizens in the moral values supportive of democracy, and serve as mediating institutions and protective buffers between the individual and the state. In this way churches and synagogues serve as agents of resistance to limit the potential tyranny of majoritarian democracy.

What can we conclude about the role of religion in American public life? I contend that the phrase "wall of separation between church and state" is an inapt metaphor. It is too rigid and absolute; it suggests an impregnable barrier between church and state—a high wall that permits churches, mosques, and temples little access to governmental institutions. It is also rather confusing. The phrase has become a separationist's mantra, routinely invoked whenever churches and government agencies appear to cooperate to address social problems such as the need for child care or healthcare. Moreover, the metaphor fails to capture adequately the many ways in American history in which religion and politics have been related—whether in social protest movements against slavery and war or in favor of civil rights and women's suffrage.

Unfortunately, we are stuck with this metaphor. It is part of our historical legacy, traceable to Roger Williams and Thomas Jefferson and invoked in several decisions by the U.S. Supreme Court. But if we fully realize the inadequacy of this phrase, perhaps we can begin discussing the cracks in the wall of separation—points of intersection between church and state where religious citizens can legitimately bring moral judgments derived from various faith traditions to bear in debating public policy. We know from American history that religious institutions and religiously motivated citizens often cooperate to improve politics and public policy and generally contribute to the common good. We also know that religiously based moral judgments can support fundamental political values such as equality, justice, and liberty—which, at the moment, are badly in need of philosophical support and intellectual buttressing.

In the end, the obligation of citizen equals in a democratic republic is to converse and deliberate about sound public policy. There is no reason why individual Americans should not bring religiously based moral judgments into this conversation—as long as such moral judgments are subjected to the rational scrutiny of all citizens. As a society, we have come to accept that one's race, gender, and ethnicity provide valuable insights and perspectives that should be brought into our civil conversation. If this is true, why exclude religion from the mix of backgrounds, contexts, and perspectives? Of course, the obligation of every citizen to respect diversity and freedom of religion obtains. At the same time, religiously devout citizens have every right to bring

faith perspectives to bear in deliberating about sound public policy and the direction of our politics. At stake here is the quality and character of American public life. As John Courtney Murray once suggested, a republic is a civil conversation; when civility stops, the republic is dead.

Notes

1. These introductory thoughts are partly inspired by a 1989 PBS video documentary "The Supreme Court's Holy Battles," with Roger Mudd as narrator (originally from WHYY in Philadelphia).

2. See James Madison's "A Memorial and Remonstrance on the Religious Rights of Man," where he argues that religion has flourished without governmental assistance (pages 132–37 in the volume).

3. Commenting on the past fifty years of the Supreme Court's church-state jurisprudence, Stephen Monsma contends that the Court took a wrong turn in its landmark 1947 case *Everson v. Board of Education of Ewing Township,* 330 U.S. 1:

> Strict separationist, no-aid-to-religion language still stands as the official interpretation of the First Amendment, yet countless forms of financial and other types of cooperation between government and religious groups continue. The Supreme Court has approved public expenditures for textbooks for religiously based schools, a paid chaplain in a state legislature, a city-owned creche as part of a Christmas display, the placement of a cross on a state capitol grounds, and public funding for religiously based colleges and universities, hospitals, and teenage counseling centers. In a recent year, 65 percent of the Catholic Charities' revenues came from government sources, as did 75 percent of the Jewish Board of Family and Children's Services' revenues, and 55 percent of Lutheran Social Ministries' revenues. . . . All this occurs in a society whose highest court has declared that its Constitution prohibits "any taxes in any amount, large or small" from going to support "any religious activities or institutions, whatever they may be called." The juxtaposition of soaring rhetoric declaring no aid to religion as a constitutional norm with a host of instances where government aids or supports religion is one of the key legacies of *Everson.*

See Stephen V. Monsma, "The Wrong Road Taken," in *Everson Revisited: Religion, Education, and Law at the Crossroads,* ed. Jo Renée Formicola and Hubert Morken (Lanham, Md.: Rowman & Littlefield, 1997), 129–30.

4. Stephen L. Carter, *The Culture of Disbelief: How American Law and Politics Trivialize Religious Devotion* (New York: Basic Books, 1993), 4.

5. William Lee Miller, *The First Liberty: Religion and the American Republic* (New York: Alfred A. Knopf, 1986), 156.

6. William Lee Miller, *The First Liberty,* 157.

7. For an overview of the Puritan legacy, see Robert Booth Fowler and Allen D. Hertzke, *Religion and Politics in America: Faith, Culture, and Strategic Choices* (Boulder, Colo.: Westview, 1995). See also Barry Alan Shain, *The Myth of American*

Individualism: The Protestant Origins of American Political Thought (Princeton, N.J.: Princeton University Press, 1994).

8. Perry Miller, *Roger Williams: His Contribution to the American Tradition* (Indianapolis: Bobbs-Merrill, 1953), 22–23.

9. Fowler and Hertzke, *Religion and Politics in America,* 6.

10. Alexander Hamilton, James Madison, and John Jay, *The Federalist* (New York: Modern Library, 1937). See especially Numbers 47, 48, 49, and 51.

11. Fowler and Hertzke, *Religion and Politics in America,* 7–8. See also Allen D. Hertzke, *Echoes of Discontent: Jesse Jackson, Pat Robertson, and the Resurgence of Populism* (Washington, D.C.: CQ Press, 1993).

12. Paul Weber, "Strict Neutrality: The Next Step in First Amendment Development?" in *Religion in American Politics,* ed. Charles Dunn (Washington, D.C.: CQ Press, 1989), 29.

13. For a discussion of religious lobbies, see Allen D. Hertzke, *Representing God in Washington: The Role of Religious Lobbies in the American Polity* (Knoxville: University of Tennessee Press, 1988). See also Daniel J. B. Hofrenning, *In Washington But Not of It: The Prophetic Politics of Religious Lobbyists* (Philadelphia: Temple University Press, 1995).

14. Scholars usually mention at least three criteria that define evangelicalism: belief in the absolute authority of Scripture, a born-again or conversion experience, and an eagerness to evangelize others. See Richard John Neuhaus, "The Public Square," in *First Things* 37 (November 1993), 48. For a fuller discussion of the meaning of the term *evangelical,* see Randall Balmer, *Mine Eyes Have Seen the Glory: A Journey into the Evangelical Subculture in America* (New York: Oxford University Press, 1989).

15. Balmer, *Mine Eyes Have Seen the Glory,* ix–xii.

16. See Martin Marty and R. Scott Appleby, *The Glory and the Power: The Fundamentalist Challenge to the Modern World* (Boston: Beacon Press, 1992).

17. Balmer, *Mine Eyes Have Seen the Glory,* xii.

18. Fowler and Hertzke, *Religion and Politics in America,* 115. See also Charles W. Dunn, ed., *American Political Theology: Historical Perspective and Theoretical Analysis* (New York: Praeger, 1984), chap. 6.

19. Fowler and Hertzke, *Religion and Politics in America,* 39. See also Jim Wallis, *The Soul of Politics: A Practical and Prophetic Vision for Change* (New York: New Press and Orbis Books, 1994).

20. Gary Potter, "A Christian America," *New York Times,* 15 October 1980, A31.

21. Robert T. Handy, *A Christian America: Protestant Hopes and Historical Realities* (New York: Oxford University Press, 1984), 3.

22. A. James Reichley, "Religion and the Constitution," in *Religion and American Politics,* ed. Charles W. Dunn (Washington, D.C.: CQ Press, 1989), 4.

23. William Lee Miller, *The First Liberty,* 153–54.

24. Reichley, "Religion and the Constitution," 4.

25. See John E. Semonche, *Religion and Constitutional Government in the United States* (Carrboro, N.C.: Signal Books, 1986); Leonard Levy, *The Establishment Clause: Religion and the First Amendment* (Chapel Hill: University of North Carolina Press, 1994); and Leo Pfeffer, *Church, State, and Freedom* (Boston: Beacon Press, 1967).

26. Madison, "A Memorial and Remonstrance," pp. 132–37 in this volume. See also Thomas Jefferson, "A Bill for Establishing Religious Freedom," in William Lee Miller, *The First Liberty,* 357–58; and Thomas Jefferson, *Notes on Virginia,* pp. 126–29 in this volume.

27. For details of Williams's life, see Perry Miller, *Roger Williams*; Edmund S. Morgan, *Roger Williams: The Church and the State* (New York: Harcourt, Brace and World, 1967); and William Lee Miller, *The First Liberty.* Recent literature on Williams includes Jimmy D. Neff, "Roger Williams: Pious Puritan and Strict Separationist," *Journal of Church and State* 38, no. 3 (Summer 1996): 529–46 and Stephen Phillips, "Roger Williams and the Two Tables of the Law," pp. 547–68, in the same publication.

28. Roger Williams, "Mr. Cotton's Letter Lately Printed, Examined and Answered" (London, 5 February 1644), reprinted in Perry Miller, *Roger Williams,* 89–100 (the quote is on 98).

29. Roger Williams, "Letter to the Town of Providence" (Providence, January 1655), reprinted in Perry Miller, *Roger Williams,* 225–26.

30. A. James Reichley, *Religion in American Public Life* (Washington, D.C.: Brookings Institution, 1985), 67.

31. Thomas Jefferson, *Notes on Virginia,* pp. 126–29 in this volume.

32. Thomas Jefferson, "Reply to the Danbury Baptist Association," p. 125 in this volume. Daniel Dreisbach has argued persuasively that the "wall of separation" metaphor was first used by James Burgh, an eighteenth-century British political writer widely read in revolutionary America. Jefferson read and admired Burgh's work but was not familiar with the writings of Roger Williams. As a Scottish dissenter, Burgh distrusted established churches and argued for religious toleration. In *Crito,* Burgh proposed building "an impenetrable wall of separation between things sacred and civil." James Burgh, *Crito, or Essays on Various Subjects,* 2 vols. (London, 1766, 1767), II: 68, as cited in Daniel Dreisbach, " 'Sowing Useful Truths and Principles': The Danbury Baptists, Thomas Jefferson, and the 'Wall of Separation,' " *Journal of Church and State* 39, no. 3 (Summer 1997): 455–501. Dreisbach also contends that Jefferson's use of the "wall" metaphor was primarily about the principle of federalism rather than about the goals of separationism. In responding to the congratulatory letter from the Danbury Baptists, Jefferson wanted to explain why he, as president, declined to issue religious proclamations for days of fasting and thanksgiving, whereas he did not hesitate to decree or call for days of prayer and fasting as governor of Virginia and as a Virginia state legislator in the 1770s. This apparent inconsistency was the context for his response to the Danbury Baptists. According to Dreisbach, "A careful review of Jefferson's actions throughout his public career suggests that he believed, as a matter of federalism, the national government had no jurisdiction in religious matters, whereas state governments were authorized to accommodate and even prescribe religious exercises." Thus, in using the "wall of separation" metaphor in his letter to the Danbury Baptists, Jefferson was not addressing the broad issue of separation between religion and all civil government (both federal and state); rather, he was addressing the narrow issue of whether a separation between the entire federal government and religion was required by the First Amendment.

33. *Everson v. Board of Education of Ewing Township* 330 U.S. 1 (1947), pp. 160–68 in this volume. See also *Everson Revisited: Religion, Education, and Law at*

112   *Mary C. Segers*

the Crossroads, ed. Jo Renée Formicola and Hubert Morken (Lanham, Md.: Rowman & Littlefield, 1997). In addition to *Everson*, the "wall of separation" metaphor was also used by the Supreme Court in *Reynolds v. United States* 98 U.S. 145 (1879).

34. Carter, *The Culture of Disbelief*, 105.

35. Carter, *The Culture of Disbelief*, 107.

36. Weber, "Strict Neutrality," 25.

37. Weber, "Strict Neutrality," 27.

38. *Lemon v. Kurtzman*, 403 U.S. 602 (1971), pp. 168–70 in this volume.

39. Statistics are from Fowler and Hertzke, *Religion and Politics in America*, chap. 2.

40. Fowler and Hertzke, *Religion and Politics in America*, 28.

41. Fowler and Hertzke, *Religion and Politics in America*, 31.

42. See *Being Right: Conservative Catholics in America*, ed. Mary Jo Weaver and R. Scott Appleby (Bloomington: Indiana University Press, 1995).

43. See *Employment Division, Department of Human Resources of Oregon v. Smith* 494 U.S. 872 (1990), pp. 171–84 in this volume.

44. *Wisconsin v. Yoder* 406 U.S. 205 (1972).

45. *Church of the Lukumi Babalu Aye v. City of Hialeah* 508 U.S. 520 (1993).

46. *The Politics of Aristotle*, ed. Ernest Barker (New York: Oxford University Press, 1962), Book III, Chapters VI–XIII, pp. 170–88.

47. See Hertzke, *Representing God in Washington*.

48. Hertzke, *Representing God in Washington*, 16.

49. See Hertzke, *Echoes of Discontent*.

50. John A. Coleman, "Under the Cross and the Flag: Reflections on Discipleship and Citizenship in America," *America* 174, no. 16 (11 May 1996): 6–14.

51. Coleman, "Under the Cross and the Flag," 7.

52. Coleman is relying on a fascinating debate among contemporary political scientists and sociologists about the relationship between political participation and a strong civic and social life in local and regional groups. He cites Robert Putnam's classic essay "Bowling Alone: America's Declining Social Capital," *Journal of Democracy* 6 (January 1995): 65–78, as well as his earlier study of civic voluntarism in Italy, *Making Democracy Work: Civic Traditions in Modern Italy* (Princeton: Princeton University Press, 1993). See also Robert D. Putnam, "Tuning In, Tuning Out: The Strange Disappearance of Social Capital in America," *PS: Political Science and Politics* 28 (December 1995): 664–83; Nicholas Lemann, "Kicking in Groups," *The Atlantic Monthly* 277, no. 4 (April 1996): 22–26; and Michael W. Foley and Bob Edwards, "The Paradox of Civil Society," *Journal of Democracy* 7:3 (1996): 38–52.

53. Sidney Verba, Kay Schlozman, and Henry E. Brady, *Voice and Equality: Civic Voluntarism in American Politics* (Cambridge, Mass.: Harvard University Press, 1995), chaps. 11 and 13.

54. Verba, Schlozman, and Brady, *Voice and Equality*, 320 and 330.

55. Coleman, "Under the Cross and the Flag," 10.

56. Verba, Schlozman, and Brady, *Voice and Equality*, 333.

57. Verba, Schlozman, and Brady, *Voice and Equality*, 329.

58. Coleman, "Under the Cross and the Flag," 10.

59. Carter, *The Culture of Disbelief*, 37.

60. See Herbert A. Deane, *The Political and Social Ideas of St. Augustine* (New York: Columbia University Press, 1964), 1–12.

61. Carter, *The Culture of Disbelief,* 16.

62. Carter, *The Culture of Disbelief,* 37.

63. Reichley, *Religion and American Public Life,* 359.

64. A. James Reichley, "Democracy and Religion," *PS: Political Science and Politics* 19, no. 3 (Fall 1986): 805.

65. Contributors to this debate include Robert Audi, "The State, the Church, and the Citizen," and Nicholas Wolterstorff, "Why We Should Reject What Liberalism Tells Us About Speaking and Acting in Public for Religious Reasons," both in *Religion and Contemporary Liberalism,* ed. Paul Weithman (South Bend, Ind.: University of Notre Dame Press, 1997). See also Michael Perry, *Religion in Politics: Constitutional and Moral Perspectives* (New York: Oxford University Press, 1997) and *Love and Power: The Role of Religion and Morality in American Politics* (New York: Oxford University Press, 1991); and Robert Audi and Nicholas Wolterstorff, *Religion in the Public Square: The Place of Religious Convictions in Political Debate* (Lanham, Md.: Rowman & Littlefield, 1997).

66. Reichley, "Democracy and Religion," 801.

67. Reichley suggests that "religious bodies can avoid social intolerance by acknowledging that human imperfection clouds and corrupts the judgments of all institutions, including the churches, or by limiting their social pronouncement to broad moral directives." However, he warns that "In practice . . . individuals or institutions claiming to represent transcendent moral authority are often tempted to attach certainty to their opinions on complex issues in secular politics." Reichley, "Democracy and Religion," 801.

68. Reichley, "Democracy and Religion," 801.

69. Robert Audi, cited in Coleman, "Under the Cross and the Flag," 14.

70. See Roger D. Hatch, "Jesse Jackson in Two Worlds," in *Religion in American Politics,* ed. Charles W. Dunn (Washington, D.C.: CQ Press, 1989), 87–101. Note the interesting comparison of Jesse Jackson and Pat Robertson in Hertzke, *Echoes of Discontent.* See also Thomas H. Landess and Richard M. Quinn, *Jesse Jackson and the Politics of Race* (Ottawa, Ill.: Jameson Books, 1985); and Adolph L. Reed, Jr., *The Jesse Jackson Phenomenon: The Crisis of Purpose in Afro-American Politics* (New Haven: Yale University Press, 1986).

71. Mario M. Cuomo, "Religious Belief and Public Morality: A Catholic Governor's Perspective," pp. 144–59 in this volume.

72. See Mary C. Segers, "Ferraro, the Bishops, and the 1984 Election," in *Shaping New Vision: Gender and Values in American Culture,* ed. Clarissa W. Atkinson, Constance H. Buchanan, and Margaret R. Miles (Ann Arbor, Mich.: UMI Research Press, 1987), 143–67.

73. Mario M. Cuomo, "Religious Belief and Public Morality," pp. 144–59 in this volume.

74. Mario M. Cuomo, "Catholics and the Commonweal," address presented at the Church of St. James, Brooklyn, New York, October 1988. The source here is the author's notes; she was present in the audience that evening.

75. David W. Hendon and James M. Kennedy, "Notes on Church-State Affairs,"

Journal of Church and State 38, no. 3 (Summer 1996): 683–85. In the 104th Congress, the bill was called H.R. 1833, the "Partial-Birth Abortion Act of 1995."

76. *New York Times,* 11 April 1996, A1 and A24. See also Clinton's defense of his veto in *New York Times,* 14 December 1996, 1 and 10. (This last is the Saturday *New York Times,* which does not use numbers with letters, but numbers only.)

77. Hendon and Kennedy, "Notes on Church-State Affairs," 684–85.

78. *New York Times,* 17 April 1996, A19. The Cardinals' letter to President Clinton is reprinted in *Origins* 25 (25 April 1996): 753–56. See also Timothy A. Byrnes, "There They Go Again: The Bishops, Abortion, and Presidential Politics," *Conscience* 18, no. 2 (Summer 1996): 3–8. The Vatican also condemned Clinton's veto; news release from the Associated Press, 19 April 1996 (from the Internet).

79. Transcript of Sunday Morning ABC News program with David Brinkley, 21 April 1996, from the Federal Document Clearing House (reprinted from the Internet).

80. "O'Connor Backs Criticism of Clinton Abortion Veto," *New York Times,* 22 April 1996, B3 and B7. See also *New York Times,* 9 August 1996, B3.

81. See the U.S. Bishops' Statement on the veto of the Partial-Birth Abortion Ban Act in *Origins* 26 (4 July 1996): 110. On September 10, 1996, eight American cardinals and the president of the National Conference of Catholic Bishops wrote members of Congress urging them to override President Clinton's veto of the proposed legislation; the letter is reprinted in *Origins* 26 (19 September 1996): 213–15. Catholic archdiocesan weekly newspapers also carried extensive coverage of the campaign to lobby Congress to override the presidential veto during the 1996 election; see, for example, *Catholic New York,* 4 July 1996, 5, and *The Catholic Advocate,* 29 May 1996, 15 (this is the weekly newspaper of the Newark archdiocese).

82. *New York Times,* 27 September 1996, A20. See also David W. Hendon and James M. Kennedy, "Notes on Church-State Affairs," *Journal of Church and State* 38, no. 4 (Autumn 1996): 941. Members of the 105th Congress (elected in November 1996) have introduced new legislation, the "Partial-Birth Abortion Act of 1997." Identical to H.R. 1833, the 1995 bill, this new bill was passed by the House of Representatives on March 20, 1997, and by the Senate on May 20, 1997. However, the Senate vote (64–36) fell three votes short of the number needed to override an expected presidential veto. On October 10, 1997, President Clinton vetoed the bill, saying again that the bill should provide exceptions to the ban for women whose life and/or health is seriously threatened. (The bill contains only an exemption to save the life of the pregnant woman.) As of this writing, Congress again faces the challenge of an override vote. See *New York Times,* 21 March 1997, A21; *New York Times,* 21 May 1997, A1; *Wall Street Journal,* 21 May 1997, A4; and *New York Times,* 11 October 1997, A9.

83. See Mary C. Segers, "Abortion Politics Post-*Webster:* The New Jersey Bishops," in *The Catholic Church and the Politics of Abortion: A View from the States,* ed. Timothy A. Byrnes and Mary C. Segers (Boulder, Colo.: Westview, 1992), 27–47.

84. Reichley, "Democracy and Religion," 805.

Select Bibliography

Ahlstrom, Sydney E. *A Religious History of the American People*, 2 vols. New Haven, Conn.: Yale University Press, 1975.

Aristophanes. "The Knights." In *Five Comedies*. New York: Fine Edition Press, 1948.

Asher, Herbert B. *Presidential Elections in American Politics: Candidates and Elections Since 1952*, 5th ed. Pacific Grove, Calif.: Brooks-Cole, 1992.

Audi, Robert. "Separation of Church and State and the Obligations of Citizenship." *Philosophy and Public Affairs* 18 (1989): 258–96.

Audi, Robert, and Nicholas Wolterstorff. *Religion in the Public Square: The Place of Religious Convictions in Political Debate*. Lanham, Md.: Rowman & Littlefield, 1997.

———. "The State, the Church, and the Citizen." In *Religion and Contemporary Liberalism*, ed. Paul Weithman. South Bend, Ind.: University of Notre Dame Press, 1997.

Bachrach, Peter. *The Theory of Democratic Elitism: A Critique*. Boston: Little, Brown, 1967.

Balmer, Randall. *Mine Eyes Have Seen the Glory: A Journey into the Evangelical Subculture in America*. New York: Oxford Univerity Press, 1989.

Bellah, Robert. "Civil Religion in America." Pp. 3–23 in *Religion in America*, ed. W. McLoughlin and Robert Bellah. Boston: Houghton-Mifflin, 1968.

Bellah, Robert, et al. *Habits of the Heart: Individualism and Commitment in American Life*. Berkeley: University of California Press, 1985.

Berger, Peter. *The Sacred Canopy: Elements of a Sociological Theory of Religion*. New York: Doubleday, 1967.

"Bishop Threatens Excommunication." *Chicago Tribune* March 28, 1996: 1:10.

Blanchard, Dallas. *The Anti-Abortion Movement and the Rise of the Religious Right: From Polite to Firey Protest*. New York: Twayne, 1994.

Blanchard, Dallas, and Terry J. Prewitt. *Religious Violence and Abortion: The Gideon Project*. Gainesville: University Press of Florida, 1993.

Bollinger, Lee C. *The Tolerant Society*. New York: Oxford University Press, 1986.

Bowers, James R. *Pro-Choice and Anti-Abortion: Constitutional Theory and Public Policy*. Westport, Conn.: Praeger, 1994.

Bradley, Gerard V. *Church-State Relationships in America*. Westport, Conn.: Greenwood, 1987.

Brisbin, Richard A. "The Rehnquist Court and the Free Exercise of Religion." *Journal of Church and State* 34 (1992): 57–76.

Carlson-Thies, Stanley W., and James W. Skillen. *Welfare in America: Christian Perspectives on a Policy in Crisis.* Grand Rapids, Mich.: Eerdmans, 1996.

Carter, Stephen L. *The Culture of Disbelief: How American Law and Politics Trivialize Religious Devotion.* New York: Basic Books, 1993.

Casanova, Jose. *Public Religions in the Modern World.* Chicago: University of Chicago Press, 1994.

Choper, Jesse. *Securing Religious Liberty.* Chicago: University of Chicago Press, 1995.

Christenson, J. A., and R. C. Wimberly. "Who Is Civil Religious?" *Sociological Analysis* 39 (1979): 77–83.

Cochran, Clarke. *Religion in Private and Public Life.* New York: Routledge, 1990.

———. "Religious Traditions and Health Care Policy: Potential for Democratic Discourse?" *Journal of Church and State* 39 (Winter 1997): 15–35.

Coleman, John A. "Under the Cross and the Flag: Reflections on Discipleship and Citizenship in America." *America* 174, no. 16 (11 May 1996): 6–14.

Cook, Elizabeth Adell, Ted G. Jelen, and Clyde Wilcox. *Between Two Absolutes: Public Opinion and the Politics of Abortion.* Boulder, Colo.: Westview, 1992.

Cord, Robert L. *Separation of Church and State: Historical Fact and Current Fiction.* New York: Lambeth Press, 1982.

Deane, Herbert A. *The Political and Social Ideas of St. Augustine.* New York: Columbia University Press, 1964.

Dorning, Mike. "Episcopal Heresy Trial Tests Gay Clergy Issue." *Chicago Tribune* February 28, 1996: 1:4.

Dreisbach, Daniel. "'Sowing Useful Truths and Principles': The Danbury Baptists, Thomas Jefferson, and the 'Wall of Separation'." *Journal of Church and State* 39, no. 3 (Summer 1997): 455–501.

Dunlap, David W. "Reform Rabbis Vote to Back Gay Marriage." *New York Times* March 28, 1996.

Dunn, Charles W., ed. *American Political Theology: Historical Perspective and Theoretical Analysis.* New York: Praeger, 1984.

Falwell, Jerry. *Listen, America!* Garden City, N.Y.: Doubleday, 1980.

———. "An Agenda for the 1980s." In *Piety and Politics: Evangelicals and Fundamentalists Confront the Modern World,* ed. Richard J. Neuhaus and Michael Cromartie. Washington, D.C.: Ethics and Public Policy Center, 1987.

Fauser, Patricia, et al. "Conclusion: Perspectives on the Politics of Abortion." Pp. 177–99 in *Perspectives on the Politics of Abortion,* ed. Ted G. Jelen. Westport, Conn.: Praeger, 1995.

Finke, Roger, and Rodney Stark. *The Churching of America, 1776–1990.* New Brunswick, N.J.: Rutgers University Press, 1992.

Fishkin, James S. *Democracy and Deliberation: New Directions for Democratic Reform.* New Haven, Conn.: Yale University Press, 1991.

Fleet, Elizabeth, ed. "Madison's 'Detached Memoranda.'" *William and Mary Quarterly* 3 (1946): 535–62.

Flowers, Ronald B. *That Godless Court? Supreme Court Decisions on Church-State Relationships.* Louisville, Ky.: Westminster John Knox Press, 1994.

Foley, Michael W., and Bob Edwards. "The Paradox of Civil Society." *Journal of Democracy* 7, no. 3 (1996): 38–52.

Formicola, Jo Renée, and Hubert Morken, eds. *Everson Revisited: Religion, Education, and Law at the Crossroads*. Lanham, Md.: Rowman & Littlefield, 1997.

Fowler, Robert Booth. *Unconventional Partners: Religion and Liberal Culture in the United States*. Grand Rapids, Mich.: Eerdmans, 1989.

Fowler, Robert Booth, and Allen D. Hertzke. *Religion and Politics in America: Faith, Culture, and Strategic Choices*. Boulder, Colo.: Westview, 1995.

Friendly, Fred W., and Martha J. H. Elliot. *The Constitution: That Delicate Balance*. New York: Random House, 1984.

Fukuyama, Francis. *The End of History and the Last Man*. New York: Free Press, 1992.

Gans, Herbert J. *Middle American Individualism*. New York: Free Press, 1988.

Green, John C. "Pat Robertson and the Latest Crusade: Religious Resources and the 1988 Presidential Campaign." *Social Sciences Quarterly* 74 (1995): 157–68.

Green, John C., James L. Guth, Lyman A. Kellstedt, and Corwin E. Smidt, "Uncivil Challenges: Support for Civil Liberties among Religious Activists." *Journal of Political Science* 22 (1994): 25–49.

Greenawalt, Kent. *Religious Convictions and Political Choice*. New York: Oxford University Press, 1988.

———. "Grounds for Political Judgment: The Status of Personal Experience and the Autonomy and Generality of Principles of Restraint." *San Diego Law Review* 30 (1993): 674–75.

Grindstaff, Laura. "Abortion and the Popular Press: Mapping Media Discourse from *Roe* to *Webster*." Pp. 57–88 in *Abortion Politics in the United States and Canada: Studies in Public Opinion*, ed. Ted G. Jelen and Marthe A. Chandler. Westport, Conn.: Praeger, 1994.

Hamer, Dean, and Peter Copeland. *The Science of Desire: The Search for the Gay Gene and the Biology of Behavior*. New York: Simon and Schuster, 1994.

Hamilton, Alexander, James Madison, and John Jay. *The Federalist*. New York: Modern Library, 1937.

Handy, Robert T. *A Christian America: Protestant Hopes and Historical Realities*. New York: Oxford University Press, 1984.

Hart, Stephen. *What Does the Lord Require? How American Christians Think about Economic Justice*. New Brunswick, N.J.: Rutgers University Press, 1992.

Hartz, Louis. *The Liberal Tradition in America*. New York: Harcourt, Brace and World, 1988.

Hatch, Roger D. "Jesse Jackson in Two Worlds." Pp. 87–101 in *Religion in American Politics*, ed. Charles W. Dunn. Washington, D.C.: CQ Press, 1989.

Hendon, David W., and James M. Kennedy. "Notes on Church-State Affairs." *Journal of Church and State* 38, no. 3 (Summer 1996): 683–85.

Hertzke, Allen. *Representing God in Washington: The Role of Religious Lobbies in the American Polity*. Knoxville: University of Tennessee Press, 1988.

———. *Echoes of Discontent: Jesse Jackson, Pat Robertson, and the Resurgence of Populism*. Washington, D.C.: CQ Press, 1993.

Hofrenning, Daniel J. B. *In Washington But Not of It: The Prophetic Politics of Religious Lobbyists*. Philadelphia: Temple University Press, 1995.

Hunter, James Davison. *Culture Wars: The Struggle to Define America.* New York: Basic Books, 1991.

———. *Before the Shooting Begins.* New York: Free Press, 1994.

Iannaccone, Laurence R. "Heirs to the Protestant Ethic? The Economics of American Fundamentalism." Pp. 342–66 in *Fundamentalisms and the State,* ed. Martin R. Marty and R. Scott Appleby. Chicago: University of Chicago Press, 1993.

———. "Why Strict Churches Are Strong." *American Journal of Sociology* (1994): 1180–211

Inglehart, Ronald. *Culture Shift in Advanced Industrial Society.* Princeton, N.J.: Princeton University Press, 1990.

Jefferson, Thomas. "A Bill for Establishing Religious Freedom." In *The First Liberty: Religion and the American Republic,* ed. William Lee Miller. New York: Alfred A. Knopf, 1986.

Jelen, Ted G. "Human Knowledge and Democratic Theory: An Analysis of Participatory Democracy." Ph.D. diss., Ohio State University, 1979.

———. "Helpmeets and Weaker Vessels: Gender Role Stereotypes and Attitudes toward Female Ordination." *Social Science Quarterly* 70 (1989): 575–85.

———. *The Political Mobilization of Religious Beliefs.* Westport, Conn.: Praeger, 1991.

———. "Religion and Democratic Citizenship: A Review Essay." *Polity* 23 (1991): 471–81.

———. *The Political World of the Clergy.* Westport, Conn.: Praeger, 1993.

———. "Religion and the American Political Culture: Alternative Models of Citizenship and Discipleship." *Sociology of Religion* 56 (1995): 271–84.

———. "Religion and Public Opinion in the 1990s: An Empirical Overview." Pp. 55–68 in *Understanding Public Opinion,* ed. Barbara Norrander and Clyde Wilcox. Washington, D.C.: CQ Press, 1996.

Jelen, Ted G., and Clyde Wilcox. "Denominational Preference and the Dimensions of Political Tolerance." *Sociological Analysis* 51 (1990): 69–80.

———. *Public Attitudes toward Church and State.* Armonk, N.Y.: M. E. Sharpe, 1995.

Kersch, Ken I. "Full Faith and Credit for Same-Sex Marriages." *Political Science Quarterly* 112 (1997): 117–36.

Kirk, Russell, ed. *The Assault on Religion.* Lanham, Md.: University Press of America, 1986.

Landess, Thomas H., and Richard M. Quinn. *Jesse Jackson and the Politics of Race.* Ottawa, Ill.: Jameson Books, 1985.

Leege, David C. "Religion and Politics in Theoretical Perspective." Pp. 3–25 in *Rediscovering the Religious Factor in American Politics,* ed. David C. Leege and Lyman A. Kellstedt. Armonk, N.Y.: M. E. Sharpe, 1993.

Lemann, Nicholas. "Kicking in Groups." *Atlantic Monthly* 277, no. 4 (April 1996): 22–26.

Levinson, Sanford. "Religious Language and the Public Square." *Harvard Law Review* 105 (1992): 2061–79.

Levy, Leonard W. *The Establishment Clause.* New York: Macmillan, 1986.

———. *Original Intent and the Framers' Constitution.* New York: Macmillan, 1988.

———. *The Establishment Clause: Religion and the First Amendment.* Chapel Hill: University of North Carolina Press, 1994.

Martin, William. *With God on Our Side: The Rise of the Religious Right in America.* New York: Broadway Books, 1996.

Marty, Martin, and R. Scott Appleby. *The Glory and the Power: The Fundamentalist Challenge to the Modern World.* Boston: Beacon Press, 1992.

Maxwell, Carol J. C. "Introduction: Beyond Polemics and toward Healing." Pp. 1–20 in *Perspectives on the Politics of Abortion,* ed. Ted G. Jelen. Westport, Conn.: Praeger, 1995.

McClosky, Herbert, and Alida Brill. *Dimensions of Tolerance: What Americans Believe about Civil Liberties.* New York: Russell Sage, 1983.

Mill, John Stuart. "De Tocqueville on Democracy in America." In *Collected Works of John Stuart Mill,* ed. J. M. Robinson (21 volumes). Toronto: University of Toronto Press, 1977.

———. *On Liberty.* London: Oxford University Press, 1975.

Miller, Perry. *Roger Williams: His Contribution to the American Tradition.* Indianapolis: Bobbs-Merrill, 1953.

Miller, William Lee. *The First Liberty: Religion and the American Republic.* New York: Alfred A. Knopf, 1986.

Monsma, Stephen V. *Positive Neutrality: Letting Religious Freedom Ring.* Westport, Conn.: Praeger, 1993.

———. "The Wrong Road Taken." Pp. 129–30 in *Everson Revisited: Religion, Education, and Law at the Crossroads,* ed. Jo Renée Formicola and Hubert Morken. Lanham, Md.: Rowman & Littlefield, 1997.

Morgan, Edmund S. *Roger Williams: The Church and the State.* New York: Harcourt, Brace and World, 1967.

National Conference of Catholic Bishops. *The Challenge of Peace: God's Promise and Our Response.* Washington, D.C.: United States Catholic Conference, 1983.

———. *Economic Justice for All.* Washington, D.C.: United States Catholic Conference, 1986.

Neff, Jimmy D. "Roger Williams: Pious Puritan and Strict Separationist." *Journal of Church and State* 38, no. 3 (Summer 1996): 529–46.

Neuhaus, Richard John. *The Naked Public Square.* Grand Rapids, Mich.: Eerdmans, 1984.

———. "The Public Square." *First Things* 37 (November 1993).

Noll, Mark A., ed. *Religion and American Politics: From the Colonial Period to the Present.* New York: Oxford University Press, 1990.

Ostling, Richard N. "What Does God Really Think about Sex?" *Time,* June 24, 1991: 48–50.

Pateman, Carol. *Participation and Democratic Theory.* London: Cambridge University Press, 1970.

Perry, Michael J. *Love and Power: The Role of Religion and Morality in American Politics.* New York: Oxford University Press, 1991.

———. *Religion in Politics: Constitutional and Moral Perspectives.* New York: Oxford University Press, 1997.

Pfeffer, Leo. *Church, State, and Freedom.* Boston: Beacon Press, 1967.

———. "The Current State of Law in the United States and the Separationist Agenda." *The Annals* 446 (December 1979): 1–9.

Phillips, Stephen. "Roger Williams and the Two Tables of the Law." *Journal of Church and State* 38, no. 3 (Summer 1996): 547–68.

Potter, Gary. "A Christian America." *New York Times,* 15 October 1980, A31.

Putnam, Robert D. "Tuning In, Tuning Out: The Strange Disappearance of Social Capital in America." *PS: Political Science and Politics* 28 (December 1995): 665–83.

———. *Making Democracy Work: Civic Traditions in Modern Italy.* Princeton: Princeton University Press, 1993.

———. "Bowling Alone: America's Declining Social Capital." *Journal of Democracy* 6 (January 1995): 65–78.

Rawls, John. *Political Liberalism.* New York: Columbia University Press, 1993.

Reed, Adolph L., Jr. *The Jesse Jackson Phenomenon: The Crisis of Purpose in Afro-American Politics.* New Haven: Yale University Press, 1986.

Reed, Ralph. *Politically Incorrect: The Emerging Faith Factor in American Politics.* Dallas: Word, 1994.

Reichley, A. James. *Religion in American Public Life.* Washington, D.C.: Brookings Institution, 1985.

———. "Democracy and Religion." *PS: Political Science and Politics* 19, no. 3 (Fall 1986): 805.

———. "Religion and the Constitution." In *Religion and American Politics,* ed. Charles W. Dunn. Washington, D.C.: CQ Press, 1989.

Richey, Russell E., and Donald G. Jones, eds. *American Civil Religion.* New York: Harper & Row, 1974.

Robbins, Thomas. "The Intensification of Church-State Conflict in the United States." *Social Compass* 40 (1993): 505–27.

Roof, Wade Clark, and William McKinney. *American Mainline Religion.* New Brunswick, N.J.: Rutgers University Press, 1987.

Rorty, Richard. "Religion as Conversation-Stopper." *Common Knowledge* 3 (1994): 1–6.

Rozell, Mark J., and Clyde Wilcox. *Second Coming: The New Christian Right in Virginia Politics.* Baltimore: Johns Hopkins University Press, 1996.

Savage, David G. *Turning Right: The Making of the Rehnquist Supreme Court.* New York: John Wiley and Sons, 1993.

Segers, Mary C. "Abortion Politics Post-*Webster:* The New Jersey Bishops." Pp. 27–47 in *The Catholic Church and the Politics of Abortion: A View from the States,* ed. Timothy A. Byrnes and Mary C. Segers. Boulder, Colo.: Westview Press, 1992.

———. "The Catholic Church as a Political Actor." Pp. 87–130 in *Perspectives on the Politics of Abortion,* ed. Ted G. Jelen. Westport, Conn.: Praeger, 1995.

———. "Ferraro, the Bishops, and the 1984 Election." Pp. 143–67 in *Shaping New Vision: Gender and Values in American Culture,* ed. Clarissa W. Atkinson, Constance H. Buchanan, and Margaret R. Miles. Ann Arbor, Mich.: UMI Research Press, 1987.

Semonche, John E. *Religion and Constitutional Government in the United States.* Carrboro, N.C.: Signal Books, 1986.

Sezer, L. Kent. "The Constitutional Underpinnings of the Abortion Debate." Pp. 131–76 in *Perspectives* on the Politics of Abortion, ed. Ted G. Jelen. Westport, Conn.: Praeger, 1995.

Sezer, L. Kent, and Ted G. Jelen. "Pornography, Feminism, and the First Amendment." Paper presented at the annual meeting of the Northeastern Political Science Association, Philadelphia, Penn., 1985.

Shain, Barry Alan. *The Myth of American Individualism: The Protestant Origins of American Political Thought.* Princeton, N.J.: Princeton University Press, 1994.

Smolin, David M. "Regulating Religious and Cultural Conflict in a Postmodern America: A Response to Professor Perry." *Iowa Law Review* 76 (1992): 1067–104.

Stark, Rodney, and Charles Y. Glock. *American Piety: The Nature of Religious Commitment.* Berkeley: University of California Press, 1968.

Sterling, Richard W., and William C. Scott, trans. *Plato: The Republic.* New York: W. W. Norton, 1985.

Stouffer, Samuel. *Communism, Conformity, and Civil Liberties.* Gloucester, Mass.: Peter Smith, 1955.

Stout, Cushing. *The New Heavens and New Earth: Political Religion in America.* New York: Harper Torchbooks, 1974.

Sullivan, John L., James Pierson, and George E. Marcus. *Political Tolerance and American Democracy.* Chicago: University of Chicago Press, 1982.

Tamney, Joseph B., Ronald Burton, and Stephen D. Johnson. "Fundamentalism and Economic Restructuring." Pp. 67–82 in *Religion and Political Behavior in the United States,* ed. Ted G. Jelen. New York: Praeger, 1989.

Thiemann, Ronald. *Religion in Public Life: A Dilemma for Democracy.* Washington, D.C.: Georgetown University Press, 1996.

Tinder, Glenn. *The Political Meaning of Christianity.* Baton Rouge: Louisiana State University Press, 1989.

de Tocqueville, Alexis. *Democracy in America,* ed. Phillips Bradley (2 vol.). New York: Vintage Books, 1945.

Toulmin, Stephen. *The Uses of Argument.* London: Cambridge University Press, 1974.

Urofsky, Melvin I. "Church and State: The Religion Clauses." Pp. 57–71 in *The Bill of Rights in Modern America,* ed. D. J. Bedenhamer and J. W. Ely. Bloomington: Indiana University Press, 1993.

Verba, Sydney, Kay Lehman Scholzman, and Henry E. Brady. *Voice and Equality: Civic Voluntarism in American Politics.* Cambridge, Mass.: Harvard University Press, 1995.

Wald, Kenneth D. *Religion and Politics in the United States,* 2d ed. Washington, D.C.: CQ Press, 1992.

Wald, Kenneth D., Dennis E. Owen, and Samuel S. Hill. "Habits of the Mind: The Problem of Authority in the New Christian Right." Pp. 93–108 in *Religion and Political Behavior in the United States,* ed. Ted G. Jelen. New York: Praeger, 1989.

Waldron, Jeremy. "Religious Contributions in Public Deliberation." *San Diego Law Review* 30 (1993): 817–48.

Wallis, Jim. *The Soul of Politics: A Practical and Prophetic Vision for Change.* New York: New Press and Orbis Books, 1994.

Warner, R. Stephen. "Work in Progress toward a New Paradigm for the Sociological Study of Religion in the United States." *American Journal of Sociology* 94 (1992): 1044–93.

Way, Frank, and Barbara Burt. "Religious Marginality and the Free Exercise Clause." *American Political Science Review* 77 (1983): 654–65.

Weber, Max. *The Protestant Ethic and the Spirit of Capitalism,* trans. Talcott Parsons. London: G. Allen and Unwin, 1930.

Weber, Paul. "Strict Neutrality: The Next Step in First Amendment Development?" In *Religion in American Politics,* ed. Charles Dunn. Washington, D.C.: CQ Press, 1989.

Wilcox, Clyde. "Feminism and Anti-Feminism among Evangelical Women." *Western Political Quarterly* 42 (1989): 147–60.

———. *God's Warriors: The Christian Right in the Twentieth Century.* Baltimore: Johns Hopkins University Press, 1992.

———. *Onward, Christian Soldiers? The Religious Right in American Politics.* Boulder, Colo.: Westview, 1996.

Wilcox, Clyde, and Elizabeth Adell Cook. "Evangelical Women and Feminism: Some Additional Evidence." *Women and Politics* 9 (1989): 27–49.

Wilcox, Clyde, and Ted G. Jelen. "Evangelicals and Political Tolerance." *American Politics Quarterly* 18 (1990): 25–46.

———. "The Effects of Employment and Religion on Women's Feminist Attitudes." *International Journal for the Psychology of Religion* 1 (1991): 161–71.

Wilcox, Clyde, Ted G. Jelen, and Sharon Linzey. "Reluctant Warriors: Premillennialism and Politics in the Moral Majority." *Journal for the Scientific Study of Religion* 30 (1991): 245–58.

———. "Rethinking the Reasonableness of the Religious Right." *Review of Religious Research* 36 (1995): 263–76.

Wilcox, Clyde, Mark J. Rozell, and Roland Gunn. "Religious Coalitions in the New Christian Right: The Decline of Religious Particularism." *Social Science Quarterly* 77 (1996): 543–58.

Williams, Roger. "Mr. Cotton's Letter Lately Printed, Examined and Answered." Reprinted in *Roger Williams: His Contribution to the American Tradition,* Perry Miller. Indianapolis: Bobbs-Merrill, 1953.

———. "Letter to the Town of Providence." Reprinted in *Roger Williams: His Contribution to the American Tradition,* ed. Perry Miller. Indianapolis: Bobbs-Merrill, 1953.

Wills, Gary. *Under God.* New York: Simon and Schuster, 1991.

Wolterstorff, Nicholas. "Why We Should Reject What Liberalism Tells Us about Speaking and Acting in Public for Religious Reasons." In *Religion and Contemporary Liberalism,* ed. Paul Weithman. South Bend, Ind.: University of Notre Dame Press, 1997.

Wood, James W. *The First Freedom: Religion and the Bill of Rights.* Waco, Tex.: J. M. Dawson Institute of Church-State Relations, Baylor University, 1990.

Part Two

Readings

1

Thomas Jefferson, Reply to the Danbury Baptist Association, January 1, 1802

To Messrs. Nehemiah Dodge and Others, a Committee of the Danbury Baptist Association, in the State of Connecticut

January 1, 1802

GENTLEMEN,

The affectionate sentiments of esteem and approbation which you are so good as to express towards me, on behalf of the Danbury Baptist Association, give me the highest satisfaction. My duties dictate a faithful and zealous pursuit of the interests of my constituents, and in proportion as they are persuaded of my fidelity to those duties, the discharge of them becomes more and more pleasing.

Believing with you that religion is a matter which lies solely between man and his God, that he owes account no none other for his faith or his worship, that the legislative powers of government reach actions only, and not opinions, I contemplate with sovereign reverence that act of the whole American people which declared that their legislature should "make no law respecting an establishment of religion, or prohibiting the free exercise thereof," thus building a wall of separation between church and State. Adhering to this expression of the supreme will of the nation in behalf of the rights of conscience, I shall see with sincere satisfaction the progress of those sentiments which tend to restore to man all his natural rights, convinced he has no natural right in opposition to his social duties.

I reciprocate your kind prayers for the protection and blessing of the common Father and Creator of man, and tender you for yourselves and your religious association, assurances of my high respect and esteem.

2

Thomas Jefferson, *Notes on Virginia*, 1781–1782

The first settlers in this country were emigrants from England, of the English Church, just at a point of time when it was flushed with complete victory over the religious of all other persuasions. Possessed, as they became, of the powers of making, administering, and executing the laws, they showed equal intolerance in this country with their Presbyterian brethren, who had emigrated to the northern government. The poor Quakers were flying from persecution in England. They cast their eyes on these new countries as asylums of civil and religious freedom; but they found them free only for the reigning sect. Several acts of the Virginia assembly of 1659, 1662, and 1693, had made it penal in parents to refuse to have their children baptized; had prohibited the unlawful assembling of Quakers; had made it penal for any master of a vessel to bring a Quaker into the State; had ordered those already here, and such as should come thereafter, to be imprisoned till they should abjure the country; provided a milder punishment for their first and second return, but death for their third; had inhibited all persons from suffering their meetings in or near their houses, entertaining them individually, or disposing of books which supported their tenets. If no execution took place here, as did in New England, it was not owing to the moderation of the church, or spirit of the legislature, as may be inferred from the law itself; but to historical circumstances which have been handed down to us. The Anglicans retained full possession of the country about a century. Other opinions began to creep in, and the great care of the government to support their own church, having begotten an equal degree of indolence in its clergy, two-thirds of the people had become dissenters at the commencement of the present revolution. The laws, indeed, were still oppressive on them, but the spirit of the one party had subsided into moderation, and of the other had risen to a degree of determination which commanded respect.

The present state of our laws on the subject of religion is this. The convention of May, 1776, in their declaration of rights, declared it to be a truth, and

126

a natural right, that the exercise of religion should be free; but when they proceeded to form on that declaration the ordinance of government, instead of taking up every principle declared in the bill of rights, and guarding it by legislative sanction, they passed over that which asserted our religious rights, leaving them as they found them. The same convention, however, when they met as a member of the general assembly in October, 1776, repealed all *acts of Parliament* which had rendered criminal the maintaining any opinions in matters of religion, the forbearing to repair to church, and the exercising any mode of worship, and suspended the laws giving salaries to the clergy, which suspension was made perpetual in October, 1779. Statutory oppression in religion being thus wiped away, we remain at present under those only imposed by the common law, or by our own acts of assembly. At the common law, *heresy* was a capital offence, punishable by burning. Its definition was left to the ecclesiastical judges, before whom the conviction was that nothing should be deemed heresy, but what had been so determined by authority of the canonical scriptures, or by one of the four first general councils, or by other council, having for the grounds of their declaration the express and plain words of the scriptures. Heresy, thus circumscribed, being an offence against the common law, our act of assembly of October, 1777, gives cognizance of it to the general court, by declaring that the jurisdiction of that court shall be general in all matters at the common law. By our own act of assembly . . . , if a person brought up in the Christian religion denies the being of a God, or the Trinity, or asserts there are more gods than one, or denies the Christian religion to be true, or the scriptures to be of divine authority, he is punishable on the first offence by incapacity to hold any office or employment ecclesiastical, civil, or military; on the second by disability to sue, to take any gift or legacy, to be guardian, executor, or administrator, and by three years' imprisonment without bail. A father's right to the custody of his own children being founded in law on his right of guardianship, this being taken away, they may of course be severed from him, and put by the authority of a court into more orthodox hands. This is a summary view of that religious slavery under which a people have been willing to remain, who have lavished their lives and fortunes for the establishment of their civil freedom. The error seems not sufficiently eradicated, that the operations of the mind, as well as the acts of the body, are subject to the coercion of the laws. But our rulers can have no authority over such natural rights, only as we have submitted to them. The rights of conscience we never submitted, we could not submit. We are answerable for them to our God. The legitimate powers of government extend to such acts only as are injurious to others. But it does me no injury for my neighbor to say there are twenty gods, or no God. It neither picks my pocket nor breaks my leg. If it be said, his testimony in a court of justice cannot be relied on, reject it then, and be the stigma on him. Constraint may make him worse by making him a hypocrite, but it will never make him a truer man. It may fix him obstinately

in his errors, but will not cure them. Reason and free inquiry are the only effectual agents against error. Give a loose to them, they will support the true religion by bringing every false one to their tribunal, to the test of their investigation. They are the natural enemies of error, and of error only. Had not the Roman government permitted free inquiry, Christianity could never have been introduced. Had not free inquiry been indulged at the era of the Reformation, the corruptions of Christianity could not have been purged away. If it be restrained now, the present corruptions will be protected, and new ones encouraged. Was the government to prescribe to us our medicine and diet, our bodies would be in such keeping as our souls are now. Thus in France the emetic was once forbidden as a medicine, the potato as an article of food. Government is just as infallible, too, when it fixes systems in physics. Galileo was sent to the Inquisition for affirming that the earth was a sphere; the government had declared it to be as flat as a trencher, and Galileo was obliged to abjure his error. This error, however, at length prevailed, the earth became a globe, and Descartes declared it was whirled round its axis by a vortex. The government in which he lived was wise enough to see that this was no question of civil jurisdiction, or we should all have been involved by authority in vortices. In fact, the vortices have been exploded, and the Newtonian principle of gravitation is now more firmly established, on the basis of reason, than it would be were the government to step in, and to make it an article of necessary faith. Reason and experiment have been indulged, and error has fled before them. It is error alone which needs the support of government. Truth can stand by itself. Subject opinions to coercion: whom will you make your inquisitors? Fallible men; men governed by bad passions, by private as well as public reasons. And why subject it to coercion? To produce uniformity. But is uniformity of opinion desirable? No more than of face and stature. . . . Difference of opinion is advantageous in religion. The several sects perform the office of a *censor morum* over each other. Is uniformity attainable? Millions of innocent men, women, and children, since the introduction of Christianity, have been burnt, tortured, fined, imprisoned; yet we have not advanced one inch towards uniformity. What has been the effect of coercion? To make one half the world fools, and the other half hypocrites. To support roguery and error all over the earth. Let us reflect that it is inhabited by a thousand millions of people. That these profess probably a thousand different systems of religion. That ours is but one of that thousand. That if there be but one right, and ours that one, we should wish to see the nine hundred and ninety-nine wandering sects gathered into the fold of truth. But against such a majority we cannot effect this by force. Reason and persuasion are the only practicable instruments. To make way for these, free inquiry must be indulged; and how can we wish others to indulge it while we refuse it ourselves. But every State, says an inquisitor, has established some religion. No two, say I, have established the same. Is this a proof of the infallibility of establishments? Our sister States

of Pennsylvania and New York, however, have long subsisted without any establishment at all. The experiment was new and doubtful when they made it. It has answered beyond conception. They flourish infinitely. Religion is well supported; of various kinds, indeed, but all good enough; all sufficient to preserve peace and order; or if a sect arises, whose tenets would subvert morals, good sense has fair play, and reasons and laughs it out of doors, without suffering the State to be troubled with it. They do not hang more malefactors than we do. They are not more disturbed with religious dissensions. On the contrary, their harmony is unparalleled, and can be ascribed to nothing but their unbounded tolerance, because there is no other circumstance in which they differ from every nation on earth. They have made the happy discovery, that the way to silence religious disputes, is to take no notice of them. Let us too give this experiment fair play, and get rid, while we may, of those tyrannical laws. . . . It can never be too often repeated, that the time for fixing every essential right on a legal basis is while our rulers are honest, and ourselves united. From the conclusion of this war we shall be going down hill. It will not then be necessary to resort every moment to the people for support. They will be forgotten, therefore, and their rights disregarded. They will forget themselves, but in the sole faculty of making money, and will never think of uniting to effect a due respect for their rights. The shackles, therefore, which shall not be knocked off at the conclusion of this war, will remain on us long, will be made heavier and heavier, till our rights shall revive or expire in a convulsion.

3

Thomas Jefferson, Virginia Statute of Religious Liberty, 1786

I. WHEREAS Almighty God hath created the mind free; that all attempts to influence it by temporal punishments or burthens, or by civil incapacitations, tend only to beget habits of hypocrisy and meanness, and are a departure from the plan of the Holy author of our religion, who being Lord both of body and mind, yet chose not to propagate it by coercions on either, as was in his Almighty power to do; that the impious presumption of legislators and rulers, civil as well as ecclesiastical, who being themselves but fallible and uninspired men, have assumed dominion over the faith of others, setting up their own opinions and modes of thinking as the only true and infallible, and as such endeavouring to impose them on others, hath established and maintained false religions over the greatest part of the world, and through all time; that to compel a man to furnish contributions of money for the propagation of opinions which he disbelieves, is sinful and tyrannical; that even the forcing him to support this or that teacher of his own religious persuasion, is depriving him of the comfortable liberty of giving his contributions to the particular pastor whose morals he would make his pattern, and whose powers he feels most persuasive to righteousness, and is withdrawing from the ministry those temporary rewards, which proceeding from an approbation of their personal conduct, are an additional incitement to earnest and unremitting labours for the instruction of mankind; that our civil rights have no dependence on our religious opinions, any more than our opinions in physics or geometry; that therefore the proscribing any citizen as unworthy the public confidence by laying upon him an incapacity of being called to offices of trust and emolument, unless he profess or renounce this or that religious opinion, is depriving him injuriously of those privileges and advantages to which in common with his fellow-citizens he has a natural right, that it tends only to corrupt the principles of that religion it is meant to encourage, by bribing with a monopoly of worldly honours and emoluments, those who will externally profess

and comform to it; that though indeed these are criminal who do not withstand such temptation, yet neither are those innocent who lay the bait in their way; that to suffer the civil magistrate to intrude his powers into the field of opinion, and to restrain the profession or propagation of principles on supposition of their ill tendency, is a dangerous fallacy, which at once destroys all religious liberty, because he being of course judge of that tendency will make his opinions the rule of judgment, and approve or condemn the sentiments of others only as they shall square with or differ from his own; that it is time enough for the rightful purposes of civil government, for its officers to interfere when principles break out into overt acts against peace and good order; and finally, that truth is great and will prevail if left to herself, that she is the proper and sufficient antagonist to error, and has nothing to fear from the conflict, unless by human interposition disarmed of her natural weapons, free argument and debate, errors ceasing to be dangerous when it is permitted freely to contradict them.

II. *Be it enacted by the General Assembly,* that no man shall be compelled to frequent or support any religious worship, place or ministry whatsoever, nor shall be enforced, restrained, molested, or burthened in his body or goods, nor shall otherwise suffer on account of his religious opinions or belief; but that all men shall be free to profess, and by argument to maintain, their opinion in matters of religion, and that the same shall in no wise diminish, enlarge or affect their civil capacities.

III. And though we well know that this assembly, elected by the people for the ordinary purposes of legislation only, have no power to restrain the acts of succeeding assemblies, constituted with powers equal to our own, and that therefore to declare this act to be irrevocable would be of no effect in law; yet as we are free to declare, and do declare, that the rights hereby asserted are of the natural rights of mankind, and that if any act shall hereafter be passed to repeal the present, or to narrow its operation, such act will be an infringement of natural right.

4

James Madison, "A Memorial and Remonstrance on the Religious Rights of Man," 1784

TO THE HONORABLE THE GENERAL ASSEMBLY OF THE STATE OF VIRGINIA

We, the subscribers, citizens of the said commonwealth, having taken into serious consideration a bill printed by order of the last session of the general assembly, entitled "A bill for establishing a provision for teachers of the Christian religion," and conceiving that the same, if finally armed with the sanctions of a law, will be a dangerous abuse of power, are bound, as faithful members of a free state, no remonstrate against the said bill—

Because we hold it for a "fundamental and undeniable truth," that religion, or the duty which we owe to our creator, and the manner of discharging it, can be directed only by reason and conviction, not by force or violence. The religion, then, of every man, must be left to the conviction and conscience of every man; and it is the right of every man to exercise it as these may dictate. This right is, in its nature, an unalienable right. It is unalienable, because the opinions of men, depending only on the evidence contemplated in their own minds, cannot follow the dictates of other men; it is unalienable, also, because what is here a right towards men, is a duty towards the creator. It is the duty of every man to render the creator such homage, and *such only,* as he believes to be acceptable to him; this duty is precedent, both in order of time and degree of obligation, to the claims of civil society. Before any man can be considered as a member of civil society, he must be considered as a subject of the governor of the universe; and if a member of civil society, who enters into any subordinate association, must always do it with a reservation of his duty to the general authority, much more must every man who becomes a member of any particular civil society do it *with the saving his allegiance to the universal sovereign.* We maintain, therefore, that in matters of religion no

man's right is abridged by the institution of civil society; and that religion is wholly exempt from its cognizance. True it is, that no other rule exists, by which any question which may divide society can be ultimately determined, but the will of the majority; but it is also true, that the majority may trespass on the rights of the minority.

Because, if religion be exempt from the authority of the society at large, still less can it be subject to that of the legislative body. The latter are but the creatures and vicegerents of the former. Their jurisdiction is both derivative and limited. It is limited with regard to the coordinate departments: more necessarily is it limited with regard to the constituents. The preservation of a free government requires not merely that the meres and bounds which separate each department of power be universally maintained; but more especially, that neither of them be suffered to overleap the great barrier which defends the rights of the people. The rulers who are guilty of such an encroachment, exceed the commission from which they derive their authority, and are tyrants. The people who submit to it are governed by laws made neither by themselves, nor by an authority derived from them, and are slaves.

Because it is proper to take alarm at the first experiment on our liberties. We hold this prudent jealousy to be the first duty of citizens, and one of the noblest characteristics of the late revolution. The freemen of America did not wait till usurped power had strengthened itself by exercise, and entangled the question in precedents. They saw all the consequences by denying the principle. We revere this lesson too much soon to forget it. Who does not see that the same authority which can establish Christianity, in exclusion of all other religions, may establish, with the same ease, any particular sect of Christians, in exclusion of all other sects? That the same authority that can call for each citizen to contribute three pence only of his property for the support of only one establishment, may force him to conform to any one establishment, in all cases whatsoever?

Because the bill violates that equality which ought to be the basis of every law, and which is more indispensable in proportion as the validity or expediency of any law is more liable to be impeached. If "all men by nature are equally free and independent," all men are to be considered as entering into society on equal conditions, as relinquishing no more, and, therefore, retaining no less, one than another, of their rights. Above all, they are to be considered as retaining an "equal right to the free exercise of religion, according to the dictates of conscience." While we assert for ourselves a freedom to embrace, to profess, and to observe, the religion which we believe to be of divine origin, we cannot deny an equal freedom to those whose minds have not yet yielded to the evidence which has convinced us. If this freedom be abused, it is an offence against God, *not against man:* to God, therefore *not to man,* must an account of it be rendered. As the bill violates equality by subjecting some to peculiar burdens, so it violates the same principle by granting to others pecu-

liar exemptions. Are the Quakers and Menonists the only sects who think compulsive support of their religions unnecessary and unwarrantable? Can their piety alone be entrusted with the care of public worship? Ought their religions to be endowed, above all others, with extraordinary privileges, by which proselytes may be enticed from all others? We think too favorably of the justice and good sense of these denominations to believe that they either covet preeminence over their fellow citizens, or that they will be seduced by them from the common oppositions to the measure.

Because the bill implies, either that the civil magistrate is a competent judge of truth, or that he may employ religion as an engine of civil policy. The first is an arrogant pretension, falsified by the contradictory opinions of rulers in all ages, and throughout the world: the second is an unhallowed perversion of the means of salvation.

Because the establishment proposed by the bill is not requisite for the support of the Christian religion. To say that it is, is a contradiction to the Christian religion itself; for every page of it disavows a dependence on the powers of this world: it is a contradiction to fact; for it is known that this religion both existed and flourished, not only without the support of human laws, but in spite of every opposition from them; and not only during the period of miraculous aid, but long after it had been left to its own evidence, and the ordinary care of Providence. Nay, it is a contradiction in terms; for a religion not invented by human policy must have pre-existed and been supported before it was established by human policy. It is, moreover, to weaken in those who profess this religion a pious confidence in its innate excellence, and the patronage of its author; and to foster in those who still reject it, a suspicion that its friends are too conscious of its fallacies to trust it to its own merits.

Because experience witnesseth that ecclesiastical establishments, instead of maintaining the purity and efficacy of religion, have had a contrary operation. During almost fifteen centuries has the legal establishment of Christianity been on trial. What have been its fruits? More or less, in all places, pride and indolence in the clergy; ignorance and servility in the laity; in both, superstition, bigotry, and persecution. Enquire of the teachers of Christianity for the ages in which it appeared in its greatest lustre; those of every sect point to the ages prior to its incorporation with civil policy. Propose a restoration of this primitive state, in which its teachers depended on the voluntary rewards of their flocks; many of them predict its downfall. On which side ought their testimony to have the greatest weight, when for, or when against, their interest?

Because the establishment in question is not necessary for the support of civil government. If it be urged as necessary for the support of civil government only as it is a means of supporting religion, and if it be not necessary for the latter purpose, it cannot be necessary for the former. If religion be not within the cognizance of civil government, how can its legal establishment

be said to be necessary to civil government? What influences, in fact, have ecclesiastical establishments had on civil society? In some instances they have been seen to erect a spiritual tyranny on the ruins of civil authority; in many instances they have been seen upholding the thrones of political tyranny; in no instance have they been seen the guardians of the liberties of the people. Rulers who wished to subvert the public liberty may have found an established clergy convenient auxiliaries. A just government, instituted to secure and perpetuate it, needs them not. Such a government will be best supported by protecting every citizen in the enjoyment of his religion with the same equal hand that protects his person and property; by neither invading the equal rights of any sect, nor suffering any sect to invade those of another.

Because the proposed establishment is a departure from that generous policy which, offering an asylum to the persecuted and oppressed of every nation and religion, promised a lustre to our country, and an accession to the number of its citizens. What a melancholy mark is the bill, of sudden degeneracy. Instead of a holding forth an asylum to the persecuted, it is itself a signal of persecution. It degrades from the equal rank of citizens all those whose opinions in religion do not bend to those of the legislative authority. Distant as it may be, in its present form, from the inquisition, it differs only in degree. The one is the *first* step, the other the *last,* in the *career of intolerance.* The magnanimous sufferer under this cruel scourge in foreign regions, must view the bill as a beacon on our coast, warning him to seek some other haven, where liberty and philanthropy, in their due extent, may offer a more certain repose from his troubles.

Because it will have a like tendency to banish our citizens. The allurements presented by other situations are every day thinning their numbers. To superadd a fresh motive to emigration, by revoking the liberty which they now enjoy, would be the same species of folly which has dishonored and depopulated flourishing kingdoms.

Because it will destroy the moderation and harmony which the forbearance of our laws to intermeddle with religion has produced among its several sects. Torrents of blood have been spilt in the world in vain attempts of the secular arm to extinguish religious discord, by proscribing all differences in religious opinions. Time, at length, has revealed the true remedy. Every relaxation of narrow and rigorous policy, wherever it has been tried, has been found to assuage the disease. The American theatre has exhibited proofs, that equal and complete liberty, if it does not wholly eradicate it, sufficiently destroys its malignant influence on the health and prosperity of the state. If, with the salutary effects of this system under our own eyes, we begin to contract the bounds of religious freedom, we know no name that will too severely reproach our folly. At least, let warning be taken at the first fruits of the threatened innovation. The very appearance of the bill has transformed that "Christian forbearance, love, and charity," which of late mutually prevailed, into animos-

ities and jealousies, which may not soon be appeased. What mischiefs may not be dreaded, should this enemy to the public quiet be armed with the force of a law!

Because the policy of the bill is adverse to the diffusion of the light of Christianity. The first wish of those who enjoy this precious gift ought to be, that it may be imparted to the whole race of mankind. Compare the number of those who have as yet received it, with the number still remaining under the dominion of false religions, and how small is the former! Does the policy of the bill tend to lessen the disproportion? No: it at once discourages those who are strangers to the light of revelation from coming into the region of it: countenances, by example, the nations who continue in darkness, in shutting out those who might convey it to them. Instead of levelling, as far as possible, every obstacle to the victorious progress of truth, the bill, with an ignoble and unchristian timidity, would circumscribe it with a wall of defence against the encroachments of error.

Because attempts to enforce by legal sanctions acts obnoxious to so great a proportion of citizens, tend to enervate the laws in general, and to slacken the bands of society. If it be difficult to execute any law which is not generally deemed necessary or salutary, what must be the case where it is deemed invalid and dangerous? And what may be the effect of so striking an example of impotency in the government on its general authority?

Because a measure of such general magnitude and delicacy ought not to be imposed, without the clearest evidence that it is called for by a majority of citizens: and no satisfactory method is yet proposed, by which the voice of the majority in this case may be determined, or its influence secured. "The people of the respective counties are, indeed, requested to signify their opinion, respecting the adoption of the bill, to the next sessions of assembly;" but the representation must be made equal before the voice either of the representatives or the counties will be that of the people. Our hope is, that neither of the former will, after due consideration, espouse the dangerous principle of the bill. Should the event disappoint us, it will still leave us in full confidence that a fair appeal to the latter will reverse the sentence against our liberties.

Because, finally, "the equal right of every citizen to the free exercise of his religion, according to the dictates of conscience," is held by the same tenure with all our other rights. If we recur to its origin, it is equally the gift of nature; if we weigh its importance, it cannot be less dear to us; if we consult the "declaration of those rights which pertain to the good people of Virginia, as the basis and foundation of government," it is enumerated with equal solemnity, or, rather, studied emphasis.

Either, then, we must say that the will of the legislature is the only measure of their authority, and that, in the plenitude of this authority, they may sweep away all our fundamental rights; or, that they are bound to leave this particular right untouched and sacred: either we must say that they may control the

freedom of the press, may abolish the trial by jury, may swallow up the executive and judiciary powers of the state; nay, that they may despoil us of our right of suffrage, and erect themselves into an independent and hereditary assembly: or, we must say, that they have no authority to enact into law the bill under consideration. We, the subscribers, say, that the general assembly of this commonwealth have no such authority; and that no effort may be omitted, on our part, against so dangerous an usurpation, we oppose to it in this remonstrance—earnestly praying, as we are in duty bound, that the SUPREME LAWGIVER OF THE UNIVERSE, by illuminating those to whom it is addressed, may, on the one hand, turn their councils from every act which affronts his holy prerogative, or violates the trust committed to them; and, on the other, guide them into every measure that may be worthy of his blessing, may redound to their own praise, and may establish more firmly the liberties of the people, and the prosperity and happiness of the commonwealth.

5

U.S. Constitution, First Amendment, 1791

Congress shall make no law respecting an establishment of religion or prohibiting the free exercise thereof; or abridging the freedom of speech, or of the press; or the right of the people to peaceably assemble, and to petition the Government for a redress of grievances.

6

U.S. Constitution, Article VI, 1787

The Senators and Representatives before mentioned, and the Members of the several State Legislatures, and all executive and judicial Officers, both of the United States and of the several States, shall be bound by Oath or Affirmation, to support this Constitution, but no religious Test shall ever be required as a Qualification to any Office or public Trust under the United States.

7

John F. Kennedy, "Remarks on Church and State," Delivered to the Greater Houston Ministerial Association, September 12, 1960

I am grateful for your generous invitation to state my views.

While the so-called religious issue is necessarily and properly the chief topic here tonight, I want to emphasize from the outset that I believe that we have far more critical issues in the 1960 election: the spread of Communist influence, until it now festers only ninety miles off the coast of Florida—the humiliating treatment of our President and Vice-President by those who no longer respect our power—the hungry children I saw in West Virginia, the old people who cannot pay their doctor's bills, the families forced to give up their farms—an America with too many slums, with too few schools, and too late to the moon and outer space.

These are the real issues which should decide this campaign. And they are not religious issues—for war and hunger and ignorance and despair know no religious barrier.

But because I am a Catholic, and no Catholic has ever been elected President, the real issues in this campaign have been obscured—perhaps deliberately in some quarters less responsible than this. So it is apparently necessary for me to state once again—not what kind of church I believe in, for that should be important only to me, but what kind of America I believe in.

I believe in an America where the separation of church and state is absolute—where no Catholic prelate would tell the President (should he be a Catholic) how to act and no Protestant minister would tell his parishioners for whom to vote—where no church or church school is granted any public funds or political preference—and where no man is denied public office merely because his religion differs from the President who might appoint him or the people who might elect him.

I believe in an America that is officially neither Catholic, Protestant nor Jewish—where no public official either requests or accepts instructions on public policy from the Pope, the National Council of Churches or any other ecclesiastical source—where no religious body seeks to impose its will directly or indirectly upon the general populace or the public acts of its officials—and where religious liberty is so indivisible that an act against one church is treated as an act against all.

For while this year it may be a Catholic against whom the finger of suspicion is pointed, in other years it has been, and may someday be again, a Jew—or a Quaker—or a Unitarian—or a Baptist. It was Virginia's harassment of Baptist preachers, for example, that led to Jefferson's statute of religious freedom. Today, I may be the victim—but tomorrow it may be you—until the whole fabric of our harmonious society is ripped apart at a time of great national peril.

Finally, I believe in an America where religious intolerance will someday end—where all men and all churches are treated as equal—where every man has the same right to attend or not to attend the church of his choice—where there is no Catholic vote, no anti-Catholic vote, no bloc voting of any kind— and where Catholics, Protestants and Jews, both the lay and the pastoral level, will refrain from those attitudes of disdain and division which have so often marred their works in the past, and promote instead the American ideal of brotherhood.

That is the kind of America in which I believe. And it represents the kind of Presidency in which I believe—a great office that must be neither humbled by making it the instrument of any religious group, nor tarnished by arbitrarily withholding it, its occupancy, from the members of any religious group. I believe in a President whose views on religion are his own private affair, neither imposed upon him by the nation or imposed by the nation upon him as a condition to holding that office.

I would not look with favor upon a President working to subvert the First Amendment's guarantees of religious liberty (nor would our system of checks and balances permit him to do so). And neither do I look with favor upon those who would work to subvert Article VI of the Constitution by requiring a religious test—even by indirection—for if they disagree with that safeguard, they should be openly working to repeal it.

I want a Chief Executive whose public acts are responsible to all and obligated to none—who can attend any ceremony, service or dinner his office may appropriately require him to fulfill—and whose fulfillment of his Presidential office is not limited or conditioned by any religious oath, ritual or obligation.

This is the kind of America I believe in—and this is the kind of America I fought for in the South Pacific and the kind my brother died for in Europe. No one suggested then that we might have a "divided loyalty," that we did

"not believe in liberty" or that we belonged to a disloyal group that threatened "the freedoms for which our forefathers died."

And in fact this is the kind of America for which our forefathers did die when they fled here to escape religious test oaths, that denied office to members of less favored churches, when they fought for the Constitution, the Bill of Rights, the Virginia Statute of Religious Freedom—and when they fought at the shrine I visited today—the Alamo. For side by side with Bowie and Crockett died Fuentes and McCafferty and Bailey and Bedillio and Carey—but no one knows whether they were Catholics or not. For there was no religious test there.

I ask you tonight to follow in that tradition, to judge me on the basis of fourteen years in the congress—on my declared stands against an ambassador to the Vatican, against unconstitutional aid to parochial schools, and against any boycott of the public schools (which I attended myself)—instead of judging me on the basis of these pamphlets and publications we have all seen that carefully select quotations out of context from the statements of Catholic Church leaders, usually in other countries, frequently in other centuries, and rarely relevant to any situation here—and always omitting, of course, that statement of the American bishops in 1948 which strongly endorsed church-state separation.

I do not consider these other quotations binding upon my public acts—why should you? But let me say, with respect to other countries, that I am wholly opposed to the state being used by any religious group, Catholic or Protestant, to compel, prohibit or persecute the free exercise of any other religion. And that goes for any persecution at any time, by anyone, in any country.

And I hope that you and I condemn with equal fervor those nations which deny their Presidency to Protestants and those which deny it to Catholics. And rather than cite the misdeeds of those who differ, I would also cite the record of the Catholic Church in such nations as France and Ireland—and the independence of such statesmen as de Gaulle and Adenauer.

But let me stress again that these are my views—for, contrary to common newspaper usage, I am not the Catholic candidate for President. I am the Democratic Party's candidate for President, who happens also to be a Catholic.

I do not speak for my church on public matters—and the church does not speak for me.

Whatever issue may come before me as President, if I should be elected—on birth control, divorce, censorship, gambling, or any other subject—I will make my decision in accordance with these views, in accordance with what my conscience tells me to be in the national interest, and without regard to outside religious pressure or dictate. And no power or threat of punishment cold cause me to decide otherwise.

But if the time should ever come—and I do not concede any conflict to be

remotely possible—when my office would require me to either violate my conscience, or violate the national interest, then I would resign the office, and I hope any other conscientious public servant would do likewise.

But I do not intend to apologize for these views to my critics of either Catholic or Protestant faith, nor do I intend to disavow either my views or my church in order to win this election. If I should lose on the real issues, I shall return to my seat in the Senate, satisfied that I tried my best and was fairly judged.

But if this election is decided on the basis that 40,000,000 Americans lost their chance of being President on the day they were baptized, then it is the whole nation that will be the loser in the eyes of Catholics and non-Catholics around the world, in the eyes of history, and in the eyes of our own people.

But if, on the other hand, I should win this election, I shall devote every effort of mind and spirit to fulfilling the oath of the Presidency—practically identical, I might add, with the oath I have taken for fourteen years in the Congress. For, without reservation, I can, and I quote, "solemnly swear that I will faithfully execute the office of President of the United States and will to the best of my ability preserve, protect and defend the Constitution, so help me God."

8

Mario M. Cuomo, "Religious Belief and Public Morality: A Catholic Governor's Perspective," Address at the University of Notre Dame, September 13, 1984

I would like to begin by drawing your attention to the title of this lecture: "Religious Belief and Public Morality: A Catholic Governor's Perspective." I was not invited to speak on "church and sate" generally. Certainly not "Mondale versus Reagan." The subject assigned is difficult enough. I will not try to do more than I've been asked.

It's not easy to stay contained. Certainly, although everybody talks about a wall of separation between church and state, I've seen religious leaders scale that wall with all the dexterity of Olympic athletes. In fact, I've seen so many candidates in churches and synagogues that I think we should change Election Day from Tuesdays to Saturdays and Sundays.

I am honored by this invitation, but the record shows that I am not the first governor of New York to appear at an event involving Notre Dame. One of my great predecessors, Al Smith, went to the Army–Notre Dame football game each time it was played in New York.

His fellow Catholics expected Smith to sit with Notre Dame; protocol required him to sit with Army because it was the home team. Protocol prevailed. But not without Smith noting the dual demands on his affections. "I'll take my seat with Army," he said, "but I commend my soul to Notre Dame!"

Today I'm happy to have no such problem: both my seat and my soul are with Notre Dame. And as long as Father McBrien doesn't invite me back to sit with him at the Notre Dame–St. John's basketball game, I'm confident my loyalties will remain undivided.

In a sense, it's a question of loyalty that Father McBrien has asked me here today to discuss. Specifically, must politics and religion in America divide our loyalties? Does the "separation between church and state" imply separation

between religion and politics? Between morality and government? Are these different propositions? Even more specifically, what is the relationship of my Catholicism to my politics? Where does the one end and other begin? Or are the two divided at all? And if they're not, should they be?

Hard questions.

No wonder most of us in public life—at least until recently—preferred to stay away from them, heeding the biblical advice that if "hounded and pursued in one city," we should flee to another.

Now, however, I think that it is too late to flee. The questions are all around us, and answers are coming from every quarter. Some of them have been simplistic, most of them fragmentary, and a few, spoken with a purely political intent, demagogic.

There has been confusion and compounding of confusion, a blurring of the issue, entangling it in personalities and election strategies, instead of clarifying it for Catholics, as well as others.

Today I would like to try to help correct that.

I can offer you no final truths, complete and unchallengeable. But it's possible this one effort will provoke other efforts—both in support and contradiction of my position—that will help all of us understand our differences and perhaps even discover some basic agreement.

In the end, I'm convinced we will all benefit if suspicion is replaced by discussion, innuendo by dialogue, if the emphasis in our debate turns from a search for talismanic criteria and neat but simplistic answers to an honest, more intelligent attempt at describing the role religion has in our public affairs, and the limits placed on that role.

And if we do it right—if we're not afraid of the truth even when the truth is complex—this debate, by clarification, can bring relief to untold numbers of confused, even anguished Catholics, as well as to many others who want only to make our already great democracy even stronger than it is.

I believe the recent discussion in my own state has already produced some clearer definition. In early summer, an impression was created in some quarters that official church spokespeople would ask Catholics to vote for or against specific candidates on the basis of their political position on the abortion issue. I was one of those given that impression. Thanks to the dialogue that ensued over the summer—only partially reported by the media—we learned that the impression was not accurate.

Confusion had presented an opportunity for clarification, and we seized it. Now all of us are saying one thing, in chorus, reiterating the statement of the National Conference of Catholic Bishops that they will not "take positions for or against political candidates" and that their stand on specific issues should not be perceived "as an expression of political partisanship."

Of course the bishops will teach—they must—more and more vigorously

and more and more extensively. But they have said they will not use the power of their position, and the great respect it receives from all Catholics, to give an imprimatur to individual politicians or parties.

Not that they couldn't if they wished to—some religious leaders do; some are doing it at this very moment.

Not that it would be a sin if they did—God doesn't insist on political neutrality. But because it is the judgment of the bishops, and most of us Catholic laypeople, that it is not wise for prelates and politicians to be tied too closely together.

I think that getting this consensus was an extraordinarily useful achievement.

Now, with some trepidation, I take up your gracious invitation to continue the dialogue in the hope that it will lead to still further clarification.

Let me begin this part of the effort by underscoring the obvious. I do not speak as a theologian; I do not have that competence. I do not speak as a philosopher; to suggest that I could would be to set a new record for false pride. I don't presume to speak as a "good" person except in the ontological sense of that word. My principal credential is that I serve in a position that forces me to wrestle with the problems you've come here to study and debate.

I am by training a lawyer and by practice a politician. Both professions make me suspect in many quarters, including among some of my own coreligionists. Maybe there's no better illustration of the public perception of how politicians unite their faith and their profession than the story they tell in New York about "Fishhooks" McCarthy, a famous Democratic leader on the Lower East Side and right-hand man to Al Smith.

"Fishhooks," the story goes, was devout. So devout that every morning on his way to Tammany Hall to do his political work, he stopped into St. James Church on Oliver Street in downtown Manhattan, fell on his knees, and whispered the same simply prayer: "O, Lord, give me health and strength. We'll steal the rest."

"Fishhooks" notwithstanding, I speak here as a politician. And also as a Catholic, a layperson baptized and raised in the pre–Vatican II church, educated in Catholic schools, attached to the church first by birth, then by choice, now by love. An old-fashioned Catholic who sins, regrets, struggles, worries, gets confused, and most of the time feels better after confession.

The Catholic church is my spiritual home. My heart is there, and my hope.

There is, of course, more to being a Catholic than a sense of spiritual and emotional resonance. Catholicism is a religion of the head as well as the heart, and to be a Catholic is to say, "I believe," to the essential core of dogmas that distinguishes our faith.

The acceptance of this faith requires a lifelong struggle to understand it

more fully and to live it more truly, to translate truth into experience, to practice as well as to believe.

That's not easy: applying religious believe to everyday life often presents difficult challenges.

It's always been that way. It certainly is today. The America of the late twentieth century is a consumer society, filled with endless distractions, where faith is more often dismissed than challenged, where the ethnic and other loyalties that once fastened us to our religion seem to be weakening.

In addition to all the weaknesses, dilemmas, and temptations that impede every pilgrim's progress, the Catholic who holds political office in a pluralistic democracy—who is elected to serve Jews and Muslims, atheists and Protestants, as well as Catholics—bears special responsibility. He or she undertakes to help create conditions under which *all* can live with a maximum of dignity and with a reasonable degree of freedom; where everyone who chooses may hold beliefs different from specifically Catholic ones, sometimes contradictory to them; where the laws protect people's right to divorce, to use birth control, and even to choose abortion.

In fact, Catholic public officials take an oath to preserve the Constitution that guarantees this freedom. And they do so gladly. Not because they love what others do with their freedom, but because they realize that in guaranteeing freedom for all, they guarantee *our* right to be Catholics: *our* right to pray, to use the sacraments, to refuse birth control devices, to reject abortion, not to divorce and remarry if we believe it to be wrong.

The Catholic public official lives the political truth most Catholics through most of American history have accepted and insisted on: the truth that to assure our freedom we must allow others the same freedom, even if occasionally it produces conduct by them which we would hold to be sinful.

I protect my right to be a Catholic by preserving your right to believe as a Jew, a Protestant, or nonbeliever, or as anything else you choose.

We know that the price of seeking to force our beliefs on others is that they might someday force theirs on us.

This freedom is the fundamental strength of our unique experiment in government. In the complex interplay of forces and considerations that go into the making of our laws and policies, its preservation must be a pervasive and dominant concern.

But insistence on freedom is easier to accept as a general proposition than in its applications to specific situations. There are other valid general principles firmly embedded in our Constitution, which, operating at the same time, create interesting and occasionally troubling problems. Thus the same amendment of the Constitution that forbids the establishment of a state church affirms my legal right to argue that my religious belief would serve well as an article of our universal public morality. I may use the prescribed processes of government—the legislative and executive and judicial processes—to con-

vince my fellow citizens, Jews and Protestants and Buddhists and nonbelievers, that what I propose is as beneficial for them as I believe it is for me; that it is not just parochial or narrowly sectarian but fulfills a human desire for order, peace, justice, kindness, love, any of the values most of us agree are desirable even apart from their specific religious base or context.

I am free to argue for a governmental policy for a nuclear freeze not just to avoid sin, but because I think my democracy should regard it as a desirable goal.

I can, if I wish, argue that the state should not fund the use of contraceptive devices not because the pope demands it, but because I think that the whole community—for the good of the whole community—should not sever sex from an openness to the creation of life.

And surely I can, if so inclined, demand some kind of law against abortion not because my bishops say it is wrong, but because I think that the whole community, regardless of its religious beliefs, should agree on the importance of protecting life—including life in the womb, which is at the very least potentially human and should not be extinguished casually.

No law prevents us from advocating any of these things: I am free to do so. So are the bishops. And so is Reverend Falwell.

In fact, the Constitution guarantees my right to try. And theirs. And his.

But should I? Is it helpful? Is it essential to human dignity? Does it promote harmony and understanding? Or does it divide us so fundamentally that it threatens our ability to function as a pluralistic community?

When should I argue to make my religious value your morality? My rule of conduct your limitation?

What are the rules and policies that should influence the exercise of this right to argue and promote?

I believe I have a salvific mission as a Catholic. Does that mean I am in conscience required to do everything I can as governor to translate *all* my religious values into the laws and regulations of the state of New York or the United States? Or be branded a hypocrite if I don't?

As a Catholic, I respect the teaching authority of the bishops.

But must I agree with everything in the bishops' pastoral letter on peace and fight to include it in party platforms?

And will I have to do the same for the forthcoming pastoral on economics even if I am an unrepentant supply-sider?

Must I, having heard the pope renew the church's ban on birth control devices, veto the funding of contraceptive programs for non-Catholics or dissenting Catholics in my state?

I accept the church's teaching on abortion. Must I insist you do? By law? By denying you Medicaid funding? But a constitutional amendment? If so, which one? Would that be the best way to avoid abortions or to prevent them?

These are only some of the questions for Catholics. People with other religious beliefs face similar problems.

Let me try some answers.

Almost all Americans accept some religious values as a part of our public life. We are a religious people, many of us descended from ancestors who came here expressly to live their religious faith free from coercion or repression. But we are also a people of many religions, with no established church, who hold different beliefs on many matters.

Our public morality, then—the moral standards we maintain for everyone, not just the ones we insist on in our private lives—depends on a consensus view of right and wrong. The values derived from religious belief will not—and should not—be accepted as part of the public morality unless they are shared by the pluralistic community at large, by consensus.

That values happen to be religious values does not deny them acceptability as a part of this consensus. But it does not require their acceptability, either.

The agnostics who joined the civil rights struggle were not deterred because the crusade's values had been nurtured and sustained in black Christian churches. Those on the political left are not perturbed today by the religious basis of the clergy and laypeople who join them in the protest against the arms race and hunger and exploitation.

The arguments start when religious values are used to support positions which would impose on other people restrictions they find unacceptable. Some people *do* object to Catholic demands for an end to abortion, seeing it as a violation of the separation of church and state. And some others, while they have no compunction about invoking the authority of the Catholic bishops in regard to birth control and abortion, might reject out of hand their teaching on war and peace and social policy.

Ultimately, therefore, the question whether or not we admit religious values into our public affairs is too broad to yield a single answer. Yes, we create our public morality through consensus and in this country that consensus reflects to some extent religious values of a great majority of Americans. But no, all religiously based values don't have an a priori place in our public morality.

The community must decide if what is being proposed would be better left to private discretion than public policy; whether it restricts freedoms, and if so to what end, to whose benefit; whether it will produce a good or bad result; whether overall it will help the community or merely divide it.

The right answers to these questions can be elusive. Some of the wrong answers, on the other hand, are quite clear. For example, there are those who say there is a simple answer to *all* these questions; they say that by history and practice of our people we were intended to be—and should be—a Christian country in law.

But where would that leave the nonbelievers? And whose Christianity would be law, yours or mine?

This "Christian nation" argument should concern—even frighten—two groups: non-Christians and thinking Christians.

I believe it does.

I think it's already apparent that a good part of this nation understands—if only instinctively—that anything which seems to suggest that God favors a political party or the establishment of a state church is wrong and dangerous.

Way down deep the American people are afraid of an entangling relationship between formal religions—or whole bodies of religious belief—and government. Apart from constitutional law and religious doctrine, there is a sense that tells us it's wrong to presume to speak for God or to claim God's sanction of our particular legislation and his rejection of all other positions. Most of us are offended when we see religion being trivialized by its appearance in political throwaway pamphlets.

The American people need no course in philosophy or political science or church history to know that God should not be made into a celestial party chairman.

To most of us, the manipulative invoking of religion to advance a politician or a party is frightening and divisive. The American people will tolerate religious leaders taking positions for or against candidates, although I think the Catholic bishops are right in avoiding that position. But the American people are leery about large religious organizations, powerful churches, or synagogue groups engaging in such activities—again, not as a matter of law or doctrine, but because our innate wisdom and democratic instinct teaches us these things are dangerous.

Today there are a number of issues involving life and death that raise questions of public morality. They are also questions of concern to most religions. Pick up a newspaper and you are almost certain to find a bitter controversy over any one of them: Baby Jane Doe, the right to die, artificial insemination, embryos in vitro, abortion, birth control . . . not to mention nuclear war and the shadow it throws across all existence.

Some of these issues touch the most intimate recesses of our lives, our roles as someone's mother or child or husband; some affect women in a unique way. But they are also public questions, for all of us.

Put aside what God expects—assume, if you like, there is no God—then the greatest thing still left to us is life. Even a radically secular world must struggle with the questions of when life begins, under what circumstances it can be ended, when it must be protected, by what authority; it, too, must decide what protection to extend to the helpless and the dying, to the aged and the unborn, to life in all its phases.

As a Catholic, I have accepted certain answers as the right ones for myself

and my family, and because I have, they have influenced me in special ways, as Matilda's husband, as a father of five children, as a son who stood next to his own father's deathbed trying to decide if the tubes and needles no longer served a purpose.

As a governor, however, I am involved in defining policies that determine *other* people's rights in these same areas of life and death. Abortion is one of these issues, and while it is one issue among many, it is one of the most controversial and affects me in a special way as a Catholic public official.

So let me spend some time considering it.

I should start, I believe, by noting that the Catholic church's actions with respect to the interplay of religious values and public policy make clear that there is no inflexible moral principle which determines what our *political* conduct should be. For example, on divorce and birth control, without changing its moral teaching, the church abides by the civil law as it now stands, thereby accepting—without making much of a point of it—that in our pluralistic society we are not required to insist that *all* our religious values be the law of the land.

Abortion is treated differently.

Of course there are differences both in degree and quality between abortion and some of the other religious positions the church takes: abortion is a "matter of life and death," and degree counts. But the differences in approach reveal a truth, I think, that is not well enough perceived by Catholics and therefore still further complicates the process for us. That is, while we always owe our bishops words respectful attention and careful consideration, the question whether to engage the political system in a struggle to have it adopt certain articles of our belief as part of public morality is not a matter of doctrine: it is a matter of prudential political judgment.

Recently, Michael Novak put it succinctly. "Religious judgment and political judgment are both needed," he wrote. "But they are not identical."

My church and my conscience require me to believe certain things about divorce, birth control, and abortion. My church does not order me—under pain of sin or expulsion—to pursue my salvific mission according to a precisely defined political plan.

As a Catholic I accept the church's teaching authority. While in the past some Catholic theologians may appear to have disagreed on the morality of some abortions (it wasn't, I think, until 1869 that excommunication was attached to all abortions without distinction), and while some theologians still do, I accept the bishops' position that abortion is to be avoided.

As Catholics, my wife and I were enjoined never to use abortion to destroy the life we created. We thought church doctrine was clear on this. Life or fetal life in the womb should be protected, even if five of nine justices of the Supreme Court and my neighbor disagree with me. A fetus is different from an appendix or a set of tonsils. At the very least, even if the argument is made by

some scientists or some theologians that in the early stages of fetal development we can't discern human life, the full potential of human life is indisputably there. That—to my less subtle mind—by itself should demand respect,
caution, indeed . . . reverence.

But not everyone in our society agrees.

And those who don't—those who endorse legalized abortions—aren't a
ruthless, callous alliance of anti-Christians determined to overthrow our moral
standards. In many cases, the proponents of legal abortion are the very people
who have worked with Catholics to realize the goals of social justice set out
in papal encyclicals: the American Lutheran Church, the Central Conference
of American Rabbis, the Presbyterian Church in the United States, B'nai
B'rith Women, the Women of the Episcopal Church. These are just a few of
the religious organizations that don't share the church's position on abortion.

Certainly, we should not be forced to mold Catholic morality to conform to
disagreement by non-Catholics, however sincere or severe their disagreement.
Our bishops should be teachers, not pollsters. They should not change what
we Catholics believe in order to ease our consciences or please our friends or
protect the church from criticism.

But if the breadth, intensity, and sincerity of opposition to church teaching
shouldn't be allowed to shape our Catholic morality, it can't help but determine our ability—our realistic, political ability—to translate our Catholic morality into civil law, a law not for the believers who don't need it but for the
disbelievers who reject it.

And it is here, in our attempt to find a political answer to abortion—an
answer beyond our private observance of Catholic morality—that we encounter controversy within and without the church over how and in what degree to
press the case that our morality should be everybody else's, and to what effect.

*I repeat, there is no church teaching that mandates the best political course
for making our belief everyone's rule, for spreading this part of our Catholicism. There is neither an encyclical nor a catechism that spells out a political
strategy for achieving legislative goals.*

And so the Catholic trying to make moral and prudent judgments in the
political realm must discern which, if any, of the actions one could take would
be best.

This latitude of judgment is not something new in the church, not a development that has arisen only with the abortion issue. Take, for example, the question of slavery. It has been argued that the failure to endorse a legal ban on
abortions is equivalent to refusing to support the cause of abolition before the
Civil War. This analogy has been advanced by the bishops of my own state.

But the truth of the matter is few, if any, Catholic bishops spoke for abolition in the years before the Civil War. It wasn't, I believe, that the bishops
endorsed the idea of some humans owning and exploiting other humans; Pope
Gregory XVI, in 1840, had condemned the slave trade. Instead it was a practi-

cal political judgment that the bishops made. They weren't hypocrites; they were realists. At the time, Catholics were a small minority, mostly immigrants, despised by much of the population, often vilified and the object of sporadic violence. In the face of a public controversy that aroused tremendous passions and threatened to break the country apart, the bishops made a pragmatic decision. They believed their opinion would not change people's minds. Moreover, they knew that there were Southern Catholics, even some priests, who owned slaves. They concluded that under the circumstances arguing for a constitutional amendment against slavery would do more harm than good, so they were silent. As they have been, generally, in recent years, on the question of birth control. And as the church has been on even more controversial issues in the past, even ones that dealt with life and death.

What is relevant to this discussion is that the bishops were making judgments about translating Catholic teachings into public policy, not about the moral validity of the teachings. In so doing they grappled with the unique political complexities of their time. The decision they made to remain silent on a constitutional amendment to abolish slavery or on the repeal of the Fugitive Slave Law wasn't a mark of their moral indifference: it was a measured attempt to balance moral truths against political realities. Their decision reflected their sense of complexity, not their diffidence. As history reveals, Lincoln behaved with similar discretion.

The parallel I want to draw here is not between or among what we Catholics believe to be moral wrongs. It is in the Catholic response to those wrongs. Church teaching on slavery and abortion is clear. But in the application of those teachings—the exact way we translate them into action, the specific laws we propose, the exact legal sanctions we seek—there was and is no one, clear, absolute route that the church says, as a matter of doctrine, we must follow.

The bishops' pastoral letter, "The Challenge of Peace," speaks directly to this point. "We recognize," the bishops wrote, "that the Church's teaching authority does not carry the same force when it deals with technical solutions involving particular means as it does when it speaks of principles or ends. People may agree in abhorring an injustice, for instance, yet sincerely disagree as to what practical approach will achieve justice. Religious groups are entitled as others to their opinions in such cases, but they should not claim that their opinions are the only ones that people of good will may hold."

With regard to abortion, the American bishops have had to weigh Catholic moral teaching against the fact that we are a pluralistic country where our view is in the minority, acknowledging that what is ideally desirable isn't always feasible, that there can be different political approaches to abortion besides unyielding adherence to an absolute prohibition.

This is in the American-Catholic tradition of political realism. In supporting or opposing specific legislation the church in this country has never re-

treated into a moral fundamentalism that will settle for nothing less than total acceptance of its views.

Indeed, the bishops have already confronted the fact that an absolute ban on abortion doesn't have the support necessary to be placed in our Constitution. In 1981, they put aside earlier efforts to describe a law they could accept and get passed, and supported the Hatch amendment instead.

Some Catholics felt the bishops had gone too far with that action, some not far enough. Such judgments were not a rejection of the bishops' teaching authority: the bishops even disagreed among themselves. Catholics are allowed to disagree on these technical political questions without having to confess.

Respectfully, and after careful consideration of the position and arguments of the bishops, I have concluded that the approach of a constitutional amendment is not the best way for us to seek to deal with abortion.

I believe that legal interdicting of all abortions by either the federal government or the individual states is not a plausible possibility and, even if it could be obtained, it wouldn't work. Given present attitudes, it would be Prohibition revisited, legislating what couldn't be enforced and in the process creating a disrespect for law in general. And as much as I admire the bishops' hope that a constitutional amendment against abortion would be the basis for a full, new bill of rights for mothers and children, I disagree that this would be the result.

I believe that, more likely, a constitutional prohibition would allow people to ignore the causes of many abortions instead of addressing them, much the way the death penalty is used to escape dealing more fundamentally and more rationally with the problem of violent crime.

Other legal options that have been proposed are, in my view, equally ineffective. The Hatch amendment, by returning the question of abortion to the states, would have given us a checkerboard of permissive and restrictive jurisdictions. In some cases people might have been forced to go elsewhere to have abortions and that might have eased a few consciences, but it wouldn't have done what the church wants to do—it wouldn't have created a deep-seated respect for life. Abortions would have gone on, millions of them.

Nor would a denial of Medicaid funding for abortion achieve our objectives. Given *Roe v. Wade,* it would be nothing more than an attempt to do indirectly what the law says cannot be done directly; worse, it would do it in a way that would burden only the already disadvantaged. Removing funding from the Medicaid program would not prevent the rich and middle class from having abortions. It would not even assure that the disadvantaged wouldn't have them; it would only impose financial burdens on poor women who want abortions.

Apart from that unevenness, there is a more basic question. Medicaid is designed to deal with health and medical needs. But the arguments for the

cutoff of Medicaid abortion funds are not related to those needs. They are moral arguments. If we assume health and medical needs exist, our personal view of morality ought not to be considered a relevant basis for discrimination.

We must keep in mind always that we are a nation of laws—when we like those laws and when we don't.

The Supreme Court has established a woman's constitutional right to abortion. The Congress has decided the federal government should not provide federal funding in the Medicaid program for abortion. That, of course, does not bind states in the allocation of their own state funds. Under the law, the individual states need not follow the federal lead, and in New York I believe we *cannot* follow that lead. The equal protection clause in New York's constitution has been interpreted by the courts as a standard of fairness that would preclude us from denying only the poor—indirectly, by a cutoff of funds—the practical use of the constitutional right given by *Roe v. Wade.*

In the end, even if after a long and divisive struggle we were able to remove all Medicaid funding for abortion and restore the law to what it was, if we could put most abortions out of our sight, return them to the back rooms where they were performed for so long, I don't believe our responsibility as Catholics would be any closer to being fulfilled than it is now, with abortion guaranteed by the law as a woman's right.

The hard truth is that abortion isn't a failure of government. No agency or department of government forces women to have abortions, but abortion goes on. Catholics, the statistics show, support the right to abortion in equal proportion to the rest of the population. Despite the teaching in our homes and schools and pulpits, despite the sermons and pleadings of parents and priests and prelates, despite all the effort at defining our opposition to the sin of abortion, collectively we Catholics apparently believe—and perhaps act— little differently from those who don't share our commitment.

Are we asking government to make criminal what we believe to be sinful because we ourselves can't stop committing the sin?

The failure here is not Caesar's. This failure is our failure, the failure of the entire people of God.

Nobody has expressed this better than a bishop in my own state, Joseph Sullivan, a man who works with the poor in New York City, is resolutely opposed to abortion, and argues, with his fellow bishops, for a change of law. "The major problem the church has is internal," the bishop said last month in reference to abortion. "How do we teach? As much as I think we're responsible for advocating public policy issues, our primary responsibility is to teach our own people. We haven't done that. We're asking politicians to do what we haven't done effectively ourselves."

I agree with the bishop. I think our moral and social mission as Catholics must begin with the wisdom contained in the words: "Physician, heal thy-

self." Unless we Catholics educate ourselves better to the values that define—and can ennoble—our lives, following those teachings better than we do now, unless we set an example that is clear and compelling, then we will never convince this society to change the civil laws to protect what we preach is precious human life.

Better than any law or rule or threat of punishment would be the moving strength of our own good example, demonstrating our lack of hypocrisy, proving the beauty and worth of our instruction.

We must work to find ways to avoid abortions without otherwise violating our faith. We should provide funds and opportunity for young women to bring their child to term, knowing both of them will be taken care of if that is necessary; we should teach our young men better than we do now their responsibilities in creating and caring for human life.

It is this duty of the church to teach through its practice of love that Pope John Paul II has proclaimed so magnificently to all peoples. "The Church," he wrote in *Redemptor Hominis* (1979), "which has no weapons at her disposal apart from those of the spirit, of the word and of love, cannot renounce her proclamation of 'the word . . . in season and out of season.' For this reason she does not cease to implore . . . everybody in the name of God and in the name of man: Do not kill! Do not prepare destruction and extermination for each other! Think of your brothers and sisters who are suffering hunger and misery! Respect each other's dignity and freedom!"

The weapons of the word and of love are already available to us; we need no statute to provide them.

I am not implying that we should stand by and pretend indifference to whether a woman takes a pregnancy to its conclusion or aborts it. I believe we should in all cases try to teach a respect for life. And I believe with regard to abortion that, despite Roe v. Wade, *we can, in practical ways. Here, in fact, it seems to me that all of us can agree.*

Without lessening their insistence on a woman's right to an abortion, the people who call themselves "pro-choice" can support the development of government programs that present an impoverished mother with the full range of support she needs to bear and raise her children, to have a real choice. Without dropping their campaign to ban abortion, those who gather under the banner of "pro-life" can join in developing and enacting a legislative bill of rights for mothers and children, as the bishops have already proposed.

While we argue over abortion, the United States' infant mortality rate places us sixteenth among the nations of the world. Thousands of infants die each year because of inadequate medical care. Some are born with birth defects that, with proper treatment, could be prevented. Some are stunted in their physical and mental growth because of improper nutrition.

If we want to prove our regard for life in the womb, for the helpless infant, if we care about women having real choices in their lives and not being driven

to abortions by a sense of helplessness and despair about the future of their child, then there is work enough for all of us. Lifetimes of it.

In New York, we have put in place a number of programs to begin this work, assisting women in giving birth to healthy babies. This year we doubled Medicaid funding to private-care physicians for prenatal and delivery services.

The state already spends 20 million dollars a year for prenatal care in outpatient clinics and for inpatient hospital care.

One program in particular we believe holds a great deal of promise. It's called New Avenues to Dignity, and it seeks to provide a teenager mother with the special services she needs to continue with her education, to train for a job, to become capable of standing on her own, to provide for herself and the child she is bringing into the world.

My dissent, then, from the contention that we can have effective and enforceable legal prohibitions on abortion is by no means an argument for religious quietism, for accepting the world's wrongs because that is our fate as "the poor banished children of Eve."

Let me make another point. Abortion has a unique significance but not a preemptive significance. Apart from the question of the efficacy of using legal weapons to make people stop having abortions, we know our Christian responsibility doesn't end with any one law or amendment. That it doesn't end with abortion. Because it involves life and death, abortion will always be a central concern of Catholics. But so will nuclear weapons. And hunger and homelessness and joblessness, all the forces diminishing human life and threatening to destroy it. The "seamless garment" that Cardinal Bernardin has spoken of is a challenge to all Catholics in public office, conservatives as well as liberals.

We cannot justify our aspiration to goodness simply on the basis of the vigor of our demand for an elusive and questionable civil law declaring what we already know, that abortion is wrong.

Approval or rejection of legal restrictions on abortion should not be the exclusive litmus test of Catholic loyalty. We should understand that whether abortion is outlawed or not, our work has barely begun: the work of creating a society where the right to life doesn't end at the moment of birth; where an infant isn't helped into a world that doesn't care if it's fed properly, housed decently, educated adequately; where the blind or retarded child isn't condemned to exist rather than empowered to live.

The bishops stated this duty clearly in 1974, in their statement to the Senate subcommittee considering a proposed amendment to restrict abortions. They maintained such an amendment could not be seen as an end in itself. "We do not see a constitutional amendment as the final product of our commitment or of our legislative activity," they said. "It is instead the constitutional base on

which to provide support and assistance to pregnant women and their unborn children. This would include nutritional, prenatal, child birth and post-natal care for the mother, and also nutritional and pediatric care for the child through the first year of life. . . . We believe that all of these should be available as a matter of right to all pregnant women and their children."

The bishops reaffirmed that view in 1976, in 1980, and again this year when the United States Catholic Committee asked Catholics to judge candidates on a wide range of issues—on abortion, yes, but also on food policy, the arms race, human rights, education, social justice, and military expenditures.

The bishops have been consistently pro-life in the full meaning of that term, and I respect them for that.

The problems created by the matter of abortion are complex and confounding. Nothing is clearer to me than my inadequacy to find compelling solutions to all of their moral, legal, and social implications. I, and many others like me, are eager for enlightenment, eager to learn new and better ways to manifest respect for the deep reverence for life that is our religion and our instinct. I hope that this public attempt to describe the problems as I understand them will give impetus to the dialogue in the Catholic community and beyond, a dialogue which could show me a better wisdom than I've been able to find so far.

It would be tragic if we let that dialogue become a prolonged, divisive argument that destroys or impairs our ability to practice any part of the morality given us in the Sermon on the Mount, to touch, heal, and affirm the human life that surrounds us.

We Catholic citizens of the richest, most powerful nation that has ever existed are like the stewards made responsible over a great household: from those to whom so much has been given, much shall be required. It is worth repeating that ours is not a faith that encourages its believers to stand apart from the world, seeking their salvation alone, separate from the salvation of those around them.

We speak of ourselves as a body. We come together in worship as companions, in the ancient sense of that word, those who break bread together, and who are obliged by the commitment we share to help one another, everywhere, in all we do and, in the process, to help the whole human family. We see our mission to be "the completion of the work of creation."

This is difficult work today. It presents us with many hard choices.

The Catholic church has come of age in America. The ghetto walls are gone, our religion no longer a badge of irredeemable foreignness. This newfound status is both an opportunity and a temptation. If we choose, we can give in to the temptation to become more and more assimilated into the larger, blander culture, abandoning the practice of the specific values that made us different, worshiping whatever gods the marketplace has to sell while we seek

to rationalize our own laxity by urging the political system to legislate on others a morality we no longer practice ourselves.

Or we can remember where we come from, the journey of two millennia, clinging to our personal faith, to its insistence on constancy and service and on hope. *We can live and practice the morality Christ gave us, maintaining his truth in this world, struggling to embody his love, practicing it especially where that love is most needed, among the poor and the weak and the dispossessed. Not just by trying to make laws for others to live by, but by living the laws already written for us by God, in our hearts and our minds.*

We can be fully Catholic, proudly, totally at ease with ourselves, a people in the world, transforming it, a light to this nation. Appealing to the best in our people, not the worst. Persuading, not coercing. Leading people to truth by love. And still, all the while, respecting and enjoying our unique pluralistic democracy. And we can do it even as politicians.

9

Selected Supreme Court Cases

Everson v. Board of Education of Ewing Township, 330 U.S. 1 (1947)

Mr. Justice Black delivered the opinion of the Court.

A New Jersey statute authorizes its local school districts to make rules and contracts for the transportation to and from schools. The appellee, a township board of education, acting pursuant to this statute, authorized reimbursement to parents of money expended by them for the bus transportation of their children on regular buses operated by the public transportation system. Part of this money was for the payment of transportation of some children in the community to Catholic parochial schools. These church schools give their students, in addition to secular education, regular religious instruction conforming to the religious tenets and modes of worship of the Catholic Faith. The superintendent of these schools is a Catholic priest.

The appellant, in his capacity as a district taxpayer, filed suit in a State court challenging the right of the Board to reimburse parents of parochial school students. He contended that the statute and the resolution passed pursuant to it violated both the State and the Federal Constitutions. . . .

The only contention here is that the State statute and the resolution, insofar as they authorized reimbursement to parents of children attending parochial schools, violate the Federal Constitution. . . .

The statute and the resolution forced inhabitants to pay taxes to help support and maintain schools which are dedicated to, and which regularly teach, the Catholic Faith. This is alleged to be a use of State power to support church schools contrary to the prohibition of the First Amendment which the Fourteenth Amendment made applicable to the states. . . .

Whether this New Jersey law is one respecting an "establishment of religion" requires an understanding of the meaning of that language, particularly with respect to the imposition of taxes. Once again, therefore, it is not inappropriate briefly to review the background and environment of the period in which that constitutional language was fashioned and adopted.

A large proportion of the early settlers of this country came here from Europe to escape the bondage of laws which compelled them to support and attend government favored churches. The centuries immediately before and contemporaneous with the colonization of America had been filled with turmoil, civil strife, and persecutions, generated in large part by established sects determined to maintain their absolute political and religious supremacy. . . .

These practices of the old world were transplanted to and began to thrive in the soil of the new America. . . .

Catholics found themselves hounded and proscribed because of their faith; Quakers who followed their conscience went to jail; Baptists were peculiarly obnoxious to certain dominant Protestant sects; men and women of varied faiths who happened to be in a minority in a particular locality were persecuted because they steadfastly persisted in worshipping God only as their own consciences dictated. And all of these dissenters were compelled to pay tithes and taxes to support government-sponsored churches whose ministers preached inflammatory sermons designed to strengthen and consolidate the established faith by generating a burning hatred against dissenters.

These practices became so commonplace as to shock the freedom-loving colonials into a feeling of abhorrence. The imposition of taxes to pay ministers' salaries and to build and maintain churches and church property aroused their indignation. It was these feelings which found expression in the First Amendment. No one locality and no one group throughout the Colonies can rightly be given entire credit for having aroused the sentiment that culminated in adoption of the Bill of Rights' provisions embracing religious liberty. But Virginia, where the established church had achieved a dominant influence in political affairs and where many excesses attracted wide public attention, provided a great stimulus and able leadership for the movement. The people there, as elsewhere, reached the conviction that individual religious liberty could be achieved best under a government which was stripped of all power to tax, to support or otherwise to assist any or all religions, or to interfere with the beliefs of any religious individual or group.

The movement toward this end reached its dramatic climax in Virginia in 1785–86 when the Virginia legislative body was about to renew Virginia's tax levy for the support of the established church. Thomas Jefferson and James Madison led the fight against this tax. Madison wrote his great Memorial and Remonstrance against the law. In it, he eloquently argued that a true religion did not need the support of law; that no person, either believer or nonbeliever, should be taxed to support a religious institution of any kind; that the best interest of a society required that the minds of men always be wholly free; and that cruel persecutions were the inevitable result of government-established religions. Madison's Remonstrance received strong support throughout Virginia, and the Assembly postponed consideration of the proposed tax measure until its next session. When the proposal came up for con-

sideration at that session, it not only died in committee, but the Assembly enacted the famous "Virginia Bill for Religious Liberty" originally written by Thomas Jefferson. . . .

This Court has previously recognized that the provisions of the First Amendment, in the drafting and adoption of which Madison and Jefferson played such leading roles, had the same objective and were intended to provide the same protection against governmental intrusion on religious liberty as the Virginia statute. Prior to the adoption of the Fourteenth Amendment, the First Amendment did not apply as a restraint against the states. Most of them did soon provide similar constitutional protections for religious liberty. But some states persisted for about half a century in imposing restraints upon the free exercise of religion and in discriminating against particular religious group. In recent years, so far as the provision against the establishment of a religion is concerned, the question has most frequently arisen in connection with proposed state aid to church schools and efforts to carry on religious teachings in the public schools in accordance with the tenets of a particular sect. Some churches have either sought or accepted state financial support for their schools. Here again the efforts to obtain state aid or acceptance of it have not been limited to any one particular faith. The state courts, in the main, have remained faithful to the language of their own constitutional provisions designed to protect religious freedom and to separate religions and governments. Their decisions, however, show the difficulty in drawing the line between tax legislation which provides funds for the welfare of the general public and that which is designed to support institutions which teach religion.

The meaning and scope of the First Amendment, preventing establishment of religion or prohibiting the free exercise thereof, in the light of its history and the evils it was designed forever to suppress, have been several times elaborated by the decisions of this Court prior to the application of the First Amendment to the states by the Fourteenth. The broad meaning given the amendment by these earlier cases has been accepted by this Court in its decisions concerning an individual's religious freedom rendered since the Fourteenth Amendment was interpreted to make the prohibitions of the First applicable to state action abridging religious freedom. There is every reason to give the same application and broad interpretation to the "establishment of religion" clause. . . .

The "establishment of religion" clause of the First Amendment means at least this: Neither a state nor the Federal Government can set up a church. Neither can pass laws which aid one religion, aid all religions, or prefer one religion over another. Neither can force nor influence a person to go to or to remain away from church against his will or force him to profess a belief or disbelief in any religion. No person can be punished for entertaining or professing religious beliefs or disbeliefs, for church attendance or nonattendance. No tax in any amount, large or small, can be levied to support any religious

activities or institutions, whatever they may be called, or whatever form they may adopt to teach or practice religion. Neither a state nor the Federal Government can, openly or secretly, participate in the affairs of any religious organizations or groups and vice versa. In the words of Jefferson, the clause against establishment of religion by law was intended to erect "a wall of separation between Church and State. . . ."

We must consider the New Jersey statute in accordance with the foregoing limitations imposed by the First Amendment. But we must not strike that state statute down if it is within the State's constitutional power even though it approaches the verge of that power. New Jersey cannot consistently with the "establishment of religion" clause of the First Amendment contribute tax-raised funds to the support of an institution which teaches the tenets and faith of any church. . . .

We must be careful, in protecting the citizens of New Jersey against state-established churches, to be sure that we do not inadvertently prohibit New Jersey from extending its general state law benefits to all its citizens without regard to their religious belief.

Measured by these standards, we cannot say that the First Amendment prohibits New Jersey from spending tax-raised funds to pay the bus fares of parochial school pupils as a part of a general program under which it pays the fares of pupils attending public and other schools. It is undoubtedly true that children are helped to get to church schools. There is even a possibility that some of the children might not be sent to the church schools if the parents were compelled to pay their children's bus fares out of their own pockets when transportation to a public school would have been paid for by the State. . . .

Similarly, parents might be reluctant to permit their children to attend schools which the state had cut off from such general government services as ordinary police and fire protection, connections for sewage disposal, public highways and sidewalks. Of course, cutting off church schools from these services, so separate and so indisputably marked off from the religious function, would make it far more difficult for the schools to operate. But such is obviously not the purpose of the First Amendment. That Amendment requires the state to be a neutral in its relations with groups of religious believers and non-believers; it does not require the state to be their adversary. State power is no more to be used so as to handicap religions than it is to favor them.

This Court has said that parents may, in the discharge of their duty under state compulsory education laws, send their children to a religious rather than a public school if the school meets the secular educational requirements which the state has power to impose. . . .

It appears that these parochial schools meet New Jersey's requirements. The State contributes no money to the schools. It does not support them. Its legislation, as applied, does no more than provide a general program to help

parents get their children, regardless of their religion, safely and expeditiously to and from accredited schools.

The First Amendment has erected a wall between church and state. That wall must be kept high and impregnable. We could not approve the slightest breach. New Jersey has not breached it here.

Affirmed.

Mr. Justice Jackson, dissenting.

I find myself, contrary to first impressions, unable to join in this decision. . . .

The Court's opinion marshals every argument in favor of state aid and puts the case in its most favorable light, but much of its reasoning confirms my conclusions that there are no good grounds upon which to support the present legislation. . . .

The Court sustains this legislation by assuming two deviations from the facts of this particular case; first, it assumes a state of facts the record does not support, and secondly, it refuses to consider facts which are inescapable on the record. . . .

What the Township does, and what the taxpayer complains of, is at stated intervals to reimburse parents for the fares paid, provided the children attend either public schools or Catholic Church schools. This expenditure of tax funds has no possible effect on the child's safety or expedition in transit. As passengers on the public buses they travel as fast and no faster, and are as safe and no safer, since their parents are reimbursed as before.

In addition to thus assuming a type of service that does not exist, the Court also insists that we must close our eyes to a discrimination which does exist. The resolution which authorizes disbursement of this taxpayer's money limits reimbursement to those who attend public schools and Catholic schools. That is the way the Act is applied to this taxpayer. . . .

If we are to decide this case on the facts before us, our question is simply this: Is it constitutional to tax this complainant to pay the cost of carrying pupils to Church schools of one specified denomination? . . .

The Court's holding is that this taxpayer has no grievance because the state has decided to make the reimbursement a public purpose and therefore we are bound to regard it as such. I agree that this Court has left, and always should leave to each state, great latitude in deciding for itself, in the light of its own conditions, what shall be public purposes. . . .

But it cannot make public business of religious worship or instruction, or of attendance at religious institutions of any character. The effect of the religious freedom Amendment to our Constitution was to take every form of propagation of religion out of the realm of things which could directly or indirectly be made public business and thereby be supported in whole or in part at taxpayers' expense. That is a difference which the Constitution sets up be-

tween religion and almost every other subject matter of legislation, a difference which goes to the very root of religious freedom and which the Court is overlooking today. This freedom was first in the Bill of Rights because it was first in the forefathers' minds; it was set forth in absolute terms, and its strength is its rigidity. It was intended not only to keep the states' hands out of religion, but to keep religion's hands off the state, and, above all, to keep bitter religious controversy out of public life by denying to every denomination any advantage from getting control of public policy or the public purse. Those great ends I cannot but think are immeasurably compromised by today's decision.

This policy of our Federal Constitution has never been wholly pleasing to most religious groups. They all are quick to invoke its protections, they all are irked when they feel its restraints. . . .

Mr. Justice Rutledge, with whom Mr. Justice Frankfurter, Mr. Justice Jackson and Mr. Justice Burton agree, dissenting.

"Congress shall make no law respecting an establishment of religion, or prohibiting the free exercise thereof. . . ."

Not simply an established church, but any law respecting an establishment of religion is forbidden. The Amendment was broadly but not loosely phrased. It is the compact and exact summation of its author's views formed during his long struggle for religious freedom. In Madison's own words characterizing Jefferson's Bill for Establishing Religious Freedom, the guaranty he put in our national charter, like the bill he piloted through the Virginia Assembly, was "a Model of technical precision, and perspicuous brevity." Madison could not have confused "church" and "religion," or "an established church" and "an establishment of religion."

The Amendment's purpose was not to strike merely at the official establishment of a single sect, creed or religion, outlawing only a formal relation such as had prevailed in England and some of the colonies. Necessarily it was to uproot all such relationships. But the object was broader than separating church and state in this narrow sense. It was to create a complete and permanent separation of the spheres of religious activity and civil authority by comprehensively forbidding every form of public aid or support for religion. . . .

"Religion" appears only once in the Amendment. But the word governs two prohibitions and governs them alike. It does not have two meanings, one narrow to forbid "an establishment" and another, much broader, for securing "the free exercise thereof. . . ."

"Religion" and "establishment" were not used in any formal or technical sense. The prohibition broadly forbids state support, financial or other, of religion in any guise, form or degree. It outlaws all use of public funds for religious purposes.

No provision of the Constitution is more closely tied to or given content by

its generating history than the religious clause of the First Amendment. It is at once the refined product and the terse summation of that history. The history includes not only Madison's authorship and the proceedings before the First Congress, but also the long and intensive struggle for religious freedom in America, more especially in Virginia, of which the Amendment was the direct culmination. In the documents of the times, particularly of Madison, who was leader in the Virginia struggle before he became the Amendment's sponsor, but also in the writings of Jefferson and others and in the issues which engendered them is to be found irrefutable confirmation of the Amendment's sweeping content.

For Madison, as also for Jefferson, religious freedom was the crux of the struggle for freedom in general. . . .

All the great instruments of the Virginia struggle for religious liberty thus became warp and woof of our constitutional tradition, not simply by the course of history, but by the common unifying force of Madison's life, thought and sponsorship. He epitomized the whole of that tradition in the Amendment's compact, but nonetheless comprehensive, phrasing. . . .

Today, apart from efforts to inject religious training or exercises and sectarian issues into the public schools, the only serious surviving threat to maintaining that complete and permanent separation of religion and civil power which the First Amendment commands is through use of the taxing power to support religion, religious establishments, or establishments having a religious foundation whatever their form or special religious function.

Does New Jersey's action furnish support for religion by use of the taxing power? Certainly it does, if the test remains undiluted as Jefferson and Madison made it, that money taken by taxation from one is not to be used or given to support another's religious training or belief, or indeed one's own. Today as then the furnishing of "contributions of money for the propagation of opinions which he disbelieves" is the forbidden exaction; and the prohibition is absolute for whatever measure brings that consequence and whatever amount may be sought or given to that end.

The funds used here were raised by taxation. The Court does not dispute, nor could it, that their use does in fact give aid and encouragement to religious instruction. It only concludes that this aid is not "support" in law. But Madison and Jefferson were concerned with aid and support in fact, not as a legal conclusion "entangled in precedents." Here parents pay money to send their children to parochial schools and funds raised by taxation are used to reimburse them. This not only helps the children to get to school and the parents to send them. It aids them in a substantial way to get the very thing which they are sent to the particular school to secure, namely, religious training and teaching.

Believers of all faiths, and others who do not express their feeling toward ultimate issues of existence in any creedal form, pay the New Jersey tax. . . .

New Jersey's action therefore exactly fits the type of exaction and the kind of evil at which Madison and Jefferson struck. . . .

But we are told that the New Jersey statute is valid in its present application because the appropriation is for a public, not a private purpose, namely, the promotion of education, and the majority accept this idea in the conclusion that all we have here is "public welfare legislation." If that is true and the Amendment's force can be thus destroyed, what has been said becomes all the more pertinent. For then there could be no possible objection to more extensive support of religious education by New Jersey. . . .

The reasons underlying the Amendment's policy have not vanished with time or diminished in force. Now as when it was adopted the price of religious freedom is double. It is that the church and religion shall live both within and upon that freedom. There cannot be freedom of religion, safeguarded by the state, and intervention by the church or its agencies in the state's domain or dependency on its largesse. . . .

Two great drives are constantly in motion to abridge, in the name of education, the complete division of religion and civil authority which our forefathers made. One is to introduce religious education and observances into the public schools. The other, to obtain public funds for the aid and support of various private religious schools. . . .

It might also be argued that parents who want their children exposed to religious influences can adequately fulfill that wish off school property and outside school time. With all its surface persuasiveness, however, this argument seriously misconceives the basic constitutional justification for permitting the exercises at issue in these cases. For a compulsory state educational system so structures a child's life that if religious exercises are held to be an impermissible activity in schools, religion is placed at an artificial and state-created disadvantage. Viewed in this light, permission of such exercises for those who want them is necessary if the schools are truly to be neutral in the matter of religion. And a refusal to permit religious exercises thus is seen, not as the realization of state neutrality, but rather as the establishment of a religion of secularism, or at the least, as government support of the beliefs of those who think that religious exercises should be conducted only in private.

What seems to me to be of paramount importance, then, is recognition of the fact that the claim advanced here in favor of Bible reading is sufficiently substantial to make simple reference to the constitutional phrase "establishment of religion" as inadequate an analysis of the cases before us as the ritualistic invocation of the nonconstitutional phrase "separation of church and state." What these cases compel, rather, is an analysis of just what the "neutrality" is which is required by the interplay of the Establishment and Free Exercise Clauses of the First Amendment, as imbedded in the Fourteenth. . . .

The dangers both to government and to religion inherent in official support

of instruction in the tenets of various religious sects are absent in the present cases, which involve only a reading from the Bible unaccompanied by comments which might otherwise constitute instruction. Indeed, since, from all that appears in either record, any teacher who does not wish to do so is free not to participate, it cannot even be contended that some infinitesimal part of the salaries paid by the State are made contingent upon the performance of a religious function. . . .

I have said that these provisions authorizing religious exercises are properly to be regarded as measures making possible the free exercise of religion. But it is important to stress that, strictly speaking, what is at issue here is a privilege rather than a right. In other words, the question presented is not whether exercises such as those at issue here are constitutionally compelled, but rather whether they are constitutionally invalid. And that issue, in my view, turns on the question of coercion. . . .

What our Constitution indispensably protects is the freedom of each of us, be he Jew or Agnostic, Christian or Atheist, Buddhist or Free-thinker, to believe or disbelieve, to worship or not worship, to pray or keep silent, according to his own conscience, uncoerced and unrestrained by government. It is conceivable that these school boards, or even all school boards, might eventually find it impossible to administer a system of religious exercises during school hours in such a way as to meet this constitutional standard—in such a way as completely to free from any kind of official coercion those who do not affirmatively want to participate. But I think we must not assume that school boards so lack the qualities of inventiveness and good will as to make impossible the achievement of that goal.

I would remand both cases for further hearings.

Lemon v. Kurtzman, 403 U.S. 602 (1971)

Mr. Chief Justice Burger delivered the opinion of the Court.

These two appeals raise questions as to Pennsylvania and Rhode Island statues providing state aid to church-related elementary and secondary schools. Both statues are challenged as violative of the Establishment and Free Exercise Clauses of the First Amendment and the Due Process Clause of the Fourteenth Amendment. . . .

In *Everson v. Board of Education,* this Court upheld a state statute that reimbursed the parents of parochial school children for bus transportation expenses. There Mr. Justice Black, writing for the majority, suggested that the decision carried to "the verge" of forbidden territory under the Religion Clauses. Candor compels acknowledgment, moreover, that we can only dimly perceive the lines of demarcation in this extraordinarily sensitive area of constitutional law.

The language of the Religion Clauses of the First Amendment is at best opaque, particularly when compared with other portions of the Amendment. Its authors did not simply prohibit the establishment of a state church or a state religion, an area history shows they regarded as very important and fraught with great dangers. Instead they commanded that there should be "no law *respecting* an establishment of religion." A law may be one "respecting" the forbidden objective while falling short of its total realization. A law "respecting" the proscribed result, that is, the establishment of religion, is not always easily identifiable as one violative of the Clause. A given law might not *establish* a state religion but nevertheless be one "respecting" that end in the sense of being a step that could lead to such establishment and hence offend the First Amendment.

In the absence of precisely stated constitutional prohibitions, we must draw lines with reference to the three main evils against which the Establishment Clause was intended to afford protection: "sponsorship, financial support, and active involvement of the sovereign in religious activity."

Every analysis in this area must begin with consideration of the cumulative criteria developed by the Court over many years. Three such tests may be gleaned from our cases. First, the statute must have a secular legislative purpose; second, its principal or primary effect must be one that neither advances nor inhibits religion; [and] finally, the statute must not foster "an excessive government entanglement with religion. . . ."

The two legislatures, however, have also recognized that church-related elementary and secondary schools have a significant religious mission and that a substantial portion of their activities is religiously oriented. They have therefore sought to create statutory restrictions designed to guarantee the separation between secular and religious educational functions and to ensure that State financial aid supports only the former. All these provisions are precautions taken in candid recognition that these programs approached, even if they did not intrude upon, the forbidden areas under the Religion Clauses. We need not decide whether these legislative precautions restrict the principal or primary effect of the programs to the point where they do not offend the Religion Clauses, for we conclude that the cumulative impact of the entire relationship arising under the statutes in each State involves excessive entanglement between government and religion. . . .

Our prior holdings do not call for total separation between church and state; total separation is not possible in an absolute sense. Some relationship between government and religious organizations is inevitable. Fire inspections, building and zoning regulations, and state requirements under compulsory school-attendance laws are examples of necessary and permissible contacts. . . .

In order to determine whether the government entanglement with religion is excessive, we must examine the character and purposes of the institutions

that are benefited, the nature of the aid that the State provides, and the resulting relationship between the government and the religious authority. . . .

Here we find that both statutes foster an impermissible degree of entanglement. . . .

The potential for political divisiveness related to religious belief and practice is aggravated in these two statutory programs by the need for continuing annual appropriations and the likelihood of larger and larger demands as costs and populations grow. The Rhode Island District Court found that the parochial school system's "monumental and deepening financial crises" would "inescapably" require larger annual appropriations subsidizing greater percentages of the salaries of lay teachers. Although no facts have been developed in this respect in the Pennsylvania case, it appears that such pressures for expanding aid have already required the state legislature to include a portion of the state revenues from cigarette taxes in the program.

In *Walz* it was argued that a tax exemption for places of religious worship would prove to be the first step in an inevitable progression leading to the establishment of state churches and state religion. That claim could not stand up against more than 200 years of virtually universal practice imbedded in our colonial experience and continuing into the present.

The progression argument, however, is more persuasive here. We have no long history of state aid to church-related educational institutions comparable to 200 years of tax exemption for churches. Indeed, the state programs before us today represent something of an innovation. We have already noted that modern governmental programs have self-perpetuating and self-expanding propensities. These internal pressures are only enhanced when the schemes involve institutions whose legitimate needs are growing and whose interests have substantial political support. Nor can we fail to see that in constitutional adjudication some steps, which when taken were thought to approach "the verge," have become the platform for yet further steps. . . . The dangers are increased by the difficulty of perceiving in advance exactly where the "verge" of the precipice lies. As well as constituting an independent evil against which the Religion Clauses were intended to protect, involvement or entanglement between government and religion serves as a warning signal. . . .

The merit and benefits of these schools . . . are not the issue before us in these cases. The sole question is whether state aid to these schools can be squared with the dictates of the Religion Clauses. Under our system the choice has been made that government is to be entirely excluded from the area of religious instruction and churches excluded from the affairs of government. The Constitution decrees that religion must be a private matter for the individual, the family, and the institutions of private choice, and that while some involvement and entanglement are inevitable, lines must be drawn.

Employment Division, Department of Human Resources of Oregon v. Smith, 494 U.S. 872 (1990)

Justice Scalia delivered the opinion of the Court.

This case requires us to decide whether the Free Exercise Clause of the First Amendment permits the State of Oregon to include religiously inspired peyote use within the reach of its general criminal prohibition on use of that drug, and thus permits the State to deny unemployment benefits to persons dismissed from their jobs because of such religiously inspired use.

I

Oregon law prohibits the knowing or intentional possession of a "controlled substance" . . . [including] the drug peyote, a hallucinogen derived from the plant Lophophprawilliamsii Lemaire. . . .

Respondents Alfred Smith and Galen Black were fired from their jobs with a private drug rehabilitation organization because they ingested peyote for sacramental purposes at a ceremony of the Native American Church, of which both are members. When respondents applied to petitioner Employment Division for unemployment compensation, they were determined to be ineligible for benefits because they had been discharged for work-related "misconduct". . . .

. . . The Oregon Supreme Court reasoned . . . that the criminality of respondents' peyote use was irrelevant to resolution of their constitutional claim—since the purpose of the "misconduct" provision under which respondents had been disqualified was not to enforce the State's criminal laws but to preserve the financial integrity of the compensation fund, and since that purpose was inadequate to justify the burden that disqualification imposed on respondents' religious practice. . . .

Before this Court in 1987, petitioner continued to maintain that the illegality of respondents' peyote consumption was relevant to their constitutional claim. We agreed, concluding that "if a State has prohibited through its criminal laws certain kinds of religiously motivated conduct without violating the First Amendment, it certainly follows that it may impose the lesser burden of denying unemployment compensation benefits to persons who engage in that conduct." Employment Div., Dept. of Human Resources of Oregon v. Smith, 485 U.S. 660, 670 (1988) *(Smith I)*. We noted, however, that the Oregon Supreme Court had not decided whether respondents' sacramental use of peyote was in fact proscribed by Oregon's controlled substance law, and that this issue was a matter of dispute between the parties. . . . [W]e vacated the judgment of the Oregon Supreme Court and remanded for further proceedings. . . .

On remand, the Oregon Supreme Court held that respondents' religiously

inspired use of peyote fell within the prohibition of the Oregon statute . . . It then considered whether that prohibition was valid under the Free Exercise Clause, and concluded that it was not. The court therefore reaffirmed its previous ruling that the State could not deny unemployment benefits to respondents for having engaged in that practice.

II

Respondents' claim for relief rests on our decision in *Sherbert v. Verner,* supra, *Thomas v. Review Board, Indiana Employment Security Div.,* supra, and *Hobbie v. Unemployment Appeals Comm'n of Florida,* 480 U.S. 136 (1987) . . . As we observed in *Smith I,* however, the conduct at issue in those cases was not prohibited by law. We held that distinction to be critical, for "if Oregon does prohibit the religious use of peyote, and if that prohibition is consistent with the Federal Constitution, there is no federal right to engage in that conduct in Oregon," and "the State is free to withhold unemployment compensation from respondents for engaging in work-related misconduct, despite its religious motivation." 485 U.S., at 672. Now that the Oregon Supreme Court has confirmed that Oregon does prohibit the religious use of peyote, we proceed to consider whether that prohibition is permissible under the Free Exercise Clause.

A

. . . The free exercise of religion means, first and foremost, the right to believe and profess whatever religious doctrine one desires. Thus, the First Amendment obviously excludes all "governmental regulation of religious *beliefs* as such." . . . The government may not compel affirmation of religious belief, see *Torcaso v. Watkins,* 367 U.S. 488 (1961), punish the expression of religious doctrines it believes to be false, *United States v. Ballard,* 322 U.S. 78, 86–88 (1944), impose special disabilities on the basis of religious views or religious status, see *McDaniel v. Paty,* 435 U.S. 618 (1978); . . . or lend its power to one or the other side in controversies over religious authority or dogma, see *Presbyterian Church v. Hull Church,* 393 U.S. 440, 445–452 (1969); *Kedroff v. St. Nicholas Cathedral,* 344 U.S. 94, 95–119 (1952); *Serbian Eastern Orthodox Diocese v. Milivojevich,* 426 U.S. 696, 708–725 (1976).

But the "exercise of religion" often involves not only belief and profession but the performance of (or abstention from) physical acts: assembling with others for a worship service, participating in sacramental use of bread and wine, proselytizing, abstaining from certain foods or certain modes of transportation. It would be true, we think (though no case of ours has involved the point), that a state would be "prohibiting the free exercise [of religion]" if it

sought to ban such acts or abstentions only when they are engaged in for religious reasons, or only because of the religious belief that they display. It would doubtless be unconstitutional, for example, to ban the casting of "statutes that are to be used for worship purposes," or to prohibit bowing down before a golden calf.

Respondents in the present case, however, seek to carry the meaning of "prohibiting the free exercise [of religion]" one large step further. They contend that their religious motivation for using peyote places them beyond the reach of a criminal law that is not specifically directed at their religious practice, and that is concededly constitutional as applied to those who use the drug for other reasons. They assert, in other words, that "prohibiting the free exercise [of religion]" includes requiring any individual to observe a generally applicable law that requires (or forbids) the performance of an act that his religious belief forbids (or requires). As a textual matter, we do not think the words must be given that meaning. It is no more necessary to regard the collection of a general tax, for example, as "prohibiting the free exercise [of religion]" by those citizens who believe support of organized government to be sinful, than it is to regard the same tax as "abridging the freedom . . . of the press" of those publishing companies that must pay the tax as a condition of staying in business. . . .

. . . We have never held that an individual's religious beliefs excuse him from compliance with an otherwise valid law prohibiting conduct that the State is free to regulate. On the contrary, the record of more than a century of our free exercise jurisprudence contradicts that proposition. As described succinctly by Justice Frankfurter in *Minersville School Dist. Bd. of Educ. v. Gobitis,* 310 U.S. 586, 594–595 (1940):

> Conscientious scruples have not, in the course of the long struggle for religious toleration, relieved the individual from obedience to a general law not aimed at the promotion or restriction of religious beliefs. The mere possession of religious convictions which contradict the relevant concerns of a political society does not relieve the citizen from the discharge of political responsibilities. (footnote omitted)

We first had occasion to assert that principle in *Reynolds v. United States,* 98 U.S. 145 (1879), where we rejected the claim that criminal laws against polygamy could not be constitutionally applied to those whose religion commanded the practice. "Laws," we said, "are made for the government of actions, and while they cannot interfere with mere religious belief and opinions, they may with practices. . . . Can a man excuse his practices to the contrary because of his religious belief? To permit this would be to make the professed doctrines of religious belief superior to the law of the land, and in effect to permit every citizen to become a law unto himself." Id., at 166–167.

Subsequent decisions have consistently held that the right of free exercise does not relieve an individual of the obligation to comply with a "valid and neutral law of general applicability on the ground that the law proscribes (or prescribes) conduct that his religion prescribes (or proscribes)." *United States v. Lee,* 455 U.S. 252, 263, n. 3 (1982) (Stevens, J., concurring in judgment); see Minersville School Distr. Bd. of Educ. v. Gobitis, supra, at 595 (collecting cases). In *Prince v. Massachusetts,* 321 U.S. 158 (1944), we held that a mother could be prosecuted under the child labor laws for using her children to dispense literature in the streets, her religious motivation notwithstanding. We found no constitutional infirmity in "excluding [these children] from doing there what no other children may do." Id., at 171. In *Braunfeld v. Brown,* 366 U.S. 599 (1961) (plurality opinion), we upheld Sunday-closing laws against the claim that they burdened the religious practices of persons whose religions compelled them to refrain from work on other days. In *Gillette v. United States,* 401 U.S. 437, 461 (1971), we sustained the military selective service system against the claim that it violated free exercise by conscripting persons who opposed a particular war on religious grounds.

Our most recent decision involving a neutral, generally applicable regulatory law that compelled activity forbidden by an individual's religion was United States v. Lee, 455 U.S. at 258–261. There, an Amish employer, on behalf of himself and his employees, sought exemption from collection and payment of Social Security taxes on the ground that the Amish faith prohibited participation in governmental support programs. We rejected the claim that an exemption was constitutionally required. There would be no way, we observed, to distinguish the Amish believer's objection to Social Security taxes from the religious objections that others might have to the collection or use of other taxes. "If, for example, a religious adherent believes war is a sin, and if a certain percentage of the federal budget can be identified as devoted to war-related activities, such individuals would have a similarly valid claim to be exempt from paying that percentage of the income tax. The tax system could not function if denominations were allowed to challenge the tax system because tax payments were spent in a manner that violates their religious belief." Id., at 260. . . .

The only decisions in which we have held that the First Amendment bars application of a neutral, generally applicable law to religiously motivated action have involved not the Free Exercise Clause alone, but the Free Exercise Clause in conjunction with other constitutional protections, such as freedom of speech and of the press, see *Cantwell v. Connecticut,* 310 U.S. at 304–307 (invalidating a licensing system for religious and charitable solicitations under which the administrator had discretion to deny a license to any cause he deemed nonreligious); *Murdock v. Pennsylvania,* 319 U.S. 105 (1943) (invalidated a flat tax on solicitation as applied to the dissemination of religious ideas); *Follett v. McCormick,* 321 U.S. 573 (1944) (same), or the right of

parents, acknowledged in *Pierce v. Society of Sisters,* 268 U.S. 510 (1925), to direct the education of their children, see *Wisconsin v. Yoder,* 406 U.S. 205 (1972) (invalidating compulsory school-attendance laws as applied to Amish parents who refused on religious grounds to send their children to school).[1] Some of our cases prohibiting compelled expression, decided exclusively upon free speech grounds, have also involved freedom of religion, cf. *Wooley v. Maynard,* 430 U.S. 705 (1977) (invalidating compelled display of a license plate slogan that offended individual religious beliefs); *West Virginia Board of Education v. Barnette,* 319 U.S. 624 (1943) (invalidating compulsory flag salute statute challenged by religious objectors). And it is easy to envision a case in which a challenge on freedom of association grounds would likewise be reinforced by Free Exercise Clause concerns. Cf. *Roberts v. United States Jaycees,* 468 U.S. 609, 622 (1983) ("An individual's freedom to speak, to worship, and to petition the government for the redress of grievances could not be vigorously protected from interference by the State [if] a correlative freedom to engage in group effort toward those ends were not also guaranteed.").

The present case does not present such a hybrid situation, but a free exercise claim unconnected with any communicative activity or parental right. Respondents urge us to hold, quite simply, that when otherwise prohibitable conduct is accompanied by religious convictions, not only the convictions but the conduct itself must be free from governmental regulation. We have never held that, and decline to do so now. There being no contention that Oregon's drug law represents an attempt to regulate religious beliefs, the communication of religious beliefs, or the raising of one's children in those beliefs, the rule to which we have adhered ever since *Reynolds* plainly controls. . . .

B

Respondents argue that even though exemption from generally applicable criminal laws need not automatically be extended to religiously motivated actors, at least the claim for a religious exemption must be evaluated under the balancing test set forth in *Sherbert v. Verner,* 374 U.S. 398 (1963). . . . We have never invalidated any governmental action on the basis of the *Sherbert* test except the denial of unemployment compensation. Although we have sometimes purported to apply the *Sherbert* test in contexts other than that, we

---

1. Both lines of cases have specifically adverted to the non-free exercise principle involved. . . . *Yoder* said that "the Court's holding in *Pierce* stands as a charter of the rights of parents to direct the religious upbringing of their children. And, when the interests of parenthood are combined with a free exercise claim of the nature revealed by this record, more than merely a "reasonable relation to some purpose within the competency of the State is required to sustain the validity of the State's requirement under the First Amendment." 406 U.S., at 233.

have always found the test satisfied, see *United States v. Lee,* 455 U.S. 252 (1982); *Gillette v. United States,* 401 U.S. 437 (1971). In recent years we have abstained from applying the *Sherbert* test (outside the unemployment compensation field) at all. In *Bowen v. Roy,* 476 U.S. 693 (1986), we declined to apply *Sherbert* analysis to a federal statutory scheme that required benefit applicants and recipients to provide their Social Security numbers. The plaintiffs in that case asserted that it would violate their religious beliefs to obtain and provide a Social Security number for their daughter. We held the statute's application to the plaintiffs valid regardless of whether it was necessary to effectuate a compelling interest. See id., at 699–701. In *Lyng v. Northwest Indian Cemetery Protective Assn.,* 485 U.S. 439 (1988), we declined to apply *Sherbert* analysis to the Government's logging and road construction activities on lands used for religious purposes by several Native American Tribes, even though it was undisputed that the activities "could have devastating effects on traditional Indian religious practices," 485 U.S., at 451. In *Goldman v. Weinberger,* 475 U.S. 503 (1986), we rejected application of the *Sherbert* test to military dress regulations that forbade the wearing of yarmulkes. In *O'Lone v. Estate of Shabazz,* 482 U.S. 342 (1987), we sustained, without mentioning the *Sherbert* test, a prison's refusal to excuse inmates from work requirements to attend worship services.

Even if we were inclined to breathe into *Sherbert* some life beyond the unemployment compensation field, we would not apply it to require exemptions from a generally applicable criminal law. The *Sherbert* test, it must be recalled, was developed in a context that lent itself to individualized governmental assessment of the reasons for the relevant conduct. As a plurality of the Court noted in *Roy,* a distinctive feature of unemployment compensation programs is that their eligibility criteria invite consideration of the particular circumstances behind an applicant's unemployment . . . As the plurality pointed out in *Roy,* our decisions in the unemployment cases stand for the proposition that where the State has in place a system of individual exemptions, it may not refuse to extend that system to cases of "religious hardship" without compelling reason. *Bowen v. Roy,* supra, at 708.

Whether or not the decisions are that limited, they at least have nothing to do with an across-the-board criminal prohibition on the particular form of conduct. Although, as noted earlier, we have sometimes used the *Sherbert* test to analyze free exercise challenges to such laws, . . . we have never applied the test to invalidate one. We conclude today that the sounder approach, and the approach in accord with the vast majority of our precedents, is to hold the test inapplicable to such challenges. The government's ability to enforce generally applicable prohibitions of socially harmful conduct, like its ability to carry out other aspects of public policy, "cannot depend on measuring the effects of a governmental action on a religious objector's spiritual development." *Lyng,* supra, at 451. To make an individual's obligation to obey such

a law contingent upon the law's coincidence with his religious beliefs, except where the State's interest is "compelling"—permitting him, by virtue of his beliefs, "to become a law unto himself," *Reynolds v. United States,* 98 U.S., at 167—contradicts both constitutional tradition and common sense.[2]

The "compelling government interest" requirement seems benign, because it is familiar from other fields. But using it as the standard that must be met before the government may accord different treatment on the basis of race, see, e.g., *Palmore v. Sidoti,* 466 U.S. 429, 432 (1984), or before the government may regulate the content of speech, see, e.g., *Sable Communications of California v. FCC,* 492 U.S. 115,—(1989), is not remotely comparable to using it for the purpose asserted here. What it produces in those other fields—equality of treatment, and an unrestricted flow of contending speech—are constitutional norms; what it would produce here—a private right to ignore generally applicable laws—is a constitutional anomaly.

Nor is it possible to limit the impact of respondents' proposal by requiring a "compelling state interest" only when the conduct prohibited is "central" to the individual's religion. . . . It is no more appropriate for judges to determine the "centrality" of religious beliefs before applying a "compelling interest" test in the free exercise field, than it would be for them to determine the "importance" of ideas before applying the "compelling interest" test in the free speech field. . . . Repeatedly and in many different contexts, we have warned that courts must not presume to determine the place of a particular belief in a religion or the plausibility of a religious claim. . . .[4]

If the "compelling interest" test is to be applied at all, then, it must be applied across the board, to all actions thought to be religiously commanded. Moreover, if "compelling interest" really means what it says (and watering it down here would subvert its rigor in the other fields where it is applied), many laws will not meet the test. Any society adopting such a system would be

---

2. Justice O'Connor seeks to distinguish *Lyng v. Northwest Indian Cemetery Protective Assn.,* supra, and *Bowen v. Roy,* supra, on the ground that those cases involved the government's conduct of "its own internal affairs," . . . [I]t is hard to see any reason in principle or practicality why the government should have to tailor its health and safety laws to conform to the diversity of religious belief, but should not have to tailor its management of public lands, *Lyng,* supra, or its administration of welfare programs, *Roy,* supra.

4. . . . Justice O'Connor . . . agrees that "our determination . . . cannot, and should not, turn on the centrality of the particular religious practice at issue." . . . Earlier in her opinion, however, Justice O'Connor appears to contradict this, saying that the proper approach is "to determine whether the burden on the specific plaintiffs before us is constitutionally significant and whether the particular criminal interest asserted by the State before us is compelling." "Constitutionally significant burden" would seem to be "centrality" under another name. . . . There is no way out of the difficulty that, if general laws are to be subjected to a "religious practice" exception, *both* the importance of the law at issue *and* the centrality of the practice at issue must reasonably be considered. . . .

courting anarchy, but that danger increases in direct proportion to the society's diversity of religious beliefs, and its determination to coerce or suppress none of them. . . . The rule respondents favor would open the prospect of constitutionally required religious exemptions from civic obligations of almost every conceivable kind—ranging from compulsory military service, see, e.g., *Gillette v. United States,* 401 U.S. 437 (1971), to the payment of taxes, see, e.g., *United States v. Lee,* supra; to health and safety regulation such as manslaughter and child neglect laws, see, e.g., *Funkhouser v. State,* 763 P.2d 695 (Okla.Crim.App.1988), compulsory vaccination laws, see, e.g., *Cude v. State,* 237 Ark. 927, 377 S.W.2d 816 (1964), drug laws, see, e.g., *Olsen v. Drug Enforcement Administration,*—U.S.App.D.C.—, 878 F.2d 1458 (1989), and traffic laws, see *Cox v. New Hampshire,* 312 U.S. 569 (1941); to social welfare legislation such as minimum wage laws, see *Susan and Tony Alamo Foundation v. Secretary of Labor,* 471 U.S. 290 (1985), child labor laws, see *Prince v. Massachusetts,* 321 U.S. 158 (1944), animal cruelty laws, see, e.g., *Church of the Lukumi Babalu Aye Inc. v. City of Hialeah,* 723 F.Supp. 1467 (S.D.Fla.1989), cf. *State v. Massey,* 229 N.C. 734, 51 S.E.2d 179, appeal dism'd, 336 U.S. 942 (1949), environmental protection laws, see *United States v. Little,* 638 F.Supp. 337 (Mont.1986), and laws providing for equality of opportunity for the races, see, e.g., *Bob Jones University v. United States,* 461 U.S. 574, 603–604 (1983). The First Amendment's protection of religious liberty does not require this.

Values that are protected against government interference through enshrinement in the Bill of Rights are not thereby banished from the political process. . . . [A] society that believes in the negative protection accorded to religious belief can be expected to be solicitous of that value in its legislation. . . . It is therefore not surprising that a number of States have made an exception to their drug laws for sacramental peyote use. But to say that a nondiscriminatory religious-practice exemption is permitted, or even that it is desirable, is not to say that it is constitutionally required, and that the appropriate occasions for its creation can be discerned by the courts. It may fairly be said that leaving accommodation to the political process will place at a relative disadvantage those religious practices that are not widely engaged in; but that unavoidable consequence of democratic government must be preferred to a system in which each conscience is a law unto itself or in which judges weigh the social importance of all laws against the centrality of all religious beliefs.

Because respondents' ingestion of peyote was prohibited under Oregon law, and because that prohibition is constitutional, Oregon may, consistent with the Free Exercise Clause, deny respondents unemployment compensation when their dismissal results from use of the drug. The decision of the Oregon Supreme Court is accordingly reversed.

It is so ordered.

Justice O'Connor, with whom Justice Brennan, Justice Marshall, and Justice Blackmun join as to Parts I and II, concurring in the judgment.*
Although I agree with the result the Court reaches in this case, I cannot join its opinion. In my view, today's holding dramatically departs from well-settled First Amendment jurisprudence, appears unnecessary to resolve the question presented, and is incompatible with our Nation's fundamental commitment to individual religious liberty.

. . .

II

The Court today extracts from our long history of free exercise precedents the single categorical rule that "if prohibiting the exercise of religion . . . is . . . merely the incidental effect of a generally applicable and otherwise valid provision, the First Amendment has not been offended." Indeed, the Court holds that where the law is a generally applicable criminal prohibition, our usual free exercise jurisprudence does not even apply. To reach this sweeping result, however, the Court must not only give a strained reading of the First Amendment but must also disregard our consistent application of free exercise doctrine to cases involving generally applicable regulations that burden religious conduct.

A

. . . Because the First Amendment does not distinguish between religious belief and religious conduct, conduct motivated by sincere religious belief, like the belief itself, must therefore be at least presumptively protected by the Free Exercise Clause.

The Court today, however, interprets the Clause to permit the government to prohibit, without justification, conduct mandated by an individual's religious beliefs, so long as that prohibition is generally applicable. But a law that prohibits certain conduct—conduct that happens to be an act of worship for someone—manifestly does prohibit that person's free exercise of his religion. A person who is barred from engaging in religiously motivated conduct is barred from freely exercising his religion. Moreover, that person is barred from freely exercising his religion regardless of whether the law prohibits the conduct only when engaged in for religious reasons, only by members of that religion, or by all persons. It is difficult to deny that a law that prohibits religiously motivated conduct, even if the law is generally applicable, does not at least implicate First Amendment concerns.

. . .

To say that a person's right to free exercise has been burdened, of course, does not mean that he has an absolute right to engage in the conduct. . . . [W]e

---

*Although Justice Brennan, Justice Marshall, and Justice Blackmun join Parts I and II of the opinion, they do not concur in the judgment.

have respected both the First Amendment's express textual mandate and the governmental interest in regulation of conduct by requiring the Government to justify any substantial burden on religiously motivated conduct by a compelling state interest and by means narrowly tailored to achieve that interest. . . .

The Court attempts to support its narrow reading of the Clause by claiming that "[w]e have never held that an individual's religious beliefs excuse him from compliance with an otherwise valid law prohibiting conduct that the State is free to regulate." But as the Court later notes, as it must, in cases such as *Cantwell* and *Yoder* we have in fact interpreted the Free Exercise Clause to forbid application of a generally applicable prohibition to religiously motivated conduct. . . .

The Court endeavors to escape from our decisions in *Cantwell* and *Yoder* by labeling them "hybrid" decision, but there is no denying that both cases expressly relied on the Free Exercise Clause, . . . and that we have consistently regarded those cases as part of the mainstream of our free exercise jurisprudence. Moreover, in each of the other cases cited by the Court to support its categorical rule, we rejected the particular constitutional claims before us only after carefully weighing the competing interests. . . . That we rejected the free exercise claims in those cases hardly calls into question the applicability of First Amendment doctrine in the first place. Indeed, it is surely unusual to judge the vitality of a constitutional doctrine by looking to the win-loss record of the plaintiffs who happen to come before us.

B

. . .

In my view, . . . the essence of a free exercise claim is relief from a burden imposed by government on religious practices or beliefs, whether the burden is imposed directly through laws that prohibit or compel specific religious practices, or indirectly through laws that, in effect, make abandonment of one's own religion or conformity to the religious beliefs of others the price of an equal place in the civil community. . . .

. . .

Indeed, we have never distinguished between cases in which a State conditions receipt of a benefit on conduct prohibited by religious beliefs and cases in which a State affirmatively prohibits such conduct. The *Sherbert* compelling interest test applies in both kinds of cases. . . .

. . . Even if, as an empirical matter, a government's criminal laws might usually serve a compelling interest in health, safety, or public order, the First Amendment at least requires a case-by-case determination of the question, sensitive to the facts of each particular claim. . . . Given the range of conduct that a State might legitimately make criminal, we cannot assume, merely because a law carries criminal sanctions and is generally applicable, that the

First Amendment never requires the State to grant a limited exemption for religiously motivated conduct.

. . .

Finally, the Court today suggests that the disfavoring of minority religions is an "unavoidable consequence" under our system of government and that accommodation of such religions must be left to the political process. In my view, however, the First Amendment was enacted precisely to protect the rights of those whose religious practices are not shared by the majority and may be viewed with hostility. The history of our free exercise doctrine amply demonstrates the harsh impact majoritarian rule has had on unpopular or emerging religious groups such as the Jehovah's Witnesses and the Amish. . . .

III

The Court's holding today not only misreads settled First Amendment precedent; it appears to be unnecessary to this case. I would reach the same result applying our established free exercise jurisprudence.

. . .

. . . [T]he critical question in this case is whether exempting respondents from the State's general criminal prohibition "will unduly interfere with fulfillment of the governmental interest." . . . Although the question is close, I would conclude that uniform application of Oregon's criminal prohibition is "essential to accomplish" its overriding interest in preventing the physical harm caused by the use of a . . . controlled substance. Oregon's criminal prohibition represents that State's judgement that the possession and use of controlled substances, even by only one person, is inherently harmful and dangerous. Because the health effects caused by the use of controlled substances exist regardless of the motivation of the user, the use of such substances, even for religious purposes, violated the very purpose of the laws that prohibit them. . . . Moreover, in view of the societal interest in preventing trafficking in controlled substances, uniform application of the criminal prohibition at issue is essential to the effectiveness of Oregon's stated interest in preventing any possession of peyote. . . .

For these reasons, I believe that granting a selective exemption in this case would seriously impair Oregon's compelling interest in prohibiting possession of peyote by its citizens. Under such circumstances, the Free Exercise Clause does not require the State to accommodate respondents' religiously motivated conduct. . . .

Respondents content that any incompatibility is belied by the fact that the Federal Government and several States provide exemptions for the religious use of peyote . . . But other governments may surely choose to grant an exemption without Oregon, with its specific asserted interest in uniform application of its drug laws, being *required* to do so by the First Amendment. Respondents also note that the sacramental use of peyote is central to the tenets of the

Native American Church, but I agree with the Court that . . . our determination of the constitutionality of Oregon's general criminal prohibition cannot, and should not, turn on the centrality of the particular religious practice at issue. This does not mean, of course, that courts may not make factual findings as to whether a claimant holds a sincerely held religious belief that conflicts with, and thus is burdened by, the challenged law. The distinction between questions of centrality and questions of sincerity and burden is admittedly fine, but it is one that is an established part of our free exercise doctrine . . .

I would therefore adhere to our established free exercise jurisprudence and hold that the State in this case has a compelling interest in regulating peyote use by its citizens and that accommodating respondents' religiously motivated conduct "will unduly interfere with fulfillment of the governmental interest." *Lee,* 455 U.S., at 259. Accordingly, I concur in the judgment of the Court.

Justice Blackmun, with whom Justice Brennan and Justice Marshall join, dissenting.

This Court over the years painstakingly has developed a consistent and exacting standard to test the constitutionality of a state statute that burdens the free exercise of religion. Such a statute may stand only if the law in general, and the State's refusal to allow a religious exemption in particular, are justified by a compelling interest that cannot be served by less restrictive means.

Until today, I thought this was a settled and inviolate principle of this Court's First Amendment jurisprudence. . . .

. . .

. . . I agree with Justice O'Connor's analysis of the applicable free exercise doctrine, and I join parts I and II of her opinion. As she points out, "the critical question in this case is whether exempting respondents from the State's general criminal prohibition 'will unduly interfere with fulfillment of the governmental interest.' " I do disagree, however, with her specific answer to that question.

. . .

. . . The State's asserted interest . . . amounts only to the symbolic preservation of an unenforced prohibition. . . .

. . .

The State proclaims an interest in protecting the health and safety of its citizens from the dangers of unlawful drugs. It offers, however, no evidence that the religious use of peyote has ever harmed anyone. The factual findings of other courts cast doubt on the State's assumption that religious use of peyote is harmful. . . .

The carefully circumscribed ritual context in which respondents used peyote is far removed from the irresponsible and unrestricted recreational use of unlawful drugs. The Native American Church's internal restrictions on, and

supervision of, its members' use of peyote substantially obviate the State's health and safety concerns. . . .

. . .

Finally, the State argues that granting an exception for religious peyote use would erode its interest in the uniform, fair, and certain enforcement of its drug laws. The State fears that, if it grants an exemption for religious peyote use, a flood of other claims to religious exemptions will follow. It would then be placed in a dilemma, it says, between allowing a patchwork of exemptions that would hinder its law enforcement efforts, and risking a violation of the Establishment Clause by arbitrarily limiting its religious exemptions. This argument, however, could be made in almost any free exercise case. . . .

The State's apprehension of a flood of other religious claims is purely speculative. Almost half the States, and the Federal Government, have maintained an exemption for religious peyote use for many years, and apparently have not found themselves overwhelmed by claims to other religious exemptions. . . .

. . .

Finally, although I agree with Justice O'Connor that courts should refrain from delving into questions of whether, as a matter of religious doctrine, a particular practice is "central" to the religion, I do not think this means that the courts must turn a blind eye to the severe impact of a State's restrictions on the adherents of a minority religion. . . .

Respondents believe, and their sincerity has never been an issue, that the peyote plant embodies their deity, and eating it is an act of worship and communion. Without peyote, they could not enact the essential ritual of their religion. . . .

If Oregon can constitutionally prosecute them for this act of worship, they, like the Amish, may be "forced to migrate to some other and more tolerant region." *Yoder,* 406 U.S., at 218. This potentially devastating impact must be viewed in light of the federal policy—reached in reaction to many years of religious persecution and intolerance—of protecting the religious freedom of Native Americans. See American Indian Religious Freedom Act, 92 Stat. 469, 42 U.S.C., § 1996 ("it shall be the policy of the United States to protect and preserve for American Indians their inherent right of freedom to believe, express, and exercise the traditional religions . . . , including but not limited to access to sites, use and possession of sacred objects, and the freedom to worship through ceremonials and traditional rites"). Congress recognized that certain substances, such as peyote, "have religious significance because they are sacred, they have power, they heal, they are necessary to the exercise of the rites of the religion, they are necessary to the cultural integrity of the tribe, and, therefore, religious survival." H.R.Rep. No. 95–1308, p. 2 (1978).

The American Indian Religious Freedom Act, in itself, may not create rights enforceable against government action restricting religious freedom, but this Court must scrupulously apply its free exercise analysis to the religious claims

of Native Americans, however unorthodox they may be. Otherwise, both the First Amendment and the stated policy of Congress will offer to Native Americans merely an unfulfilled and hollow promise.

. . .

For these reasons, I conclude that Oregon's interest in enforcing its drug laws against religious use of peyote is not sufficiently compelling to outweigh respondents' right to the free exercise of their religion. Since the State could not constitutionally enforce its criminal prohibition against respondents, the interests underlying the State's drug laws cannot justify its denial of unemployment benefits. . . .

I dissent.

Index

About the Authors

Clarke E. Cochran is professor of political science and adjunct professor, Department of Health Organization Management, at Texas Tech University, where he has won the President's Award for Excellence in Teaching. He is the author of *Character, Community, and Politics* (University of Alabama Press, 1982), *Religion in Public and Private Life* (Routledge, 1990), (coauthor) *American Public Policy: An Introduction* (St. Martin's Press, 6th ed., 1999), and numerous articles in such journals as *American Political Science Review, Journal of Politics,* and *Polity.* He has served as chair of the Religion and Politics Section of the American Political Science Association. During 1998–99 he is senior research fellow in the Erasmus Institute, University of Notre Dame.

Mary C. Segers is professor and director of the Graduate Program in Political Science at Rutgers University in Newark, New Jersey. She teaches courses in political theory, religion and politics, and women and politics. Segers has written widely about religious and ethical values underlying public policy. Her recent books include *Church Polity and American Politics* (1990), *The Catholic Church and Abortion Politics: A View from the States* (1992) with Timothy Byrnes, and *Abortion Politics in American States* (1995) also with Timothy Byrnes.

Ted G. Jelen is professor and chair of the Department of Political Science at the University of Nevada at Las Vegas. He has published numerous books and articles on religion and politics, public opinion, and the politics of abortion.

DATE DUE

MAR 0 7 2007			

*To my beloved mother and father, Anna Pearl
and William Henry—Cosby, of course.*

*And to those people with no children but who
think they'd like to have them some day to
fulfill their lives. Remember: With fulfillment
comes responsibility.*

Contents

I am not a psychologist or a sociologist. I do have a doctorate in education, but much more important than my doctorate is my delight in kids. I devote a part of my professional life to entertaining and educating them. I like children. Nothing I've ever done has given me more joys and rewards than being a father to my five. In between these joys and rewards, of course, has come the natural strife of family life, the little tensions and conflicts that are part of trying to bring civilization to children. The more I have talked about such problems, the more I have found that all other parents had the very same ones and are relieved to hear me turning them into laughter.

Yes, every parent knows the source of this laughter. Come share more of it with me now.

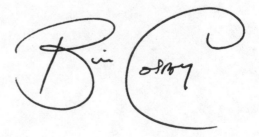

FATHERHOOD

Introduction

by Alvin F. Poussaint, M.D.

Bill Cosby's triumph in this book is to remind us through laughter that models for successful American fatherhood have been changing dramatically over the past several decades. He has sometimes been as dumbfounded as other contemporary dads: "Many men have wondered: Just what *is* a father's role today?" Then he rightly commiserates that the new American father has more responsibilities than ever. Bill recognizes that, though we are closer today to a consensus on the healthy ingredients in a balanced fathering role, many uncertainties remain.

The father's importance in rearing children and his ability to manage families, until quite recently, was not only downplayed but often totally neglected by child-care experts. The general public, supported by pronouncements by leading psychologists and psychiatrists, believed that women, due to "natural instinct," were best suited to raise children and supervise the related duties in the home. Women carried and bore the baby and were physically equipped to breast-feed them, so it was reasonable to assume that they possessed innate "mothering" talents. The ability to nurture children was not only believed to be a woman's God-given gift, but her duty as well.

The father's role was prescribed to be more ethereal and remote from the children. He was primarily conceived as the authority figure who disciplined and taught the children the ways of the outside world. Many famous psychiatrists, including Freud, argued that the mother-child bond was the one most critical to the healthy development of children. And lurking in the minds of many, as a wicked afterthought, was the belief that men, even if they so desired, were not equipped biologically or psychologically to assume the "mothering," nurturant role with children.

No wonder then that, until recently, rearing children has been considered the primary responsibility of mothers. A division of labor evolved, in keeping with strong sex-role stereotypes, that created the model nuclear family, comprised of the stay-at-home mother/housewife and the outside-wage-earner father/provider. Most of us have an image of what motherhood entails, but few of us recognize the different models for fatherhood and their significance in the rearing of children.

More men and women, husbands and wives, fathers and mothers, the divorced and the married, and single parents too, have been taking a fresh look at the phenomenon of fatherhood. As Bill Cosby asks: Just what is it? Bill, who spans the time of the "old" fatherhood to the "new" fatherhood, challenges us with exciting and amusing tales of his own experiences at fathering, to reflect on the dimensions of the enigmatic and complicated issue of fatherhood.

For better or for worse, Bill and I, as contemporaries, grew up under a more rigid definition of traditional male and female family responsibilities. Our own experiences must to some degree color our values today, though Bill and I support the validity of much of the "modern" approach to fatherhood.

In my boyhood home, for example, Papa's chief role was to work: to be the breadwinner, the provider. My mother was a housewife whose chief function was to raise, nurture, and provide custodial care for me and my seven brothers and sisters. Momma relied on Papa, though, on those occasions when we were provocatively disobedient, to be the heavyweight disciplinarian. She would snap, "Wait until your father gets home, you're really going to get it." "It" usually meant a beating, but her threat alone was enough to keep us in check. Fathers were to be feared and respected. "Talking back" to Papa was totally unacceptable. We could "get away" with things with Momma partly because our relationship with her felt more accessible and humane. There was more give-and-take with Mother, while Father tried hard (but not always successfully) to keep the children, and sometimes Momma, strictly "in line."

My father's superior "head of household" attitude toward my mother was also reflected in the way he treated his sons and daughters. Generally, he believed that girls should learn to cook, clean, sew, marry a "good" man, and become a housewife. That was his vision of their fulfillment, and Momma, as a traditional wife, agreed. Papa downright discouraged my sisters from going to college, but two of them did anyway. The boys were expected to work hard in school, go to college, get a job, get married, and, I suppose, become a father like he was. Despite this sex-role typing, my father (and mother too) required that the boys learn how to grocery-shop, cook, clean, paint, and fix things in the house because "a man needed to know how to take care of himself." So there was some degree of flexibility in the children's sex roles but, overall, Papa had the typical old-fashioned attitudes about males and females. But perhaps more significantly, he remained remote and authoritarian with us, sons and daughters alike.

In this traditional father role, Papa was distant and difficult to get to know. It was often hard to relax with him or even to talk to him. But even though fathers were not supposed to be "expressive," Papa occasionally let down his guard and let the warmth shine through to us. I feel, retrospectively, that he was uneasy about showing too much warmth and affection toward us because it might have been viewed by others as a reflection of a lack of manliness. With the aplomb of a general, my father was the authority-in-charge and most definitely the "head-of-the-household." In Bill Cosby's material, there are images of the besieged father, Bill, struggling to stay tough and in charge but frequently giving in to his tender feelings toward his children, striking a better balance than my dad's.

But before anyone starts criticizing my father's approach, let us acknowledge that my dad was not atypical of the fathers of his day. In fact, in many respects he satisfied the requirements well enough to be given a "good father award" because he responsibly carried out his chief role of dependable breadwinner. We ate and we had a roof over our heads, and my dad even at times played with us, argued with us, and disciplined us enough to keep us on the path of righteousness. In contrast, I had friends who did not eat well, barely had a roof over their heads, and had fathers who were absent.

Being a good provider, of course, did not mean that a father had to raise you to the level of even the lower working class. What it meant in my neighborhood was that the father had a job and kept the family off the welfare rolls. This is an act of responsibility to be respected because if more fathers today were merely "good providers" and financially supported their offspring, we would not have so many millions of children living in poverty. This limited role of the father, therefore, is not without value and certainly is not deserving of belittlement. Feeding your children, after all, is one important way of saying you care.

We all know that feeding a child alone is not enough to produce an emotionally balanced, healthy adult. But Momma was there to provide the missing nurturant ingredients for a healthy childhood. Yet it is difficult to decide in retrospect whether Papa's role was good or bad, helpful or harmful, in relation to our growth: Some of us did well and others not so well. Ironically, some social scientists have reported that many children turn out to be emotionally troubled adults because they didn't have my kind of father around.

Psychiatrists and psychologists in the past suggested that the absence of a "strong father" in the home was sufficient cause to account for the many persons who ended up in mental hospitals or jails. There were some mental health specialists who mistakenly believed that the absence of a "strong" dad could turn young boys into gay men. Most of these theories have now been debunked.

The "strong father" role (which doesn't have to be associated with beatings and remoteness) is not to be totally discounted as part of the recipe for raising healthy children, if it is executed skillfully and given in measured doses at the most appropriate of times, as Cosby's crafty accounts illustrate. The new factor that we must acknowledge is that mothers play this "strong" role too!

My mother was definitely "strong." She changed our diapers, fed us by breast or bottle, cooked for us, washed our clothes and dressed us, did the ironing, made the beds, cleaned house, mopped the floors, did the grocery shopping, took us to the doctor, took us to school, made our lunches, and kept us "in line" with everyday matter-of-fact discipline. She also hugged and kissed us, cried over our successes and failures, and counseled us to respect Papa. My mother waited on my father and knew when not to argue back with him and when to "keep her place." The children sometimes felt sorry for Mother (and perhaps ourselves) as this somewhat mysterious authoritarian figure of a father swept in and out "bringing home the bacon."

However, now that I am grown, enlightened, and a psychiatrist, I can ask the critical question: Was my dad missing something? Were we, the children, being deprived of the chance for a warm, closer relationship with Papa? I can at least speculate that my father's style of parenting required that he pay some emotional price. He *was* missing something by not sharing in some of the everyday trials and tribulations and joys and pleasures of the children, family, and home. It was a loss for the children and Mother, and it was a loss for Father. Papa didn't get to know us intimately because he did not participate in any of the activities of parenting that were considered exclusively women's work.

As I grew up, I felt that I was missing something too. I wanted to feel closer to my father and wanted to know him better. He was not an unfriendly man, but he was too stuck in his image of the role of father as presented to him by the mores of his generation to change. He died when I was in my mid thirties, but he allowed me to feel much closer to him during the few months before his death than he had during my whole life. It was a deeply moving experience. I knew then that, as a father, I wanted to be closer to my own children, for my sake as well as theirs.

Since my father's generation there has been a growing and reviving interest in the role of the father. After many decades where the mother was seen as the exclusive or primary caretaker, social scientists and parents are beginning to reexamine old concepts. The women's movement, in particular, has raised questions about the legitimacy and healthiness of the fixed roles for mothers and fathers in the American family, but men also have been questioning the traditional father role. Social and economic demands, too, have coalesced to put greater pressure on fathers and mothers to modify their perspectives in order to meet the child-rearing demands of changing family patterns, no longer typified by the so-called nuclear family. There are more divorced, single-parent, and dual-career families than ever before. Though the responsibility of child rearing still remains primarily with women, more men have been drawn or forced into new and more active fathering roles. Some men have changed out of necessity, but many others have a new desire to participate and share more directly in child rearing and family activities now that they have been given permission to do so.

Men have been struggling with the unfamiliar demands and challenges of this new model of fatherhood. Many have modified their behaviors to some degree in order to adapt more comfortably to changing social and family patterns. In the process of this change, many fathers have seen new possibilities for their own fulfillment by taking a greater part in child-rearing responsibilities. A new movement has been spawned that has been pushing American men and women closer to the acceptance of androgynous fatherhood—men who take a significant share of nurturing responsibilities for children and the home, tasks that were previously assigned exclusively to women.

As with movements of all types, there is support coming from scholars and a new breed of family and child experts. University professors, cognizant of their previous neglect of the subject of fatherhood, are rushing to restore balance to the parenting role. Recent evidence suggests that the fathering role, or the ability of fathers to support their children's healthy growth, is equivalent to mothers if men develop the attitudes and skills to be good parents. This often requires that they give up old-fashioned ideas about so-called manliness, "who wears the pants in the family," and what constitutes "women's work" as opposed to "men's work." There is perhaps no mystique of motherhood that a man cannot master except for the physical realities of a pregnancy, delivery, and breast feeding. All other ingrained notions about which sex makes the more natural parent are at least challengeable. Men too can be "primary care givers" and can provide "mother love."

Divorced fathers, often sharing custody of their children, want to be more than "Disneyland Daddys" or weekend fathers. Fathers in dual career families who are no longer the sole breadwinners must share more child care and household chores with their spouses. These new requirements for fatherhood have caught many men unprepared because they were reared according to the old ideologies of fatherhood. Nonetheless, some men are changing their old outlook and experiencing wonderment, and often joy, as they assume duties usually assigned to the category of motherhood.

We can see today that the new fatherhood demands a change of attitude on the part of both fathers and mothers toward their male and female offspring. There is a need to eliminate sexism and sex-role typing in child rearing and strive for a more balanced, androgynous approach that maximizes the opportunities and options for both boys and girls. Children brought up with a mix of "masculine" and "feminine" qualities will be better suited to adapt to demands of both the new fatherhood and motherhood.

Many people will continue to ask: Can there really be pleasure for Father in changing a baby's diaper, feeding her a bottle, bathing her, dressing her, and nursing her when she's ill? Can playing peek-a-boo and patty-cake with your toddler be a legitimately rewarding activity for an adult male? Can a father bond with his baby, his child, as easily as the mother can? Is it preordained that fathers cannot be as nurturing a parent as the mother in the development of his offspring? These questions have not yet been conclusively answered by researchers, scholars, or even the parenting public, but the new fatherhood is catching on in many families across socioeconomic classes and among different ethnic and religious groups. No one is sure what the future will hold. Yet, a growing number of fathers enjoy parenting so much that they have become "househusbands."

Although we can by no means put Bill Cosby in this category, the comedic insights about marriage, children, and family in this volume will be recognized by all fathers who choose to be deeply involved in the business of raising children. Bill gives hope to all fathers: "The answer, of course, is that no matter how hopeless or copeless a father may be, his role is simply to *be* there, sharing all the chores with his wife. Let her *have* the babies; but after that, try to share every job around."

Every father—and future father—can benefit from reading Bill Cosby's perceptive, touching, and hilarious accounts of parenthood.

That Bill has taken the time to write this book shows his own commitment to the important role of the father. He has written a very funny book about fatherhood, but his underlying message to all dads is quite serious: Care for, nurture, and discipline your children, and do it all with love!

1

Is Three a Crowd?

The Baffling Question

So you've decided to have a child. You've decided to give up quiet evenings with good books and lazy weekends with good music, intimate meals during which you finish whole sentences, sweet private times when you've savored the thought that just the two of you and your love are all you will ever need. You've decided to turn your sofas into trampolines, and to abandon the joys of leisurely contemplating reproductions of great art for the joys of frantically coping with reproductions of yourselves.

Why?

Poets have said the reason to have children is to give yourself immortality; and I must admit I did ask God to give me a son because I wanted someone to carry on the family name. Well, God did just that and I now confess that there have been times when I've told my son not to reveal who he is.

"You make up a name," I've said. "Just don't tell anybody who you are."

Immortality? Now that I have had five children, my only hope is that they all are out of the house before I die.

No, immortality was not the reason why my wife

and I produced these beloved sources of dirty laundry and ceaseless noise. And we also did not have them because we thought it would be fun to see one of them sit in a chair and stick out his leg so that another one of them running by was launched like Explorer I. After which I said to the child who was the launching pad, "Why did you do that?"

"Do what?" he replied.

"Stick out your leg."

"Dad, I didn't know my leg was going out. My leg, it does that a lot."

If you cannot function in a world where things like this are said, then you better forget about raising children and go for daffodils.

My wife and I also did not have children so they could yell at each other all over the house, moving me to say, "What's the problem?"

"She's waving her foot in my room," my daughter replied.

"And something like that *bothers* you?"

"Yes, I don't *want* her foot in my room."

"Well," I said, dipping into my storehouse of paternal wisdom, "why don't you just close the door?"

"Then I can't see what she's doing!"

Furthermore, we did not have the children because we thought it would be rewarding to watch them do things that should be studied by the Menninger Clinic.

"Okay," I said to all five one day, "go get into the car."

All five then ran to the same car door, grabbed the

same handle, and spent the next few minutes beating each other up. Not one of them had the intelligence to say, "Hey, *look*. There are three more doors." The dog, however, was already inside.

And we did not have the children to help my wife develop new lines for her face, or because she had always had a desire to talk out loud to herself: "Don't tell *me* you're *not* going to do something when I tell you to move!" And we didn't have children so I could always be saying to someone, "Where's my change?"

Like so many young couples, my wife and I simply were unable to project. In restaurants, we did not see the small children who were casting their bread on the water in the glasses the waiter had brought; and we did not see the mother who was fasting because she was both cutting the food for one child while pulling another from the floor to a chair that he would use for slipping to the floor again. And we did not project beyond those lovely Saturdays of buying precious little things after leisurely brunches together. We did not see that *other* precious little things would be coming along to destroy the first batch.

Sweet Insanity

Yes, having a child is surely the most beautifully irrational act that two people in love can commit. Having had five qualifies me to write this book but not to give you any absolute rules because there *are* none. Screenwriter William Goldman has said that, in spite of all the experience that Hollywood people have in making movies, "Nobody knows anything." I sometimes think the same statement is true of raising children. In spite of the six thousand manuals on child raising in the bookstores, child raising is still a dark continent and no one really knows anything. You just need a lot of love and luck—and, of course, courage because you'll be spending many years in fear of your kids.

In talking to audiences around the country, I have conducted my own Cosby Poll, asking parents, "Why did you have children when all your other acts were rational?" And I have gotten answers that almost made sense:

"Because I wanted someone to carry on the family name."

"Because a child will be an enduring reflection of ourselves."

"Because I wanted someone to look after me in my old age."

"Because we wanted to hear sounds around the house."

I don't care how bright people are, I have yet to receive a sound reason that would move a man to go out into the street, find a mate, and say, "I want to impregnate you so I can have one of these."

There was, however, one shining exception in this Cosby Poll. One day I found a woman who was the mother of six children; and with simple eloquence, she explained to me why she'd had them.

"Because," she said, "I kept falling asleep."

Some people call a baby "a symbol of our love," feeling that just the two of them would not be symbol enough. The sad truth is, there are people who marry, grow a·vay from each other, get divorced, and then take this symbol of their love and tell it to hate the other mate.

It seems to me that two people have a baby just to see what they can make, like a kind of erotic arts and crafts. And some people have several children because they know there are going to be failures. They figure that if they have a dozen, maybe one or two will work out, for having children is certainly defying the odds. The great sports writer Ring Lardner once said that all life is eight-to-five against. Well, trying to raise a child to come out right is like trying to hit the daily double—which my father used to do when he whacked my brother and me.

Raising children is an incredibly hard and risky business in which no cumulative wisdom is gained:

each generation repeats the mistakes the previous one made. When England's literary giant Dr. Samuel Johnson saw a dog walking on its hind legs, he said, "The wonder is not that it be done well but that it be done at all." The same thing is true of raising children, who have trouble walking straight until they're nineteen or twenty.

We parents so often blow the business of raising kids, but not because we violate any philosophy of child raising. I doubt there can *be* a philosophy about something so difficult, something so downright mystical, as raising kids. A baseball manager has learned a lot about his job from having played the game, but a parent has not learned a thing from having once been a child. What can you learn about a business in which the child's favorite response is "I don't know"?

A father enters his son's room and sees that the boy is missing his hair.

"What happened to your head?" the father says, beholding his skin-headed son. "Did you get a haircut?"

"I don't know," the boy replies.

"You don't *know* if you got a haircut? Well, tell me this: Was your head with you all day?"

"I don't know " says the boy

Beware, Your Foolish Heart

People who have no children say they love them because children are so truthful. Well, I have done extensive fieldwork with five children and can tell you as
scientific fact that the only time they tell the truth is
when they are in pain.

A baby, however, sells itself and needs no advertis-
ing copy; few people can resist it. There is something
about babyness that brings out the softness in people
and makes them want to hug and protect this small
thing that moves and dribbles and produces what we
poetically call poopoo. Even *that* becomes precious, for
the arrival of a baby coincides with the departure of
our minds. My wife and I often summoned the grand-
parents of our first baby and proudly cried, "Look!
Poopoo!" A statement like this is the greatest single
disproof of evolution I know. Would you like a *second*
disproof? Human beings are the only creatures on
earth that allow their children to come back home.

A baby overwhelms us with its lovableness; even its
smell stirs us more deeply than the smell of pine or
baking bread. What is overpowering is simply the fact
that a baby is life. It is also a mess, but such an appealing one that we look past the mess to the jewel under-
neath.

We even love the messy babies of lower species. One night on TV, I saw a show about turtles. Dozens of them came out of a hole on the beach and they were full of a disgusting slime from the eggs, on top of which was now a coating of sand. A baby turtle has to be the ugliest baby around, with sand all over the eggwhite sauce and arms bent in the wrong direction. Nevertheless, in spite of all this ugliness, I watched that show and found myself saying, "Awwww, look at those sweet little baby turtles."

A baby's cry tells us it is wanted; and so, with a baby we cannot lose. For a new father, this little person is something he can hold and love and play with and even teach, if he knows anything. Without always being aware of it, this father has been loving babies almost since the time he was one himself. Even a three-year-old says, "Awwww, look—baby!" and goes over to touch it. Then we have to teach the three-year-old not to remove the baby's eyes. Of course, this three-year-old is also capable of loving a baby panther.

"Awwww, a little kitty cat," she will say.

"No, a little panther," you reply.

"Can I play with the kitty?"

"No, only lion tamers play with kitty," you say to her.

Yes, a baby is so powerfully appealing that people are even entertained watching it sleep. Just notice how grown people tiptoe to a crib and look down at a baby. Perhaps such a journey finally answers the great question about why people have babies who will soon start saying, "I don't know" and "Mine! Mine! Mine!" and start walking around with their flies always open. The decision to have such a thing is made by the heart, not the brain.

2

With Bouquets
and
Back Rubs

Because It's There

It's love, of course, that makes us fathers do it—love for the woman we've married and love for every baby we've ever seen, except the one that threw up on our shoes. And so, in spite of all our reservations about this scary business of reproduction, we must admit that people look happy when they're carrying babies. The male looks especially happy because he has someone to carry it for him, his darling packager.

But his wife is happy too, because she feels she's fulfilling herself as a woman. I've heard so many females say that they became mothers because they wanted to feel like women, as if they felt like longshoremen at all other times. And so many others have said, "I had the baby because I wanted to see if I could," which sounds like a reason for climbing Mount Everest or breaking the four-minute mile. If a chimpanzee can have a baby, the human female should realize that the feat is something less than an entry for the *Guinness Book of World Records*.

The new father, of course, feels that his mere impregnation of his mate, done every day by otters and apes, is Olympic gold medal stuff. Even if he's afraid of garter snakes, he feels positively heroic. He feels that

he and his wife have nobly created something that will
last. He never thinks that they may have created one of
the top ten underachievers in their town.

Try a Little Tenderness

The male has got to get rid of the feeling that inflating
his wife makes him a man, that mere fertilization is a
reason for a high five. He has to stop feeling smugly
triumphant.

If you really love your wife, her pregnancy is a time
to test your attention span. You have to pay attention
when she says, "It's moving! Wake up and feel it!" You
have to respond as if she's pointing out a replay of a
touchdown pass. Remember that the demands of your
wife for attention and affection don't come close to the
demands that the *baby* will be putting on you.

Not only is her figure changing, but her personality
is too. There will be sudden flashes of anger and tears,
and from time to time she will blame you for everything from her backaches to the balance of trade. She
feels ugly, no matter how many friends tell her that
her skin glows.

"If carrying this thing for nine months makes a person look so great," she wants to say, "how'd *you* like to
carry it around and put a glow on *your* skin?"

Although you don't have to agree to carry it for her, you *should* make an effort to keep helping her and to keep expressing your love. Make sure that she sits in comfortable chairs; and then help her out of the chair when it's time to leave, or else you'll find yourself in the street without her because she'll still be in the chair, flapping her arms and trying to get airborne.

You have to understand that she has lost more than her mobility and her figure: she has also lost the fun of sleeping on her face. Her new hobby is finding a comfortable position for sleeping, so she needs you to put pillows under her back and head and knees; and she needs your help during her drop into the bucket seat of your car, the car you bought when you entertained the wonderfully silly thought that just the two of you would be living a sporty life, enjoying only each other.

She even needs your help in giving birth.

Almost as Smart as Neanderthals

Before we had children, my wife and I felt educated. She was a college graduate, a child psychology major with a B-plus average, which means, if you ask her a question about a child's behavior, she will give you eighty-five percent of the answer. And I was a physical education major with a child psychology minor at

Temple, which means if you ask me a question about a child's behavior, I will advise you to tell the child to take a lap.

Because we were college graduates, we studied things that people have always done naturally, like have children; and so, we decided to have our first child by natural childbirth. Childbirth, of course, *is* a natural thing: the pains come automatically, the muscles contract and push down, and all you need, as they say, is hot water. Neanderthals delivered children without training manuals.

At any rate, these classes give the father a diploma so that he can attend the birth. And what the classes teach him is how to be a cheerleader in the delivery room: how to say, "Push! Push! Push 'em out, shove 'em out, waaay out!"

My wife's job was to keep breathing, but she had studied how to do this in the course, so she was breathing at the top of her class. By the time we had finished the class, we were well prepared for natural childbirth, which means that no drugs can be given to the female during delivery. The father, however, can have all he wants.

One day near the end of the ninth month, my wife came running to me, breathing rapidly, and she cried, "Bill!"

"Push!" I said.

But then I remembered something from the class: You have to go to a hospital. And so we did, at 120 miles an hour, with my wife moaning all the way.

When we got to the hospital, we went right to the delivery room, where I put the booties on my shoes. Her legs went up into the stirrups, while the obstetrician sat awaiting the delivery, like Johnny Bench.

When the first big pain hit her, I merrily said, "Push!"

Like every man, of course, I had no understanding of how a labor pain really feels. Carol Burnett said, "If you want to know the feeling, just take your bottom lip and pull it over your head."

When the second big pain hit, she cried out and stood up in the stirrups.

"Morphine!" she said. "I want morphine!"

"But dear," I sweetly replied, "you *know* that morphine—"

"*You* shut up! You did this to me!"

And at the next contraction, she told everyone in the delivery room that my parents were never married. Then she continued breathing while I continued cheering from the sidelines: "Push! Push! Push!"

"I don't *want* to push anymore," she said. "Bill, tell them to give me something."

"No, dear, the class forbids—"

"I'm dropping out of *school!*"

"But you can *do* it!"

Meanwhile, Johnny Bench was still sitting there, waiting for the delivery.

"Look!" I suddenly said. "Isn't that the head?"

"I believe it is," he replied.

"Well, go *get* it."

"It's stuck."

"Then get the salad spoons, man."

So he got the salad spoons, the baby came out, and my wife and I were suddenly sharing the greatest moment in our lives. This was what we had asked God for; this was what we wanted to see if we could make. And I looked at it lovingly as they started to clean it off, but it wasn't getting any better.

And then I went over to my wife, kissed her gently on the lips, and said, "Darling, I love you very much. You just had a lizard."

What's in a Name?

Even though all the millions of births are pretty much alike, what will set your child apart from the others is its name. Always end the name of your child with a vowel, so that when you yell, the name will carry. I do not see how a mother can hang out of her window and do anything much with a cry of "Torvald!" A nervous mother needs an "o" or an "i" or an "e" because they last long enough to get the kid home for his beating. That mother also can't be heard by her other son, Dag, because the "g" sound doesn't stretch any better than the "d."

If you must put consonants in your child's name,

put them in the middle, where an "n" or two "n's" or even four will work, as long as there's a vowel at the end. For example, if your child were named Winnou, you could linger on the "Winn" for a long time and then finish up strong with the "oooo." You could get past more than two sewers with that name: you could get a couple of blocks.

My own father violated this rule by giving me a name that ended in "t," but you have to admit that this name was an exception. He called me Jesus Christ. Often he turned to me and said, "Jesus Christ!"

My brother had a name that also ended in a consonant: "Lookdammit." Addressing the two of us, my father would say, "Lookdammit, stop jumping on the furniture! Jesus Christ, can't you ever be still?"

My father, however, did sometimes get me and my brother mixed up. One day when I was out playing in the rain, he came to the door and said, "Lookdammit."

And I replied, "Dad, I'm Jesus Christ."

In spite of these names for my brother and me, my father did try hard not to curse, an effort that often rendered him semi-articulate. Having to squelch the profanities that he dearly wanted to lavish on me reduced him to saying such things as, "If you ever . . . because you're a . . . and I'll be . . . because it's just too . . . and I swear I'll . . ." For many years, in fact, I thought my father was a man unable to complete a sentence. I made him swallow curses like after-dinner mints.

I always corrected my father respectfully because,

although he never gave me a beating, he did often hit for distance. Many times when I was flying by, a neighbor would say, "Tell your father I said hello."

"I brought you into this world," my father would say, "and I can take you out. It don't make no difference to me. I'll just make another one like you."

So my father would not have been particularly interested in a book like this about fathering, although he did like to read. In fact, it was sometimes hard to make him take his face out of a book. One day when my father was reading in the living room, my brother and I decided that we could play basketball without breaking anything. When I took a shot that redesigned a glass table, my mother came in with a stick and said, "So help me, I'll bust you in half."

Without lifting his head from his book, my father said, "Why would you want twice as many?"

3

These Beggars
Are
Choosers

Like the Marines, Be Prepared

In spite of my father's feelings, I presume that you still have decided to have a child instead of a hamster. A hamster, however, would give you more privacy in the bathroom.

Bathroom privacy is something that you and your wife have taken for granted, the same way you have taken for granted a quiet ride in the car, a civilized dinner out, and not having to file for bankruptcy because of investments in toy stores. A new father quickly learns that his child invariably comes to the bathroom at precisely the times when he's in there, as if he needed company. The only way for this father to be certain of bathroom privacy is to shave at the gas station.

The new father also loses privacy for taking naps and for working at home. To a young person, naps don't mean much; he casually takes them in English class. But to a father, a nap is a basic need; and he soon learns that this need can best be met in a local theater.

Whether the father is trying to shave or nap or work, small children come to him like moths to a flame.

"Now look," he says, "I want you to *stop* that. I want

you to go outside because Daddy is working. I've bought you three-and-a-half-million dollars' worth of toys and dolls. You even have a *beauty parlor* for the dolls, which you begged me to buy because it was the only thing you really wanted—except, of course, the motorbike. It isn't that I don't love you. It's just that Daddy doesn't have time for you to rearrange his desk right now. I really do love you—you're better mentally and physically than anything I'd ever hoped for— but right now your hand is on the thing that's causing our problem. That thing is part of Daddy's job. *Your* job is to go upstairs and try to find something in that three-and-a-half-million-dollar room that can amuse you for five or ten minutes. Why don't you take Barbie to the beauty parlor?"

I guess the real reason that my wife and I had children is the same reason that Napoleon had for invading Russia: it seemed like a good idea at the time. Since then, however, I've had some doubts, primarily about my intelligence. I began entertaining these doubts when my first daughter was about eighteen months old. Every time I went into her room, she would take some round plastic thing from her crib and throw it on the floor. Then I would pick it up, wipe it off, and hand it back to her so she could throw it back to the floor.

"Don't throw that on the floor, honey," I'd tell her. "Do you understand Daddy? Don't throw that on the floor."

Then I would give it back to her and she would

throw it again. Picking it up once more, wiping it off, and returning it to her, I again would say, "Look, I just *told* you not to throw this on the floor, didn't I?"

And, of course, she would listen carefully to me and then throw it again.

This little game is wonderful exercise for the father's back, but it is his *mind* that needs developing. Sometimes a father needs ten or fifteen droppings before he begins to understand that he should *leave* the thing on the floor—or maybe put the child down there too.

During this little game, the child has been thinking: *This person is a lot of fun. He's not too bright, but a lot of fun.*

Toilet Training—for You

Except for the cost of the child, which may lead you to consider joining organized crime, fathering is easier today than it was when I began. Take diapering. A father today doesn't have to try to figure out how to fold a cloth diaper, and he doesn't have to keep making little holes in his fingers with safety pins, and he doesn't have to drop the diaper in the toilet bowl.

I do not often get nostalgic about the days when I dropped diapers with their contents into the toilet bowl because I didn't have time to properly clean them off. And then my neighbor would come, I'd forget that the diaper was in the toilet bowl, and when the neighbor went to use the bathroom, I had the kind of moment that encourages people not to have children.

I remember traveling with two babies in those medieval days of cloth diapers. I was always overweight on planes because I needed an extra suitcase with nothing but diapers. A father today has disposable diapers and plastic bottles. The only thing left to invent is a plastic toy that will hit the floor and then bounce back into the crib.

Some things, however, never change. For example, you still have to put newspaper under the child's chair to catch all the food he misses. Eventually, of course, you can sit down and have a picnic on the floor because more food is down there than in the child's stomach.

To the Poorhouse with a Smile

Because you are feeding both the child and the floor, raising this child will be expensive. The Lord was wise enough to make a woman's pregnancy last nine months. If it were shorter, people with temporary insanity might have two or three kids a year, and they would be wiped out before the first one had learned to talk. You know why John D. Rockefeller had all that money? Because he had only one child, so he didn't have to spend ninety thousand dollars on Snoopy pens and Superhero mugs and Smurf pajamas and Barbie Ferraris.

It doesn't make any difference how much money a father earns, his name is always Dad-Can-I; and he always wonders whether these little people were born to beg. I bought each of my five children everything up to a Rainbow Brite jacuzzi and still I kept hearing "Dad, can I get . . . Dad, can I go . . . Dad, can I buy . . ."

Like all other children, my five have one great talent: they are gifted beggars. Not one of them ever ran into the room, looked up at me, and said, "I'm really happy that you're my father, and as a tangible token of my appreciation, here's a dollar." If one of them had ever done this, I would have taken his temperature.

A parent quickly learns that no matter how much money you have, you will never be able to buy your kids everything they want. You can take a second mortgage on your house and buy what you think is the entire Snoopy line: Snoopy pajamas, Snoopy underpants, Snoopy linen, Snoopy shoelaces, Snoopy cologne, and Snoopy soap, but you will never have it all. And if Snoopy doesn't send you to the poorhouse, Calvin Klein will direct the trip. Calvin is the slick operator who sells your kids things for eighty-five dollars that cost seven at Sears. He has created millions of tiny snobs, children who look disdainfully at you and say, "Nothing from Sears." However, Dad-Can-I fought back: I got some Calvin Klein labels and sewed them into Sears undershorts for my high fashion junkies.

Sometimes, at three or four in the morning, I open the door to one of the children's bedrooms and watch the light softly fall across their little faces. And then I quietly kneel beside one of the beds and just look at the girl lying there because she is so beautiful. And because she is not begging. Kneeling there, I listen reverently to the sounds of her breathing.

And then she wakes up and says, "Dad, can I . . ."

Help from a Second Opinion

You other fathers will be happy to learn I have found a way for you to exploit this juvenile frenzy to own everything that was ever made. At the peak of Michael Jackson's fame, when I had girls of six and ten who lived amid Jackson paraphernalia, I discovered that I could use *him* as a proxy disciplinarian.

"Michael Jackson loves all his fans, but he has a special feeling for the ones who eat broccoli," I said one night at dinner, and two of his fans quickly swallowed both that story and broccoli too.

"You girls know Michael Jackson's great big eyes?" I said to them at another meal.

His anti-vegetarian fan club smiled.

"Well, they were *tiny* until he started eating Brussels sprouts," I said.

The problem was that this bond to Michael was also putting pressure on *me*.

"Dad, *you* know people like Michael Jackson," one of my daughters said. "Take us to his house."

"I'd love to," I said, "but he's in Europe."

"Then take us to Europe."

"And what will you do when you meet him? Thank him for the Brussels sprouts?"

"No, I will die."

"Well, I don't want you to die."

"Oh, I'm not going to die."

"Then why did you say that?"

"Dad, it's just a figure of speech."

"What would you do if you saw him?"

"I'd pass out."

"Still no good," I said. "I don't want you fooling around with your mind. I want you to have all your mental powers when you get the Snoopy Porsche."

4

Are They
Evolution's
Missing Link?

Dr. Spock Never Promised Us a Rose Garden

When a man has children, the first thing he has to learn is that he is not the boss of the house. I am certainly not the boss of *my* house. However, I have seen the boss's job and I don't want it, for sometimes the boss ends up sitting alone in a room and talking to herself as if the enemy were there: "What do you *mean* you don't want to do it? When I *tell* you to do something, you *do* it and you don't stand there practicing for law school!"

In spite of all the love, joy, and gratification that children bring, they do cause a certain amount of stress that takes its toll on parents. My wife and I have five children, and the reason we have five is that we did not want six.

Before we were married, my wife was a stunningly beautiful woman. Today she is a stunningly beautiful woman whose mouth droops and who has conversations with herself. She also sounds like my mother: "I'm gonna knock you into the middle of next week!" The middle of next week, by the way, is where their father wouldn't mind going: I would have four days by myself.

From time to time, my wife also threatens to knock the children to Kingdom Come. If she ever *does* knock them there, she's going to ask me to go get them, and I will not know where it is.

"You know where it is," she'll say. "You just don't want to find them."

You new fathers will learn that almost all mothers are like my wife and have conversations with themselves. These maternal monologists, however, have developed a lovely retaliation. They put a curse on their children: *I just hope that when you get married, you have children who act just like you.* (And, of course, the curse always works, proving that God has a sense of humor.) My own wish is not a curse but a simple prayer: I just want the children to get out of the house before we die.

There is no wisdom I can give you new fathers more profound than what I said at the start of this chapter: you are *not* the boss of this house that you want the children out of within thirty years and you are *not* allowed to give them permission for anything. When one of them comes to you and says, "Dad, can I go explore the Upper Nile?" your answer must be, "Go ask your mother."

Only once did I make the great permission mistake. One of the children came to me and said, "Dad, can I go out and play?"

"Sure," I replied. "I don't see why not."

That was the last time I couldn't see why not. My wife came in and said, "Did you let that child go out?"

"Yeah," I said.

"Well, the next time you check with *me*. He's being punished."

From that day on, I knew my place; and whenever a child starts to say, "Dad, can I . . ." even though it's my name, I always reply, "What did your mother say?"

And even if the child says that she got permission, I still say, "Very fine. Just bring me a note from your mother. It doesn't have to be notarized. A simple signature and date will do."

Ironically, even though the father is not the boss of the house, the mother will try to use him as a threat: "When your father comes home, he's going to shoot you in the face with a bazooka. And this time I'm not going to stop him."

My Wife's Clean Hands

You see, the wives *pretend* to turn over the child-raising job to us fathers, but they don't really mean it. One day, my wife said to me, "He's *your* child. I wash my hands of him."

Where is this sink where you can wash your hands of a child? I want to wash my hands too, and then the boy can go free.

For someone who supposedly had washed her hands of the child, my wife still sounded unwashed to me.

"You go and talk to him right now."

"I certainly will," I said.

"But the thing is, Bill, you always let him have his own way."

"Look, you've washed your hands; he's not yours, he's mine. So let me handle it."

"I want you to be hard on him."

She was singing this song now; but three years before, when I had wanted to set him on fire, she'd said, "Oh, *please* don't. He's such a little boy."

And I had said, "No, burn him now."

Yes, amid all the love, there are still dark threats in any normal family, especially if a man and woman have been reckless enough to allow the joy of making love to lead to something as dangerous as children.

The problem is consistency: there isn't any. New parents quickly learn that raising children is a kind of desperate improvisation. If *I* ever get angry at the children, my wife collects them under her wing and says, "Come away with me, darlings. Your father's gone mad."

Of course, people who spend more than six minutes trying to discipline children learn that consistency and logic are never a part of things. Usually, however, my wife gives the orders in our house. Late one afternoon, I came home from playing tennis, gave her a warm kiss on the cheek, and said, "How ya feeling, pud?"

And she softly replied, "I want you to go upstairs and kill that boy."

"Very fine," I said, feeling pretty happy because *I* wasn't the one in trouble.

When I reached the boy's room, we had that nice thoughtful talk I mentioned earlier, the one in which he could not remember when he had shaved his head; and then, being a father who likes to probe to the very souls of those I love, I said, "So tell me, son, how are things?"

"Okay," he said.

"Is there any problem you'd like to discuss with Dad?"

"It's okay."

And, as every father knows, "Okay" means "*I haven't killed anyone.*"

Such descriptions of his own good behavior do not seem to stop his mother from making the poor boy the target of a hit, and I'm not the only one with a contract. His four sisters—two older, two younger—are also interested in wiping him out. Because some girls are both cleaner and more mature than boys, they had a meeting recently about his habit of leaving the toilet seat up. They conducted this meeting with the maturity that they all possess; and when it was over, they decided to fix him. You see, the two most important things to the American female are man's prevention of nuclear war and man's putting the toilet seat down. Their brother can't seem to learn the latter and may have to pay the ultimate price.

A father has a right to get tired of such constant sibling rivalry. Unfortunately, a father's job is *not* to get tired of what he has a right to get tired of: for example, small people who keep doing things that you tell them not to do, and when you ask them why they keep doing these things, they reply, "I don't know."

It is also possible to get tired of a small person who yells to another, "Will you stop *touching* me!"

"What's going on?" you say.

"She's *touching* me!"

"Look, don't touch her anymore, okay?"

"But she touched me *first.*"

And then you resolve the dispute with wisdom worthy of Solomon: "I don't want anyone in this house to touch another person as long as you live."

Tales from the Funny Farm

No matter how calmly you try to referee, parenting will eventually produce bizarre behavior, and I'm not talking about the kids. *Their* behavior is always normal, a norm of acting incomprehensibly with sweetly blank looks. But *you* will find yourself strolling down the road to the funny farm—like my mother, who used to get so angry that she would forget my name:

"All right, come *over* here, Bar—uh, Bernie . . . uh,

uh—Biff . . . uh—what *is* your name, boy? And don't lie to me 'cause you live here and I'll find out who you are and take a stick and knock your brains out!"

All during my stormy boyhood years, I wanted to get some calves' brains and keep them in my pocket. Then, when my mother hit me in the head, I would throw them on the floor. Knowing her, however, she merely would have said, "Put your brains back in your head! Don't *ever* let your brains fall out of your head! Have you lost your *mind?*"

And thus, in spite of the joys that children do bring, does parenting take its toll on both father and mother. Mothers who have experience in the trenches of family warfare are sometimes even driven to what I call anticipatory parenting. They ask a child a question, he tries to answer, and they say, "You shut up! When I ask you a question, you keep your mouth shut! You think I'm talking to hear myself talk? *Answer* me!"

This is a pitiable condition in a mother, but my hold on my own sanity has also been a tenuous one because of the behavior of what was created by a few delightful seconds of sex. Believe me, I have paid for those delights. My three-year-old, for example, used to grab things belonging to her close relatives and cry, "Mine! Mine! Mine!" It was a sound that ricocheted through the house for a while and then went up your spinal cord: "Mine! Mine! Mine!" If you followed the sound to its source, you would always find an older child pulling on the end of what the three-year-old had stolen, saying, "You took this from my *room!*"

"Why don't you let her have it?" I would tell the older one. "Don't you hear how it's upsetting her?"

Okay, so I *haven't* been Solomon, perhaps because I've felt more like Noah, just lost at sea. But the truth is that parents are not really interested in justice. They just want quiet.

No matter how much the pressure on your spinal cord builds up, *never* let these small people know that you have gone insane. There is an excellent reason for this: they want the house; and at the first sign that something is wrong with you, they will take you right to a home.

When I reach sixty-five, I plan to keep a gun in my hand, for I know that the moment I spill something on my lap, they'll come to me and say, "We're sorry, Dad, but you can't control yourself and you've got to go."

Whether or not I manage to avoid eviction, I hope that these young adversaries appreciate that my wife and I have tried not to make the mistakes that our parents made with us. For example, we have always been against calling the children idiots. This philosophy has been basic for my wife and me. And we proudly lived by it until the children came along.

5

A Guru Would
Give Up Too

Good Morning, Opponents

If a family wants to get through the day with a minimum of noise and open wounds, the parents have to impose order on the domestic scene. And such order should start with breakfast, which we all know is the most important meal of the day. My wife certainly thinks so. A few weeks ago, she woke me at six o'clock in the morning and said, "I want you to go downstairs and cook breakfast for the children."

"But, dear," I said with an incredulous look at the clock, "it's six in the morning."

"You tell time very nicely. Now go down and cook breakfast for the children. They have to go to school."

"But to eat at six . . . isn't that bad for the stomach? I mean, they just ate twelve hours ago."

"Bill, get out of this bed and go downstairs and cook breakfast for your children!"

I would like to repeat a point I made before: I am not the boss of my house. I don't know how I lost it and I don't know where I lost it. I probably never had it to begin with. My wife is the boss, and I do not understand how she is going to outlive me.

"But here's the thing, dear," I said, now a desperate man, "I don't know what they want to eat."

"It's *down* there."

I went back to sleep. I dreamed I was with Scott in the Antarctic, perhaps because my wife was pouring ice water over my head.

"Have you given any more thought to cooking breakfast?" she said as I awoke again.

And so, downstairs I went, wondering about the divorce laws in my state, and I started slamming things around. I had bacon, sausages, and eggs all lined up when my four-year-old arrived, looking so adorable with her cute face and little braids.

"Morning, Daddy," she said.

"Okay," I said, "what do *you* want for breakfast?"

"Chocolate cake," she replied.

"Chocolate *cake?* For *breakfast?* That's ridiculous."

Then, however, I thought about the ingredients in chocolate cake: milk and eggs and wheat, all part of good nutrition.

"You want chocolate cake, honey?" I said, cutting a piece for her. "Well, here it is. But you also need something to drink."

And I gave her a glass of grapefruit juice.

When the other four children came downstairs and saw the four-year-old eating chocolate cake, they wanted the same, of course; and since I wanted good nutrition for them too, I gave each of them a piece.

So there my five children sat, merrily eating chocolate cake for breakfast, occasionally stopping to sing:

Dad is the greatest dad you can make!
For breakfast he gives us chocolate cake!

The party lasted until my wife appeared, staggered slightly, and said, "Chocolate cake for *breakfast?* Where did you all get *that?*"

"*He* gave it to us! *He* made us eat it!" said my five adorable ingrates in one voice; and then my eight-year-old added, "*We* wanted eggs and cereal."

A Law Newton Missed

My eight-year-old was given to me just for love because she certainly doesn't *do* anything. The new American father has more responsibilities than ever, but the children seem to have fewer. Ask any eight-year-old why she can never bring herself to do her chores and she will reply, "But I caaan't. I'm only a little person."

This little person who can jump rope nonstop for twenty-seven minutes says that her chores are too great a strain on her fragile little body. This little person who could ride a bicycle up Mount Washington cannot muster the strength to pick up the coat and sweater she dropped on her way to the kitchen. (To be fair, she may have left that trail of clothes so she could find her way *back* from the kitchen.)

One day, my eight-year-old was fooling around, undoubtedly because I had told her not to fool around, and she knocked over a big bucket of popcorn.

"You have to clean that up," I said.

"But it's so maaany, Dad."

"No, I'm afraid you have to clean it up. We're not leaving it down there for the birds."

And so, she began to pick up the popcorn. She was doing fine for five or six seconds, when she turned to me and said, "I'm so *tired*, Dad," and she started to walk away.

"Come back," I said, recognizing this approach to work from my days in the Navy. "Does that look cleaned up?"

"Well, I did the best I could. It's so maaany, Dad. And my arms got tired. I think I wanna go to bed now."

I am not a physicist, but I'm sure that the theory of the conservation of energy was discovered while watching an eight-year-old pretend to work.

Play It as It Lays

It is no profound revelation to say that fathering has changed greatly from the days when my own father used me for batting practice. However, the baffling behavior of children is exactly the same today as it was when Joseph's brothers peddled him to the Egyptians. And in the face of such constantly baffling behavior, many men have wondered: Just what *is* a father's role today? As a taskmaster, he's inept. As a referee, he's hopeless. And as a short-order cook, he may have the wrong menu.

The answer, of course, is that no matter how hopeless or copeless a father may be, his role is simply to *be* there, sharing all the chores with his wife. Let her *have* the babies; but after that, try to share every job around. Any man today who returns from work, sinks into a chair, and calls for his pipe is a man with an appetite for danger. Actually, changing a diaper takes much less time than waxing a car. A car doesn't spit on your pants, of course, but a baby's book value is considerably higher.

If the new American father feels bewildered and even defeated, let him take comfort from the fact that whatever he does in any fathering situation has a fifty percent chance of being right. Having five children has taught me a truth as cosmic as any that you can find on a mountain in Tibet: There are no absolutes in raising children. In any stressful situation, fathering is always a roll of the dice. The game may be messy, but I have never found one with more rewards and joys.

You know the only people who are *always* sure about the proper way to raise children? Those who've never had any.

High Anxiety

On a recent cross-country flight, I saw a dramatic example of why being a parent is a harder job than being President of the United States. In fact, the scene I saw could have been a commercial for birth control.

On that flight were a mother and her four-year-old son, whose name was Jeffrey. Everybody on the plane knew his name was Jeffrey because his mother spent a major part of the trip talking to him, generally from a distance:

"Jeffrey, don't *do* that!"

"Jeffrey, will you get *down* from there!"

"Jeffrey, now look what you've done!"

All of the passengers knew not only Jeffrey's name but also his age because, as he merrily ran about kicking their legs, he kept crying, "I'm four years old!" I happened to have been spared his kicking my particular legs. Instead, he merely smeared chocolate on my shirt.

And so, as our terror flight moved west, sleep was made impossible by the counterpoint of the voices of mother and son:

"Jeffrey, get down!"

"I'm four years old!"

"Jeffrey, now *look* what you've done to the man!"

"I'm four years old!"

If the passengers had been given a choice between riding with Jeffrey and riding with a hijacker, I know what their choice would have been. The hijacker might have allowed a few of us to sleep; and even if he hadn't, he certainly would not have kept saying, "I'm twenty-three years old!"

As the plane moved west, the feelings of the passengers toward Jeffrey grew more intense. When we reached the continental divide, one gentleman invited him into the lavatory to play with the blue water.

At last, however, there was mercy and Jeffrey fell asleep—five minutes before we landed. When the plane reached the terminal and the passengers began to leave, a few of them took special pains to wake up Jeffrey and say good-bye. And their hearts went out to his mother, who had aged ten years in five hours. Her hair was disheveled, her mascara had run, and exhaustion had seeped into her face. After every other person had left, she summoned the last traces of her strength, picked up Jeffrey, and carried him off the plane, as if she were taking out the garbage.

And there, at the end of the ramp, was Jeffrey's father. He was smiling, he had a deep tan, and he was wearing a clean white shirt and brightly checkered pants. The mother handed Jeffrey to this man and then quietly told him to go to hell.

The First Parent Had Trouble Too

Whenever your kids are out of control, you can take comfort from the thought that even God's omnipotence did not extend to His kids. After creating the heaven, the earth, the oceans, and the entire animal kingdom, God created Adam and Eve. And the first thing He said to them was "Don't." To the animals, He never said, "Don't"—he hurled no negatives at the elephant—but to the brightest of His creatures, the ones who get into Yale, He said, "Don't."

"Don't what?" Adam replied.

"Don't eat the forbidden fruit."

"Forbidden fruit? Really? Where is it?"

Is this beginning to sound familiar? You never realized that the pattern of your life had been laid down in the Garden of Eden.

"It's over there," said God, wondering why He hadn't stopped after making the elephants.

A few minutes later, God saw the kids having an apple break and He was angry.

"Didn't I *tell* you not to eat that fruit?" the First Parent said.

"Uh-huh," Adam replied.

"Then why *did* you?"

"I don't know," Adam said.

At least he didn't say, "No problem."

"All right then, get out of here! Go forth, become fruitful, and multiply!"

This was not a blessing but a curse: God's punishment was that Adam and Eve should have children of their own. And so, they moved to the east of Eden, which was still the good part of town, and they had your typical suburban family: a couple of dim-witted boys. One of these boys couldn't stand the other; but instead of just leaving Eden and going to Chicago, he had to kill him.

Thus the pattern was set and it never has changed. But there is reassurance in this story for those of you whose children are not doing well. If you have lovingly and persistently tried to give them wisdom and they haven't taken it, don't be hard on yourself. If *God* had trouble handling children, what makes you think it would be a piece of cake for you?

The Doctors of Dumbness

In America, there are many experts on child raising who have no children. They are people who have never met Jeffrey, the four-year-old. One of my great pleasures is listening to these people because they are an endless source of richly comic stupidity. They say things like "When I have children, I want them to be very close friends so they can share each other's things."

To be fair, however, I must admit that from time to time children do like to share with siblings. For example, once in a while a brother will try to remove his sister's arm so he can play with it.

These childless experts fail to understand that, for the last nine million years, ever since the first child crawled out of the slime (where his mother had told him not to play), children have had just one guiding philosophy and it is greed:

Mine! Mine! Mine!

Of *course* these small people like to share. The way Hitler shared Czechoslovakia.

The childless experts on child raising also bring tears of laughter to my eyes when they say, "I love children because they're so honest." There is not an agent in the CIA or the KGB who knows how to conceal the theft of food, how to fake being asleep, or how to forge a parent's signature like a child. I have looked it up: the last honest child died in 1843 at the age of ten. He was driven to his death by other children for making them look bad.

6

She's Got
the Whole World
in Her Glands

Prepubescent and Preposterous

Not long ago, my eight-year-old, who is the size of a well-built flea, walked past me singing, "Give it to me all night long."

So I called her over and nervously said, "Give you *what* all night long?"

"I don't know," she replied.

"Then why do you want it all night long?"

"Because it feels so good."

Her fingers had encountered difficulty curling around that heavy popcorn on the floor, but she had the strength to take something unknown all night long.

In the last chapter, I said it must have been an eight-year-old who inspired the discovery of the law of the conservation of energy. Well, at nine, new problems of physics arise, such as trying to hold a glass upright. Have you ever taken a nine-year-old to a movie? It's easy to find one for her today because most movies are made for nine-year-olds. Some, in fact, seem to have been made *by* nine-year-olds.

At any rate, a movie for a nine-year-old is the most exciting thing in her life—except, of course, for avoiding work. The nine-year-old likes to absorb the entire essence of movieness, a procedure that excludes watching the movie.

About ten minutes after the movie has begun, she will say, "I want some popcorn."

So you give her a dollar and tell her to go out to the lobby and get it. When she returns with the seventy-five-cent popcorn, sits down, and turns to the screen, you say, "Do I get any change?" (You have realized by now that if you want to be a father, you had better be prepared to spend twenty years asking for change.)

Well, she almost succeeds in giving the change to you, but instead she decides to roll the quarter down the aisle. She will be happy to retrieve it, right after she returns to the refreshment stand for a soda. You give her more money for the soda and a few minutes later she comes back to you with half a cup. Did she have enough money for only half a cup? No, she had enough money for both a whole cup *and* a bar of candy that you did not authorize; but she spilled half the cup on her way back to you. Since she has spilled out half a cup many times before, you suddenly are struck by the insight that this small person does not understand how the law of gravity affects a liquid. By the age of thirty-five, her father has learned the way to put something down on a flat surface; so at least you know she'll get the hang of it in another twenty-six years.

Often we take for granted that children can do simple things, but simple things can be the hardest for them. Your five-year-old, for example, may fall down at any time, three years after he has learned how to walk. The problem is not an inner ear imbalance: the problem is just that he falls down. It is a talent that is handed down from one generation to the next, for many times my mother said to me, "Can't you *walk?*" My wife and I, however, vowed that we would never say such things to our children. And our children will make the same vow about theirs.

Down Mammary Lane

At eleven, the imbalance in a child, especially a girl, moves from the physical to the mental. At eleven, a girl stands at the window a lot and stares out into space. She is waiting for her breasts to come. The strange look on her face moves you to ask, "Are you all right?"

"Well, sort of, I guess," she says. "They didn't come today."

When the child is twelve, your wife buys her a splendidly silly article of clothing called a training bra. To train *what?* I never had a training *jock*. And believe me, when I played football, I could have used a training jock more than any twelve-year-old needs a training bra. I used to get training knees in my crotch.

Girls at eleven and even twelve are physiologically like boys. And these boys are not ready for them yet;

they are still involved with lower species. They are wandering around with frogs, sleeping with lizards, and cutting the heads off flies. The poor girls, meanwhile, are trying to look as lovely as they can for these little zookeepers.

When these boys do allow themselves to be involved with girls, it is often to push them around. While the girls polish their nails, curl their hair, and prayerfully put on their training bras, they look at the boys and wonder: *How much longer will they be nitwits?*

And then one day, in the kind of miracle of nature that Disney liked to capture, it suddenly happens. One morning, I saw it in my son's face while we were driving to school.

"Dad," he said reverently, "there's a lot of women in the world, right?"

At the moment that a boy of thirteen is turning toward girls, a girl of thirteen is turning on her mother. This girl can get rather unreasonable, often saying such comical things as, "Listen, this is my *life!*"

This remark is probably her response to her mother having said, "You are *not* going to South Carolina alone to see a boy that you talked to on the telephone for ninety seconds."

"But Mother, I've *got* to see him. This is my *life* and you're *ruining* it! *You're* from the olden days. *Your* life is *over!*"

When I heard my daughter say this to my wife, I went upstairs and packed, for there was no point in staying with a woman whose life was over.

I did, however, change my mind and I decided to hang around a while longer because my wife is definitely worth staying with, no matter how washed up she may be.

"And where do you think you're going in that Madonna get-up?" she said to my daughter a few days later.

"But the boys are *ready*," my daughter replied. "They're through with frogs and lizards. I've waited so *long* for them to be ready."

"Well, you're going to stay right *here*. You're not going to any mall to look at nasty boys."

"But, Mother, this is my *life!*"

A father who hears this intellectual exchange is rooting for the mother, of course. He knows exactly what those boys at the mall have in their depraved little minds because he once owned such a depraved little mind himself. In fact, if he thinks enough about the plans that he used to have for young girls, the father not only will support his wife in keeping their daughter home but he might even run over to the mall and have a few of those boys arrested.

They Need Ventriloquists

The problem is that your daughter has given her heart to a fifteen-year-old boy, and a fifteen-year-old boy does not yet qualify as a human being. If this boy happens to be yours, he has you in a constant state of embarrassment, especially when you make the mistake of introducing him to people.

"This is my son," you say proudly to some man you know. "Son, this is Mr. Clark."

And there is silence. Perhaps the boy was momentarily distracted by working on a calculus problem in his head; so again you say, "Son, this is Mr. Clark."

"Hello, Mr. Clark," the boy finally manages to produce.

"Hello," says Mr. Clark. "What a fine-looking boy. You're really tall. How tall *are* you?"

And another silence descends. This is the kind of question that you hope will not be on the SAT, or else your son will have to skip college and go right to work at a car wash.

"I said, how tall are you?" says Mr. Clark again, wondering if English is the boy's first language.

But the boy just cannot handle this stumper about his height. He certainly *looks* ready to speak; in fact, his mouth is always half open; but no signals from the brain ever arrive. It's too bad that you can't run a string from his mouth out through the back of his head.

Nevertheless, even though your kids may not be paying attention, *you* have to pay attention to them all the way. And if you really pay attention to them from the very beginning, then you'll know the moment they start to swallow or sniff things that rearrange their brain cells. When Willie Loman in *Death of a Salesman* said, "Attention must be paid," he was speaking the four most important words a parent can know, even more important than "Dad, she's not pregnant."

And with the attention, of course, must be all the love you can give, especially in the first twelve or thirteen years. Then, when the kids start doing strange things under the guise of independence, they will always know that they are loved and that the lines are always open for them to send a message back to earth.

You see, you *can't* wash your hands of them. You have to keep those hands dirty with the kids you love.

People sometimes ask me how I like to spend my spare time. The answer is, I like to go home from the studio and stare at my wife and kids.

Sounds Like One of Mine

Sometimes I wonder if I pay too *much* attention. For example, many parents say that they can tell without even looking when their own child is crying or calling them in a crowd; but I cannot. In fact, I think that every child I hear is mine.

One day in a department store, I heard a voice say, "Daddy," and I whirled around and said, "Yes, honey?" But this honey belonged to another hive. When the child's mother looked at me with a smile, I said, "Sorry, but I have five, and whenever I hear Daddy . . ."

And the woman said, "Daddy . . ."

"Yes," I replied.

"Would you buy me this necklace?"

"I'd love to, but I'm afraid you've missed the cutoff for 'Daddy.' It stops at six."

There is, however, one sound from my own children that I cannot bear: the sound of one of them crying. And the most piteous crying comes not from an injury to your daughter's body but to her feelings. It starts low and then heartbreakingly builds, with fluid flowing from a variety of outlets: her eyes, her mouth, and her nose. Desperately you try to calm her while wiping her face and seeking the name of the person who reduced her to this state. But your plans to kill that person are changed when you learn that the person is another daughter of yours.

"She's *bossing* me!" the little weeper says about her sister.

It turns out that the tragedy has been caused by her sister stopping her from putting on one of her mother's silk scarves. And the very telling of this awful tale now triggers even more tears.

At once, you turn from the dripping victim and call in the older sister, that dastardly girl.

"But Mom says you can't *wear* that," the sister tells the little one.

"I *know*, but you still can't boss me and snatch it away," the little one says with her own wondrous logic.

And she underscores her point by starting to cry again and flinging herself on the bed. She has lost so much fluid that you fear she needs an IV of saline solution.

After thanking the older sister for her information, you quickly go to the mother and plead the little one's case.

"Our youngest daughter is having a nervous breakdown because she wants to wear your scarf for a little while," you say. "Is there any particular reason why she can't wear it?"

The mother now gives you a particular reason: because she says so. As you return to the child, you are filled by anguish over her plight. She, however, not only has stopped crying, but she is happily playing with something else. Because fathers shift gears much more slowly than crying children, you will be brooding about this whole business for another hour or so, long after your little one has forgotten it. Call it the anguish gap. Call it just another part of being a father: trying to catch up to both misery and joy.

7

The Fourth R
Is Ridiculousness

No Problem, But It Needs a Solution

When your fifteen-year-old son does speak, he often says one of two things: either "Okay," which, as we know, means "I haven't killed anyone," or "No problem."

"No problem" has been my son's philosophy of life. Two years ago, he was one of the top ten underachievers in our state and whenever you asked him how he was doing in school, he always said, with simple eloquence, "No problem." And, of course, his answer made sense: there *was* no problem, no confusion about how he was doing. He had failed everything; and what he hadn't failed, he hadn't taken yet. (Undoubtedly, F's had even been penciled in for next year.) He had even failed *English*.

His failing his native tongue piqued my curiosity, so I said, "How can you fail English?"

"Yeah," he replied.

Hoping to get an answer that had something to do with the question, I said again, "Please tell me: how can you fail English?"

"I don't know," he said.

"Son, you didn't really fail *English*, did you? You failed handing in reports on time, right? Because you can understand people who speak English, can't you? And when you talk, *they* can understand *you*, can't they? So the teacher *understood* what you had written but just didn't care for the way you put it, right? You just failed *organization*, right? I mean, the teacher who failed you in English also said, 'He can do the work,' right? It's just that you don't *want* to do it yet. And all it'll take is maybe leaving you out in the wilderness with no food or money in the middle of winter. Just a dime to make a collect call saying that you're ready to study."

"No problem," he said.

The Five Worst Words

He can do the work.

I talked before about the four most important words a parent can hear. Well, *these* are the five *worst* words a parent can hear: *He can do the work.* If the teachers could keep themselves from putting these words on report cards, all would be fine because the kids don't *look* that smart. When you see them walking around the house, they look as though their entire body of knowledge is the location of the refrigerator. And so, if the teacher said on the report card, *This kid is a total and hopeless jackass who may have trouble learning his zip code*, then the parent wouldn't be teased by the possibility of scholastic success.

This is a boy whose mind goes out of neutral only when giving reasons why he didn't turn in his work on time. On one occasion, he said that the dog ate his book report; and another time he said that he was robbed of his homework. The thief took no money, just the homework.

He called me the other day, my splendidly underachieving son. He is in a fine school now with four teachers for every child—two in front and two in back. He called to give me a detailed report on his progress to date.

"No problem," he said.

Then, however, he suddenly waxed articulate and said, "Dad, I want to be able to control my own destiny."

"Oh, God," I said, "does this mean LSD?"

And I had visions of him going airborne in his room. He probably would have wanted a movie on the flight, too.

Your Own Grades

When your child is struggling in school, you have such a strong desire to help that you often find it easier just to do the work yourself than to use a middleman. A few weeks ago my daughter came to me and said, "Dad, I'm in a bind. I've got to do this paper right away."

"All right," I said, "what's your plan of work?"

"You type it for me."

Once again, I typed her paper; but when I had finished and looked at the work, I said, "I'm afraid there's just one problem."

"What's that?" she said.

"This is awful. As your secretary, I can't let you turn this in."

Needless to say, I rewrote it for her and I picked up a B minus. I would have had a B plus if I hadn't misspelled all those words.

And so, I've now done high school at least twice, probably closer to three times; and I've gone through college a couple of times, too. Sending your daughter to college is one thing, but going to college *with* her is a wonderful way for the two of you to grow closer together.

Although we try hard to inspire our kids to do good work on their own, the motivation for such work always has to come from inside them; and if the kids really don't want to study, don't want to achieve, then we must not feel guilty; we are not at fault. You can make your boy come home from school at three-thirty, but you can't go up to his room and stand there to make sure that he immerses himself in the three R's instead of rock and roll.

The problem is one that every parent knows well: no matter what you tell your child to do, he will always do the opposite. This is Cosby's First Law of Intergenerational Perversity. Maybe the way to get a child to do his schoolwork is to say, "I want you to forget about school and spend the next two weeks at the mall."

No, Cosby's Law would be suspended for that. He would *go* to the mall and he would take your Visa card, too.

And here's the whole challenge of being a parent. Even though your kids will consistently do the exact opposite of what you tell them to do, you have to keep loving them just as much. To any question about your response to a child's strange behavior, there is really just one answer: give them love. I make a lot of money and I've given a lot of it to charities, but I've given all of myself to my wife and the kids, and that's the best donation I'll ever make.

Try Indirection and Prayer

No matter how much love you give, of course, you will still have the endlessly maddening job of trying to get your child to do the right thing, both in and out of school. For example, there is no moment in parenting more distressing than when your child goes to someone else's home and forgets to call you. It is not easy to forget such a call because you have told him nine times that he should make it; but the achievement of forgetting is one that he manages nonetheless.

One weekend, my oldest daughter left home to visit a friend who lived about thirty miles away. I missed her terribly, of course, and I also wondered if she had arrived safely, so I called her.

"Hey, Dad," she said, warming my heart by remembering who I was.

"Honey, I just wanted to make sure you were safe," I said.

"Of *course.*"

"But I didn't *know.*"

"Oh, yeah. I forgot."

"Well, the next time I'll just leave it up to the State Police, okay? I'll just have them call me and let me know that you arrived. I'm sure they have a service like that for frantic fathers."

"Oh, Dad, that's not fair."

"True. I told you less than ten times to call me, so you may have missed the message. You see, all I want to know is that you got someplace safely—someplace far away, that is. It doesn't count for local trips. I mean, you don't have to call and say, 'Dad, I made it to the bank.' Wait a minute—*I* see what happened: you forgot our number."

But then I realized it was unlikely she'd forgotten our number because it was the number she called for money. In fact, those trips to the bank are just walks to my den.

What is equally maddening about the visit of your child to some distant home is the call you get from the mother or father there telling you how lovely and helpful your child has been.

"I just can't tell you what a polite young gentleman he is," the mother says. "He straightened his room and he made his bed and he even offered to do the dishes."

At moments like these, you truly feel that you have fallen down the rabbit hole.

8

Speak Loudly
and Carry
a Small Stick

Batter Up

Let me repeat: *nothing* is harder for a parent than getting your kids to do the right thing. There is such a rich variety of ways for you to fail: by using threats, by using bribery, by using reason, by using example, by using blackmail, or by pleading for mercy. Walk into any bus terminal in America and you will see men on benches poignantly staring into space with the looks of generals who have just surrendered. They are fathers who have run out of ways to get their children to do the right thing, for such a feat is even harder than getting my daughter to remember her own telephone number.

I succeeded once. It happened after my son, who was twelve at the time, had sent me on a trip to the end of my rope. He had taken up a new hobby: lying; and he was doing it so well that he was raising it to an art. Disturbing letters were coming from school—disturbing to me, not to him, for he was full of the feeling that he could get away with anything; and he was right.

"No longer are we going to *ask* you to do something," I told him one day, "we're going to *tell* you that you'd better do it. This is the law of our house: you do

what we *tell* you to do. Thomas Jefferson will pardon
me, but you're the one American who isn't ready for
freedom. You don't function well with it. Do you understand?"

"Yes, Dad," he said.

A few days later, I called from Las Vegas and
learned from my wife that this law of the house had
been broken. I was hardly taken by surprise to learn
that the outlaw was my son.

"Why didn't you do what you were told?" I said to
him on the phone. "This is the second time I've had to
tell you, and your mother's very upset. The school also
says you're not coming in with the work."

"Well, I just don't feel like doing it," he said.

"Very well. How does this idea strike you? When I
come home on Thursday, I'm going to kick your butt."

Now I know that many distinguished psychologists
feel that kicking butt is a reversion to the Stone Age.
But kids may have paid more attention in the Stone
Age. When a father said, "No shrinking heads this
week," his boy may have listened.

On Thursday, I came home, but I couldn't find the
boy. He didn't make an appearance at dinner, and
when I awoke the next morning, he still wasn't there.
So I assembled my staff and solemnly said, "Ladies,
where is my son?"

"He's around here *somewhere*," one of my daughters
said. They were the French underground hiding one
of their heroes from the Nazis.

At last, just before dinner, he entered the house, tired of wandering in the wilderness.

"Young man," I said, "I told you that when I came home, I would kick your behind."

"Yes, Dad," he replied.

"And you know why, don't you?"

"Yes, Dad."

"Then let's go over to the barn."

He may have been slow in his studies, but by now he must have suspected that I wasn't planning a lesson in animal husbandry. When we reached the barn, I said, "Son, we are now going to have a little talk about breaking the law and lying."

As the boy watched me roll up my sleeves, his usual cool gave way to fear, even though I was a father with absolutely no batting average: I had never before hit him or any of the other children. Was I making a mistake now? If so, it would just be mistake number nine thousand, seven hundred, and sixty-three.

"Dad, I know I was wrong," he said, "and I'm really sorry for what I did. I'll never do it again."

"I appreciate your saying that," I said, "and I love you; but I made a promise to you and you wouldn't respect me if I broke it."

"Oh, Dad, I'd respect you—I'd respect you like crazy!"

"Son, it's too late."

"It's never too late!"

He was reaching heights of legal eloquence, which

didn't help him because I've often wanted to hit law-
yers, too.

"Just turn around," I said. "I want you to know that
this is a form of punishment I truly do not believe in."

"I hate to see you go against your *principles*, Dad."

"I can make an exception. I also won't say that this
will hurt me more than it will hurt you. That would
be true only if I turned around and let you hit *me*. This
is simply a barbaric form of punishment, but it happens to match your barbaric behavior."

And then I hit him. He rose up on his toes in the
point position and the tears began.

"Now do you understand my point about never lying again?" I said.

"Oh *yes*, Dad!" he said. "I've never understood it
better."

"Fine. Now you can go."

He turned around to leave and I hit him again.
When he turned back to me with a look of having been
betrayed, I said, "I'm sorry; I lied. Do you ever want
me to lie to you again?"

"No, Dad," he said.

And to this day, he has not lied again to me or my
wife. Moreover, we received a letter from his school
taking credit for having done a wonderful job on our
son. I'm glad I had been able to supplement this work
by the school with my own parent-student conference
in the barn.

Could I have done anything else to put him on the
road to righteousness? My wife and I spent long hours

pondering this question. The problem was that the reservoir was empty: we had tried all the civilized ways to redirect him, but he kept feeling he could wait us out and get away with anything. And we loved him too much to let him go on thinking that.

The week after our trip to the barn, a friend of mine, Dr. Eddie Newman, said something that clicked with the boy.

"My boy is having his problems being a serious student," I told Eddie.

"Well, your studying is very important," Eddie said, while the boy sat smiling a smile that said: an old person is about to hand out some Wisdom. Could this please be over fast? "You know, a jet plane burns its greatest energy taking off; but once it reaches its cruising altitude, it burns less fuel. Just like studying. If you're constantly taking off and landing, you're going to burn more fuel as opposed to taking off and staying up there and maintaining that altitude."

A few days later, I ran into my son in the house. (He was around a lot more now that he knew the designated hitter had retired.)

"How's school?" I said.

Without a word, he raised his arm and laid his palm down and flat like a plane that had leveled off. He suddenly knew it was the only way to fly.

There are many good moments in fathering, but few better than that.

Pride and Prejudice

It is easy for a father to say that a child who will not behave is not his problem but the problem of the boss of the house, his wife. Real fatherhood, however, means total acceptance of the child for better or worse; and once in a while, as you have seen, better comes along.

Many fathers feel that one of these better moments is sitting in the stands of a stadium and watching your son carry a football to glory. As a former Temple halfback on a truly nondescript football team, I've been guilty of such quaint machismo, such yearning to see a son who is my reincarnation on a football field, such desire to see a projection of myself get a second chance to break a leg. I have dreamed of sitting in the stands and having a man beside me point to something streaking down the field and say, "Is that your son?"

"Yes, that's my boy," I'll reply. "The galloping ghost with the name Cosby on his back. I'd be doing the galloping myself, but the team has a funny rule about using postgraduate students of forty-eight, so I decided to give the boy the business. He's now in charge of running for touchdowns."

Training my son to succeed in the business has guaranteed that there will be no more trips to the barn because he is now much stronger than I am, and three inches taller, too. Conservationists will pardon me, but I have even taught him how to attack trees. It has all been preparation for the moment when his college plays on national TV and he catches a short pass and then proceeds to run not around but *over* several members of the other team. And after he scores, he will turn to the network camera and stirringly say, "Hi, Mom."

9

Drowning in Old Spice

Who Dressed This Mess?

The father of a daughter, especially one in her teens, will find that she doesn't like to be seen walking with him on the street. In fact, she will often ask him to walk a few paces behind. The father should not take this outdoor demotion personally; it is simply a matter of clothes. His are rotten. Every American daughter is an authority on fashion, and one of the things she knows is that her father dresses like somebody in the Mummers Parade.

In schools, you can always identify the children who were dressed by their fathers. Such children should have signs pinned on their strange attire that say:

Please do not scorn or mock me. I was dressed by my father, who sees colors the way Beethoven heard notes.

Whenever I travel with my kids, the moment I open my suitcase in a hotel, I see the instructions from my wife:

The red blouse goes with the gray skirt.

Do not let her wear the green striped shirt with the purple plaid pants.

The pink paisley pants and pink paisley sweater go together.

They may jog or sleep in their sweat suits, but no one is to wear a sweat suit into the hotel dining room.

The problem is that men are less studied than women about the way they dress. They never see what a woman sees—for example, that those khaki pants do not cover their ankles. Therefore, the child who goes out to be seen by the public represents the mother; and if this child is out of fashion, an observer will say, "Who dressed that little girl? Some woman at Ringling Brothers?"

"No," will come the answer. "That is Mrs. Cosby's child."

"You're kidding! In spite of her choice of husband, I've always thought that woman had taste."

"It must have been Bill who dressed the child today."

"Oh no, he's not allowed to dress them."

Unless he happens to work for Halston, the American father cannot be trusted to put together combinations of clothes. He is a man who was taught that the height of fashion was to wear two shoes that matched; and so, children can easily convince him of the elegance of whatever they do or don't want to wear.

"Dad, I don't want to wear socks today."

"Fine."

"Or a shirt."

"That's fine, too."

Mothers, however, are relentless in dressing children and often draw tears.

"Young lady, you are not going to wear red leotards

outside this house unless you're on your way to dance *Romeo and Juliet*."

"But, Mom, everyone at *school* is wearing them."

"Then I'm helping you keep your individuality. You're wearing that nice gray skirt with the blue sweater and the white lace blouse."

"But, Mom, I *hate* that white lace blouse. It makes me look like a *waitress*."

"Which is what you will be if you don't wear it 'cause you won't be leaving the house to go to school, and a restaurant job will be *it*."

And now come the tears, which move a father deeply. His heart breaks for this child crying at seven in the morning, and he fears that this moment will leave a scar on her psyche. He wonders if Blue Cross covers psychiatry. Couldn't his wife back off a bit? After all, *he* would allow red leotards. He would *also* allow green combat boots.

However, a few minutes later at breakfast, where his darling little girl appears with swollen eyes, a runny nose, and the white lace blouse, she and her mother are getting along beautifully.

Of course, it is not hard to get along beautifully with my wife—certainly not for *me*. After twenty-two years of marriage, she is still as feminine as a woman can be; she has fine taste, especially in husbands; and we have many things in common, the greatest of which is that we are both afraid of the children. (The sternness with which she disciplines them is just a front.) I am happi-

est when she is happy, which means I am happy most
of the time.

No Hope on a Rope

Except on Father's Day. I am never as happy as I deserve to be on Father's Day. The problem is my presents. I trust my family to get them instead of simply
buying them for myself; and so, I get soap-on-a-rope.

In the entire history of civilization, no little boy or
girl ever wished on a star for soap-on-a-rope. It is not
the dumbest present you can get, but it is certainly
second to a thousand yards of dental floss. Have you
ever tried to wash your feet with soap-on-a-rope? You
could end up with a sudsy hanging.

Of course, soap-on-a-rope is not the *only* gift that can
depress a father on Father's Day: there are many others, like hedge cutters, weed trimmers, and plumbing
snakes. It is time that the families of America realized
that a father on Father's Day does not want to be
pointed in the direction of manual labor.

We could also do without a ninety-seventh tie or another pair of socks, and we do not want a sweater in
June. We appreciate the sentiment behind the buying
of the sweater: it was on sale; but we still would rather
have a Corvette.

Mothers do not permit Mother's Day to be run like this. Even General Patton would have lacked the courage to give his mother soap-on-a-rope. Mothers, in fact, organize the day as precisely as Patton planned an attack. They make a list of things they want, summon their children, and say, "Go see your father, get some money from him, and surprise me with some of these."

The kids then go to the father and say, "Dad, we need eight thousand dollars for some presents for Mom."

Mothers stress the lovely meaning of Mother's Day by gathering their children and tenderly saying, "I carried every one of you in my body for nine months and then my hips started spreading because of you. I wasn't built like this until you were born and I didn't have this big blue vein on the back of my leg. *You* did this to me."

For Father's Day, however, this woman comes to you and says, "It's one of those compulsory holidays again, one of those meaningless greeting-card things, so the kids are under pressure to buy some presents for you and the money is certainly not coming from *me*. Twenty bucks for each of them should do it—unless you'd rather have me put it on your charge."

You have five children, so you give her a hundred dollars. The kids then go to the store and get two packages of underwear, each of which costs five dollars and contains three shorts. They tear them open and each kid wraps one pair of shorts for me. (The sixth pair is saved for a Salvation Army drive.) Therefore, on this

Father's Day, I will be walking around in new underwear and my kids will be walking around with ninety
dollars change.

Not every year, of course, do I get Old Spice or underwear. Many times a few of my kids are away from
home on this special day, but they always remember to
call me collect, thus allowing the operator to join in
the Father's Day wishes too. I have, in fact, received so
many of these calls that I'm thinking of getting an 800
number.

On Father's Day, which is almost as exciting as
Ground Hog Day, I sometimes think of a famous
writer named Dorothy Parker, who said that men
were always giving her one perfect rose but never one
perfect limousine. Well, I understand just how she felt.
For just *one* Father's Day, I would like the kids to forget about the underpants, the tie, and the tin trophy
saying WORLD'S GREATEST FATHER and instead surprise
me with a Mercedes. Just put two hundred dollars
down on it and I'll gladly finish the payments.

It will never happen, of course, because fathers are
good actors who lie well. A father can sound convincing when he says that he is delighted to have another
bottle of Old Spice because he is down to his last six. A
mother, however, will refuse to accept such a bottle or
a little tin trophy and will send the children back to
the store to get it right. After all, it's the thought that
counts. And did you kids think she was crazy?

On every day of the year, both mothers and fathers
should be given more recognition than a jock or a tro-

phy. I am still waiting for some performer to win an award and then step to the microphone and say, "I would like to thank my mother and father, first of all, for letting me live."

Academic Masquerade

Most fathers are such good people that they don't even mind having their wardrobes looted by the daughters they love, a point that brings us back to the subject of clothes. A few months ago, one of my sweaters disappeared; and then, two weeks later, another sweater disappeared, soon followed by a third. Were it not for my fourteen-year-old daughter's allergy to makeup, I would still be wondering what happened to those sweaters, or perhaps to my mind.

One day during that crime wave, my wife and I were summoned to school by the nurse because our daughter's face had suddenly swollen. Had she come down with the mumps in geometry? Or had she been attacked by killer bees? No, she had been attacked by the makeup she was putting on at her locker, the lipstick and eyeliner and blusher that she was secretly wearing at school to become a person I wouldn't have recognized. The other part of this disguise was a choice of my sweaters: her locker contained three of them, and one of my sports jackets too.

And so, I learned that part of my daughter's schedule at school was a fashion elective: every day she shed the drab clothes her mother had chosen and became Miss Supercool, with clothes that belonged to me and makeup I unwittingly had paid for when I'd thought I was giving her money for magazines.

On certain girls, this makeup looks like something out of a police lineup: funky stuff that complements pants rolled high above her socks, half-laced sneakers with holes artfully punched in them, and one of your sweaters with a shirttail showing below. She had to steal three of your sweaters, of course, because she certainly couldn't be seen wearing the same one two days in a row. But she still looks better in your clothes than you ever did, and you can't wait to kiss that grease-painted cheek.

10

Your Crap or Mine?

Turn That Crap Down

Nothing separates the generations more than music. By the time a child is eight or nine, he has developed a passion for his own music that is even stronger than his passions for procrastination and weird clothes. A father cannot even convince his kids that Bach was a pretty good composer by telling them that he made the cover of *Time* a few years ago. The kids would simply reply that he isn't much in *People*.

"Okay," says the father grimly, standing at his stereo, "I want you guys to forget that Madonna stuff for a few minutes and hear some Duke Ellington."

"Duke Ellington?" says his son. "Is he a relative of Prince?"

Yes, the kids will listen to neither the old masters nor the great popular music that Mom and Dad loved in their own youth, the modern classics like "The Flat Foot Floogie" and the immortal ballads like "Cement Mixer (Put-ti Put-ti)."

When I was a boy, Patti Page made a record called "That Doggie in the Window." It swept the country, but it wouldn't sell ten copies today because it couldn't be filmed for a video. A cocker spaniel scratching himself in a pet store window lacks the drama a video needs, unless the dog were also coming into heat and fifty dancing veterinarians were singing, "Go, you bitch!"

Today's parents grew up with the silly notion that music was meant to be heard, that one picture was superfluous to ten thousand words. We now have learned, of course, that music has to be *seen*, that the *1812 Overture* is nothing unless you also see twenty regiments of Russian infantry. Duke Ellington was lucky to have done "Take the 'A' Train" when he did. If Duke were doing the song today, he would have to play it in the subway, with the lyrics being sung by a chorus of break-dancing conductors.

I doubt that *any* father has ever liked the music his children did. At the dawn of time, some caveman must have been sitting on a rock, contentedly whistling the song of a bird, until he was suddenly jarred by music coming from his son, grunting the sound of a sick monkey. And eons later, Mozart's father must have walked into the parlor one day when Mozart was playing Bach on the harpsichord.

"Turn that crap down," the father must have said.

And Mozart must have replied—in German, of course—"But, Dad, this stuff is *fresh.*"

The older generation is simply incapable of ever appreciating the strange sounds that the young one calls music.

One day last year, my daughter, who is eighteen now, came to me and said, "Dad, can I have ten dollars?"

As a typical father, I knew that I would be giving her the money; and, as a typical father, I also knew that I would be making her squirm before I gave it.

"What do you want it for?" I said.

"I want to buy a new album."

"A new album by whom?"

"The Septic Tanks."

When I was a kid, singing groups were named after such things as birds: we had the Ravens, the Robins, and the Orioles. But only the Vultures or the Pigeon Droppings could be singing groups today. And the lyrics are even worse than the names: these groups are singing the stuff that sent Lenny Bruce to jail. What my wife and I have always fondly known as sex is just foreplay today. Against a background as romantic as the Battle of Guadalcanal, these singers describe oral things that you never heard from your dentist.

The grotesque violence of some of these rock videos reflects a philosophy that many kids seem to hold:

"Well, it's *your* fault that everything will be destroyed."

But the kids have it *backward*. If they don't like the idea of destruction, then why don't they show us nymphs and shepherds merrily dancing on the grass instead of a guy who looks as though he is being electrocuted by his guitar?

About an hour after I had given my daughter ten dollars for her music, she came home with an album, and for the next twenty minutes I heard:

> *Slish-slish,*
> *Boom-boom,*
> *Slish-slish,*
> *Boom-boom.*
> *Grick, grack, greck*
> *And dreck.*

During this performance, the dog wandered in, glanced at the stereo, and sat down to listen. The dog loves this kind of music; he likes to breathe to it. At last, after the melody had segued to a noise that sounded like eruptions of natural gas, some singing began; and this singing was perfectly matched to the quality of the instrumental that had preceded it:

> *Oh, baby,*
> *Uhh-uhh, uhh-uhh.*
> *Come to my place*
> *And sit on my face.*

The Way It Was

When I was thirteen, my father used to sit in our living room and listen on our Philco radio to strange music by people named Duke Ellington, Count Basie, and Jimmie Lunceford. Sometimes when I walked by, I saw him leaning back in his armchair and smiling blissfully. My mission was to sneak *past* that living room before he caught me and made me come inside for a music appreciation lesson on the old-timey music that I couldn't stand.

"Come here and sit down," he'd say. "Now this is Jimmie Lunceford." He pointed to the Philco and smiled, while I tried to adjust my ears to the low volume. And when the piece was over, he'd say, "Now *that's* music. I don't know what you call the crap you hear upstairs, but *that's* music."

During each of these command performances, I would smile respectfully and move my head back and forth in rhythm as if I really enjoyed this junk; and after my own performance was over, I would pat my father on the knee, say, "Thank you, Dad," and tell him I had something important to do. The something important, of course, was to get away from that music. And then I would go upstairs and wonder how I could negotiate these walks past the living room and out of the house without having my father use his Philco to damage my brain. For a while, I considered putting a ladder against my window, but it also would have let a burglar in.

Had a burglar made it into my room, he would have had a wonderful time hearing Sonny Rollins, John Coltrane, Dizzy Gillespie, Miles Davis, Thelonious Monk, Bud Powell, and Philly Joe Jones. He would have been able to hear them right through any ski mask because I always played them at top volume. The greatest advantage of top volume was that I couldn't hear the grownups when they came in to tell me to turn that crap down.

From time to time my father would come by, kick the door open, and then stand there under the assault of the music. He had the look of a sailor standing on deck in a typhoon. And then his lips would start to move. I couldn't hear him, but I didn't have to, for he was sending an ancient message:

Turn that crap down.

I then would turn the sound down about halfway, moving him to say, "Turn it down, I said." I'd then turn the dial to the three-quarters point and he'd say, "More." Giving him more, I would say, "Dad, it's off."

"And that," he would say, "is what I want."

Music has changed so drastically since the days when I first heard the wonders of John Coltrane and Bud Powell. Today a guitar is a major appliance whose volume guarantees that the teenager playing it will never be aware of the start of World War III. This teenager will merely see the explosions and will probably think that they are part of a publicity campaign for a new English group called the Armageddons.

I know I don't sound hip talking like this, but no matter *how* he talks, a father cannot sound hip to his children. (I wonder if even the Duke sounded hip to Mercer Ellington, or if Mercer just humored the old man.) He can give high fives until his palms bleed; he can say "Chilly down" so much that he sounds like a short order cook; but the father will still be a man who lost all his hipness at the age of twenty-three.

The day he started paying rent.

Remember Cosby's First Law of Intergenerational Perversity? Well, it also applies to being hip. Anything that *you* like cannot possibly be something your kids like too, so it cannot possibly be hip. You know what would end Madonna's career? If enough parents suddenly started to like her.

The Tender Trap

The volume of "that crap" is my own fault, of course. No one *made* me buy that complex stereo system for my decibel-hungry darlings. The day I went into the electronics store to see the equipment, those two BOX 95s and Bowie Twin Triple Hitter treble, woofer speakers, and double-headed action didn't *seem* too much for a twenty-by-fifteen bedroom, as long as there was no bed. I even failed to notice the gleam in my daughter's eye that resembled the gleam in Dr. Frankenstein's eye when he first decided to make a mobile. I had been too busy falling into the great American trap: trying to make a child happy by buying something for her.

If the children's name for me is Dad-Can-I, then my name for them is Yes-You-May. (My response is weak but *grammatical.*) You may have the tuner, the amplifier, the tape deck, and those two speakers that belong at a pregame rally at Grambling State. I must confess, however, that all this permissiveness was not entirely altruistic: I figured that whenever she wasn't home, I could rent her room as a recording studio.

And so I bought the stereo. The price was surrealistic, but what I got for my money was more than just equipment that belonged in Yankee Stadium: I got a smile that said that I was the greatest father in the world.

When I brought the equipment home, I simply opened the instruction book, which was slightly shorter than *Pride and Prejudice*, and flipped past the Chinese, Italian, French, and Turkish until I got to the English, which had been written by a foreigner. Only two hours later, the unit was assembled and I was issuing wise paternal advice:

"Now the thing to know is you needn't turn this unit up so loud. Leave the volume control on two and a half and your ears will adjust to every little nuance."

"Yes, Dad," my daughter said, still feeling that I was a wonderful person; and going to the stereo, she put on a record that sounded like a train derailment, which I pretended to like. I was trying to reach out to her generation, to understand that there might be more to music than just melody, harmony, and rhythm.

Then I went downstairs. A few minutes later, the doorbell rang (the first good music I had heard all day) and some of my daughter's friends came in. As I told them she was upstairs, I believe I heard one of them say that I was the greatest father since Abraham. And then, when they went upstairs, I sat down for lunch with my wife in the dining room, which is just beneath my daughter's bedroom.

Moments later, things began to move that ordinarily had no locomotion: the plates, the cups, the silverware, and the salt and pepper shakers.

"I was unaware," I told my wife, "that this house is sitting on a major geological fault."

When the chandelier began to swing and the chairs began to dance, I said, "If these are my last words, I want you to know only the greatest truth that is in my heart. I love you profoundly, and I never played halfback in that game against Penn."

While the glasses, plates, and utensils danced, my wife listened intently to a deep rhythmic thumping—two short thumps and one long one—that filled the house. And after listening to this extraterrestrial sound for about a minute, she turned to me and said, "That stereo is too damn loud."

You can see that I married above my IQ.

At once, I sprang into action. I rushed upstairs and kicked open the door to my daughter's bedroom like a man arriving at a fire. With the skin on my face feeling as though it were being pushed away from my skull, and with a vein struggling to free itself from the center of my forehead, the greatest father since Abraham cried the words that Abraham himself must have cried when Isaac brought home his new ram's horn:

"Turn that crap down!"

11

Unsafe
at Any Speed

Wheeler-Dealer

Buying a stereo is merely a father's practice for the Big Buy: a car. When his child requests a car, a father will wish that he were a member of some sect that hasn't gone beyond the horse.

"Dad, all my friends say I should have my own car," the boy says earnestly one day.

"Wonderful. When are they going to buy it?"

"No, Dad. They think that you and Mom should buy me the car."

"Is there any particular reason why we should?"

"Well, that's what parents *do*."

"Not *all* parents. Did Adam and Eve get Abel a car? And he was the *good* one. Tell me this: why do you *need* a car?"

"To go places by myself."

"Well, you'd be surprised how many people manage to do that on public transportation. Elderly *ladies* do it every day. It's called a bus and I'd be happy to buy you a token. I won't even wait for your birthday."

"Dad, *you* know a bus isn't cool. My friends say I shouldn't have to ride on a bus now that I'm sixteen."

"They say that? Well, they couldn't be *good* friends

because buses are so much fun. They expand your social circle. You meet new people every three blocks."

"That's cute, Dad."

"I know you don't go particularly deep in math, but do you happen to know what a car costs?"

"I'll get a *used* one."

"Terrific. And we'll have a family lottery to try to guess the day it will break down."

"Okay, *slightly* used."

"Which is slightly more or less than five thousand dollars, not counting insurance."

"Insurance?"

"You getting some used insurance too?"

"I'll drive it real carefully."

"And there's a chance you will," you say, suddenly picturing people all over town bouncing off your son's fenders.

"Dad, I just *have* to have a car. Say, what about *yours?* Then you could buy yourself a *new* one. Dad, you *deserve* a new car."

"That's very thoughtful, son," you say, now having heard the ploy you've been expecting.

"Think nothing of it, Dad."

And so, the moment has come for you to gently remind your son precisely how worthless he currently is —without bruising his ego, of course.

"You see," you tell him, "the thing is that unless a wonderful offer came in last night, you have no job. You are sixteen years old, you have no job, and you have an excellent chance of failing the eleventh grade."

"Not *Driver's Ed!* I'm *creaming* that!"

"I'm happy to hear it. You'll go on to college—if we can find one in Baja California—and you'll major in Driver's Ed. Maybe you'll get your M.A. in Toll Booths and even your Ph.D. in Grease and Lube."

"Dad, I wish you wouldn't keep bringing up school. I'm just not motivated."

"To improve your mind, that is. But you *are* motivated to get a car. The bus may not go to the unemployment office."

"Come on, Dad; *you* know what a car means. I need it to *go* places."

"Like a fast-food joint, where your career will be. Because with the grades you have right now, if you somehow *do* happen to be graduated from high school, which the Vatican will declare a miracle, you'll be competing with only ten million others for the job of wrapping cheeseburgers."

"Dad, I'd love to talk more about my career, but I gotta tell you something really exciting that s gonna change your mind: I just saw an ad for a sensational sixty-nine Mustang."

"Really? How much?"

"Just two thousand dollars."

"Just two thousand dollars. Did you happen to ask if it had an engine? And are brakes optional?"

"Dad, I can't understand why you're being so unreasonable."

"That's what fathers are. It's one of the qualifications."

"But my friends keep saying I should *have* a car."

"And they certainly have the right to buy you one. I'll tell you what: how's *this* for reasonable? Bring your friends over here and we'll have a collection, a matching funds collection. Whatever you get from them, I'll match it."

The boy winds up with ninety-six cents.

Was That Me Driving By?

What I forgot to tell my son during this stimulating intellectual exchange was that my wife and I had already made a solemn decision about Cosby transportation: we would not allow any of the children to have a driver's license as long as he or she was living with us. Does this sound unreasonable to *you?*

One memorable day, one of these children *did* drive to town just to see if she could do it while unencumbered by a license. It was a Saturday morning and my wife and I had just finished breakfast. I walked over to the sink to rinse out a glass and there I suddenly saw our car going past the kitchen window. Turning to my wife, I said, "Dear, did you just drive by here?"

"No," she replied.

"Well, am *I* in this kitchen?"

"As far as I can tell."

"Then why did I just go by in the car?"

"You didn't," she said, moving toward the toolbox for something to tighten my screws.

A few minutes later, an idiot who happened to be my daughter came into the kitchen. I use the word idiot only in the narrow automotive sense, for my daughter is one of the brightest people her school has ever seen avoid work. In her defense, however, I must say that she does have a special philosophy about school: she feels that it is pointless to waste intelligence there.

"Dad, you didn't have to call me an idiot," she said after I had cooled off.

"That's true," I said. "But somehow the word seemed to fit."

"You don't understand. You just don't understand."

"No, I *do* understand. I just don't accept. Because when you drive with no license or insurance, you could run someone down, make him an instant millionaire, and send your mother and me back to the projects. And then you'll leave *us* because we won't be making enough money for you. And if you ever *do* get a driver's license, you know what they'll stamp on it? Legally stupid."

In Spite of Mutiny

Just as your children are not afraid to let you know
that they are not perfect (they let you know it night
and day), you must not be afraid to let them know that
you're not perfect too. The most important thing to let
them know is simply that you're there, that you're the
one they can trust the most, that you're the best person
on the face of the earth to whom they can come and
say, "I have a problem."

If *only* more kids would say "I have a problem" instead of "No problem."

Your children have to know it's their responsibility
to come to you when they are in trouble, even if it
means their earning the title of idiot.

Let's say that you do buy a car for your daughter.
It's an act of love and she is very happy to have it, both
the love and the car. And you say, "Now I don't want
anybody driving this car when they're drinking. In
fact, I don't want this car to move with any hands on
the steering wheel but yours. This car is not to be
loaned like a sweater or a Duran Duran album, not
even to go around the block. You could get hurt. And I
could get sued for the trade deficit of the United
States."

Now the rules have been set and the responsibility
has been placed. But there is other pressure on the
child too: the pressure of wanting to be liked. And so,
it happens, and the moment has come for you to let the
child know that something will be learned, though this
is not your favorite school. And you also have to let the
child know that there will be forgiveness, even when
you hear the police say that liquor was involved.

"Look, kids do this," the police say.

"Yes, *other* kids," you say; "but we've *talked* about it."
Then you say to your daughter, "Didn't I *tell* you?"
And she replies, "Yes, but I didn't think . . ."

I didn't think.

If any words can describe the teenage years, these
are the ones. A famous actor with two daughters once
told me, "When a girl hits thirteen, you can just watch
her lose her mind. Luckily, she gets it back; but during
all the time that it's misplaced, you can lose your
own."

In these trying years, as I have said, and can't say too
often, a father just has to keep hanging around and
loving and knowing that his baby needs guidance because her own rudder hasn't started working yet. To
extend the nautical image, a father during these years
has to do everything in his power to keep a tight ship,
even though he knows the crew would like to send
him away in a dinghy.

The Impossible Dream

Americans are often in love with their cars, so I'm not surprised when I travel around the country and find teenagers who would rather have cars than roofs over their heads. That is, the roofs they want are from General Motors.

For example, early last year, when I was performing at Lake Tahoe, I noticed a boy of about fourteen sitting quietly near the stage. He clearly wasn't enjoying the show, so I decided to bring him into it and then he'd be partly responsible for not having any fun.

Walking over to him, I said, "Son, do you like cars?"

"Oh, yes," he replied, perking up.

"What kind of car do you like?"

"A Corvette."

"And how much does a Corvette cost?"

"Around thirty thousand dollars."

"Tell me, how are you doing in school?" I said.

"Okay." The sweeping meaning of which you and I already know.

"You mean your grades are okay?"

"Well, uuhhh . . . some C's . . . and   . ."

"Some C's and what? Some A's?"

"No, D's."

"In what were the D's?"

"Well, I got one in English."

"English? Were you born here?"

"Yes."

"And what language did your parents speak around the house?"

"English."

"And your newspapers were in English too?"

"Yes, they were."

"And television. Did your parents put on only Spanish or Bulgarian stations?"

"Oh, no."

Suddenly I was back on old familiar ground: another American boy whose native tongue was a foreign one.

"Okay, never mind that," I said. "So you got some C's and D's. Have you been told that you could do better?"

"Yes, I have."

"Teachers have told you that you're much brighter than your grades?"

"Yes."

"But you're just not motivated."

"That's right."

Once again, familiar ground. It sounds as though method acting has been brought to American schools. Before a child can play the part of a student, he has to say: *Well, what is my motivation here? Why am I doing this homework instead of hanging out at the mall? Can I look convincing going to class?*

"Okay," I said to the boy, "so let me see where you

are. Right now, you're somewhere below mediocre; and as far as I know, there are not too many corporate recruiters looking for a sub-mediocre person who doesn't want to do anything. You see, you've got enormous competition for that position of not wanting to do anything. By the way, do you have any real reason for wanting a car?"

All right, all together now, let's sing out his answer: *To go places.* How refreshing it would be if a child told his father that he wanted a car for robbing banks.

And speaking of robbing banks, for the next few minutes, I talked to the boy about raising the thirty thousand dollars. I discovered he hadn't completely worked out every detail of the financing. To distract him from this pressure, I changed the subject and told him a way to do his homework that had never occurred to him: read the assignments every night. And then, at the end of my little commercial for scholarship, I finally said, "Now, son, do you *still* think it's important to have a thirty-thousand-dollar Corvette?"

"No," he said thoughtfully. "I think I'll go for a Volkswagen."

12

The Attention Span of a Flea

Remembrance of Things Upstairs

That boy at Lake Tahoe had trouble remembering the address of his school, but he is typical of young people. I have found that children remember only what they want to. It's a talent they develop from the very beginning.

For example, suppose you are sitting in your living room and suddenly realize that you need something from upstairs, but you feel too lazy to make the trip. Luckily, however, you have co-produced a five-year-old who goes upstairs just for fun and who also speaks your language. Moreover, at this moment, the child is in your very room, about to destroy an antique.

"Come here," you say to this child and she understands perfectly and moves directly to you. "I want you to get something from my bedroom and bring it down to me."

"*Sure*, Daddy!" the child says, delighted to be honored with such a mission. And this is why you are sending her: because the mission is an honor for her but would do nothing for you.

And now you tell the child not only the exact location of your glasses (on the table to the right of the bed), but also the exact location of your bedroom, as if she has never been in the house before. She is, after all, only five.

Within moments, however, you realize the child is having trouble remembering the difference between the left hand and the right.

"*This* hand," you say. "This hand is the *right* one, okay?"

"If you say so, Daddy."

"I want you to go to the table on Daddy's side of the bed, so here's what you do. Make this hand into a fist, hold it way out, and go upstairs. Leave it balled up in a fist so that when you go through the door, you can go in *its* direction. Won't that be *fun?* As much fun as chocolate cake for breakfast or taking a shower in your clothes. Now you do remember where our bed is, don't you? The one you like to come into when Mommy and I want to be alone."

"Uh-huh."

"Good! So you just go around to the side that's on the same side as your balled-up hand and then go to the table on that side. You know the one with the lamp on it?"

"Uh-huh."

"Well, my glasses are there. Bring Daddy's glasses right down here. Now what did I say?"

"Go upstairs to your room and look on the table," says the child. "With the right hand balled up."

"You are going to do brilliantly on the SATs. Just bring those glasses down to Daddy."

"Okay."

And so, you return to your reading, trying to guess what the words are because your glasses have not yet arrived. After a while, you sense that too much time has passed since you sent the child for the glasses; and then you see this very child walking past your living-room chair, but she says nothing to you. She is simply walking around, so you call her over and say, "Sweetheart, I thought I asked you to get my glasses."

And the sweetheart says, "Oh, yeah. Uh, I didn't see them."

Drawing her closer, you say, "Did you go up to my room?"

"Yeah."

"My room in *this* house?"

"Yeah."

"And you looked on the table?"

"Yeah."

"And you didn't see them?"

"Yeah."

"With your hand balled up?"

"Yeah."

"Okay, now you just go back upstairs and look on that table nice and hard because I know I left them there."

"Well, Dad, I didn't see them. I looked for them and I didn't see them."

"Did you look on the *other* table?"

"No."

At once, you're aware of your own stupidity in not having asked the child to look on both tables. And so,

you say to her, "Sweetheart, go up again. Keep your
hand balled up on that side and look for the glasses.
Keep your *hand* balled up, but nothing else."

And the child goes upstairs again, and this time she
comes back, so definite progress has been made.

"They're not there, Dad," she says.

"You definitely looked on the other table?"

"Yeah."

And so you lead the child upstairs. Both of you have
your right hands balled up because this is a learning
experience.

"Now we put our hands straight out," you tell her
as you enter the bedroom, "and we follow them like
this."

And there, on the table, are your glasses.

You start to get angry, but you cannot sustain it, for
how can you be angry at a child who is so pretty and
biteable? Sustaining anger at a biteable daughter has
been a father's timeless problem. I doubt it can ever be
solved.

"*Here* are my glasses," you say. "I thought I *told* you
they were here."

"But, Dad," she sweetly replies, "they weren't here
when I *looked* for them."

"You came over to this side?"

"Yeah."

"And you looked?"

"Yeah."

"And they weren't there?"

"No, Dad. Not there at all."

There are many times during the fathering years when you wonder about the condition of your mind, and this is one of them. I don't think *anyone*, not even a magician or a psychic, could have said whether or not those glasses were on the bedside table when the child went up to look for them. The psychic might have told you, "I see this as a great learning experience."

And she would have been right: you have learned to get your glasses by yourself. Moreover, your child has learned a little something about remembering directions. It may take several more trips to fetch things before her mind will be as well trained as a golden retriever's, but you will keep trying. You will keep trying and keep having patience.

And *that* is fatherhood.

Be It Ever So Rent Free

Your reward will be that some day your daughter will come home to you and stay, perhaps at the age of forty-three. More and more children these days are moving back home a decade or two after they have stopped being children because the schools have been making the mistake of teaching Robert Frost, who said, "Home is the place where, when you go there, they have to take you in." Why don't they teach *You Can't Go Home Again* instead?

I recently met a man and woman who had been married for fifty years and they told me a story with enough horror for Brian DePalma. Their forty-six-year-old son had just moved back in with them, bringing his two kids, one who was twenty-three and one who was twenty-two. All three of them were out of work.

"And that," I told my wife, "is why there is death."

Who wants to be seven hundred years old and look out the window and see your six-hundred-year-old son coming home to live with you? Bringing his two four-hundred-year-old kids.

I have five children and I love them as much as a father possibly could, but I confess that I have an extra bit of appreciation for my nine-year-old.

"Why do you love her so much?" the other kids keep asking me.

And I reply, "Because she's the last one. And I never thought that would occur. If I'm still alive when she leaves at eighteen, my golden age can finally begin."

I find there is almost music to whatever this child does, for, whatever she does, it's the last time I will have to be a witness to that event. She could set the house on fire and I would say, "Well, that's the last time the house will burn down."

She is as bad as the others, this nine-year-old; in fact, she learns faster how to be bad; but I still look at her with that extra bit of appreciation and I also smile a lot because she is the final one.

I sympathize with the older ones for not understanding. They are perplexed because things they did that annoyed me are now adorable when done by the nine-year-old. When the older ones took pages from a script I was writing and used them for origami, I was annoyed; but when the last one does it, I feel good all over.

After their last one has grown up, many fathers think that the golden age of solitude has arrived, but it turns out to be fool's gold, for their married children have this habit of getting divorced; and then they drop off the children at your house while they go to find another spouse.

And sometimes it is not only the children but animals too.

"Dad, I wonder if you could watch our horse while we're away."

"Well, what if your mother and I decide to go someplace?" you say.

"You people are *old*. You don't *go* anywhere."

The only reason we had children was to give them love and wisdom and then freedom. But it's a package deal: the first two have to lead to the third. Freedom—the thing so precious to Thomas Jefferson. He didn't want *his* kids coming back either, especially because he had *six* of them.

In spite of all the scientific knowledge to date, I have to say that the human animal cannot be the most intelligent one on earth because he is the only one who allows his offspring to come back home. Look at anything that gives birth: eventually it will run and hide.

After a while, even a mother elephant will run away from its child and hide. And when you consider how hard it is for a mother elephant to hide, you can appreciate the depth of her motivation.

Look Homeward, Sponger

When you and your wife are down to one child and that child is nineteen, when you are in the home stretch of the obstacle course that is leading you to the golden years, *never* buy a bigger house. And if, for reason of insanity, you do buy one, make sure that it's in Samoa or else the children will see it and say, *"Look! They're there!"* Moreover, some of these children have studied biology and know you're going to die, so they express the kind of feeling that is found in the major poets:

"Whoever's in the house when they die, gets it!"

For generations, fathers have been telling sons who are nearing the end of their college days, "Son, your mother and I don't care *what* career you finally decide to pursue because the important thing is that you will be going forth."

The key word here is *forth*. Every time you attend a graduation, you hear a dean or president say, "And so, young men and women, as you go forth . . ."

For years, I had thought that forth meant going out into the world on their own; I had thought that forth meant leaving home. But then I discovered that I was wrong. Every time that they go forth, they come back, so forth must mean home.

My father, however, gave to forth its old traditional meaning. On the day I was graduated from college, he presented to me a Benrus watch and then he said with a smile, "All right, now give me the keys to the house."

"Why, Dad?" I replied.

"Because you're going forth, which is any direction but to this house."

But I got my mother to let me back in.

"He's just a baby," she said.

This baby lived with his parents until he was twenty-four years old. It was a good life: food was free, there was hot and cold running water, and my laundry was done—eventually. It took a while to have my laundry done because my hamper was the floor of my room. I learned what many young men have learned: if you leave your clothes on the floor of your room long enough, you can wait your mother out. Sooner or later, she will pick them up and wash them for you. The price you pay will merely be her noisy disgust:

"All these stinking, moldy clothes . . . just a disgrace . . . at twenty-four . . . he must think I'm his slave . . . he must think I want to start some kind of *collection* of rotting clothes."

Fathers, however, are a little tougher about such earthy living. My father set my clothes on fire.

"Unfit for man or beast," he said. "Not even fair to the *garbage* men to make 'em handle stuff like that."

After I had been living at home for a while at the age of twenty-four, my mother and father had a meeting about me and they decided to charge me rent. The figure they chose was seven dollars a week; and I considered this figure fair because I was producing forty dollars' worth of laundry.

Once I began paying rent, I had the right to tell my mother that she wasn't doing this laundry well enough for my sartorial style.

"Now look, Mom," I said, "if you want this seven dollars a week, then you've got to improve your work on these collars. If I ever want to *wear* a damp one, I'll tell you."

I really took advantage of those people; but if you can't take advantage of your mother and father, then what do you have them for?

I have known parents who are even harder on adult child boarders than mine were, parents who charge their children as much as eleven or twelve dollars a week. Sometimes this money has to come from the adult child's allowance, thus creating the financial version of a balanced aquarium.

"I'm telling you now, you're gonna pay us rent," the father says. "You're gonna give us twelve dollars a week."

"Don't worry, you can skip the week of your birthday," the mother says.

The best thing about living at home is the way your

parents worry about you. Of course, they have *reason* to worry about you. They know you.

I.O.U. Aggravation

The flow of money between generations always seems to be a problem in American families. Now that my father is a grandfather, he just can't wait to give money to my kids. But when I was *his* kid and I asked him for fifty cents, he would tell me the story of his life: how he got up at four o'clock in the morning when he was seven years old and walked twenty-three miles to milk ninety cows. And the farmer for whom he worked had no bucket, so my father had to squirt the milk into his little hand and then walk eight miles to the nearest can. For five cents a month.

And I never got the fifty cents.

But now he tells *my* children every time he comes into the house, "Well, let's just see if Granddad has some money for these wonderful kids."

And the moment they take the money out of his hand, I call them over and take it from them. Because that's *my* money.

13

Ivy-Covered
Debt

Hail to Thee, Bankruptcy

I was wrong when I said that the big expense for you would be buying a car. Let us now discuss the cost of college—unless you would rather do something more pleasant, like have root canal work.

As you know, I have always put the highest value on education. However, one day last year, my eighteen-year-old daughter came in and told my wife and me that she had decided not to go to college because she was in love with a boy named Alan.

At first, my wife and I went crazy.

"What?" I cried. "You're standing there and telling your mother and me that you're *not* going to—"

And then a light went on in one of the musty corners of my mind: her decision would be saving me a hundred thousand dollars.

"—not going to college, which you have every *right* to tell us. Alan, you say? Well, he just happens to be the one I'm exceptionally fond of. I hope he's feeling well. Would you like me to send him to Palm Beach for a couple of weeks to get a little sun?"

A father like me with five children faces the terrifying prospect of sending five to college. When my oldest one went, the bill for her first year had already reached thirteen thousand dollars. I looked hard at this bill and then said to her, "Thirteen thousand dollars. Will you be the only student?"

I am lucky enough to make a lot of money; but to the average American father today, thirteen thousand dollars (which has now gone up to seventeen) is more than just a sum of money: it is the need for a winning lottery ticket.

When I saw my oldest daughter's first college bill, I multiplied thirteen thousand times four, added another thirty thousand for incidentals during these four years, and got the sum of eighty-two thousand dollars that I would be spending to see my daughter pick up a liberal arts degree, which would qualify her to come back home.

You think I'm exaggerating that extra expense for incidentals? For her freshman year, I had to spend another seventeen hundred for a tiny room just a quarter mile from a toilet. And then the college said that if my wife and I really cared for our child, we would pay another three hundred for the gourmet special. We wound up sending another five hundred to our daughter personally so that she would not have to eat the gourmet special but could get pizza instead.

"Dad, the food is terrible," she kept saying.

"But I enrolled you in *gourmet* food," I said.

"That's worse than the other. I want pizza."

And then, on top of the five hundred dollars a year that we sent for pizza, we also had to keep flying her home because her clothes kept getting dirty. She was studious, so she was unable to remember to wash her clothes. She simply flew them home every few weeks and put ten thousand dollars' worth of laundry into our washing machine.

At this college, my daughter did not major in mathematics. *No* children learn mathematics at college, even when they take the courses; I have never met a college student who knows how to count. You give one of them a certain amount of money and a budget precisely broken down to cover all her expenses.

"This is for this," you say, "and this is for that."

The child listens carefully and calls you forty-eight hours later to say she is broke.

"And, Dad, the telephone company is being really *unreasonable.*"

"Did you pay the bill?"

"We're certainly *planning* to. And *still* they want to turn it off."

"But I *gave* you enough—there's money in your *budget* for the telephone bill."

"Oh, we used that money for important things."

In my daughter's sophomore year, one of these important things was housing: she and her roommates decided that they just had to have their own apartment. They no longer could stand living in the dorm, where the shortsighted dean had objected to their putting up pictures of naked people playing guitars.

I discovered these pictures on a surprise visit, which I had made to tell my daughter that her mother and I loved her, wanted her to work hard, and were behind her all the way. Upon entering her room, I expected to see pictures of little kittens playing with thread, but instead I saw a young man who looked as though he was making music at an Army physical. My daughter, of course, was not supposed to be majoring in anatomy.

You Could Major in Spackling, Too

The eighty thousand dollars that you will be spending for college might not leave you quite so depressed if you knew that the school's curriculum were solid. I am afraid, however, that the curriculum has turned to cottage cheese.

When I went to college, I sometimes cut classes to go to the movies; but today the movies are the *class*— sorry, The Film Experience. There are also such challenging courses as The History of Western Belching, the Philosophy of Making Applesauce, and Advanced Lawn Mower Maintenance. It is no surprise to hear a college student say on his graduation day, "Hopefully, I will be able to make an input. College was a fun time, but hopefully now I'll have a viable interface with software." The software is his *brain*. The degree he is truly qualified to be given is one in Liberal Semi-Literacy.

I do not mean to sound stuffy or old-fashioned. I just

feel that for eighty thousand dollars a student should spend four years in a school where English comes up from time to time. I cannot stand to see it being scaled *down* to the students. The students should be reaching up to *it* because success in life demands the use of intellect under pressure. Also knowing how to spell.

A freshman today will change his schedule if he finds he has signed up for a course that requires books. He wants courses that will enable him to both sleep late and get rich, so he will test his intellect with such things as The Origins of the Sandbox, American National Holidays, and the Principles and Practices of Billing.

I have mentioned my feeling about grade school teachers who keep saying, "He can do the work," my feeling that if only one of these teachers would call the boy a certified idiot, I would say, "Fine; we'll get someone to work with him." Well, in college the teachers don't say, "He can do the work." They say, "What kind of work would he like to do?" And it is this new trend of letting students shape their own curriculum that leads a student to tell his advisor, "I'd like to study the number of times every day that the average light at an intersection turns green. I want to major in Traffic."

14

Full-Time Job

In from the Cold

Some authority on parenting once said, "Hold them very close and then let them go." This is the hardest truth for a father to learn: that his children are continuously growing up and moving away from him (until, of course, they move back in). Such growth is especially bittersweet with a daughter because you are always in love with her. When she is very small, she comes to you and says, "Daddy, I have to go to the bathroom," and you proudly lead her there as if the toilet were a wedding chapel. You drop to your knees, unbutton her overalls, and lovingly put her on the seat.

And then one day it happens: she stops you from unbuttoning her and pushes you away because she wants privacy in the bathroom. It is your first rejection by this special sweetheart, but you have to remember that it means no lessening of her love. You must use this rejection to prepare yourself for others that will be coming, like the one I received on a certain day when I called my daughter at college. Someone in her dorm picked up the phone and I asked to speak to my daughter. The person left and returned about a minute later to say, "She says she's sleeping right now."

I was hurt to have my daughter put me on hold, but intellectually I knew that this was just another stage in her growth; and I remembered what Spencer Tracy had said in *Father of the Bride:* "Your son is your son till he takes him a wife, but your daughter is your daughter for all of your life." You are stuck with each other, and what a lovely adhesion it is.

There is no commitment in the world like having children. Even though they often will drive you to consider commitment of another kind, the value of a family still cannot be measured. The great French writer André Malraux said it well: "Without a family, man, alone in the world, trembles with the cold."

Yes, it is even better to have Jeffrey, that wee airborne terror, than to have no child at all. Just make sure that you travel in separate planes.

This commitment, of course, cannot be a part-time thing. The mother may be doing ninety percent of the disciplining, but the father still must have a full-time acceptance of all the children. He never must say, "Get these kids out of here; I'm trying to watch TV." If he ever does start saying this, he is liable to see one of his kids on the six o'clock news.

Both mother and father have to work to establish an *honesty*. The child doesn't have to tell them *everything*, but he *should* be talking to his parents the same way he talks to someone who is not in charge of his life. When your son has his first wet dream, you don't want him to have it interpreted in the boys' locker room. And if your daughter's period is late, you want her to feel as comfortable going to you as to a confidante at the mall.

Sometimes I tell my son that the meaning of his name is "Trust nobody and smile." But that certainly doesn't apply to his parents: my wife and I have tried to stay tuned in to him and the girls from the very beginning. We have shown all five of them constant attention, faith, and love. Like all parents since Adam and Eve (who never quite seemed to understand sibling rivalry), we have made mistakes; but we've learned from them, we've learned from the *kids*, and we've all grown together. The seven of us will always stumble and bumble from time to time, but we do have the kind of mutual trust that I wish the United Nations had. And, with breaks for a little hollering, we smile a lot.

Afterword

by Alvin F.
Poussaint, M.D.

Bill Cosby makes fatherhood come alive. He takes us on a comedic yet insightful journey through the awesome shifting sands of parenthood. Along the way, he selects for emphasis those stages of fatherhood through which most men, who elect to participate actively in the great spiritual and psychological adventure of parenting, must pass.

The experience of fatherhood begins, as Cosby notes, long before the birth of your first child. It then passes through the stages of infant, toddler, preschool, school-age, preteen, teenager, and adult. There are new, different, and challenging issues at each stage of development that parents must face and resolve. These stages frequently merge and overlap, producing significant individual variations. Parents are also changing, developing, and experiencing their own life stages as their children grow. The child/parent interactions at any given stage, therefore, are more complex than it at first appears.

Because of the new interest in the role of fathering, a significant body of information, gathered by scholars and laymen alike, has shed new light on the most effective approaches to the different stages of fatherhood. Bill Cosby, in beginning this book, warns: "I doubt there can *be* a philosophy about something so difficult, something so downright mystical, as raising kids." To a large degree he is correct.

Child-care experts caution us that there is no single "right" approach; much variation exists in successful parenting styles. In addition, the mores of one's culture, religious orientation, country, community, and family influence the kind of role mothers and fathers assume in child-raising. Relatively speaking, there is no such thing as a perfect father any more than there is a perfect mother. All parents make mistakes and in most instances children can successfully overcome their caretakers' shortcomings if they are raised in a loving, caring, and disciplined environment.

Let us begin, then, at the point at which Bill Cosby starts this book: expectant fatherhood ("So you've decided to have a child."). Most men decide to be fathers for similar reasons that women want to be mothers: to reproduce themselves and undertake the challenge and fulfillment of successfully raising and interacting with a child from birth to adulthood. Men who elect to be participatory fathers look forward to the birth of a child with the same sense of anticipation, joy, doubt, and anxiety as most expectant mothers.

Both old observations and new research have shown that the expectant father, particularly one who gives it no forethought, begins his journey when he learns his partner is pregnant. From this point on for the duration of the pregnancy, the expectant father, besides his own reactions, is affected by the experiences that his partner undergoes as the pregnancy progresses to reach its endpoint: the birth of a baby.

Pregnancy is divided conveniently into trimesters, each with its special qualities, pleasures, and discomforts for the woman, to which the man responds. During the first trimester, women may experience "morning sickness," during which they feel nauseated and may vomit. They often feel fatigued, bloated, and may have a variety of minor physical complaints as their body changes to accommodate the developing baby. Their moods may vary from joy to depression, depending on their previous mental state or their current feelings about being pregnant. Often pregnant women at this stage may report that they feel vaguely "different" because of the many psychological and physiological changes they are undergoing.

The father-to-be during this period must be supportive and patient with his partner, while also realizing that he is experiencing joy, excitement, and nervousness of his own. He must respond to not only his wife's pregnancy, but also his own vicarious reactions to her pregnancy. He may feel proud, boastful, and even powerful because his "manhood" is being demonstrated by his own fertility. A few may experience "sympathetic" pregnancy symptoms because of strong identification with their pregnant spouse. Yet the reality of the pregnancy may cause many men to anxiously assess their own preparedness for fatherhood and its accompanying responsibilities. For the expectant couple the beginning of pregnancy can be an exciting mix of stress, sharing, and joy.

In out-of-wedlock pregnancies, such anxieties cause some men to panic and then flee to avoid both the financial and the psychological responsibilities of parenting. Some males, unfortunately, are interested only in impregnating a woman to become a biological father and have no interest in becoming a psychological father: a man who helps to raise and support his children. Fathers who willingly abandon their offspring are shortsighted and irresponsible. They shortchange their children, their families, society, and themselves. Absent fathers, due to whatever cause, are missing the opportunity for an unparalleled form of self-fulfillment and emotional satisfaction, including involvement in their partner's pregnancy.

For participating fathers, the second trimester brings another set of experiences that make the baby seem much more of a reality. The first movements of the baby can now be felt. Bill recalls when his wife woke him up in the middle of the night and yelled: "It's moving; wake up and feel it!" These movements are called "quickening" and the parents are now convinced that there is something "alive and kicking in there." The expectant father should participate in feeling the baby move. But men should be aware that, even though it may feel great to them, the movements of the baby sometimes may be uncomfortable for the mother. Yet the father's sharing of the experience will help him to understand and empathize more appreciatively with his wife's responses.

The last trimester brings new excitement but new stresses as well. Mother's abdomen is growing large and protruding. There is considerable weight gain, about twenty to thirty pounds. Often women experience "puffiness," swollen ankles, insomnia, and an aching back. Physical movements become awkward and, as Bill Cosby indicates, simply getting up and sitting down may become an ordeal for the pregnant woman. Women—and their mates—may be filled with worries about the normality and health of the baby. Thoughts about the sex of the child become prominent, as do the many preparations for her or his arrival. Sexist attitudes may surface if the father goes overboard in his preference for a son and implies that girls are not worth as much. Attitudes of this type in either parent may be disturbing to the other.

As the day of delivery approaches, fathers may worry about their sexual needs and are anxious to consult their physicians about when to abstain. Men also fret about the details of getting their partner to the hospital when labor begins. Bill describes the chaotic excitement that characterizes this event in the beginning of this book. Once in the hospital, birthing center, or attended at home, the experience of the delivery looms as a deep and lasting experience for both mother and father.

Not many decades ago, fathers were not permitted in the delivery room. Today, this has changed. Many couples attend courses on labor and delivery so that they can share and experience the birth together. Husbands are able to assist their wives, comfort them, and participate in the birth in the delivery room. A family feeling is established, and both mother and father can begin to bond immediately with the child.

The adjustment to the new baby causes some stress as home routines and styles change in response to baby's demands. For men who are confused or in conflict about their role as fathers, this is a critical time. If they are traditional, they may retreat and leave all or most of the custodial tasks such as feeding, bathing, and diapering to the mother. Traditional mothers, also, may try to push men away from these "feminine" chores and conflicts may result. To avoid misunderstandings, it is important for the couple to discuss and decide on their respective "feminine" and "masculine" roles and responsibilities *before* the baby arrives.

Fathers who want to bond closely with their babies should share in caretaking. As Bill says, "For a new father, this little person is something he can hold and

love and play with and even teach, if he knows anything." Bill mentions many humorous getting-to-
know-you incidents that occurred while he was engaged in such routine activities as feeding and dressing
his children. It should reassure any male readers growing anxious at this point that the new fatherhood
movement sanctions such activities as "masculine."
There is no cause here for men to worry about their
manhood.

Paternal participation in caretaking offers enormous
support to the mother and strengthens the bonds between the couple. When older children are in the family, the father can also play an active role in helping
his children cope with the new baby and their own
periodic feelings of jealousy, displacement, and sibling
rivalry. He can also assist them in engaging in helpful
activities with their new sibling. This kind of father
involvement is especially important because a new and
tired mother is often not as available as before to her
other children. A daddy can fill the gap!

Today, there are more and more men taking time off
from work, or requesting paternity leave, to spend this
critical early period learning parenting tasks expected
of the modern father. Fathers, by the way, are often
just as interested in and delighted with their newborns
as the mother. Indeed, there are many occasions when
Dad is more "high" on the baby than Mom, because
Mom, having gone through the physical stress of the
delivery, may be feeling more exhausted than "high."
(A word of caution: fathers should not get so wrapped

up in their baby that they neglect their relationship with their wives.)

As the baby begins to grow, besides the custodial care required, fathers can take an active role in helping their children in social, physical, and intellectual development. This is best accomplished during the activities that are considered play. Fathers who are less androgynous in their orientation may feel more comfortable in playing games and reading to their young ones than in changing their diapers and dressing them. They should make use of toys and games that aid in their child's exploration of his or her environment. Dads also enjoy holding, touching, rocking, and lifting their children. These physical games and exercises are important for a child's motor development and coordination. Fathers who think they should get involved only when they can begin to teach their child (usually the son) sports are way off base. Child-care specialists report that early involvement of parents in stimulating play with their youngsters facilitates their growth.

Modern fathers must try to check inclinations to "rough house" with their sons and not with their daughters. All games and sports are as appropriate for girls as they are for boys. Child-care experts have strong evidence that restrictive and often damaging sex-role typing begins early in infancy and is perpetuated in many subtle ways by fathers—and mothers. It is worthwhile for fathers and mothers to reflect periodically on their attitudes toward male and female roles. Through self-examination they may avoid personal biases that impede their sons' and daughters' healthy development.

Divorced and out-of-wedlock fathers should realize that constructive involvement with their children is an important ingredient in shaping their offspring's growth and identity. Psychological fathers in all categories serve as role models who can significantly influence their children's personalities and development. Fathers, for instance, can contribute greatly to the management of the preschool and school-age child.

Children going off to school marks a major transition for parents. When Bill and I were boys, this took place at age five, when we went to kindergarten in the public schools. It is different today. Because of changing family patterns—more women in the work force, and growing numbers of single-parent families—there has been a great need for child-care services outside of the home for very young children. Adding to this pressure for services is the belief by some parents and teachers that formal education and socialization outside the home should begin sooner than age five.

As a result, more and more children are beginning "school" in the form of Head Start, day-care, and nursery school at ages two and three. There are even day-care centers that specialize in infant and early toddler care. Many have educational programs that occasionally go overboard in "hurrying" children's development. Some experts criticize programs that utilize high-pressure, "flash card" educational techniques to produce "super" children. Parents should scrutinize such programs to be sure their youngster is not being needlessly overstressed.

For many fathers and mothers, involvement in a child's "school" activities begins earlier than in the past. Because working parents often have conflicting schedules, fathers and mothers have to juggle their schedules to get their children ready for school, drop them off, and pick them up. Modern fathers who take an active interest in their children's progress are involved in exploring school programs, meeting with teachers, and dealing with educational problems as they arise. For instance, both parents should review report cards; praising, scolding, and counseling should be, when possible, a joint affair. In the past, many school duties were performed solely by the mother. A father's participation not only eases a mother's burden, but benefits the school-age child as well.

Some fathers may begin to identify more closely with their sons when relating to the older school-age child (age five to six) and wish to be role models and guides for them. This is healthy as long as Dad is not neglecting or rejecting his daughters, or sex-typing them into limited roles and opportunities. Fathers can be very helpful during this stage. Children of elementary-school age love outings, trips, and exploration. They also have great curiosity and are generally anxious to know more about their environment. Trips to the grocery store are an opportunity to educate them about money and arithmetic. Trips to a restaurant are a chance to teach social skills. Outings to movies and museums can be just plain fun for both children and father and have educational value.

Fathers who work should explain to their growing youngsters what kind of job they perform. They can bring their child to their workplace so that they can see this other world where Daddy, or Mommy, participates. In the old days it remained a mystery to many children exactly what their fathers did when they "went to work." Fathers will seem less remote when children are not left in the dark about their parents' outside activities.

Children ask many questions at elementary-school age, including questions about sex. The old practice of fathers referring these questions to mothers is no longer acceptable. Fathers should, with their daughters as well as sons, respond to such intimate questions in a manner appropriate to the child's age. Preteens will frequently have questions, particularly about the sexual development of their bodies. Bill mentions that he would want his son to talk to him if he has questions about "wet dreams" and he would want his daughters to express any worries to him about a missed period. This open attitude will lay the groundwork for children to talk more comfortably about intimacies and feelings with father as well as with mother.

Some fathers, unfortunately, hold back expressions of affection to their challenging children of school age because they fear that it might interfere with their "strong" image and diminish their effectiveness as a stern disciplinarian. Fathers who are too stern and too often play the role of the whiplasher make their children too frightened of them. This interferes with a comfortable father/child relationship. Parents do not have to frighten children excessively or make threats of violence to make them obey.

Bill Cosby, in some of his comic material, refers to whacking his son on the behind on one occasion and getting good results when other approaches had failed. There is much controversy surrounding spanking as a means of discipline. There is, nevertheless, much anecdotal material that suggests that corporal punishment of children is an effective form of discipline. Even the old adage states: Spare the rod and spoil the child. Parents, however, too often use spanking to vent their own frustrations and anxieties. In such cases, spanking becomes an attack on their children and not a genuine attempt at constructive discipline.

Most psychiatrists and psychologists discourage the use of violence in any form to discipline children. On the other hand, there are times when children can be so exasperating that most parents will lose control and give their child "a good whack." If this happens occasionally to loving parents, there is no reason to feel excessive guilt. There is no evidence that it produces psychological harm unless the "whack" is of the force to constitute child abuse. Fathers who physically harm their children must be legally restrained at the same time that they seek counseling to prevent future abusive behavior.

Parents will be most effective in getting obedience

from their youngsters by explaining the reasons why certain behavior is not allowed. And often these lessons have to be repeated again and again to children, so patience is required. Modern mothers should avoid casting the father as a would-be child executioner. Fathers can best participate in discipline by recognizing that rewards and punishments for good and bad behavior are more likely to produce the desired result than a spanking. Most child specialists recommend the reward/punishment style of discipline mixed with consistency and love. Praise a child for desired behavior and reprimand or ignore a child displaying unacceptable behavior. Saying, "Go to your room and don't come out until you can behave," may be more productive, and certainly less painful to father and child, than a beating.

To better manage some of these frustrating discipline issues, father should be in harmony with mother on disciplinary techniques and should not allow a child to pit them against one another and manipulate them. Cosby satirically deals with these issues in much of his comic material and is correct in trying to motivate his children to behave without his playing the role of Bill the Policeman.

Wise parents know that good discipline in a child's early years prevents some of the headaches that come when their child reaches adolescence, which is about age twelve these days. Adolescent children can be especially difficult for fathers who have had an unbending, tough attitude about absolute obedience. Teenagers normally challenge and frequently rebel against the authority of their parents as they move toward greater independence and realization of their own adulthood.

Teenagehood is a time that calls for the maximum of parental flexibility and patience. A father might find himself faced with a previously obedient and compliant child, or at least one who had quietly gone about accepting Dad's word as law, suddenly telling him to "Go chuck it!" Fathers who respond too harshly, or who try to beat teenagers, may find themselves hit back by them or may soon have a young runaway. Teenagers feel a great sense of indignity when parents try to use physical force to discipline them. Again, reason and the use of rewards and nonviolent punishment is the best approach.

Parents have to be ready to take some adolescent challenges as a matter of course and allow teenagers to make as many of their own decisions as possible, so long as they do not endanger their own well-being or the well-being of others. Adolescents usually like to experiment and "try out things" for themselves. They are not as likely to "take your word for it" as they were as children. Some of their activities and challenges to the father's authority may reawaken conflicts in the father—and mother—about sex, drugs, smoking, and different forms of behavior. If a father believes his teenage son or daughter is moving in a direction away from his—the father's—expected aspirations, he may become anxious as well as angry. Failures at school or "hanging out with the wrong crowd" may be particularly exasperating to fathers who feel that, as the "head of the household," they should be in control.

One of the tasks for a father during his child's progression through adolescence is to give up more and more control at the same time that he tries to guide his teenage child in the right direction. But, as Bill Cosby recognizes in his presentations, there is a contradiction and conflict here: adolescents are usually still economically dependent on their parents, particularly the father if he is the primary breadwinner. The attitude of many fathers is: I'm taking care of you, so you do what I say. The implied afterthought is: If you don't like it, move out.

This approach will work to some degree, but it may also drive a strong wedge between the adolescent and Father, simply because the teenager does not want to feel totally controlled by him or Mother, particularly with the threat of withdrawing financial support. Many will take on the challenge, run away, live in the streets, and eventually get into all kinds of dangerous and unlawful activities just to spite Dad and Mom.

It is important, at this stage of development, to help adolescents reach independence in constructive ways. Foremost, fathers should maintain an active interest in their teenager and not retreat because they are feeling a sense of angry impotence. Teenagers, despite their disclaimers, need strong parental involvement and will appreciate it in later years. Secondly, opportunities to participate in decision-making along with sharing some adult responsibilities such as helping maintain the household should be available to them. This includes having part-time jobs, taking on major household chores like cooking and cleaning, and deciding on how they would like to spend their summer vacation. The object is to reward adult behavior and to remain as patient as possible when childish acting-out aggravates you. Adolescents will at times make unrealistic demands and are very ambivalent about their real dependence on their parents. That they have to ask parents for things, particularly money, is a constant reminder that they are not yet independent adults.

Adolescents, even those with part-time jobs, will need money from their parents for clothes and other items. Bill Cosby jokes frequently about the demands of adolescent children for clothes, cars, and other luxuries. This is certainly a real issue and the challenge is to satisfy some of their needs when possible but not to overindulge them. Whenever possible, adolescents should be required to contribute to purchases of large items such as stereos and cars. Bill moans that the more he buys his kids, the more they seem to want. Many parents would agree with him. On the whole, fathers should be willing to give, particularly when it supports the responsible growth of their budding adult.

Some adolescents will become independent earlier than others. There are those who drop out of high school to work, others who graduate from high school and go to work, and those who go on to college to drop out or to graduate. Among these varied patterns, parents should remember that many adolescents may be "late bloomers." There are many stories of adolescents who early on seriously foundered but significantly achieved at a much later age.

College-bound children are financially dependent and, if their children go on to graduate or professional school, parents may be supporting a child into their mid and late twenties. Fathers in intact homes who are primary breadwinners, and single fathers and mothers, may be particularly burdened with what seems to be the never-ending financial burdens of parenting. Indeed, economic times being as hard as they are, some grown children may be returning home to live if the parents allow it.

Just as a father feels it is all ending and his children are off to start their own families, a new role begins. In mid-life, Dad may experience his second "fatherhood" as a grandparent. Bill Cosby playfully reminds his own children that someday they will be parents and he will sit back and chuckle as they struggle with their children in the same way he struggled with them. "I just hope that when you get married, you have children who act just like you."

Grandfathers do have a special place in the lives of their children's children. They can delight and play with them and even indulge them in ways that they did not indulge their own children. Grandfather knows that after the fun and games are over with his adorable grandchildren he can return to the quiet of his own home and peacefully reflect on this phenomenon of fatherhood.

Bill Cosby's willingness to share many of his own fatherhood experiences in this book will encourage men everywhere to participate more actively in parenting. Though this volume is titled *Fatherhood*, its effect will be to strengthen the entire family. Bill, who has relentlessly demonstrated his concern for kids, knows: Strong families raise strong, healthy children!